Cat Schield is an award-winning author of contemporary romances for Mills & Boon Desire. She likes her heroines spunky and her heroes swoonworthy. While her jet-setting characters live all over the globe, Cat makes her home in Minnesota with her daughter, two opinionated Burmese cats and a goofy Doberman. When she's not writing or walking dogs, she's searching for the perfect cocktail or travelling to visit friends and family. Contact her at catschield.com

USA TODAY bestselling author **Naima Simone**'s love of romance was first stirred by Mills & Boon books pilfered from her grandmother. Now she spends her days writing sizzling romances with a touch of humour and snark. She is wife to her own real-life superhero and mother to two awesome kids. They live in perfect domestically challenged bliss in the southern United States.

Discover more at millsandboon.co.uk

HOW TO CATCH
A BAD BOY

CAT SCHIELD

SECRETS OF A
ONE NIGHT STAND

NAIMA SIMONE

MILLS & BOON

First Published in Great Britain 2021
by Mills & Boon, an imprint of HarperCollins*Publishers* Ltd
1 London Bridge Street, London, SE1 9GF

www.harpercollins.co.uk

HarperCollins*Publishers*
1st Floor, Watermarque Building,
Ringsend Road, Dublin 4, Ireland

How to Catch a Bad Boy © 2021 Harlequin Books S.A.
Secrets of a One Night Stand © 2021 Naima Simone

Special thanks and acknowledgement are given to Cat Schield for her contribution to the *Texas Cattleman's Club: Heir Apparent* series.

ISBN: 978-0-263-28301-3

0821

MIX
Paper from
responsible sources
FSC™ C007454

This book is produced from independently certified FSC™ paper to ensure responsible forest management.

For more information visit: www.harpercollins.co.uk/green

Printed and bound in Spain
by CPI, Barcelona

HOW TO CATCH
A BAD BOY

CAT SCHIELD

To Bri and Ella.

Thanks for all your support so
I could get this book written.

One

Asher Davidson Edmond lay on the jail cell's hard bunk, arm thrown over his eyes to block out the gray concrete walls and dingy ceiling. How the hell had he gotten here? Correction: he knew how. A police escort in the back of a cruiser. As to the chain of events that had landed him in this mess, he'd been completely blindsided.

Despite some of the risky behavior he'd demonstrated in his thirty-one years, he'd never imagined landing behind bars because of something he hadn't done. And he definitely *hadn't* been embezzling funds from the festival. He might've bent or even broken a law or two in his youth, but that had been petty stuff. Stealing for his own gain was the last thing he'd do.

"Hey, rich boy."

The mocking voice belonged to the blocky, muscular cop who'd escorted him back to his dank, windowless cell after his arraignment. Asher's molars ground together at the man's taunt. Apparently, he'd gone to high school with

Deputy Vesta's younger sister and hadn't treated the girl too well. He had to take Vesta's word for it because he didn't remember those teenage years all that well. Something about laughing at her when she'd asked him to prom… Not one of his finest moments, obviously.

"Yeah?" Asher responded, not bothering to move. Quashing his jittery emotions, he packed as much sardonic boredom as he could into the single word, all too aware that he wasn't doing himself any favors by acting like a jerk. Still, nothing would change Vesta's rock-solid perceptions of him, and after years of coping with his adopted father's nonstop disapproval, he reflexively retreated into behaving like a sullen, entitled prick.

"You've got a visitor."

Hope exploded in Asher's chest.

Had Ross and Gina changed their mind about his guilt after failing to support him at yesterday's bail hearing? While his siblings' abandonment had aroused panic and uncertainty, Asher had known better than to expect his adopted father to show. Nor did he expect Rusty Edmond had come to see him now, unless to drive home his acute regret for adopting his second wife's son.

Asher had his own complaints on that score. Why had Rusty bothered with a legal connection when he'd never truly embraced Asher as one of his own? Or maybe he had—the man demonstrated little affection toward either of his biological children and between criticizing Ross's abilities and dismissing Gina's talents, none of the Edmond offspring had a great relationship with him.

That hadn't stopped Asher from spending his teen years fighting an uphill battle to win Rusty's affection though. And when all his efforts had failed, Asher had begun acting out. If he couldn't win his stepfather's approval, then he figured he would become truly worthy of Rusty's disdain.

Yet as difficult as his relationship with his stepfather

was, Asher's connection with his stepsiblings was as close as if they were blood relations. Ross had been twelve and Gina ten when fifteen-year-old Asher had come to live with them. He'd enjoyed playing big brother to the pair and the trio had bonded immediately. Even though Rusty had only been married to his mother for three years, they'd been formative ones for all three kids and they'd remained tight even after Rusty and Stephanie divorced and Asher headed off to college.

Which was why the silence from the Edmond siblings was so ominous. Since his arraignment, he'd consoled himself by speculating that Rusty—intent on teaching his adopted son a lesson—had barred Ross and Gina from showing up in court. But as the hours stretched out and he'd not heard from either of his siblings, Asher started to worry that they believed he was guilty and had turned their backs on him.

Unrelenting panic swelled in his chest. At the arraignment he'd learned the charges against him were worse than he'd been led to believe. It wasn't just the theft of the funds—that could've been handled locally—but the money had disappeared from the banks, sent by wire transfer and that meant the feds were involved. Even if he'd wanted to, Rusty couldn't use this as a teachable moment for his adopted son and make the charges go away.

Asher was in *deep*.

With his bank accounts frozen thanks to the embezzlement charges, he hadn't been able to post his own bail. Naturally he'd hoped that his family would believe that he'd never do anything like what he'd been accused of and help him out. But as the hours passed, his despair had grown. Only now it appeared as if he'd been worried for nothing. One or both of them had decided to help him out.

"You've got five minutes," Deputy Vesta said, his tone brisk.

Asher sat up and blinked in the sudden brightness. As his eyes adjusted, he focused on the person standing on the other side of the bars. The individual was neither his tall, lanky brother nor his stylish sister, but a petite woman in figure-hugging jeans and high-heeled boots, her long black hair slicked back into a neat, low ponytail. Probably another fed come to pick at him about the missing funds.

But then she stepped closer and he glimpsed her features. *"Lani Li?"*

He could barely breathe as recognition landed a sharp jab to his gut. Then he rallied and pushed to his feet, fighting to remain upright as his emotions executed a wild swing between delight and confusion at her appearance. Had she heard about his plight and come rushing to help him? His heart hoped so. It thumped hard against his ribs as he processed his outstanding luck.

However his euphoria dissipated as he noticed the glower in her mink-brown eyes. Spots of color flared in her cheeks, marring the uniform perfection of her pale skin. She'd compressed her luscious lips into a flat line that broadcast her disdain and the only thing keeping her arched brows from touching was the bottomless vertical indent between them. To say she looked less than pleased to see him was an understatement, but putting aside his desperate need for rescue, her arrival flooded his mind with vivid, racy memories.

Until she spoke…

"Asher." Her tone was all business.

"What a surprise," he murmured, advancing toward her, drawn like a bee to a flower.

Her scent hit him before he wrapped his hands around the bars and leaned in. She smelled like warm vanilla and spicy cinnamon, all lush sweetness and mouthwatering delectability. He remembered burying his nose in her hair and drawing her unique perfume into his lungs. How she'd tasted like sweat and sunshine as they'd made love beside a raging river, crushing pine needles beneath their straining bodies and releasing the astringent scent. The simple act of breathing her in now slowed his heart rate and soothed his restless nature.

"What's it been?" he continued blithely. "Five years?"

She gave a curt nod. "About that."

"Long time."

"Yep." Lani narrowed her eyes and scanned him from the top of his close-cropped brown hair to the toes of his brown Berluti loafers. "You look like hell."

"Well," he drawled with a lazy shrug while his brain scrambled to process that she was standing there. "I have been locked up in here for a day and a half, so…"

While finishing the sentence, he trailed his gaze over her, following the buttons of the white button-down shirt she wore beneath a practical navy blazer, over the swell of firm breasts and the flat plains of a taut abdomen to the waistband of the dark denim. He knew that body. He *adored* that body. Curves in all the right places. Honed muscle beneath silky soft skin. He'd spent long hours guiding his lips and hands over every inch, learning what made her shiver, moan and whimper.

"You look really great," he drawled, recalling that time he'd nipped the firm mound of her perfect butt and made her squeak in surprise. "So, what brings you by?" Asher posed the question lazily, chatting her up as if they'd bumped into each other at a barbecue rather than a jail cell. One corner of his mouth kicked up as he delivered a smoky look her way.

"I've gotta say, you're the last person I expected to see here."

"I'm on a case," she told him.

"I'm intrigued. Care to tell me about it?"

"I'm investigating the theft of the festival funds."

"Who do you think did it?" he asked.

She cocked her head and shot him an incredulous look. "You."

"So, you're on the Asher-is-a-thief train." He nodded, unsurprised by her answer. "I thought you might believe I was innocent."

With a long-suffering sigh, she swept aside her blazer and set her hand on her hip. The gesture exposed an empty holster clipped to her belt. He stared at the telltale harness as lust blindsided him. The thrill wasn't entirely sexual. Since he was a kid, Asher had lived for the next great adventure and had spent most of his twenties chasing anything exciting or dangerous. The thought of Lani packing heat turned him on in so many ways. His skin tingled and the tips of his fingers began to buzz with the need to touch her.

"Looks like you became a special agent after all," he said, his gaze drifting up her torso, pausing momentarily to revisit the enticing curve of her breasts before making contact with her hostile glare. "What are you? FBI? ATF? DEA?"

Her sooty eyelashes flickered. "I'm a private investigator."

"You don't say." This intrigued him.

Lani had been on the cusp of attending graduate school when they met five years earlier and planned to study criminal justice. She'd graduated college with a degree in sociology and a passion to make the world a better place. Despising injustice, she'd decided a career in federal law enforcement would offer her the best chance to make a difference.

"Well," he continued, "get me out of here and you can do all the private investigating you want."

Even before her eyes flared in outrage, Asher regretted flirting with her. She was the only person who'd come to see him and he was treating her like some random chick he'd met at a bar instead of the dazzling prize he'd foolishly let slip through his fingers.

Her full lips, bare of lipstick, puckered as she let an exasperated breath escape. As if they'd last kissed yesterday instead of five years ago, he recalled how her lip balm had tasted like strawberries. How her long silky hair had tickled the back of his hands as he'd drawn her close. From their first kiss to their final heartbreaking embrace, he hadn't been able to get enough of her.

"You're still the same frat boy, aren't you?" Her words splashed icy water on his libido.

"I'm not."

The nickname stung the way it had five years earlier. They'd met while she'd been employed as a waitress on Appaloosa Island in Trinity Bay off the coast of Texas. He'd been lazing around before what had turned out to be his final season playing professional polo. Intrigued as much by her brilliant wit as her killer body and gorgeous face, every time he ate at the resort's restaurant, he'd made sure to be seated in her section.

To his chagrin, nothing about him had charmed her. Unimpressed with the giant tips he'd left her, she'd sized him up as idle and aimless and dubbed him "frat boy" even though he'd left college behind half a decade earlier.

"These days I'm the vice president of operations in charge of The Edmond Organization's Bakken business." He puffed out his chest, wondering if he could impress upon her that he was serious and successful, someone who had a plan and stuck to it instead of roaming around the world chasing one polo season after another.

Although his practiced tone was one of pompous confidence, it didn't reflect his true feelings. In fact he hated the endless dull details demanding his attention and made the barest effort to manage his team. He'd been with the company for a little over nearly two years, bullied into taking the position because Rusty was tired of subsidizing Asher's "unproductive lifestyle" and threatened to cut off all support unless Asher did something to earn the money.

"Yet you're barely ever in the office," she said, her skeptical expression indicating she'd already heard an earful about him.

"I've been busy with the Soiree on the Bay festival." An exaggeration. He'd had little to do with the practical aspects of organizing the luxury food, art and wine extravaganza.

"Yes," she murmured dryly, "that seems to have led to your current state of incarceration."

As much as Asher wanted to argue, what could he say? The steel bars blocking him from freedom said it all. Nor could he point to anything he'd done since they'd parted ways that would meet with her stringent standards. She was one of the most focused and task-oriented people he'd ever met. From the beginning she made it perfectly clear that his lack of ambition frustrated her. In every way that mattered, they were opposites. Yet he was drawn to her by an undeniable hunger that proved as distracting as it was intoxicating.

While it might have been her striking looks that first attracted him to her, what inflamed his pursuit in the face of one rejection after another was her courage, unflinching strength of character and no-nonsense outlook.

And he loved a challenge.

Her aloofness fired his determination to discover the woman hiding behind her prickly exterior. Yet as satisfying as the chase had been, catching her had surpassed his wildest dreams. Nor had his attention shifted to his next conquest after getting her into bed. She'd proved to be more exhilarating than any woman he'd ever known. And through the course of their whirlwind affair, she'd had a profound effect on him.

During those blissful summer months, he'd become

someone...*different*. Someone who stopped joyriding through life and started to question his purpose. Someone who considered another's hopes and desires might be just as important as his own.

Yet it couldn't last. They were heading down two completely different paths. She was off to graduate school in the fall, destined to make something of herself. Faced with losing her, he'd relapsed into the aimless, restless, the unreliable "frat boy" she'd christened him. And often in the intervening years, he'd wondered what would've happened if he'd been a better man.

Lina raised a slim black eyebrow and shook her head. "Do you have any idea how much trouble you're in?"

Her stony demeanor brought him back to the predicament facing him. "I'm starting to," he grumbled, his panic surging once more. If he could only get her on his side... "It's all a huge misunderstanding."

"Is it?" she countered. "The evidence against you is pretty damning. Millions are missing from the festival accounts and all the withdrawals appear to be in your name."

"I swear I didn't steal a single cent."

For days Asher had been denying any knowledge of where the money had disappeared to. No one believed him. Not his family. Nor the authorities. He appeared responsible, so everyone believed he was guilty.

"I've talked to the investigators," Lani went on as if she hadn't heard Asher protest his innocence. "There were payments made to a tech firm, a music company, a luxury jet charter enterprise. Many of the transfers seemed as if they could be legitimate, but the companies don't exist and money was siphoned out of the accounts as soon as it was put in."

This was more information than he'd previously heard. Fake corporations with real bank accounts. That sort of thing took calculation and finesse. And if anything pointed to Asher's innocence, it was that his planning skills were subpar, just ask his team at The Edmond Organization.

While he'd been mulling his shortcomings, Lani's gaze rested heavily on his face, her expression grave and expectant. "No one has any idea where the money is now."

"Me included." Heat flared in his face as frustration bubbled up inside him. It was one thing for the Edmonds to believe his guilt, but he needed Lani's help if he was going to get out of this mess. "I didn't take any of it."

Unfazed by his continued denials, she continued to assess him with cool detachment. "There's a condo in the Maldives with your name on it."

"It isn't mine." Anger flared. Where was all this damning evidence coming from? With the money trail leading directly to him, was it any wonder no one believed his innocence? "I don't even know where the Maldives is."

"It's an island off the coast of India." She paused and studied him through narrowed eyes. "More importantly, there's no extradition treaty with the US."

"Meaning I intended to take the money and run."

He barely restrained a wince at her obvious disgust. *Damn.* As hard as it had been to glimpse the betrayal and disappointment on his family's faces as he'd been escorted out of the Edmond headquarters in handcuffs, the scorn rolling off Lani cut even deeper. He'd never admit it, but once upon a time he'd wanted to be her hero. Obviously his need for her admiration hadn't dimmed.

"I'm telling you that I didn't steal any of the festival's funds and I didn't buy a condo in the Maldives." Asher gave his head a vigorous shake. "I didn't do this. Why won't anyone believe me?"

Lani glared at Asher, unable to believe that five minutes ago, as she'd walked through the door leading to these jail cells, she'd been besieged by an attack of butterflies—*but-*

terflies!—at the thought of seeing him again. She braced her will against the pull of his striking good looks, broad shoulders and overwhelming masculine appeal and cursed the part of her that revisited the bliss of his hard body surging into hers and the peaceful aftermath snuggled against his big warm chest. The double-barreled shot of mind-blowing sex and tender romance had torn her defenses apart.

She'd spent the last five years putting her walls back up. Yet when it came to Asher Edmond, she always underestimated his charisma. Her throat clenched. She remained as woefully susceptible to him as ever. At least she hadn't let on how her heart had leaped at her first glimpse of him. Or given any hint of how she'd rushed from a client meeting with the famous musician Kingston Blue, to this jail cell in Royal, Texas, breathless and giddy and all too aware that this new case would bring her into close proximity with Asher once again. Last time she'd almost ruined her life because of him. She must *not* be led astray again.

Recognizing that she was grinding her teeth, Lani unlocked her jaw with an effort. "If you didn't do it, then who did?"

"I have no idea."

His denials didn't surprise her. Given the serious charges facing him, Asher would be a fool to admit wrongdoing. At least not until his lawyer had plea-bargained his sentence down for cooperating with the investigation.

"It would be good for you if the money was returned." A pause. "I could help with that." Kingston Blue wanted answers. She intended to get them.

"If you think I have a clue where the missing funds have gone, then you're going to be disappointed."

"When it comes to you," she retorted without considering her words, "I'm used to being disappointed."

For a second he looked stricken and Lani wished she'd guarded her tongue.

"What I mean is…" Rummaging through the ashes of their brief romantic fling to dig up all the old hurts and disappointments was not the way to get him to trust her. "Look, I'm here to do a job. I'm not here as your friend. We had a lot of fun that summer, but let's not pretend that we ever intended on seeing each other again once we parted ways."

Asher winced. "I'm sorry for how things ended between us."

Lani scoured his expression to determine if he truly felt remorse or if he was merely spouting more of his pretty words. *Fool me once…*

"Don't give it another thought." She pressed her lips into a grim line. The man already thought too much of himself. Why give him an inkling that their breakup had bothered her at all? "I haven't."

That summer everyone had warned her about him. She should've listened, should've followed her initial gut instincts and steered clear. Especially after her parents voiced their disapproval of their relationship when Lani had started reconsidering whether she should head to graduate school as planned or take a gap year and spend the time with Asher. She'd been such an idiot to think he'd been at all serious about her.

"I know I was a bit of a tool back then," Asher said as if she hadn't brushed off their fling as inconsequential. "But those days are behind me. I'm not that guy anymore."

His reputation said otherwise. He had an active love life, playing as fast and loose with women's hearts as he had with the festival's bank accounts. Every social media post featuring him should be captioned *#heartbreaker*.

"Forgive me if I have a hard time believing that given that you're behind bars at the moment."

"Like I said, I'm innocent." A muscle ticked in his jaw. "I was set up."

Don't be taken in by his earnest denials. Lani steeled herself against the agony in his intense brown eyes, but couldn't quell the sudden frantic pounding of her pulse. His silver tongue had drawn her in all those years ago and she'd almost given up her dreams to be with him. She just couldn't allow a lapse in judgment to happen again.

"Do you have any evidence of being framed? Or a theory who might be involved?" When she spied the way his chiseled lips thinned in frustration, Lani nodded. "That's what I thought."

For a long moment they stared at each other and Lani couldn't decide if she wanted him to be innocent or guilty. For his sake, the part of her that had once loved him hoped that he had been set up, but the heartbroken portion needed him to be a bad guy. Since they'd parted, she'd been telling herself that she was better off without him. Misery loomed if she stopped believing that.

"I guess that's it then. Your mind is made up. There's nothing more I can say to convince you." He looked so despondent that Lani's heart contracted in sympathy. "Well, it's been really great catching up with you. Good luck with the investigation."

Crap. Well, she'd done an outstanding job of alienating him before learning anything. "If you're innocent, you could use…help." She couldn't bring herself to say *my help*. Sucking in a steadying breath, she tried again. "My client wants me to find the money…"

"Did my father hire you?" Asher looked hopeful. "He was very impressed by you back when we dated. In fact, his only criticism was why a woman with your brains and ambition would waste your time with me."

"My client would prefer to remain anonymous."

Which wasn't true. Kingston Blue had given her no such instructions, but she was here to get information, not give it out.

The musician had agreed to perform at Soiree on the Bay and, like many people, he was out a lot of money thanks to Asher's embezzlement. Kingston Blue had deep pockets and wasn't in any desperate financial straits, unlike many of the vendors and attendees of the aborted festival, but he was a savvy businessman who didn't take lightly to being swindled. He'd met the entire Edmond clan and was quite convinced that there was more to the story than Asher Edmond acting alone to defraud all the people who'd put money into the festival.

Lani had been surprised when a high-profile client like Kingston Blue had contacted her about the case, but it became clear right away that the singer had done his homework and knew all about her connection to Asher Edmond. Kingston also knew that their fling hadn't ended amiably, at least not on Lani's part.

Professional ethics prompted her to warn Kingston that her prejudice against Asher might affect her work, but the musician believed her familiarity with the family made her the perfect person to investigate them and find the money. After the first obvious leads had panned out, progress had stalled on discovering the bulk of the missing funds. The feds had stopped investigating other suspects once all the evidence solidly pointed at Asher.

Despite her misgivings, in the end, the outrageous retainer Kingston offered was too tempting to resist. Plus, a check in the win column would open the door to other prominent clients. This case was the gateway to turn her fledgling business into the most sought-after investigative firm in Dallas.

But first she had to find the money Asher had stolen and for that she needed his cooperation.

"Sure. Okay. I understand." Asher raked his fingers through his short dark hair. "But when you see my dad, tell him I've learned my lesson. It would be great if he could bail me out now."

Lani saw no reason to correct Asher's assumption that his father had hired her. If he believed that Rusty wanted him to cooperate with her investigation, all the better.

"Let me go see what I can find out about that," she said, suddenly eager to escape.

Asher stared at her intently, his gaze growing ever more piercing as the seconds ticked by. Heat flared beneath her skin at the intensity of his stare. His look wasn't sexual in nature, yet she'd always been so aware of his body and keyed into his moods. She saw now how longing and relief mingled in his expression as he believed, perhaps for the first time since his arrest, that someone might be willing to stand in his corner and believe in him.

"Thanks."

"Don't thank me." She needed to find the money. He was her ticket to do that. "I'm on a case. I think you can help me with it. That's all. Don't read anything more into it."

"Sure. Whatever you say." His even, white teeth flashed in a relieved grin as she turned to go. "And, Lani…"

She hated the way her heart spasmed as she headed for the exit. The powerful lure of their shared history was a stronger temptation than she'd expected. But she couldn't let herself be ensnared by her longing for him. He'd been bad for her back then, and he'd be even worse for her now.

"Yeah?" Standing before the door, waiting for the buzz that would indicate it was unlocked, she made the mistake of glancing Asher's way.

A smile of genuine delight lit up his brown eyes and softened his lips into sensual curves. "Seeing you again is the best thing that's happened to me in a long, long time."

The buzz sounded. Without uttering another word, Lani yanked open the door with far more force than necessary and left. She collected her phone and keys from the deputy guarding the cells, and then she was run-walking through the police station and stepping out into the blistering hot August afternoon. She didn't stop moving until she'd reached her SUV in the parking lot. Breath coming in ragged gasps, she bent forward and set her hands on her knees while the blood pounded in her ears.

As her pulse slowed, she unlocked her vehicle and slid behind the wheel. She couldn't do this. Pulling out her phone, she began to scroll through her contacts in search of Kingston Blue's name. To hell with the money or the boost to her reputation this case offered, working in close contact with Asher was going to mess with her emotions again.

"Lani," Kingston's smooth deep voice soothed her ragged nerves. "I didn't expect to hear from you so soon. Did you meet with Asher Edmond?"

"Yes." She searched for a way to extract herself from the case without damaging her credibility. "He claims he's innocent."

"Do you think he is?"

Did she? "The evidence suggests he's guilty."

"But you know the guy. What's your take?"

"It's all a little too obvious." Lani didn't realize this fact had been bothering her until right now. "Asher isn't stupid or naive. How could he possibly think he could get away with it?"

"So, you agree that there's something more going on."

"Maybe. I don't make assumptions this early in a case."

"Fair enough." Despite Kingston's neutral tone, his inflection reflected disappointment. "So what's your next step?"

"Well, having Asher behind bars makes getting information from him about the festival bank accounts nearly impossible, and since the feds froze his assets and his family isn't stepping forward to help, it doesn't look like he can make bail."

"If I put up the money to get him out, I'm counting on you to make sure he doesn't run. That means he's your responsibility twenty-four/seven."

"That's…"

Impossible. Outrageous. Too much to expect from her.

She couldn't handle that much contact with Asher. There had to be another way. Yet even as she scrambled for a logical excuse to give Kingston, she knew there was only one answer.

"Doable."

"Great, then get me the details so we can get his bail paid and let's hope our boy can lead you to the missing money."

Two

Confronted with spending another miserable night cooling his heels in jail, Asher set aside his dinner of a roast beef sandwich, snack-size bag of potato chips and fruit cup. No doubt refusing the simple fare would be perceived as snobbishness, but in truth, the acid churning in his stomach left him unsure if he could keep anything down.

"Your bail's been posted," Deputy Vesta said in clipped tones as he unlocked the door to his cell.

Asher lacked the energy to hide his overwhelming relief as he pushed to his feet and approached the opening. "Was it my dad?"

Even though Lani hadn't confirmed that Rusty had hired her, he was leaning into the hope that his father had come around to believing his adopted son was innocent.

Vesta scowled in disgust. "Do I look like I care?"

No doubt the deputy—along with most of the town— believed he deserved to remain permanently behind bars and was disappointed at this turn of events. Suspecting further questions would irritate Vesta further, Asher kept his mouth shut. Per the terms of his release, he was fitted with a court-mandated ankle monitor and instructed about the rules surrounding his release.

After collecting his belongings, he stood in the police station lobby while the public defender assigned to his case talked on the phone. Asher peered through the glass front door into the golden sunshine of early evening, wondering who had paid his bail and when they would show up to give him a ride back home.

His spirits rose as he spied his sister approaching the police station entrance. Gina was looking at her phone as she pushed through the door and didn't see him until he greeted her.

"Gina, hey," Asher called. He stepped forward to intercept her, his arms open wide. "It's great that you're here. I'd almost given up on anyone coming to pick me up."

"You're out?" Gina stopped dead, and then actually backed up several steps and cast her eyes around frantically as if desperate for someone to rescue her. "How?"

"You paid my bail…?" Asher trailed off at her headshake. "Well, *someone* did. Maybe it was Ross?" Doubts began to close in when she continued to look panicked and confused. "Or dad. I think he hired an investigator to help find the missing money."

Asher trailed off as his sister's knuckles whitened on the hand that clutched her purse strap. The strain she'd been under these last few weeks was fully evident in her ashen skin and the tick at the corner of one dry red-rimmed eye.

"Dad didn't post your bail. He still believes you're guilty." A pause. "Everyone does."

Disappointment filled him as she emphasized *everyone*. "Then why are you here?"

"The detectives have more questions for me." She

dodged his gaze. "I don't know how much more I can tell them. I didn't put through any payments. You did."

"Damn it, Gina, you know me!" Asher tempered his tone when she flinched, and finished, "How can you think I had anything to do with it?"

"What else am I to think?" Her eyes flashed. "You authorized all the financial transactions that went missing."

"I didn't make those payments. I swear everything I did was legitimate."

"Obviously not, or the money wouldn't have vanished." She paused for a second, before adding with low vehemence, "Can't you just admit what you did and take responsibility?"

Asher recalled how the public defender had presented what would happen if he admitted what he'd done and returned the money or kept pleading his innocence and took his chances in court. Guilty or not, he was screwed.

"I'm not going to admit to something I didn't do."

Gina's expression closed down. Her next words demonstrated that she didn't have the tiniest amount of sympathy for him. "You don't seem to realize that the entire family is suffering because of what happened with the festival. Our family name is ruined. And there's talk that we could be kicked out of the Cattleman's Club because of this."

Her words gutted him. Asher stood rooted to the spot as she dodged around him and headed toward the reception desk. In a daze, he made for the exit, forgetting that he was no longer free to move around at will until he reached the sidewalk and became aware of the electronic monitor's unfamiliar weight rubbing against his ankle.

He was on house arrest until his trial. Whenever that was. While this situation was better than being stuck in jail, he still chaffed at the restrictions. Of course, he could venture out in Lani's company. As long as she notified the officials of their movements, he could accompany her on excursions. He had only to persuade her he could help her investigation.

Bolstered by determination, Asher glanced around, unsure how he was supposed to get back to Elegance Ranch to begin his court-ordered confinement. No doubt his car remained at The Edmond Organization. He doubted anyone had thought to remove it from the parking lot. Should he head there to pick it up? How much trouble would he be in if he didn't go straight home?

Asher started to pull his phone out of his pocket only to remember that it had been seized as evidence. How was he supposed to arrange a ride home without it? He could probably go inside and borrow a phone to call someone, but then remembered how Gina had acted toward him. What if everyone said no? He was a pariah now. No one would want to touch him with a ten-foot pole.

Cursing under his breath, he stood on the sidewalk and struggled to recall a moment when he'd felt more helpless. He'd been in plenty of dicey situations where he'd survived thanks to skill and/or good luck. His current predicament was unique and terrifying because he had no clue how to fix what was happening to him.

He couldn't run or charm his way out of the situation. This was a problem he had to face head-on. Usually when disquieting emotions erupted, he'd turn his attention to something pleasant. Naturally Lani's image popped into his head, and as he recalled their conversation earlier that day, the frantic thrumming of his nerves eased.

Almost as if his powerful need had summoned her, a black SUV pulled up to the curb and the passenger-side window rolled down. The woman behind the wheel turned her head in his direction. Her eyes, hidden behind aviator sunglasses, Lani regarded him for a heartbeat, assessing him. A moment later, she issued a two-word command.

"Get in."

Asher didn't hesitate. He needed help and Lani had appeared as if in answer to his prayer. Grinning at this uptick in his fortune, he opened the door and got in.

"Thanks for—"

"Save it."

Her grim expression declared just how untrustworthy he'd become in her eyes. Yet for some reason this didn't set him back the way it should. As dark as things had become in the last few days, Lani was here. She'd come to his rescue. No matter what she said, deep down, some part of her believed he wasn't capable of stealing millions of dollars.

"How did you know I was out of jail?"

"Because I'm the one who paid your bail. I need access to you in order to do my job and that's impossible with you behind bars."

Not the rousing endorsement of his innocence he was hoping for, but he was thrilled to have her on his team even if his freedom was nothing more than a means to an end for her.

"Thanks," he repeated. Not wanting to irritate her further, he quelled the urge to say more.

She took her foot off the brake and the car rolled forward. Lani drove with the same focus she applied to everything. As if by sheer force of will, she could control what happened next. Yet Asher perceived several hairline cracks in her confidence. His former lover gripped the steering wheel like it was the gunnel of a pitching boat while her attention remained locked on the road ahead of them as if expecting sinkholes to open up out of nowhere.

"My car is at The Edmond Organization," he said, noticing that she was headed in the opposite direction. "If you want to drop me off."

"It's not there."

"What do you mean it's not there?"

"Your car has been seized by investigators. They are going over it now."

Asher's skin prickled. "Why?"

"They're looking for evidence."

"In my car?" he demanded.

"Your car. Your devices. Your home and office."

As if spending the night in jail and being shunned by his family hadn't been stressful enough, it appeared as if nothing in his life was going to escape unscathed by this mess.

He squashed his disappointment and lapsed into resigned silence as they headed out of town in the direction of Elegance Ranch, the Edmond family estate. The thought of being stuck in his apartment over the barn for the uncertain future gave Asher the chills. He hated being tied down... It was part of the reason his job at Edmond Oil frustrated him. There was no thrill or exhilaration being tied to a desk.

And that was why he'd jumped at the chance to be involved with the festival. It was a much-needed break from his routine. If only the whole thing hadn't failed so spectacularly. Maybe it would've turned out if he'd kept a better eye on everything. Not that he could've predicted the tornado that destroyed the place. But if he'd paid more attention to what was going on, maybe he wouldn't have been caught flat-footed with millions of dollars missing and all signs pointing straight at him like a ring of laser sights aimed at his head and heart.

"I want to hire you," Asher declared abruptly, turning his head to stare at her elegant profile. "To prove I'm innocent," he clarified, determined to do or say whatever it took to get her on his side.

"I already have a client."

He refused to be deterred. "You can work for both of us at the same time."

"You can't afford me," she reminded him with a hint of a smirk. "Your assets are frozen."

"I have ways of generating cash."

Her dark eyebrows rose above her sunglasses. "You've found someone else to steal from?"

He ignored the flippant jab. "I have twelve horses I'm training as polo mounts. They aren't all ready to go, but selling a couple of them would pay your fees."

Lani shook her head. "It's not just about the money. It would be a conflict of interest to work for you while I've been hired to investigate the theft and find the money."

"The way I see it, he hired you to get to the truth." Asher kept a close eye on her reaction to his reasoning. "I know I didn't steal the money. So, if I hire you for the same reason, then you don't have to be worried about any conflicts of interest."

She rolled her gaze his direction before returning her attention to the highway. "My intention is to find out what's going on. I'm not going to stop until I get to the bottom of what happened to the money."

"Good. Then we're on the same side."

"We're *not*." His assumption had obviously set a spark to her temper. "Just to be completely clear, I believe you had the means and the opportunity to steal that money. I'm really good at what I do. I will find out what happened and where the money went. And when I do, I'll know who's guilty and who's not."

Asher pressed his point. "That's fine with me because I swear to you that I didn't take the money."

"Gaslighting won't work on me." She paused and took in his confused expression. "Gaslighting. Where you keep saying something over and over in the hopes that I'll eventually believe that it's reality."

"If I'm repeating the same thing over and over, it's because I'm telling the truth."

"Let's just agree to disagree," she said, echoing something he'd said to her before they parted ways five years earlier.

It hadn't been the words as much as his dismissive tone as he'd delivered the cliché. Afterward she spent a lot of time thinking about how that abrupt breakup made her feel. What bothered her at the time was how he hadn't taken her concerns seriously. She'd not felt heard. Her feelings had been swept aside as if they hadn't matter. As if *she* hadn't mattered to him.

And that, in a nutshell, was what had been wrong with their relationship the whole time. It hadn't just been a summer fling for her. She hadn't had enough experience with men to be able to lock her heart in a box and engage in some truly phenomenal sex as if it were some sort of trendy new aerobic exercise.

Maybe if he hadn't been her first, she would've been more emotionally sophisticated. More capable of keeping their relationship in perspective. Of realizing that no matter how special he treated her in an effort to get her into bed, it was all just a means to an end. She'd been little more than a distraction that summer, a fact that had become clear when he'd never contacted her again.

Neither one of them spoke until Asher gave her the key code to unlock the gate.

"Are you still in the apartment above the stables?" she asked, angling toward the driveway that led past the main house.

"I prefer the horses to Rusty's company."

Lani shored up her resolve as a smile ghosted across his lips. The last thing she needed was to get sucked in by Asher's attempt to manipulate her emotions. He needed her on his side, a friendly ear to fill with his tales of woe. Well, she wasn't going to fall for his tactics. She wasn't on his side. And nothing he said or did was going to change that.

She parked the SUV behind the stables and while Asher

slid out of the vehicle, Lani reached for the duffel bag she'd stashed in the back. He glanced at it as she joined him at the base of the stairs that led to the two-bedroom apartment above the barn.

"What's in the bag?"

A little tingle of excitement danced across her skin. "I'm planning on staying here while I get to the bottom of what's going on."

"Staying here?" he echoed, his expression softening with interest. "With *me*?"

Oh, no. She recognized that look. Her pulse jumped at the implications. Whatever assumptions he was making, she needed to shut him down ASAP.

"This isn't a booty call," she declared, wincing at her raspy tone. "You have two bedrooms. I'm planning on using the one you don't sleep in."

"You're welcome to, of course," he murmured, watching her from beneath heavy lids, a smoky glow kindling in his gaze. "But are you sure you'll be comfortable alone here with me?"

Oh, she'd definitely be uncomfortable sharing four walls with him, but with the future of her business riding on this investigation, she intended to keep things professional between her and Asher.

Don't worry about my comfort, frat boy. Worry about the mountain of evidence against you. It's what she should've shot back. But that's not what came out.

"I have no intention of sleeping with you ever again." Even as the declaration escaped her, Lani knew she'd overreacted.

"Okay." He drew the word out while peering at her expression. "It seems to me that you had no intention of sleeping with me five years ago, but look how great that turned out."

Lani noted the heat surging through her veins at his

smugness and registered annoyance and impatience. Not desire. Not yearning. She was angry at him for reminding her of something she couldn't forget.

"I didn't know what I was doing back then."

"Maybe not at first," he agreed, misinterpreting her response. While she sputtered in mortified dismay, one side of his mouth kicked up into a wicked grin. "But you sure got the hang of things. And if I remember correctly, you even managed to teach me a thing or two."

Cheeks flaming, Lani silently cursed. From the moment she'd agreed to take this gig, she'd warned herself to remain focused on the case and not rehash how their summer romance had played out.

"Why don't we concentrate on the present," she suggested in a desperate rush, once again questioning her wisdom in taking on this assignment.

He gave a lazy one-shoulder shrug. "You're the one bringing up our past."

She set her foot onto the stairs and stomped up the stairs ahead of him. Why hadn't she argued more vigorously against Kingston Blue's insistence that she was a perfect investigator to take on the mystery of the missing millions? Every time she tried to follow her instincts when it came to this man, the best way forward was always murky.

Reaching the landing at the top, she shifted to one side and waited for Asher to enter the unlock code, but he merely turned the knob and pushed open the door.

"After you," he gestured with exaggerated gallantry.

Lani stared at the door. "You don't lock it?"

"What's the point? There's fencing all around the property and a gate at the entrance. Who should I worry about getting inside? Ross? Gina? Rusty?"

"They're not the only people who live here. What about Ross's college friend?"

"Billy Holmes?" Asher chuckled. "The guesthouse

where he's staying is way nicer than this. Besides, he doesn't seem the type to show up uninvited."

"But there are parties on the property. And staff. How many people have access to your apartment?"

"I never thought about it." He made a shooing gesture to urge her inside. "And anyway, I don't keep anything of value for someone to steal."

"That watch you're wearing isn't cheap."

He glanced down at the Breitling on his wrist and from his surprised expression, he obviously didn't register the ten-thousand-dollar accessory as being anything out of the ordinary. Lani didn't know whether to laugh or hit him. Five years ago, dating him had opened up a whole new world for her. She'd grown up in a comfortable middle-class home and never lacked for anything, but once she'd been drawn into Asher's circle, she'd gotten a firsthand glimpse into all the finest things money could buy.

Not that this had anything to do with why she'd gone out with him that first time. In fact his determination to buy her affection with huge tips had reinforced her resistance to his pursuit. Still, dating him had swept her into a fairy tale and she'd enjoyed being a princess for a little while.

"Holy sh—"

Asher's shock roused Lani from her musings. The apartment was torn apart—every cabinet in the kitchen was open, plates, cups, pans and silverware all over the countertops and floor. The couch cushions had been pulled apart and the small desk near one of the windows had been ransacked.

"What did they think I was hiding?"

His shoulders sagged as he rubbed his face. Sympathy whiplashed through Lani before she could steel herself against it. To her dismay, the profound defeat gripping Asher did little to distract from his sex appeal. In fact she was seized by an overwhelming urge to slide her arms around his broad shoulders and revisit the intense physical connection she'd only known with one man. *This* man.

Lani ground her teeth and slapped some sense into her emotions. She might no longer be in love with him, but his ability to burrow beneath her skin was alive and well.

"This is definitely worse than I expected," she murmured, bemused by the devastation. "Why don't you go grab a shower while I clean up."

After tossing her duffel bag into the empty bedroom, Lani put in earbuds and set to work putting the kitchen back together. Given that the theft had happened electronically, they could've been looking for a thumb drive and something that small could be anywhere. She swept scattered pasta and cereal into the trash and loaded the dishes and drinkware back into the cabinets. Sorting the silverware into the drawers took some time and as she worked, Lani couldn't help but wonder if the investigators had left the mess as a warning to Asher or if they'd had a limited amount of time to complete a thorough search.

She didn't notice Asher had returned until a light tap on her shoulder caused her to whirl around. He was standing right there, inches away, smelling of soap and minty toothpaste. Her brain went off-kilter as she stared at his lips, moving as they formed words she couldn't hear because...

He plucked her left earbud free and before she could make a grab for it, he'd fitted it into his ear. One eyebrow shot up as he listened to the song.

"I thought you only listened to Lowercase when you were worried about something."

His question was the yummy center of a raspberry-filled donut. Her mouth watered as if the sugary-sweetness flowed across her taste buds. How was it possible that he'd remembered her obscure taste in music after all this time?

"It helps me think." Lowercase was a music genre built around unheard ambient sounds.

"What are you thinking about?"

Lani held her hand out for the earbud, not wanting him to read anything into tonight's musical choice. His fingertips grazed her palm as he dropped the one he'd taken back into her keeping. Weathering the zing of pleasure at the contact, she popped both earbuds back into their case and slid it into her jacket pocket.

"This case. My next steps."

"You always have a plan, don't you?" He sounded resigned.

"It beats running around without direction, hoping something will develop."

"If you plan for everything, nothing will surprise you." He spun her around and tugged the elastic band down her ponytail, freeing her long hair. "I've really missed this," he murmured, threading his fingers through the dark curtain, fanning it over her shoulders. Several strands spilled over her cheeks, tickling her skin. "Your hair is like satin. I've never known anything like it."

She stood transfixed as he gathered her hair together and then proceeded to separate the strands into three sections. The gentle pull as he began braiding launched her into the past. The first time he'd done this for her she'd been surprised by his skill. He'd explained that while a polo horse's mane was shaved to keep it from interfering with the reins, the tails were braided and taped up for competition.

"There you go," he murmured, securing the bottom of the braid and giving an affectionate little tug the way he always did. "Ready for bed."

With her skin awash in goose bumps, Lani turned to face him. They were standing so close. As he leaned into her space, she gathered soft folds of his T-shirt, clutching the material between trembling fingers, needing something to ground her.

Cupping the back of her neck, he lowered his forehead until it was touching hers. "Thank you."

These weren't the words she'd been expecting him to say and frustration spiked.

"Asher." His name whispered out of her in protest, in longing. "Please stop thanking me."

"I can't," he murmured. "You're the only one who's helping me."

"I'm on a case. That's all there is to it." Yet even as she restated her purpose, her spine arched ever so slightly to bring her torso into contact with his. After an instant of contact, her breasts grazing his chest, she retreated.

This was madness. She had to stop this. To back away. But with his breath caressing her heated skin, she couldn't move. All it would take for their lips to come together was the slightest shift from either of them.

Temptation gnawed at her common sense. Her whole body ached with longing. She hadn't been celibate in the years since they'd parted, but no man awakened her hunger like Asher. It wasn't fair that his body could drive her wild with pleasure when his temperament clashed with everything she believed in.

Tingles shot down her spine as the tips of his fingers caressed her nape, moved along the side of her neck. Lani nerves sang. Desire moved through her like a ghost, terrifying her. How long had they been standing here like this? Seconds? Minutes? Time blurred when Asher touched her.

Kissing him would set a bad precedent. Her professionalism was a press of lips away from being thrown out the window. On the other hand, her job was to find the festival funds. A kiss hinted that her belief in his guilt was fading. Pretending to be on his side could convince him to trust her. What happened after she figured out where Asher had hidden the money was a problem for the future.

"Lani." The low throb in his voice intensified the ache blooming between her thighs.

"Yes?"

As he grazed his knuckles along her jaw, her lips parted in anticipation and her breath rushed out in agitated puffs as every nerve in her body went on full alert. He set his thumb beneath her chin, a promise of what came next. Craving a barely-there brush of her lips against his, she rose on tiptoe just the tiniest bit. She'd lost control of her purpose. But instead of a kiss that curled her toes and inspired her to dance in the moonlight, he planted his lips against her forehead.

"See you in the morning."

Lani reeled back a step and cleared her throat, blathering out the first thing that popped into her mind. "Sure. I'll be here when you get up."

"Sleep well."

Before he walked away, his dark eyes searched hers, and a small perceptive smile tugged at the corners of his lips. If her skin weren't already on fire, she was certain she'd be flushing scarlet beneath his knowing look. She'd thought to play him and instead he'd expertly turned the tables on her. Lani sighed. She'd been a fool to suppose a single kiss would propel Ash to confess his guilt and spill his guts. She was playing with fire letting the old chemistry between them ignite once more. Yet the tactic could still work if she could manage to act the part without getting sucked in.

Five years ago she'd been slow to trust Asher, but eventually his persistence and irresistible sex appeal had worn her down. Once her hormones had seized the wheel, they'd driven her heart straight into a solid brick wall of misery.

This time, while she might be too wise to tumble head over heels for his effortless charm and handsome face, if she kept missing signs and misinterpreting signals, she could be in way too deep before she knew what hit her.

* * *

Despite not having slept at all in the jail cell the night before, Asher lay in the middle of his king-size bed, hands tucked beneath his head, ankles crossed, eyes tracing shadows on the ceiling. He'd retreated to his bedroom a couple hours ago, but adrenaline still surged through his veins, keeping him awake.

Lani Li was here. In his home. Sleeping ten strides from where he lay. The thrill of it kept his exhaustion at bay. He pictured her curled on her side, long braid coiled around her throat, her thick straight lashes a dark smudge against her ivory cheeks.

Not one thing about her had changed in the last five years. She continued to be the most intense, uptight, no-nonsense female he'd ever met. Except in bed where uptight and no-nonsense had given away to curious and naughty.

He'd been her first. The shock that delivered to his system had cemented her as the most memorable woman he'd ever had in his bed.

His lips still tingled from the silken heat of her skin when he'd kissed her forehead. They'd both been on the verge of moving too fast, of losing themselves in the fierce chemistry between them. Last time she'd been an innocent and he'd won her by awakening her sensual appetites. And then he'd lost her because he'd failed to treat her heart with the same care.

Asher hadn't realized how much he'd missed her until she'd appeared in front of his jail cell. Probably because after they'd ended things, he'd gone out of his way to purge her from his system.

With his thoughts filled with Lani, he finally fell asleep and woke with her foremost in his mind late the next morning. From the position of the light, he could tell it was mid to late morning. Reaching toward the nightstand for his phone, he remembered the police still had it. Cursing, he sat up and noticed the scent of coffee mingling with bacon. His stomach growled, reminding him that he'd skipped dinner the night before.

Pulling on worn jeans and a black polo shirt, he shuffled into the open-concept kitchen and living room and spied Lani at the kitchen island, typing away on her laptop.

"You made breakfast," he murmured unnecessarily, checking out the pan on the stove. "Have you already eaten?"

She didn't look up from her computer. "Hours ago."

"I didn't sleep at all the night before." He clamped down on further excuses and poured a cup of coffee, topping hers off in the process. After doctoring his cup, he pushed the sugar and creamer in her direction.

The eggs were freshly cooked and exactly as he liked them. His heart bumped against his ribs as he surveyed the scrambled eggs with fried onions and cheddar cheese melted through. He finished them off in record time and stood watching her work, gnawing on the final piece of thick-cut bacon.

"Stop staring at me," Lani muttered, picking up the coffee cup near her elbow and sipping the strong brew.

"Why?" He ran hot water over the pan and dishes before sliding them into the dishwasher. "You're the most interesting thing around."

"You can stop right there. I'm not susceptible to flattery."

"The fact that you felt the need to tell me that makes me think otherwise." He sent his gaze trailing over her features. She was even more beautiful than she'd been five years earlier. "And I'm not trying to flatter you. It's the truth. You fascinated me from the moment I first laid eyes on you."

"Don't confuse what happened between us five years ago to what's going on between us today. You are a *job*. Nothing more. I bailed you out because I need you to tell me where you stashed the money."

He was pondering how long she would stick around before his inability to provide the information she needed would cause her to give up on him...again...when she let out an impatient huff.

"Shouldn't you be doing something productive right now?" She jerked her head, indicating the apartment's front door.

He had horses he could exercise, but they would keep for a little while longer.

"I thought you needed my help with your case."

"Not right this second."

Coming around to her side of the island, he leaned his forearm on the cool countertop and peered at her laptop screen. Their shoulders bumped and he hid a grin as she shifted away. Obviously his presence bothered her. He could work with that.

"You are always so single-minded. At first, I thought that was just a cute personality quirk until I got to know you better. Then I realized how incredibly sexy your intense focus could be."

He'd barely finished speaking when she slapped the laptop closed and slid off the barstool.

"To be clear," she said, sliding the computer into a protective sleeve, "I am not here because I have any interest in starting up anything with you again. Let's just keep things between us professional."

"I don't see why I should have to do that. It's not as if I'm a client or anything."

"I'm investigating you," she reminded him.

"You're looking for the missing festival funds and trying to discover the real story. That puts us on the same side. Nothing wrong with hooking up with a fellow truth-seeker, is there?"

"Hooking up...?" Outrage crackled in her voice. "Don't even get me started on how wrong it is."

"You used to find me irresistible."

"You had your moments." She slipped into the same blazer she'd worn the day before and slung a tote bag over her shoulder, signaling her plans to leave. "Your situation was completely different back then."

Meaning that he might have been a *frat boy* but, as far as she knew, he hadn't been a criminal. Was his appearance of guilt all that stood between them? Would she relent once it became clear he hadn't stolen any money? Or should he get her back into his bed so she'd be motivated to clear him? Either way he would win. Cleared of all wrongdoing and Lani as his lover once more.

The whole thing seemed so simple until he remembered the strong evidence mounted against him. Just because he hadn't stolen from the festival, didn't mean he wouldn't go to jail for the theft. So far, his denials hadn't convinced anyone of his innocence. Nor should he expect to be taken at his word. Buying that damning house in his name in the Maldives had been clever. Somebody was setting him up. But who? Was it possible that someone had stolen his identity? He recalled Lani's reaction to his unlocked door. Maybe it wasn't far-fetched. But how did he go about proving something like that? No doubt she had the resources to follow the money. But how did he steer her to look for whoever had framed him when she was so convinced he was the bad guy?

"Where are you off to?" he asked.

"I have to meet a new client."

Asher loathed the idea of being left all alone with his problems. "Can I come along?" Even as he offered her his most-winning smile, he felt like a puppy begging to go for a car ride.

"No."

He strode into the kitchen and selected the largest knife in the drawer. Lani watched him through narrowed eyes as he set his foot on the counter and slid his finger beneath the strap that kept the electronic monitor on his ankle.

"What do you think you're doing?" Lani's voice rang with annoyance.

"I suffer from separation anxiety," he declared, carrying the dog metaphor beyond the absurd. "There's no telling what I'll get up to if you leave me alone here."

"Don't be ridiculous," she snapped, but her eyes remained glued to the knife. "You are perfectly fine on your own."

"Normally." He tested the edge of the blade with his thumb. A line of red appeared. Damn, it was sharper than he'd expected. "But I'm under a great deal of stress at the moment and I might do something completely rash without someone to keep an eye on me. Like maybe remove this monitor." He paused. "How much is my bail?"

"A hundred thousand." She ground out the number between clenched teeth.

"That's a lot. And you're responsible for me, right?"

Her nostrils flared as she sucked in a sharp breath. "Asher."

"Let me come along and I swear I won't be any trouble."

"Your middle name is trouble," she muttered. "Fine. I'll call and let the people monitoring you know that we're heading to Dallas."

"I'll put on some shoes."

Ten minutes later they were speeding toward Dallas with Lani behind the wheel and Asher studying her profile. She was trying to appear impassive, but her tight lips betrayed her inner turmoil.

"So, how come you're a private investigator?" he said, breaking the stony silence between them. "What happened to becoming a fed?"

"I got in." Her knuckles turned white as she clutched the steering wheel. "But in the course of my training, the amount of gender discrimination I encountered was more than I could stand. The good ol' boy network is alive and well at the FBI. Eighty percent of the trainees discharged prior to graduation are women and that's mostly because the people in charge dismiss mistakes made by male trainees as isolated incidents and declare them to be retrainable at a disproportionately higher rate than their female trainee counterparts."

"I'm sorry," he murmured, hearing the pain she was trying to mask with a clinical recitation of facts. "I know that was important to you."

So important that she'd chosen to pursue the dream over him.

"Tell me more about your firm,"

"I started it two years ago after finishing up with my master's degree. I worked with an investigator for a year before striking out on my own."

"You must be doing pretty well."

A shadow passed over her face before she mustered an off-handed shrug. "I'm doing okay."

But not as well as she'd like to be doing. Asher tapped his fingers on his thigh. His restless nature intensified when he was stressed or bored. Usually being around Lani calmed him, but he'd picked up on her tension and found himself uneasily pondering why she hadn't pursued law enforcement the way she'd intended.

"What sort of investigations do you do?"

"I've made a name for myself as a financial investigator. Divorces. Fraud. Embezzlement." Her gaze twitched his direction at the last word.

"You carry a gun," Asher pointed out. "Is there a lot of violence in financial investigations? I would've figured it would be done by being in an enclosed room with a computer."

"I do what needs to be done. I have a technical guy that

does contract work for me, a cyber specialist who can get all sorts of information."

"Legally?"

A muscle jumped in her jaw. "If you're asking whether he can dig into everything you do online, then the answer is yes. There aren't too many secrets that escape Donovan."

"So, he's looking into me." He paused, giving her room to answer, but when she remained silent, he continued, "When you find out that I'm an open book with no secrets at all, will you trust me then?"

"*Trust* is a word I don't use lightly when it comes to you."

"But if you don't find anything," he persisted, "you'll have to believe me when I tell you I had nothing to do with the missing money."

"Or you're just real clever."

Asher gave a wry snort. "Well, at long last I have something to crow about. Lani Li just called me clever."

She shot him a look. "You make it sound like I think you're stupid. That's never been the case. What I think you are is underachieving."

He winced at her blunt, if mostly accurate, declaration. As a teenager, when he'd failed to win his adoptive father's approval, frustration had led to resentment. The things Asher had a passion for, activities he excelled at—polo, extreme sports, playing the stock market—were never going to impress Rusty.

Yet deep down he still clung to the hope that one day the impossible old man would be proud of his adopted son. It was part of what had prompted Asher to switch gears and take a job he hated with The Edmond Organization. But as the months went by and Rusty was as indifferent as ever, Asher realized he'd made a mistake.

Maybe if his dad had lived and Asher could've had a father who loved him unconditionally, he might have had a solid foundation to build something out of his life. Often he'd wished for a positive paternal figure who'd listen to him and offered advice based on what he enjoyed doing. Instead, Rusty had ignored or criticized him in turns. With support, he might've been able to focus on what he loved. To fully commit instead of fighting against other people's expectations and always falling short.

"You're right about that," Asher said, not letting his angst slip into his tone. "Ask anyone in the family. I'm the quintessential underachiever."

"You don't seem thrilled to be working at The Edmond Organization," she said. "So, why are you doing it?"

"Rusty got tired of supporting me and decided to give me the choice of working for the company or being cut off." At least that's what everyone assumed was going on because that was part of the bargain he'd made with Rusty.

"Let me get this straight." She took her eyes off the road and speared him with a dubious look. "You gave up polo and came to work for the company in order to keep your lifestyle intact?"

"Seems like the obvious choice, don't you think?"

She didn't react to his flippant tone. "Obvious, maybe, but you don't seem happy."

"Since when are you an expert on what makes me happy?" he shot back, still pained by her blunt opinion of him all those years earlier.

What made the sting so much sharper is that she hadn't been wrong. He'd loved playing polo, but he hadn't played up to his abilities. He hadn't had to with Rusty's money backing him.

"I'm not," she said, her voice somewhat softening with regret. "I'm sorry I said that. I don't know you at all and have no business making assumptions."

"No, I'm sorry." He rubbed his chest where a tight knot had formed. Damn. "It's just that I never imagined our reunion happening because I was accused of embezzlement and that you'd believe I was guilty."

"Wait." She frowned in confusion. "You imagined that we'd have a reunion?"

"Sure."

"Unbelievable," she muttered, tossing an indignant look his way. "Then why haven't I heard from you in five years?"

Three

Lani breathed slowly in and out through her nose, struggling against the anguish that had just blindsided her. Damn it. Why had she asked that ridiculous question? Now the infuriating man would think it bothered her that they'd never reconnected.

"I don't have a good answer," Asher admitted, sounding more subdued than he had a moment earlier.

"Of course you don't."

Why couldn't she stop being surprised when he disappointed her? After all, she'd traveled to Royal to investigate him for embezzling millions of dollars.

"Did you want me to?"

"I…" Had she?

Lani's heart began to race. Once upon a time she'd prided herself on being straightforward and honest with people. Experience had taught her that this tactic didn't always produce the results she desired. Bottom line? She learned to mislead people in her pursuit of the truth or justice for her clients.

Kingston Blue had chosen her because of her past romantic connection with Asher. Was it wrong to take advantage of that to get him to trust her? If she appeared to believe he was innocent, maybe he'd drop his defenses and slip up.

"Well?" he prompted.

"It would've been nice to hear from you," she admitted, keeping her tone from revealing her inner conflict.

"Really?" He practically vibrated with curiosity. "The way things ended, I thought you'd be happy never to hear from me again."

"Yes…well." She couldn't give in immediately or he'd be suspicious. He had to work for it.

"You were pretty mad the last time we talked," he reminded her.

"You told me a long-distance thing between us would never work after I told you I thought I was falling in love you, and then when I asked how you felt about me, you said you liked me, but didn't think it was that serious between us." Acutely aware of Asher's gaze on her, Lani stared straight ahead and resisted the urge to glance his way. She focused on calm thoughts to reduce the heat scorching her cheeks as she revisited the humiliating scene. "And then you said it wasn't your intention to upset me."

"See, I was right. You are still mad at me."

"For pulling that typical guy crap and turning the whole disagreement back on me? You bet I am!" Her temper flared. "As if I was being unreasonable because I wanted to keep things going."

"Even though it would never have worked?"

Lani released a frustrated breath. "We could've at least tried." But agreeing to attempt a long-distance relationship would mean he had feelings for her and that had obviously not been the case.

"What can I do to make it up to you?"

He could tell her where the money went. "Not a damned thing."

"I don't believe that."

"Really. I don't want you to make anything up to me. We went our separate ways five years ago and it was for the best. In fact, I should thank you. Dragging things out in an effort to make it work and then failing would've been a lot harder in the end."

"Lani…"

She gave her head a vigorous shake to keep him from saying something that would make her wonder…was there a way they could find their way to each other this time?

"Let's just keep the past where it belongs and focus on keeping things professional between us."

To her relief, Asher lapsed into silence and focused his attention on the landscape speeding past them. Lani let out an inaudible sigh.

Why was she surprised to be no closer to figuring out what made him tick than she had been all those years ago? Back then, little had seemed to bother him. The only thing that seemed to get under his skin was the way his adoptive father treated him with such indifference and even when she'd asked him about it, Asher had shrugged it off as Rusty's issue, not his.

Asher was an expert at putting up a good front, never admitting anything was wrong, never asking for help. His reluctance to dwell on anything that made him uncomfortable had made it hard for them to develop the sort of intimate connection Lani craved. Not that this stopped her from falling deeper under his spell with each day that passed. And yet, despite his unwillingness to share how his father's death had affected him, she sensed that the loss left him unsure how to let people in.

Maybe if he'd opened up to her, shown that he needed her, she might not have given up on him so easily. But she couldn't figure out where she fit in his life and in the end she'd let him go.

Which had relieved her parents to no end. They'd been afraid she'd put off her education to run around the world with some rich, entitled polo player, thus ruining her life. While staying on the path she'd laid out for herself had been sensible, her decision wasn't without regret. Especially after her dreams of a career in the FBI had abruptly ended. Add in her struggles to build her business, and she sometimes wondered if she could've been happy following Asher from Argentina to England and all over the US.

One thing was for sure, she never imagined he'd take a position at the family organization. She knew he must have hated being tied down and yet didn't Rusty's threat to cut him off if he quit feed perfectly into a motive for Asher to steal the money? The amount that had gone missing would've funded his polo playing for many years. Or had he planned to roam the globe in search of thrilling adventures?

Yet Asher made it sound like he was relying on the Edmond family fortune when she'd noticed that he'd moved up the ranks and started doing really well as a professional polo player. His Twitter feed reflected numerous endorsements and photo shoots he'd done, capitalizing on his good looks. He'd engaged in a fair amount of philanthropic work, as well. So why was he promoting the impression that he'd been barely getting by without Rusty's money?

"Tell me something about the client you're meeting," Asher prompted, pulling Lani from her thoughts.

For a moment she thought of refusing, but talking about her work beat brooding over this man. "She came to me because her husband is cheating on her and she wants to make sure she has a clear financial picture to take to her divorce lawyer."

"I don't know why men do that."

"Do what?" she quizzed, shooting a sidelong glance his way. "Get married, cheat or hide money?"

"Get married and then cheat." Was he thinking about Rusty who'd been married four times—once for three years to Asher's mother—and was currently single and definitely mingling? "What's the point of agreeing to love someone 'til death do you part only to change your mind a few years later?"

"Is that why you never got married?" she found herself asking.

"I never got married because playing professional polo kept me from settling down with the right woman."

Was he talking in generalities or had his heart been claimed before or since they'd been together? The question raised all the insecurities she'd experienced that summer. The vividness of her reaction was like standing next to a warning siren when it went off. Her muscles twitched in response, sending a pulse of adrenaline through her.

"You seem to have settled down now, so why haven't you reached out?"

"Who says I haven't?"

"Is she in a relationship or married?"

"Neither. But she doesn't really trust that I'm not the same man she once knew."

Lani wasn't sure how to answer him. Nor could she figure out why she was pouring lemon juice on an old cut that had never fully healed. At least she knew why he hadn't wanted to try a long-distance relationship with her. Obviously he'd never gotten over the woman he'd once loved.

"You should get in touch with her. She might surprise you."

"She might," Asher murmured, his expression pensive.

With the mood between them growing incredibly awkward, Lani was thrilled that her office was only five minutes away. She pulled into the underground parking garage and slipped into her dedicated spot. Now that she and Asher had arrived, Lani was quite sure that agreeing to let him tag along had been the wrong decision.

"There's a café and lounge on the first floor where you can wait," she said, snagging her laptop out of the back seat and slipping from the SUV. "My meeting shouldn't take too long."

"Do you mind if I come along? I'd like to see your office."

"It would be better if you didn't."

Asher pointed to his ankle monitor. "Separation anxiety, remember?"

Since Lani couldn't trust him to refrain from doing something that might blow back on her, she had no choice but to agree. And she couldn't ignore that she wanted to show off a little. The spot she'd chosen for her firm was north of downtown Dallas in a glass-enclosed building with great views. Her office was on the eighth floor. She shared a spacious waiting area with a lawyer and an accountant and had done work for both of them in the year since she'd moved in.

"This is me," she declared unnecessarily a few minutes later, unlocking the door to the dual-office suite and making her way down the hall.

Entering her airy workspace with its glass walls and north-facing windows, she circled her desk and woke up her computer to check if any email had come in during the drive from Royal.

Asher glanced around the space, noting the light spilling in the floor-to-ceiling windows. The room was spacious enough to accommodate a table with four chairs, her desk and a pair of guest chairs.

"Who works there?"

Lani looked up. His attention had shifted toward the empty workspace they'd passed. "No one at the moment." Seeing his curiosity hadn't been satisfied, she sighed. "When I leased the space, I'd hoped to expand. Add an associate. I still plan to. It's just that I don't have enough business at the moment." Hopefully that would change once she completed this job for Kingston Blue. "So, now that you've seen my office…" She hoped he'd take the hint and leave her to await her client in peace. "Like I said, there's a café downstairs. Or you can sit in the waiting room."

"Why not there?" He indicated the empty office. "No one's using it."

Before Lani could argue, a woman appeared in the open doorway from the waiting room. Shooting Asher a withering glare, Lani smoothed her face and stepped forward to greet the newcomer.

"Hello, I'm Lani Li."

"Mika Sorenson."

Sensing that he'd already pushed his luck too far with Lani, Asher waited until the women were seated before he popped into Lani's office.

"Can I get you anything?" he offered. "Water? Coffee? Soda?" He'd spied a small interior room with a copier, storage and a beverage cooler.

"Nothing for me." Mika gave him an appreciative smile. "Thank you."

"Ms. Li?" The way her eyes flashed, Asher could tell he'd gone too far.

"I'm fine." Her teeth were firmly clenched as she added, "Thank you."

With a smirk Lani's client did not see, Asher ducked out of the room and headed straight into the empty workspace. Because the building was going for a sophisticated modern aesthetic with industrial vibes, glass walls divided this office from the larger one where Lani sat. Asher settled back in the office chair with his back to Lani, and strained to hear the conversation. The women spoke in subdued voices, making it impossible to discern more than a word here or there. Asher had resigned himself to the fact that he wasn't going to learn anything, and was about to head down to the café when a tall man wearing an expensive suit and a stormy expression strode into the office.

When the man's furious gaze locked on Mika Sorenson in Lani's office and his fingers curled into fists, Asher was on his feet and standing in the man's path before the guy had taken more than two steps.

"Can I help you?" Asher demanded in a tone that said he had no intention of being the least bit cooperative.

"That's my wife."

"Okay."

Before Asher could say more, Sorenson's red face contorted in rage and he made as if to charge into Lani's office and take his bad temper out on both women. He set his hand on the man's shoulder, determined to get the guy out of there, but Sorenson was completely focused on his wife.

"You stupid bitch," the man yelled, pushing his weight against Asher in an effort to power past him. "Who the hell do you think you are hiring a private investigator to spy on me?"

The situation was deteriorating fast and Asher had to get the guy out of there. He caught the man's arm in a tight grip. "Let's go."

Although Asher and Sorenson were the same height, the other man lacked Asher's strength. But what Sorenson lacked in muscle, he made up for in outrage.

"Who the hell are you? Let go of me."

"You need to leave," Asher said.

"The hell I do. I'm not going anywhere without my wife."

Asher didn't need to look over his shoulder to know that Mika Sorenson was afraid. And that Lani was not. Years of playing polo had given him the ability to widen his senses and track the ever-changing dynamic of a game where eight players, each riding a thousand-pound horse and swinging a three-foot mallet, all raced after a fist-sized ball. He knew Lani was going to get in the middle of this scuffle and that she might get hurt. Sorenson needed to go before that happened.

"Call security," Asher advised Lani, his gaze never leaving the other man.

Sorenson didn't seem to hear. "Get out of my way."

Keeping his tone mild, Asher responded, "I can't do that."

When the man's fist came toward his face, Asher leaned out of the way. Off balance from the wild swing, Sorenson wasn't at all ready when his opponent snagged his foot and used his own momentum to send him toppling to the floor. Asher winced when Sorenson's head bounced off the hardwood flooring. Convinced Sorenson wasn't about to jump up and go for round two, Asher glanced toward Lani.

Her eyes had gone wide as they bounced from him to the man on the ground. Already adrenaline surged through his veins from the altercation, but seeing the unbridled hunger in Lani's mink-brown gaze, his whole body went up in flames.

"Security," he rasped, wanting nothing more than to take her in his arms and claim the passion parting her soft lips. "You can thank me later." The declaration was both a warning and a promise. Unlike the previous night, there would be no chaste kiss on her forehead. He intended to accept her gratitude in spades.

In the end, with some sense knocked into him, Sorenson left on his own, escorted to the elevator by Asher. When he returned to Lani's office, a white-faced Mika Sorenson was making an appointment with a divorce attorney and Lani was arranging a safe place for her client to temporarily stay.

Lani was standing at her office window, staring out at the storm blowing out of the west when Asher returned from walking Mika to her car in the parking garage. Lightning flashed and the building rumbled as thunder rolled over them. Asher crossed to stand beside her, noting that her tension was as charged as the atmosphere outside.

"Thank you," she muttered, sounding not one bit convincing.

"Oh, you're going to have to do better than that."

She turned toward him, eyes fierce, arms crossed. "Fine. Thank you very much."

Asher snaked his left arm around her waist and brought her up against him hard. "Better," he coaxed, his tone lifting on the latter syllable.

"I don't know what more you want."

"Oh, I think you do." Dragging his knuckles over her flushed cheek, he lowered his head until his lips hung a whisper above hers. "I want you to say it."

"Say what?" The mutinous line of her mouth wavered even as her muscles softened, bringing her pliant curves into sizzling contact with his hard planes.

"Say that you were glad I was here to take care of you and your client today. How having me around was a good thing."

"I could've handled him just fine." She let loose a shocked gasp as he slid his palm up her spine, wrapped his fingers around her ponytail and gave it a sharp tug. "But I'm glad you were here so I didn't have to."

"Better."

The uneven cadence of her breath matched his as he

covered her mouth with his in a deep kiss meant to remind her how they'd once burned up the nights. Electricity danced down his spine as his stomach somersaulted. Rain battered the window beside them. And lightning flashed once more, this time behind his eyes as her tongue darted forward to tangle with his. Her sultry moan filled his ears while her warm skin scented the air with roses and jasmine. She lifted her fingertips to his face and ran them over his stubbly cheek. He loved when she touched him like this.

This made sense. Her lips. Kissing her. Feeling once again like some part of him was complete. Why did it only happen when she was in his arms? Everything inside him quieted, making room for this amazing explosion of fulfillment and joy.

Lani angled her head, taking him deeper into her mouth, breathing him in as her fingers tunneled through his hair, nails digging into his scalp. Her lashes were a butterfly kiss against his skin as she pulled him closer, pressing her breasts into his chest and sliding her knee up his thigh as if by wrapping herself around him, they could meld and become one.

Asher lowered his hand to her hip and was seconds away from cupping her butt and lifting her off her feet when an annoying buzzing sound began. Lani noticed it too and rolled her head back, disengaging from the kiss.

"Ignore it." Issuing the command, he fanned his fingers over her lower back to keep his iron-hard erection firmly pressed into her slowly rocking hips. "Stay just like this," he murmured, in awe of her power over him.

"We shouldn't be..." She twisted free of him, her chest heaving as if she'd finished a mile-long sprint. Scrambling to where her phone was still buzzing madly on her desk, she raked a trembling hand over the tendrils that had escaped her neat ponytail. "Yes?"

Asher leaned back against the cool glass window and shuddered while another boom of thunder rolled through the building. Or was that just the reverberation of his pounding heart? He couldn't catch his breath. The shock of that kiss. Lani's ardent response. How lust had transformed her into living flame... It was all so *exhilarating*. He'd forgotten how intoxicatingly blissful kissing her could be.

He loved her complexities. Straightforward and practical in her role as an investigator and her pursuit of her career goals. Recklessly passionate when it came to her heart. She'd trusted him when she shouldn't have and doubted him when he'd been most honest with her.

While she settled behind the desk and started typing on her keyboard, he let his gaze roam over her lips. She was gnawing on the lower one and he had to look away as sweat prickled his skin.

"Is everything okay?" he asked as she concluded her call.

She'd sat back, narrowed eyes glued to the computer screen. In the space of ten minutes, she'd cooled to focused professionalism. Meanwhile his defenses were down and his anticipation was sky-high.

"Everything's fine." She did a slow blink and seemed to return from whatever deep dive her brain had done. "Are you ready to go back to Royal?"

"I thought maybe while we're in Dallas we could have dinner." Somewhere romantic and far away from the accusing eyes in Royal so he could lavish his charm on her and see if he could soften her attitude toward him.

She glanced at her phone. "We really need to get back. I already have dinner plans."

"Here in Dallas?" A spike of jealousy caused his voice to harden. Until this moment he hadn't considered that she might be involved with someone. But if she was, would she have kissed him like that?

"No," she said. "In Royal."

"Something having to do with the investigation?" With their passionate embrace sparking his baser instincts, Asher was feeling possessive and didn't come off nearly as nonchalant as he'd hoped.

"At the moment the investigation is my main focus."

A non-answer. And from the look on her face, all she was planning to give.

Four

Lani's dinner engagement with Rusty Edmond had stirred a fair amount of interest amongst the members of the Texas Cattleman's Club. Given his family's connection to the Soiree on the Bay debacle, she'd been a little surprised that the oil tycoon wanted to meet in such a public venue. She'd thought he'd prefer to keep a low profile and share a quiet meal somewhere discreet. Instead, as the hostess led her to a table in the middle of the TCC's large dining room, Lani realized that she would be a headliner performing on the center stage.

Great.

It made sense that a man like Rusty Edmond wouldn't be chased away by some negative gossip about his family. No doubt he'd ruffled a lot of feathers while amassing his enormous fortune. What did he care if people whispered about him behind his back?

"Ms. Li." Rusty stood as she approached, his cordial smile not reaching the winter gray of his assessing gaze.

"Mr. Edmond," she countered, wondering if he remembered he'd invited her to call him Rusty the last time they'd met.

The nickname struck her as a blatant attempt to make the man approachable. It was ridiculous. Russell Edmond Sr. was an intimating man by nature. One of the richest oilmen in Texas, he had a mercurial temperament and a roving eye when it came to women.

"Call me Rusty," he rumbled in warm tones, his eyes taking in her measure, lingering a little too long on her breasts for Lani's comfort. Which made her doubly glad she'd resisted the impulse to wear something more flattering. He stuck out his hand as she drew within reach. "May I call you Lani?"

"Of course." As her hand was swallowed in his grip, she was struck by the man's imposing physical presence, as well as the aggressive potency of his personality. "Thank you for agreeing to meet me."

"I understand you bailed my son out of jail."

Okay, so they were diving right in. "I've been hired to investigate where the missing money has gone." *And who took it.*

"Have you asked Asher?" Rusty's expression gave her no clue to whether this was a serious question or if the man was being droll.

"Yes. He claims he didn't steal the money." Lani paused for a beat, waiting for the older man's reaction. "I'm not sure he gains anything by taking it."

Rusty snorted. "He gains millions of dollars."

"Yes, but the theft was so obviously done by him. Why hadn't he fled before the funds were discovered to be missing? He used part of the money to buy a house in the Maldives. Surely he had to know that would make him the prime suspect."

The waitress stopped by their table and took Lani's drink

order. Rusty already had a mostly-empty crystal tumbler sitting in front of him and ordered another whiskey.

"So, you think Asher is innocent." A statement, not a question. "Even though he purchased a house in the Maldives."

"I'm not sure that he did. And he's not the only one with access to the festival accounts who needed money. You disinherited Ross."

Lani paid careful attention to how Rusty reacted to her pointing a finger at his biological son, unsurprised by the man's cold glare. The oil tycoon had cut off Ross several months ago after finding out he'd slept with an employee and fathered a son with her. The tension between Ross and Rusty had eased somewhat in recent weeks, but it was completely possible that Ross might've started skimming the festival funds after such a dramatic reversal in his fortune.

"My son isn't a thief."

Which son? Lani's heart clenched in sympathy for Asher.

"I'm just pointing out that Ross had means, motive and opportunity. And he could've misdirected the investigation so that all the evidence points to Asher."

"Are you trying to say that Asher was set up?"

"It's a possibility."

Skepticism rolled off Rusty. "You two dated a while back." His lips twisted into disdain. "Are you sure this isn't personal for you?"

Despite preparing to be asked this question, Lani's cheeks heated. The incendiary kiss she and Asher had shared earlier made any denial she might make now a big fat lie.

"I was hired to find the missing money. If the federal investigators believe Asher is guilty, they won't be following any other leads." Lani's gaze clashed with Rusty's wintery one. "If neither Asher nor Ross are guilty, do you have any idea who else might have stolen the funds?"

"I don't." Nor did Rusty Edmond look happy about that. He was a man of decisive action. It must be difficult for him to sit by and let the situation play out. He finished his drink as the waitress set the new tumbler before him and swept away the empty glass. "I recommend the rib eye."

Lani didn't order the eighteen-ounce bone-in steak. Instead she chose a center-cut filet mignon that melted in her mouth. Five years ago Asher had brought her here for dinner. That night she'd been a starry-eyed girl unaccustomed to such lavish service and exquisite cuisine. Watching Rusty attack his own dinner with relish, Lani wondered if any of the Edmond family could survive without their cushy safety net of wealth and privilege.

Although her dinner companion kept turning the conversation away from any further talk of the failed festival or the tornado that had devastated Appaloosa Island the month before, Lani repeatedly circled back. From the way Rusty spoke about Ross, Gina and especially Asher, his pessimistic opinion of them predated any mishandling of Soiree on the Bay. Lani was utterly depressed by the time he waved away the waitress's attempts to list off the daily dessert specials.

She was gathering breath to thank the oil mogul for his time when someone approached their table. Lani recognized Ross's friend Billy Holmes from her preliminary research into everyone connected to the festival. The man's chiseled cheekbones, dark hair and assessing blue eyes combined into a face of arresting handsomeness. Maybe his long nose was a shade too narrow, the cant of his mouth a bit self-indulgent. But as he sized her up in turn, she sensed he knew how to work a room.

Rusty lit up as he and Billy exchanged greetings, startling Lani. She'd heard that Billy had Rusty's ear when his own children couldn't get his attention. Seeing the way the man oozed charm, she understood why Rusty liked him.

And apparently so did many of the women. Lani spied four at nearby tables that gazed at Billy with a range of fondness and hunger.

As much as she'd have loved to stick around and ponder this fascinating rapport between the patriarch and his son's good friend, Lani realized her audience with Rusty Edmond had come to an end. Murmuring thanks for the meal, she headed for the exit, eager to share her thoughts with Asher.

But when she arrived back at the ranch, she discovered he wasn't in his apartment. Before panic seized hold, she decided to check the barn. Sure enough, she found him in a grooming stall running a brush over a gray gelding.

"How'd dinner with my father go?" he asked, his voice cool.

Lani winced. She should've known better than to keep quiet about her meeting with Rusty. No doubt her evasiveness had fortified the barriers between them. Maybe subconsciously that had been her plan. Their kiss had shaken her confidence. How could she do her job if emotion disrupted reason? Would she overlook something because she wanted him to be innocent? Worse, what if she found out he was guilty and couldn't bring herself to send him to jail?

"It went okay."

She picked up a brush and went to work on the opposite side of the horse, running the soft bristles over his shoulder and down his front leg.

"Is he the one who hired you to figure out where the money went?" He'd asked the question before and she'd refused to answer. Silence reigned between them for several uncomfortable seconds. "You don't want to talk about it."

"Not really."

As much as Lani wanted to tell Asher that she'd been hired by Kingston Blue, thinking his father had hired her was keeping Asher off balance and she needed whatever advantage she could get if she was going to find the money.

If he was actually responsible for the theft.

While they worked without further conversation, Lani couldn't stop her gaze from chasing the strong lines of Asher's cheekbones and the delectable curve of his lower lip. She shivered as that afternoon's kiss replayed in her mind. The same raw masculinity that had tantalized her five years ago was no less potent, nor had her susceptibility to it dimmed. He'd grown harder in the intervening years. Less indulged rich boy and more a man who wasn't happy with how his life was going.

It's what made him even more interesting. She'd prepared herself to resist his meaningless flirtation and dodge his sexual banter. The melancholy beneath his glib sophistication was more pronounced than ever. He hid it well, but most people probably didn't bother looking past his easy charm and playful humor. She'd trained herself to see into those in-between moments and easily detected the dissatisfaction that plagued him.

"I thought tomorrow I'd head to Appaloosa Island," she said, the idea having come to her on the drive back to the ranch. "I haven't seen the festival site."

"Neither have I."

"I'm surprised," she said. "Didn't you go check on the damage after the tornado hit?"

"No."

"Would you like to come along?"

She was surprised when he didn't answer right away. He'd always been restless and up for anything.

"I guess I'd better take advantage of my freedom for as long as I can."

Asher wasn't feeling particularly chatty during the three-hour car ride to Mustang Point, an elite waterside community with a large marina in Trinity Bay. Because Appaloosa Island was only accessible by helicopter and boat—a ferry crossed to the island daily—the Edmond family kept several boats for their own use.

The investigators had returned his car and Asher had insisted he drive. The luxury sedan was far more comfortable for a road trip than Lani's utilitarian SUV. Plus, with him behind the wheel, she could spend the trip working on her laptop. If she noticed his reserve, she gave no sign. Which, of course, only fueled his frustration.

Being investigated by his ex-lover was bad enough. That his father had been the one to hire her cut deep. And how could he talk to her about how betrayed he felt without plunging deep into the complex emotional crap that defined his relationship with Rusty?

Maybe he should just go ahead and tell her what was really going on. Why he'd quit polo and gone to work for The Edmond Organization. More than any time before, he wanted her to know the man he truly was. For her to choose to have faith in him. To recognize that not only was he innocent of stealing the festival funds, but that he would never in a million years stoop to something so low.

And what if he told her everything and it didn't change her perception? He sensed that it was habit for her to regard him with a jaundiced eye. As with his adoptive father, she found it easier to write him off. To her, he would remain "frat boy" and his pride rejected having to prove that he was no longer that guy.

They had lunch at the marina restaurant before heading to the dock. The forty-foot boat that Asher had been staying on when he first met Lani had been replaced by a sixty-foot model that handled like a dream. He keyed in the code to unlock the double-glass doors and swept his arm in a grand gesture for her to precede him inside. Far from looking pleased by his gallantry, she shot him a repressive frown before entering the comfortable cabin with panoramic views from the wraparound windows.

The sleek open space held a lounge area with a comfortable sectional couch and a large well-appointed kitchen with tons of countertop space for food prep and an eat-in banquette.

"Are you thirsty?" he asked, determined to play the part of a good host. "The boat is fully stocked with everything you could ever want."

Her eyebrow arched at that. "I'll take a sparkling water if you have it."

"I know we do." Practically everything Gina drank had to have bubbles. "We also have that jalapeño vodka you like so well. I make sure the boat is stocked with it. You know, just in case…"

Her lips parted as if she wanted to ask, *In case of what?* But she settled for shaking her head in disapproval before continuing to survey the elegant surroundings.

"This looks new," she murmured as he pulled out glasses, filling them with ice and a slice of lime.

Still annoyed that she'd had dinner with his father the night before and refused to tell him why or what they'd discussed, he shot back, "Is that your way of asking me if I used the festival funds to buy a new boat?"

"You need to take this more seriously." She regarded him steadily as he poured sparkling water over the ice. "You're in big trouble and flippant remarks like that are not making my job any easier."

He coped with stress by making light of things. *Never let them see you sweat.* No one knew the amount of anger, insecurity or frustration he'd bottled up over the years. But he'd learned that if you play the part of someone unbothered by problems, then those difficulties have less of a chance of wearing you down.

"I didn't steal the funds and the boat doesn't belong to me." Summoning a weary half smile, Asher held the glass out to her. "But you already know that." For several seconds the only sound in the space was the happy explosions of a hundred tiny bubbles. "I'm not the villain here."

He could probably say it a million times and she'd never believe him until the truth came out, proving his innocence. What he wouldn't give for someone, anyone—but *especially* her—to believe he wasn't a thieving asshole.

His patience was rewarded when she stepped forward to accept it and their fingers grazed, sending an electric current of longing through him. Lust flared, compelling and dangerous. If he took her in his arms and kissed her the way he wanted to, they would be naked and on the floor in minutes.

But passion was easy. It was the moments in between that made a relationship grow and flourish. Or fail miserably. Whatever came, he wanted a shot with Lani.

Reacting to his volatile mood, she sipped her water in silence.

"I mean," he continued mercilessly, "if I were to steal millions of dollars, I wouldn't spend it on a boat or a house in the Maldives. I'd choose someplace more interesting than some remote island to buy real estate."

Lani studied him. "I don't get you."

"I assure you, I am quite simple to understand."

"Maybe once." She spun away from him, gliding toward the open glass doors that led to the semi-circular couch off the back of the boat. "I'm not sure I believe that anymore."

Asher trailed after her. "What's changing your mind? Am I wearing you down with my incessant claims of innocence?"

Suddenly he saw the clever trap he'd made for himself. Although it was in his best interest to convince her that he hadn't stolen the money, as soon as he stopped being a suspect, she'd be off chasing new leads. And he wasn't ready to let her walk out of his life just yet.

"Never mind." She rubbed her temple. "I must be tired.

I don't know what I'm saying anymore." Still, she gave him a long searching look before speaking again. "Should we be going?"

"Don't you want a tour of the yacht first?"

"It's a boat. I'm sure I can find my way around if I need to."

"There's two state rooms," he narrated as if she hadn't already shut him down. "You can have your pick, although I have to say the views from the one in the stern are much better."

She looked surprised, and then worried. "This is a day trip. Out and back. We're not staying here overnight."

"I thought it'd be fun." His smile was all innocence. "For old times' sake."

Bright color burned in her cheeks at his words even as outrage made her eyes snap in irritation. Her spine stiffened as she seemed to gather breath to deliver whatever scathing rebuttal she hoped would shut him down. His remark hadn't been the least bit suggestive, but she certainly took it that way. *Interesting.* Obviously she was remembering how things had been between them all those years before.

"Is there a problem?" He continued before she could argue. "I mean we're living in close quarters at the ranch. It's not different if you're alone with me here, is it?"

"Of course not," she shot back. "I just thought we'd head to the festival site and then go back to Royal. I wasn't planning on making a night of it."

"It was a long drive. Let's just spend the night and head back tomorrow."

"I didn't pack for an overnight stay," she reminded him.

"Not to worry, Gina always keeps an assortment of clothes on board. I'm sure she wouldn't mind if you borrowed something."

"I guess we can spend the night." She gave in with a grimace, looking less sure of herself by the minute.

"Great." Asher didn't put too much energy into his voice, not wanting her to realize how delighted he was to have won this standoff. "I'll start the engine and then cast off the lines."

"I've got it."

Five years earlier they'd spent a lot of time together on the previous yacht and she was familiar with the routine. Still, Asher was surprised when she headed for the mooring lines and began removing each one from the cleats. He'd been out on a variety of boats with a lot of women, but none of them lifted a finger to help. They believed their contribution was to parade around in bikinis, providing eye candy. While he wasn't opposed to beautiful, scantily clad women, he'd always appreciated Lani's helpfulness. Just another way she stood out in his mind.

To his surprise, she came up to the bridge as he reversed the yacht out of the slip. One level above the lounge, the fly bridge came equipped with top-of-the-line electronics and offered impressive views. Asher registered disappointment as Lani settled into the spacious seating area to his left. Seriously, what had he expected? She wasn't about to come snuggle beside him the way she used to back in the day. Forcibly tamping down his emotions, he navigated out of the marina and pointed the sixty-foot yacht into the bay.

The distance from the marina to the festival site on Appaloosa Island was a quick fifteen-minute trip. They'd chosen to locate the event on the undeveloped side of the island, far from the resort where Asher and Lani had met for the first time and away from the expensive homes that lined the waterfront.

Despite his initial excitement over the festival, after the preliminary idea generation and brainstorming sessions, he'd left the organizing to others and focused on the vendors. He'd been involved in several charity events during his years of playing polo and endorsements were a big part of that. Plus, his family had rejected many of the suggestions he'd made about the location and vision for the festival, leaving him feeling less and less connected to the nuts-and-bolts aspect of organizing the event. When he'd stopped attending board meetings, no doubt his family had chalked it up to yet another time that Asher failed to follow through on something. But he had a hard time sticking with anything when his heart wasn't in it.

As the boat neared the festival grounds, his gaze swept over the ruin of what had been the hopes and dreams of so many. His stomach gave a sickening wrench. No wonder everyone hated him.

Five

As the boat idled past the festival site's devastation, Lani kept her attention fixed on Asher's face. Convinced she'd glimpse something that would establish he'd been guilty all along, her righteous triumph faded as his shock and horror never wavered. The torment in his eyes as he gazed over buildings wrecked by the tornado made her throat tighten.

The dock had been spared, but Asher made no attempt to head that way. Instead he moved parallel to shore and pushed a button on the control panel. A muffled thunk reached her ears and then the floor beneath her feet began to vibrate as the anchor chain emptied from the hold.

"What are you doing?" she asked, shivering at the grim set of his expression.

"Anchoring," came his clipped answer.

When they'd first met, she'd viewed Asher as a charming libertine, engaged in an unending pursuit of entertainment. And watching him now as he skillfully maneuvered the giant yacht, she was reminded of how in the early days

of getting to know him, his easy confidence with everything he did had won her over. She was a woman whose
self-reliance had been encouraged by her parents. And
was used to doing things for herself. So, sitting back and
relying on someone else for a change had been a unique
and thrilling experience and one she still struggled with.

"There's no way we can tie up to that dock." His attention appeared fixed on the process of making sure the anchor latched onto the floor of the bay, but a frown appeared
as he shot glances toward the island. "Even if I trusted that
the storm hadn't damaged the dock, it wasn't built for boats
this size. What happened to the one that could accommodate twenty or more yachts?"

The answer was so obvious that Lani just stared at Asher
in bemusement. She couldn't process how genuinely baffled
he looked. Her instincts told her he was utterly mystified,
but how was that possible? He would've been involved with
the festival organization from the start. Didn't he know
what had been going on here?

"Or did they manage to build it and it was destroyed by
the tornado?" He continued to voice his troubled thoughts
out loud.

At moments like these, moments like when he lavished
his attention on his string of polo horses, dedicating himself to their health and welfare, she questioned if he was
as irresponsible as he seemed.

"As far as I know, this was the only dock that was ever
built," Lani said, her voice gentler than she'd meant it to be.

Once he seemed satisfied that the anchor was secure,
he shut off the motor and remained where he was, staring
at the shore. "So many people were counting on the festival," he murmured. "We'd promised to fund Valencia Donovan's horse rescue charity with a portion of the proceeds
from the festival ticket sales. She was going to expand
her property and start an equine therapy program. And I

know Rafe Cortez-Williams took out a second mortgage on his restaurant to invest in the festival." He screwed his eyes shut and rubbed his face. "With all the losses they're facing, it's selfish of me to think only about my problems. But someone set me up. Someone close to me. I feel so betrayed." The anguish in his voice tore at her.

"I'm sorry this is happening to you," she said, the words coming before she'd considered them.

Asher's dismay was getting to her. And that couldn't be allowed to happen. Feeling sorry for him was the wrong way to go. This was his fault, after all. *He* caused this problem when he stole the money. Which meant he didn't deserve her sympathy or support. He'd done a terrible thing and ruined countless lives.

Yet if this were true, why did she keep falling for his denials? If she was so convinced of his guilt, shouldn't she be able to see right through his excuses? Granted, it had been ages since she'd last seen him, but why would he have done something so obvious? He had to know he was going to get caught. Asher might be reckless, but he wasn't an idiot. What was his endgame? She recalled his reaction when she told him about the house in the Maldives. He'd genuinely looked clueless as to where that was.

"Come on."

"How are we going to get over there?" She looked at the thirty or so feet of open water between the boat and the dock.

"We could swim."

"I don't have a suit."

"I'm sure one of Gina's bikinis would fit you."

His gaze drifted down her body, a slow, lazy leer that made her skin pebble at the thought of his hands trailing over her flesh. Despite the afternoon's humidity, she shivered. It wasn't fair that the man could turn her on with a mere look. But the heat moving into her cheeks wasn't fired by irritation. It kindled as she recalled other afternoons when they'd swum together off these waters while golden sunlight sparkled on the blue surface. And she'd never forget that one night when they'd gone skinny-dipping, clad in nothing but moonlight. Asher had licked the cool salty water droplets off her naked breasts as he'd dipped his fingers into the slippery heat between her legs. The memory of that encounter hit her like a freight train and Lani's hands began to shake.

Coming here had been a bad idea. She'd brought him to the island to face reality. To show him the damage he'd caused. Instead, he'd reacted in a way that made him seem more victim than villain. She'd lost control of the situation and the only person learning a lesson here was her.

He was dangerous. To the people around him who he'd stolen from, and to her own peace of mind. She'd spent years telling herself that she'd been a fool to be taken in by Asher Edmond. Time and distance had allowed her to believe that she'd never be misled by him again. Yet here she was lost in the past, remembering only the good times and doubting what she knew to be true. That Asher had a knack for telling people what they wanted to hear and making them believe he was a better man than he actually was. Or was that just her wounded heart talking?

"Isn't there some sort of a dinghy we can take over to the island? I don't feel like swimming."

Asher regarded her silently for a moment. The lush sweep of his lashes shadowed his brown eyes, making his expression hard to read. Lani tried not to think about how much she loved that soft fringe tickling her skin or how the raspy glide of his stubble over the sensitive area where her shoulder and neck connected had driven her mad with desire. She'd been so weak back then, so susceptible to every sensation Asher visited upon her inexperienced body. Was it any wonder she'd fallen head over heels for him when he given her such pleasure? When every grace of his fingertips or the heat of his gaze could set off a maelstrom of unquenchable yearning.

"The dinghy it is," he said, his matter-of-fact tone at odds with the questing weight of his gaze.

When he turned away toward the ladder that descended from the fly deck to the main level, Lani sagged. Only as he disappeared below did she realize she'd been using all her strength to withstand the pull of longing he evoked.

Asher used a crane mounted on the bow to lower the dinghy into the water. As he worked, the wind caught the edges of his unbuttoned shirt and spread it wide. Lani ogled his lean, muscular torso, all too aware that the familiar surroundings were triggering long-buried emotions. Fighting to quell her rioting hormones, she joined Asher at the back of the boat where a swim platform extended off the stern. He'd maneuvered the small inflatable there and tied it to the structure.

"Give me your hand," he said. "The dinghy is a little unsteady."

She waved him off. "I've got this."

"You know," he began, his tone tight and impatient, "you could let me take care of you."

To her dismay, Lani's skin flushed. The first time they'd made love Asher had calmed her nerves by whispering, *Let me care of you.* And then he proceeded to do just that. She'd had a half-dozen orgasms that night, mind-blowing explosions of pleasure that he'd given her. Afterward, she'd been grateful to have been initiated into the physical act of love with that level of expertise. Unfortunately starting off with such an outstanding lover had its downside. Since then, numerous disappointing sexual experiences had followed with men who were not Asher.

Lani stiffened her spine, refusing to let him get to her again. How could she claim to be a professional if spending two days with her ex-lover turned her into a pile of needy mush?

Determined to avoid touching him again and risk revisiting the longing for still more physical contact, Lani ignored Asher's hand, choosing to board the dinghy unassisted. What began as an inelegant clamber onto the inflatable's unstable surface ended in a scene out of a rom-com when the wobbly craft shifted as she stood with one foot in it and one on the swim platform. The next thing Lani knew, she was off balance and pitching sideways. Her shoulder hit the edge of the structure. Pain shot through her as cold water closed over her head. Shock held her in its grasp for several immobilizing seconds before the need for air awakened in her lungs. Lani swept her arms out and down, wincing as the movement sent a sharp twinge through her bruised shoulder.

She surfaced, gasping and splashing, only to be hauled unceremoniously out of the water by big strong hands. Her butt settled onto the swim platform with a thump. She blinked water from her eyes and became aware that Asher cupped her head with one hand while the fingers of his other whisked drops from her cheeks.

"Are you okay?" His deep voice held an unexpected hint of panic that warmed her faster than the hot August sun.

The urge to cry rose up in her so fast that she gasped in dismay. She hated that Asher's concern for her made her feel weak and fragile. She was a street-smart private investigator, prepared for any and all emergencies. Not some silly female who needed a man to take care of her. Yet damned if she didn't appreciate being rescued by Asher. Even if it was his fault in the first place that she'd fallen in.

Scowling, she pushed Asher's hands away. "Leave me alone. I'm fine."

He opened his mouth as if to argue, but then the corners of his eyes crinkled as mirth replaced worry. He pressed his lips together as his shoulders began to shake with suppressed laughter. Lani glared at him in rapidly escalating indignation as she sat in her sopping wet clothes, overcome by embarrassment.

"It isn't funny," she snapped, shoving her palm into his shoulder, taking her discomfort out on him. "And it was all your fault that I fell in."

"Not true. If you'd let me help you into the boat, none of this would've happened." His amusement dimmed. Beneath bold dark eyebrows, his gaze became somber and intense. "Too bad you're always so determined to reject assistance."

"You say that like it's a bad thing that I rely on myself."

"It's not a bad thing to rely on yourself, but when you can't let yourself count on anyone else, then it stops being something positive."

Stung, she jumped on offense. "I don't think you're the best person to give advice on how I should act."

His face wore a mask of bland indifference. "You're probably right." He held out his hand. "Want to try again?"

"You go, I'm going to dry off."

With a brief shrug, he nimbly stepped into the dinghy and untied it. Lani huddled in her wet clothes and shivered, watching as Asher started the outboard and steered the inflatable toward the island.

Asher roamed the festival site for an hour, barely able to process how the whole damned thing had gone so wrong. Even without the tornado damage, the missing funds meant a lot of people had been ruined. If not for the storm, it wouldn't have come out that no payment had been made to the insurance company that was supposed to protect them against such a tragedy. Yet even before the winds had ripped apart buildings and uprooted trees, the festival had been sabotaged. How could things have gotten so bad?

And who in the hell had set him up for stealing the money?

It had to be someone close to him, or someone actively involved in the festival organization. He just couldn't imagine anyone he knew doing something so nefarious. Or who might have been opportunistic enough to embezzle. Obviously Lani was an expert at these sorts of investigations, but with her gaze focused directly on him, how hard would she look at anyone else?

In a grim mood, Asher returned to the boat. Lani was nowhere to be found so he headed into the lounge, poured himself two fingers of whiskey and shot back the alcohol. As the spirits seared his chest, warming his whole body, he closed his eyes and reviewed the day's events.

Lani so clearly believed he was the villain. And frankly, after looking at everything that had been done and scrutinizing the financials, he was starting to see why everyone thought he'd stolen the money. Nor did his current situation inspire anyone to give him the benefit of the doubt. He was living at his father's estate, working in a job that had been handed to him because of his connection to Rusty. He had little that he hadn't been given. It didn't cast him in the most flattering light. One thing was for sure, his current predicament was a major wake-up call. He'd given Rusty two years at The Edmond Organization. Time to make a new plan and dive into his future.

That is, if he *had* a future. The way things were going, it was looking pretty likely that he'd have many years behind bars to ponder the errors of his ways and figure out a better way to go forward.

He didn't realize his eyes remained closed until he felt a stirring in the air and realized he was no longer alone in the lounge. Pushing out a steadying breath, he got his expression back under control and opened his eyes.

Lani stepped into the kitchen and leaned against the cabinet near the sink with her arms crossed. She wore a pair of tropical-print wide-leg pants with a shoulder-baring crop top in royal blue. Her bare toenails peeked from beneath the flowing hem. Although the resort wear suited Lani, it also stripped away the professional veneer that made her so attractive to him.

She was a woman of substance, someone he valued for her authenticity, her intelligence and her drive. In so many ways they were complete opposites. She was focused and organized. While he tended to career through life, moving from one experience to another.

"Are you planning on getting drunk?" she asked, glancing pointedly at the tumbler in his hand.

"Don't you think I deserve to?" Since he was still standing by the bar, he poured himself another shot of whiskey and then began to accumulate the ingredients for Lani's spicy margarita. "Feel like joining me? There's an ice-maker there." He indicated the stainless-steel door beside the beverage cooler. "And you'll find limes and fresh jalapeños in the fridge beside it. I'm afraid you'll have to do with off-the-shelf sweet-and-sour mix, but in that cabinet you'll find chili salt."

"This isn't a party," Lani said, crossing her arms over her chest and refusing to move. "We're here on business."

"And you've never met a client over drinks?" Like the night before when she'd dined with his father at the Texas Cattleman's Club.

"You're not a client. And I don't think you should be drinking."

"Too late." He toasted her with his glass, downed the whiskey and lifted the bottle once more.

She was right to say he shouldn't be drinking. The alcohol wouldn't help defuse the tension in his gut put there by what he'd seen on the island. Nor could it dim his urgent pleasure at having her back in his life even under these terrible circumstances. As for diminishing the temptation to cross the room, wrap his arms around her and slide his lips onto the strong pulse in her throat…

"Lani." He lowered his chin and blinked slowly as warmth raced through his veins. She was so beautiful. He'd missed the way she crossed her arms and glared at him. Or how she looked so sleepy and sweet in the mornings. The corners of his mouth curled up in a slow grin. "Do you remember how we loved to picnic on the boat, make love all night and then have breakfast in bed the next morning?"

"Stop it right now." She leveled her finger at him. "I'm not doing this with you. We are not going to sleep together."

Her lips said no, but her eyes weren't quite as convincing.

"Because you don't want to?" he taunted. "Or because it would be unprofessional?"

"Both."

"I don't believe you." He spoke each syllable with deliberate care so she wouldn't miss his point.

"I don't care what you believe." She glowered at him a little too aggressively. "It's the truth."

Wondering what it would take to get her back on his side, Asher raked his hand through his hair. Once upon a time he'd been able to convince her to take a chance on him by capitalizing on the sizzling sexual energy that exploded between them whenever they touched. Yet while hormones had raged during those sultry summer months they spent together, he'd gotten the impression that he was some sort of curiosity to her. The good girl wanted to walk on the wild side just once before settling down to a career steeped in rules and regulations.

"Is it the truth?" he demanded, tired of her denials. "Or is that what you tell yourself at night when sleeping all alone in your bed?"

These words were not at all what he wanted to say to

her, but with frustration and longing a tangled knot inside his gut, hollow charm lost out to desperate honesty.

"You're so sure I'm sleeping alone?" She was so obviously bluffing that he almost smiled.

"Yes," he said, chest tightening as she scowled at him. "Am I wrong? Have you found somebody that gets you?" Because he hoped she wouldn't settle for anything less.

Needing something to do, Asher moved into the kitchen. He ignored her obvious show of maintaining a safe distance from him as he opened the refrigerator and pulled out the produce he'd mentioned earlier. Finding a cutting board and a sharp knife, he gestured for her to join him. Then he began fixing a spicy margarita just the way she liked it.

"Someone who gets me." She gave a rough laugh as she rinsed the jalapeño, before picking up the knife. "Don't act as if you give a damn about my love life."

Asher's mouth went dry. He took a step in her direction and lowered his voice. "Of course I give a damn. I want you to be happy—"

"Don't." She whirled on him with a twelve-inch blade extended in his direction. He gulped. The stainless steel glinted wickedly in her hand. Her stormy eyes practically begged him to say more. "Don't pretend that you care. I'm not going to fall for you ever again."

Fall for you.

Five years earlier he hadn't understood what he was doing when he'd relentlessly pursued her. At first she'd been a challenge. Resisting him at every turn. Refusing to give him a chance. Reluctant to let him in. And even when he'd broken through her well-fortified defenses, she'd kept the key to her heart well hidden.

Until the lazy summer days began to grow short and he realized he didn't want to lose her. He'd invited her to come to Argentina for the polo season and she'd told him that she loved him, but that she couldn't give up on grad school. He'd been terrified by the gift she'd offered him and clueless how to keep their good thing going now that the summer fling had turned into a serious romance.

"I did care about you," he countered, shaken by the mistake he'd made all those years ago when he'd chosen his freedom over her love.

"Oh, please. I watched you hit on women for a week before you even noticed me."

She looked plenty put out that she hadn't been his first choice. Except that wasn't the case at all. From the moment he had spotted her waiting on adjacent tables, he'd been mesmerized. He just hadn't been ready for the emotions that had slammed into him. Lust he could handle. Longing had caught him by surprise.

"What do you want to hear? That you were unlike any other woman I'd ever met and I didn't know how to handle that?"

"I'm only interested in what's real," she declared, slicing the lime with malevolent force.

"That is the truth." But he could see from her ramrod-straight spine that nothing he could say would convince her.

"Just be straight with me." She set the knife down and shot him a hard look. "Tell me where you put the money. That's the only truth I'm interested in hearing."

Six

"Where are we off to today?" Asher asked the morning day after their impromptu visit to Appaloosa Island.

If she'd hoped that compelling him to confront the damage to the island would provoke his confession about the missing funds, she'd been completely wrong. While he'd seemed disturbed by all he'd seen, he hadn't confessed or behaved in a way that confirmed his guilt.

Lani scanned his handsome face, fighting the sheer enjoyment of his gorgeous smile and ready energy. Yet even as she fell into the trap of wanting to do whatever made him happy, she recognized that he could be putting on an act.

She searched for evasion in his lively brown eyes, but saw only genuine curiosity and good-natured enthusiasm. It sucked that she no longer trusted her own judgment. Five years ago, his ability to twist her emotions and make her lose control of her sensibilities had almost been her ruin. Fortunately, she'd woken up just in time. While turning down his invitation to go with him to Argentina had been the hardest decision she'd ever made, no good would've come from giving up her carefully crafted plans. And Lani was convinced that even if she'd followed Asher Edmond into an uncertain future, they never would've lasted. So what if her days weren't as bright and shining without him in it. Look at how he'd ended up. Eventually he would've dragged her down with him.

"*I'm* going to visit Abby Carmichael," she said, emphasizing the first-person singular pronoun. Letting him help with this investigation was a really bad idea.

"Abby... Carmichael. The name is familiar."

"She was filming a documentary on the festival."

"Oh, sure, she interviewed all of us." Asher arched his eyebrows. "What's your interest in her?"

"She has footage of what was going on with the festival."

"What do you think you'll find on it?" His lips twisted into a sardonic quirk. "Video of me sneaking off with bags of money and burying them in the sand somewhere?"

Although he spoke in a light, mocking tone, Lani recognized his dark humor masked concern. Her time training to be an FBI agent hadn't been a waste. In those moments when she could put her emotional response to him aside, she saw his anxiety clearly.

"That would be really helpful," she responded, arching her eyebrows at him. "Especially if they are marked with big dollar signs, indicating that the bags are full of cash."

As her not-so-witty repartee made him relax, Lani sighed in weary frustration with herself. She came out of her thoughts and caught Asher regarding her intently. It was in moments like these when she glimpsed his somber watchfulness that she knew there was more to this man than he let people see.

"Can I come along?" he asked. "Maybe a third set of eyes could be helpful."

Against her better judgment, Lani found herself nodding. "Sure, why not."

Why did she keep pandering to his needs? What was she *thinking*? That if they could work the investigation together, then maybe they'd have some sort of shot in the future?

He wasn't good for her. Once she got him out of this situation, she'd probably never hear from him again. The thought made her heart clench. Five years ago she'd foolishly believed if she told him that school was important to her, then he would agree to try the long-distance thing. She'd hoped that maybe by the time she graduated, he would've settled down and their differences would've stopped being an issue.

But clearly fate had other things in store for them both.

"Thanks." He looked as if he wanted to say more, but then just gave her a smile that didn't quite reach his eyes.

Before she acted on her need to reassure him, Lani grabbed her jacket and headed for the apartment door. Before she could reach it, Asher was there, gazing down at her with his most-earnest expression. The heady scent of his cologne encircled her, causing an uptick in her pulse.

"I really mean it," he said, fingertips skimming her arm. The light contact aroused a flood of longing, but if it showed on her face, he didn't appear to notice. "It means the world to me that you are giving me the benefit of the doubt."

I'm not...

She might've been able to resist if he'd swept her into a passionate embrace and kissed her with wild abandon. Bracing against his onslaught of sensual persuasion was her first instinct. Instead, her steely resolve was being chipped away by his fleeting touches, the unexpected flashes of sincerity, his apparent gratitude that she was going to bat for him because she believed in his innocence. Guilt swept through her. Did he recognize how little she trusted him? Or did he think his tactics were working?

"Asher…"

Before she could figure out what she planned on telling him, he dropped the sweetest, lightest, most-affectionate kiss on her lips. The gentle pressure came and went so fast it was like being kissed by a butterfly, but she doubted her whole body would've lit up from a glancing brush of gossamer wings.

"It's enough that you're letting me come along." He swallowed her fingers in his warm, strong hand and drew her out the door. "You don't need to warn me that I'm still suspect number one. It's just nice to have some control over my fate."

A warning trembled on her lips. He had no control whatsoever. But his optimistic expression overwhelmed her caution. Why crush his hopes when there was nothing concrete to do the stomping?

Instead she gave his fingers a quick squeeze and said, "Let's go."

The day before she'd made this appointment to meet with Abby Carmichael at Carter Crane's ranch. Two months earlier the filmmaker had arrived to capture background on the town, the Edmond family and many of those participating in the Soiree on the Bay festival.

Lani had heard that the couple was an opposites-attract pair who'd met and fallen in love in the midst of the festival development. Abby was a city girl. Carter a rancher. Lani couldn't help but compare the couple's romantic destiny to what had happened between her and Asher. While Abby had moved to Royal, letting romance upended her world, Lani had sacrificed her personal life in favor of her career. She was eager to see how Abby was faring in the aftermath of her decision.

The woman who answered the door had long straight dark hair, inquisitive brown eyes, and a beautiful light brown complexion. A cropped white T-shirt and skinny jeans showed off her lean body and her smile was positively gleeful as her gaze landed on Asher.

"I don't suppose I could get you to sit for another interview."

Lani stiffened protectively. She'd forgotten that word around town was that Abby intended to change the focus of her documentary to an exposé on the failed festival and the scandalous missing funds.

"Maybe after I'm exonerated," Asher replied with a suave grin that made Lani's toes curl even though she wasn't on the receiving end of his attention.

"You don't think he's guilty?" Abby's eyes went wide as her gaze bounced between Asher and Lani.

"I'm investigating the missing festival funds," she said, irritation firing as she reminded the filmmaker of the reason they were here.

She knew better than to let her personal feelings for Asher get in the way of doing her job. No matter how bad the case looked against him, she had blurred the lines between doing the job Kingston Blue had hired her for and saving her former lover from jail. That the two missions might be on a parallel course would only work for her as long as Asher was innocent.

"May we see the footage?" Lani prompted.

"Of course," Abby demurred, leading them toward a large workstation with several monitors, keyboards and other computer equipment. "I pulled footage from the various visits to the island with the organizers of the event. I also have interviews with everyone involved." Her gaze flicked to Asher. "Any idea what you're looking for?"

The massive volume of video the documentarian had recorded was overwhelming. But helpful.

"Let's start with the footage from the visits to the island."

Abby began scrolling through various files, clicking on several in search of what she was looking for. "There are a lot of people involved. Between the Edmond family, the construction crew, marketers, food vendors. The list goes on and on..."

With the embezzlement evidence pointing directly at Asher, the investigators had stopped searching for other suspects and begun building a case against him. No one else would be looking at what Abby had recorded.

To Lani's mind, the people who were closest to the Edmond family were at the top of her list of suspects. Specifically Ross Edmond. Despite Asher's assurance that his brother couldn't have stolen the money, and then taken the extra step of framing Asher, Lani intended on taking a good look at him.

"That's odd," Asher murmured.

Lani braced herself for whatever had caught his eye. She'd worried that even if there was nothing of interest in what Abby had filmed, Asher would create some sort of distraction that would lead her down a divergent tunnel. His specialty was deflection and the man had a knack for getting inside her head. Who knew what crazy theory she would be chasing next if he got his way.

But it was Abby, and not Lani, that took the bait. "What's odd?"

"I wasn't along on this particular visit to the festival site." He turned to Abby. "Can you run this back about ten minutes?"

"Sure."

"Look." The footage that had caught Asher's attention was a shot of Rusty and Ross walking the grounds, looking relaxed in each other's company. From the state of the building going on and the lack of a rift between the father and son, the footage must've been shot several months earlier.

"What are we looking for?" Abby asked eagerly and Lani was happy to let her lead.

Asher hesitated before answering, his focus locked on

the monitor. "That." He pointed to a corner of the screen where Billy Holmes appeared. Although at first his expression appeared innocuous, on closer viewing, his charming veneer had slipped, replaced by a cold glare.

"He's staring at Ross and Rusty like they've done something to annoy him," Asher said, sounding triumphant. "Which is strange because I've never ever seen him looking anything but absolutely pleased with himself."

Wow. Interesting indeed.

"Well, he certainly isn't looking so happy there." Asher sounded intrigued. "How much more footage is there of this day?"

While Abby and Asher leaned forward, scanning the images on the monitor, Lani pondered this new development. Was this a significant lead or just a red herring?

"You know, when I interviewed Billy around the time that this was shot, he let it slip that some money was unaccounted for from the accounts." Abby turned in her chair and faced Asher. "He said the oddest thing. He called it a family matter and then said that *we're* handling it." She emphasized the inclusive pronoun. "He acted very protective of Ross. At the time I just thought it was because they were such good friends." Abby's gaze strayed back to the monitor and a dent appeared between her eyebrows.

Lani had never considered Billy as a suspect because he hadn't had access to the festival accounts. But she remembered Kingston Blue's theory that Ross was involved. Could they be in on it together?

If so, why did it upset Billy that Ross and Rusty seemed to be getting along?

They spent another hour reviewing footage, but nothing else jumped out. Nevertheless Lani asked Abby for copies of whatever she had featuring the Edmond family and Billy, including the individual interviews with the Edmonds.

Following the meeting with Abby Carmichael, Lani was in a thoughtful mood as they headed back to Elegance Ranch. Asher was wondering if he was being too optimistic to think that he was starting to see cracks forming in the thick wall of doubt Lani had constructed to keep him at bay.

"Weird about the way Billy was glaring at Ross and Rusty," he muttered as his curiosity grew too overwhelming to bear in silence. "What do you suppose that means?"

She took one hand off the steering wheel and rubbed her temple as if trying to alleviate pain. "I don't know."

But by watching her, seeing the telltale tightening of her lips and a slight indent between her brows, she obviously *did* know, and whatever was bothering her had caused some sort of shift in perception. Hope blared in him like a car alarm. Could she be coming around to believing that he hadn't stolen the money?

"I had no idea Billy was the one spreading word of missing funds," Asher said, continuing to chew on one of the many disturbing things he'd discovered today. "I mean, what did he think he was doing? He had to know the news would hurt our family."

"Explain to me again about Billy's relationship with Ross and how he came to be living in one of the guesthouses on the estate."

"He and Ross were good buds in college," Asher told her. "He showed up in Royal a couple years ago. As to why he's living in the guesthouse..." He thought back. "Rusty took to him right away." He made no effort to hide the bitterness in his voice. "I guess all it takes to get on Rusty's good side is to kiss his ass twenty-four/seven. Billy's an expert at that."

"You don't like him."

Asher had a ready answer. "Do I sound like a jerk if I admit that it bugs me that this guy comes out of nowhere and gets my dad to like him when I've spent my whole life waiting for Rusty to acknowledge me for doing a good job at anything?"

"I think you are justified to want Rusty's attention. He's the only father you've ever known. It makes sense that you want him to be proud of you."

Venting about being slighted by his father left Asher feel like he'd been kicked in the gut. Sharing that hadn't been easy and he appreciated Lani's empathic response. They didn't talk until she stopped the SUV behind the barn.

Asher turned to her as something electric and powerful sizzled in the air between them. "Are you heading back to Dallas right away or can you stay for dinner?"

The festival case wasn't the only one she was working. Lani was helping several clients.

"I have time for dinner."

Five words that flooded him with excitement. "Great."

She preceded him up the stairs to his apartment and keyed in the code. At her urging, he'd started locking his door. Until she came along, he hadn't considered that his stuff or his person could be in danger and her insistence on security was adorable. He didn't want her to think he wasn't taking her seriously, but the truth was, the only thing of value worth locking up was his heart and the more time he spent with her, the less confident he was at being able to keep it safe.

"Pour me a shot of whiskey," she said, setting down her laptop and slipping her blazer off her shoulders. "I'll be right back."

Asher did as she asked and then began hunting in his refrigerator for what he could use to put together a meal. He had steak and pasta. She liked Gorgonzola cheese. Would she remember the recipe they'd made on the boat that summer?

It wasn't until ten minutes passed that he noticed the water running in the bathroom. She was in the shower, probably thinking through what they'd learned that day. While he waited for her to reemerge, he sipped at his whiskey and stared in the direction of the guesthouse where Billy Holmes stayed.

"Is this mine?"

The sound of her voice broke Asher out of his thoughts. He turned around and the sight of her made the room tilt.

He blinked.

She wore a large blue button-down shirt that had definitely come out of his closet and nothing else. The sight of her pale bare legs and unbound silky black hair made his chest seize. As he stared at her in astonishment, she tipped the crystal tumbler and tossed back the entire contents. He watched her throat as she swallowed the whiskey and savored the widening of her eyes at the impact of the fiery liquid.

Asher wasn't sure if the intensity of his gaze or the liquor put color in her cheeks, but two bright patches appeared over her cheekbones.

"I hope you don't mind but I borrowed one of your shirts," she said. "I jumped into the shower before remembering that I didn't have any clean clothes. I tossed my things in the washer. They'll be clean and dry by the time we're done with dinner."

She was *naked* underneath his shirt? Damn it. Now he was the one with fire raging in his veins.

"I'm afraid I can't have you wearing my clothes," he joked, somehow managing to maintain a humorous demeanor despite the hunger clawing at him. "Take it off."

He definitely succeeded in surprising her because her lips parted in a soft *O*. It took him a second to realize she didn't intend to complain. Instead her eyebrows rose boldly in answer to his challenge.

She set her hands on her hips. "Did you miss the part where I have nothing else to wear?"

"Don't you think it's rude to take things without asking permission?" he countered, advancing in her direction.

A smile played around her lips, sizzling sweet as she methodically backpedaled toward the hall that led to the bedrooms. His gaze followed the trail of her hand as she slipped one button after another free, baring more creamy skin with each step. She was taunting him, daring him to catch her before she reached the guest bedroom. But he could move faster. That is, until his shirt smacked him in the face, blinding him just long enough for her to disappear.

Instinct took over. He tossed the shirt aside and charged after her. Three enormous strides and he closed in on her. Snatching her around the waist, he lifted her off her feet, intending to haul her into his bedroom. He had to find a bed. *Now.* While her passions were all lit up. Before her brain kicked in.

But the instant her naked body careened against his, he found the first solid surface available and set her back against the wall beside the door leading to the master bedroom.

Sliding one hand under her round butt cheek, he sank his fingers into her soft flesh and lifted her. She latched her arms around his shoulders, encircled his waist with her thighs and flicked her tongue into the sensitive skin beneath. His shoulder muscles bunched as a tsunami of arousal pounded through him.

"I need you to take me right here." She purred the demand against his skin, nipping his neck for emphasis, knowing it would drive him crazy. "Right now."

"Hell, yeah."

Her mouth bashed into his, lips parting, tongue searching. He dove straight into the hungry assault, sucking, kissing, erasing their years spent apart. Her skin grew slick as the tempest burned hot between them. He pulled back, determined to shift them to the bed in his room, but her thighs tightened around him.

"Here and now, frat boy," she taunted, rocking her hips and grinding against his arousal, making him moan.

He lost the will to argue with her. If she wanted it hard and fast up against the wall, he would give it to her. Later he could spend lazy hours chasing her curves with his fingers and lips, but for now he thought he'd die if he couldn't bury himself in her hot tight heat.

Sliding his hand over her rib cage, he cupped her breast, grazing her tight nipple with his thumb. Her breath grew ragged as he leaned forward, kissing her soft skin where shoulder met neck and trailing his tongue into the hollow of her collarbone. She ground against him, her muscles flexing in a familiar rhythm. He longed to be moving with her, *in* her. She was an addiction he'd never recovered from.

He reached down to unfasten the button holding his jeans closed and slid down the zipper. Her fervent arousal called to him as his dick sprang free. She gyrated wildly, bringing her slick heat into contact with his erection. He was an instant away from plunging into her when the need for protection struck him.

What was he doing? He'd dreamed about a moment like this for nearly five years. Why was he rushing? With her thighs clamped around his body, he spun them both and moved toward the bed. Before they went any further, he needed to get as naked as she was and to make sure she was safe.

She seemed to understand what drove him because as soon as her back touched the mattress, she sat up and began to tear at his shirt. While she stripped it off, he strained toward the nightstand drawer. To his relief, his fingers located a condom on the first try. Skimming off his jeans and boxers, he tore open the wrapper and sheathed himself.

Then he was on her, lips seeking hers, legs tangling, fingers splayed over her lower back to bring their naked skin together. Her lips were designed for his kisses. He'd memorized every curve until all he had to do was close his eyes and let his imagination run riot.

He nuzzled his lips into her neck as she pushed her bare breasts against his chest. A delicate mewling sound came from her throat as he eased his hand over the gorgeous curve of the nearest one and scraped his fingertips over her tight nipple. His mind was already fast-forwarding to how she would writhe as his mouth closed over the sensitive peak, feeling it turn into a hard pebble as he applied suction. With her slender leg trapped between his, she clung to him, purring with delight as he turned his attention to the other breast.

Her hands moved lazily over his shoulders, palms drifted up his neck before she tunneled her fingers into his hair. He trailed his fingers along her abdomen, letting the tips tickle over her belly in a way that made her squirm. Her thighs parted to let him glide along the crease that hid her sex. He dipped into her slippery wetness, lightly stroked her until she cried out, and then withdrew to circle her clit. Her body quaked as he toyed and teased before retreating. Lost in her pleasure, she trembled and bucked her hips, chanting his name. With each second he grew impossibly harder, but refused to stop what he was doing until she came for him.

"That feels *incredible*," she murmured, her chest heaving. "I'm so close…"

As if that triggered her, Lani threw her head back and howled. She climaxed in a rush. Her muscles tensing. Nails biting into his shoulders. He rubbed himself against her hip, caught up in her pleasure. The explosion that ripped through her was almost strong enough to take him with her.

He wanted to laugh at the sheer perfection of it, of her, but he needed her to experience even more. He slid his finger into her and pressed the heel of his palm against her clit. Legs spread wide, she thrashed her head from side to side, drove her mound hard against him and cried out for more.

Oh. Hell. Yes! This is what he'd missed. His senses magnified each harsh rasp of her ragged breath, the scent of her musk mingling with the delicious earthiness of her spicy perfume. Asher smiled as their tongues danced, the taste of whiskey invigorating his nerve endings. And the way her thighs clamped around him as she strained toward another orgasm, her smoky gaze locked with his, set him on fire.

Settling between her thighs in the welcoming cradle that had always felt like coming home, he waited for her to wrap her arms around his neck before pulling his head down to hers. He had to focus hard on not slamming into her. Despite her obvious burning need to meet her body with his, he wanted to remind himself of the texture of her skin, get his mouth on her breasts and glide his fingers over her tantalizing curves.

"Asher." His name was an urgent plea.

"Easy," he coaxed. "Let me take care of you."

"I love it when you say that," she whispered fiercely.

Her nails scraped down his spine and sank into his butt muscles. A curse escaped his lips when she barely paused before reaching between them. She latched her fingers onto his aching erection and drew him into contact with her hot, wet arousal.

"Now, Asher. I need you *now*."

He needed her, as well. More than needed. He'd craved this for five long years. Having her beneath him on his bed was a dream come true. The moment deserved as much smoldering all-in passion as he could produce. But the heat between them had a mind of its own and all too soon the head of his shaft was pressed against her tight entrance while she panted inarticulate words of encouragement between breaths. Heavenly voices sang in his head as he thrust into her searing heat. He groaned at the firm clasp of her inner muscles around him and lost himself in the homecoming that was Lani Li.

With the magic of the moment consuming his soul, he

began to move inside her. Fanning his fingers and gathering her butt in his palm, he began a slow withdrawal, culminating with a teasing hesitation to drive up anticipation. He waited for her to open her eyes and meet his. She always did this. Every time.

When her lashes lifted, baring her mink-brown gaze, her pure, unapologetic joy was the sexiest thing he'd ever seen. He dusted a kiss across her forehead, before he lowered his chin and grazed her lips with his.

"I've missed this," he whispered. "You have no idea how much."

Her tremulous sigh tickled his jaw. "So have I."

What she did to him was unique and one-of-a-kind. He was on fire and she was the gasoline that turned him into a raging inferno. They moaned together as he plunged into her once again, rejoicing as she took all of him. Stroke after stoke, he dove deep, thrusting smoothly while hoarse, hungry cries emanated from her throat.

Shudders slammed through him as desire wrestled for control of his muscles. He struggled to stay present and hold off, fighting to withstand the orgasm bent on claiming him. He needed her to come a second time. He moved harder, changed the angle of his deepening thrusts and watched her strain for her release, her rocking hips driving him mad.

She must've known what he wanted for her because she lifted her head and sank her white teeth into his earlobe. The painful nip sent lightning streaking straight to his groin and shattered his willpower.

"More," she commanded, meeting every one of his nearly frantic thrusts with equally reckless abandon.

This wasn't the Lani Li he knew from these last few weeks. This was a return to the wild, wanton woman he'd known that smoking hot, oh-so-memorable summer. Sex with her had ruined him for anyone else. No one matched her curiosity or her focus. She'd investigated his body and discovered all his pleasure spots with the same level of curiosity she'd shown while attacking the embezzlement case.

Pleasure drove him on. The air around them seemed to waver from the heat pouring off their bodies. He struggled for breath that wasn't there. Still, he persisted. The pounding rhythm of her pants pushing him harder. She thrashed her head from side to side, long hair tangling on her sweaty shoulders. Her legs tightened around him, the strength of the vise letting him know she was close.

Her back arched, head rolling back, baring her throat. "Come with me." The guttural order spilled from her parted lips.

She possessed just enough air to call his name before her muscles went taut, the rhythmic pulse of her release triggering his own. He wanted to hold off, to push her harder, give her more, but her power over him was too potent. There would be plenty of time later to take her past the fiery edge of satisfaction. Right now it was more important for them to be together in this momentous rejoining of body and soul.

He'd love to say he let himself go, but the truth was she grabbed hold of him and yanked him hard into a bone-jarring, roaring avalanche of satisfaction and unending joy. *She* did this to him. She made him crazy and so incredibly happy.

He collapsed into her arms and caught sight of her blissful smile before he entwined their sated bodies. As their skin cooled in the aftermath, Asher stroked back the hair from her face and let his lips drift over her damp shoulder. He hooked the comforter over both of them and grinned as she snuggled her nose into his throat.

When it was just the two of them like this, he could imagine everything would be okay. He'd just stay focused on that for tonight and enjoy that for a little while his life made sense again.

Seven

With her favorite Lowercase album pouring from Asher's Bluetooth speakers, Lani pushed back from her laptop and rubbed her tired, dry eyes. Over the past week, one lead after another had dried up, including any connection between Ross and the missing funds. Faced with a plethora of dead ends, she'd become aware of a growing panic. Was Asher guilty? Lani hoped not. She wouldn't have renewed their physical relationship if she didn't question the validity of the evidence stacked against him. At least she hoped not. She would hate it if she on the verge of making a colossal mistake.

Between long hours at her computer and late nights in bed with Asher, making up for lost time, she'd been lost in a bubble of work and sex. And Lani couldn't remember the last time she'd been this happy.

"Come on," Asher coaxed, his hands sweeping her long hair away from her neck so he could glide his lips over her skin. "You've done enough work for one day. I think you should take a break."

"What kind of a break did you have in mind?" She glanced up at him, anticipation making her breathless.

"I have twelve polo ponies in training and they need exercise. Wanna help?"

Lani blinked at him, adjusting to this unexpected development. "Help how?"

"How long has it been since you've been on a horse?"

"A while."

When they first met, he'd been intrigued that she'd been a barrel racer when she was young. He'd persuaded her to take him to visit her parents' hobby farm. Introducing him to her horse had gone a lot smoother than meeting her parents. Once they found out he was a professional polo player, they'd definitely not approved and campaigned for her to break things off.

Maybe part of her recognized that she and Asher were too different to work, but she'd waved away their concern, telling her parents that it was just a summer fling and ignoring their exchanged looks that said they believed otherwise.

"What's *a while*?"

Although her folks hadn't sold her horse, she'd been too invested in starting up her investigation firm to take time for recreation. "A year."

"That's too long. Why don't you throw on your boots and I'll saddle Royal Flush for you. She's the best I have and she'll take care of you."

"I guess I could use a break," she said and went to change her footwear.

When she entered the barn, Lani found he had pulled out two horses and was in the process of saddling one of them. She sidled up to the closest one and extended one of the carrots she'd brought as a treat.

"This is Cactus," Asher said, reaching beneath his horse's belly to snag the end of the girth and buckle it into place. "And Royal Flush."

"Hello, beautiful." She scratched the chestnut's shoulder and felt her lean into the caress. Her own horse always seemed to have an itch at this exact same spot. It made her smile.

Asher slid the halter off the bay and plucked the bridle off his shoulder. He threw the reins over the horse's head and poised the bit against the mare's long yellow teeth.

"You're using a gag bit," Lani murmured, recognizing the three-part bit with two joints. "When I raced, I used something similar because Reggie tended not to bend around the barrels and the gag bit really helped with that."

"The gag bit in polo came into popularity in Argentina because the players there were always looking for ways to improve their game. And they found that this style of bit made the horses more linear and less lateral."

"Do you miss it?" Her question caused Asher to still for a moment.

"Do I miss galloping down the field with seven other guys' mallets whizzing past my head as we pursue a little white ball?" His mocking grin flashed, knocking the breath from her body. "Hell ya, I miss it."

"So why aren't you still doing it?"

"Do you think you can manage an English saddle? Or should I put a Western one on Royal Flush?"

The difference between an English and Western saddle was pretty significant. A Western saddle had a deep secure seat with a substantial horn atop a pommel at the front and a high cantle behind. Weighing upward of twenty-five pounds, the design enabled cowboys to stay firmly seated while on bucking broncos and chasing down erratically moving cattle.

English saddles, on the other hand, were flatter and less bulky by comparison and required the rider to work to stay balanced atop their mount. That being said, because of the reduced weight, it was the saddle of choice for jumpers and polo enthusiasts.

Lani could see the dare in Asher's gaze and knew he was trying to divert her attention from the question she'd asked. Still, she gave her options serious consideration. She'd ridden English before, but never while running full tilt across a polo field or while trying to hit a ball with a mallet.

"I think if I plan to stay on, I'd better take the Western saddle."

Ten minutes later they were leading the horses out of the barn and toward a large fenced field. She'd mistaken it for a turnout before this. Instead the groomed grass indicated that this was Asher's training ground. Out of habit she tested the girth before fitting her foot into the stirrup, making sure it remained snug around Royal Flush's belly.

"You don't trust I can saddle a horse?" he teased, swinging up on the bay with no effort whatsoever.

Lani's muscles protested this unaccustomed exercise and she grunted at the effort it took to swing her leg over the Thoroughbred's back. Seating herself with an ungainly thump, she shot a glance Asher's way, hoping he hadn't seen her struggle. While Royal Flush stood still despite her awkward landing, Asher had his hands full keeping his own mount in place.

"Reggie loved to hold his breath when I saddled him and I always had to double check the girth after I walked him around a bit."

While Royal Flush stood perfectly still, waiting for Lani to cue her, Cactus was full of impatient energy as she sidestepped and backed up.

"She's new," Asher explained, his calm handling of the antsy equine demonstrating a level of patience and skill that was having a dangerous effect on her hormones. He didn't saw on the reins in an effort to control the horse, but sat quietly letting his legs and seat tell the horse what to do. "I adopted her from Donovan Horse Rescue. She's a former racehorse, purchased by an inexperienced rider and badly neglected before Valencia Donovan got her. I guess she was skin and bones. Valencia thinks she might've been abused. But she's fast and loves to run—it's the slowing and turning that we have to work on."

"How come you have so many horses? I thought a string was two or three."

"That's typical for a hobbyist. Three to four is common for a more serious player and if you're professional, a string can be up to ten."

"Are you training these horses because you're considering going back on the professional circuit again?"

"No, these days I play to give these guys experience. It's hobbyist-level action, but I can't give it up entirely. I enjoy the training far too much." He urged his mount forward and used his head to indicate she should come along.

"So once they're trained, then what?"

"I'll sell. I have several people coming to look at horses over the next week or so."

She could hear the ache in his voice. This wasn't something he was doing lightly.

"Why?"

He gave her question a negligent shrug. "Since it doesn't seem as if my family's going to help me and I'm going to be facing some pretty stiff legal bills, I thought I should generate some cash."

They rode in silence for several minutes while Lani processed Asher's pain.

"Are you ready?" he asked, stroking the bay's sweaty neck. The mare had worked herself into a lather before they'd walked to the end and back.

"Ready?" Lani echoed, unsure what he had in mind.

A second later he and Cactus shot away at a gallop. Lani felt Royal Flush gather herself to follow and keyed the mare.

As the ground whizzed by, she realized how much she'd missed this. Losing the battle to contain her excitement, a whoop ripped free. All too soon she had to slow the horse as the far fence loomed.

As she drew back on the reins, the chestnut slowed to a smooth canter. Lani's heart was thundering in her ears and she was sure she was grinning like an idiot from the amusement on Asher's face.

"How did that feel?" he asked, sidestepping his mount over to the fence where a couple of mallets sat propped against the railing.

Lani was breathing hard from the exertion. "She's really fast."

"Argentinian born and bred. They take their polo ponies seriously down there. I bought her as a two-year-old and trained her. She's the best I've ever owned."

And yet he was selling her because his family refused to help him out. Once again Lani had to withstand the urge to comfort him. Still, she hoped the mare went to a good home.

"Let's see how you do with one of these." He handed her a mallet, his wicked grin on full display. "Head weight on that one is six ounces, which is on the lighter end. You should be able to handle it without problems."

As Lani swung the mallet to get the feel of it, she braced herself against the challenge in Asher's expression. Five years earlier, after discovering a mutual love of climbing, white-water rafting and mountain biking, they'd pushed each other to do all sorts of crazy stunts. Afterward, hyped up on adrenaline and endorphins, they'd fallen upon each other in ravenous desire.

Feeling a familiar tingle between her thighs, Lani shifted in the saddle, but this only pressed her sensitive areas against the leather's firm surface, intensifying the ache there. A breeze blew across her hot skin, and she savored the cooling caress. Damn it! The man could get her hot and bothered just by being in the same vicinity.

She was glad when Asher started demonstrating the finer arts of polo. Riding a horse while holding the mallet was challenging enough. Successfully connecting the mallet with the ball absorbed all her focus and energy. They played for an hour and with each minute that passed Lani's appreciation for Asher's talent grew.

"I won't be able walk tomorrow," she groaned, the overworked muscles of her inner thighs protesting as she mounted the stairs to his apartment.

"You just need a hot bath and a massage." His eyes kindled. "I can help with both."

Lani emerged from the bedroom, dressed for work, jeans, boots, white button-down shirt and black leather jacket. Asher sat at the breakfast bar, a mug of coffee within easy reach as he texted. She wondered if his sister had responded to any of his messages. He'd reached out to her once a day since being released.

In the seconds before he noticed her arrival, she snatched the opportunity to regard him. Worn jeans hugged his lower half while a blue polo shirt molded to the muscles of his shoulders and chest. The faint scent of hay and horse hung in the air. He sat perched on a barstool, the heel of his left boot caught on the lower rung. He looked ready to spring into action. All this inactivity was clearly driving him crazy. He hummed like a live wire, his energy zapping and sizzling with the need to go and do.

She didn't know if she made a sound or if he was just so tuned in to her presence that he became aware he was no longer alone in the room. His eyes lifted from the phone screen and darted her way. The impact of his gaze raised goose bumps on her arms. A familiar breathless state came over her. This was bad. She never should've started up things with him again, but he was irresistible and she was powerless against her own longing.

"Have you heard back from Gina?" she asked, needing a distraction from her thoughts.

"Yeah." His neutral tone gave away none of his feelings. "She knows if anyone can find the money it will be you." His gaze roved ever so slowly over her outfit. "Looks like you're dressed for business. I guess we're not going to spend the morning in bed."

"You're the one who got up."

Her response was a little too tart. But honest all the same. Because deep down she was disappointed that he'd left her in bed to go tend to his horses. It had always been that way with her. She'd been so starved for his attention that any distraction left her feeling bereft and insecure.

"I didn't realize..." He set down his phone, held out his hand, a silent command to come to him and one she lacked the strength to ignore.

All too aware that a week earlier she might have flung up some sort of defense against him, Lani let herself be drawn toward him, nearly purring as his long fingers stroked her cheek and tangled in her hair. Her whole body swooned with pleasure as he hooked her hip with his other hand and drew her between his thighs. His lips grazed the sensitive skin below her ear and she shivered. Damn the man for being so good at this.

"You didn't realize what?"

There was a catch in her voice as she asked the question. He couldn't fail to hear it, couldn't fail to understand what caused it. When he touched her, she became someone else. Someone who forgot who she was, forgot right or wrong, up or down. There was just his touch anchoring her to him, helping her make sense of the emotional maelstrom inside her. All she needed was this man. His deep passionate kisses. His body possessing hers. The rest of the world didn't exist when he was kissing her.

"I didn't realize how much you miss me." He curved his hand over her butt and pulled her pelvis against the growing hardness behind his zipper. "When I'm not around."

Although it was true, confronting this chink in her armor was a puff of icy air against her hot skin. She stopped clinging to his impressive biceps and shoved against his chest. Not hard, nor with any vigor, but with enough pressure to part them, allowing her to take a half step back.

"I have a meeting in half an hour that I need to get to," she said, refusing to notice the smug light in his eye.

"May I come?"

Lani tugged her jacket straight, all too aware of the unfulfilled ache in her breasts and the clammy texture of her overheated skin. "Not a good idea."

"Because it's about the investigation?"

Plucking an elastic tie off her wrist, she fastened her hair into a low ponytail. "That *is* why I'm here."

"I hope that isn't the only reason why you are here."

He had her there. She'd already determined that he had no intention of skipping town. And the electronic bracelet around his ankle would allow the cops to track him down in a heartbeat if he ventured beyond the estate without her. She really didn't need to babysit him. In the beginning she'd stuck around to get inside his head. She could entertain the theory that he'd been set up and go back to her apartment in Dallas.

Yet the thought of being parted from him awoke a sharp pang of reluctance. She wasn't ready to move on from the long passionate nights in his arms. Or to ponder what might happen in the days to come.

"I really have to go," she said, uncomfortable with the direction her thoughts had gone.

"Who are you meeting?"

"Zach Benning."

The social media influencer had come to Royal to promote the festival and fallen in love with Lila Jones, Royal's Chamber of Commerce representative.

"I'd heard he's living in Royal now. Moved in with Lila Jones." Asher's gaze sharpened as it rested on her. "Gave up his entire life in LA just to be with her."

Lani found herself bristling at his thoughtful tone. What point was he trying to make? That she should've given up her plans for a master's degree five years earlier and trailed after him like some lovesick idiot? For how long? He'd offered her nothing she could count on. Made no promises. He had no plan for what they would do in Royal. She was a girl who needed a set of achievable goals to move her forward. Playing things by ear was *not* in her comfort zone.

"Yes, well…" She glanced toward the kitchen, dodging his assessing gaze. "I'd love a cup of coffee, but there's no time. I don't suppose you have a to-go mug?"

"I always have a to-go mug," he said, his lips lifting into a sardonic quirk. He was no stranger to their differences, but rather than ignore them, he was more likely to lean into the problems created between them. "I'd really like it if you'd let me go along. Where are you meeting him?"

As he spoke, he went into the kitchen, pulled out a travel mug. Once he poured in the coffee and doctored it the way she liked, he handed it to her. Appreciation threatened as she took the mug. Damn him for being so good to her.

Against her better judgment, Lani felt herself softening toward his entreaty. Why not bring him along? He'd already proven a handy guy to have around and by sleeping with him she'd crossed a professional line. Plus, if she really believed that he wasn't responsible for taking the money, then maybe having his perspective would prove useful. Oh, hell. She was making excuses. Before this case she'd always worked alone and liked it. Relying on anyone besides herself meant she couldn't control the outcome.

"At the Royal Diner." She wondered if the public location would deter Asher.

He wasn't exactly anyone's favorite Edmond right now. A lot of people had suffered in town because of the failure of the festival. Keeping a low profile was a better way for him to go; but one thing about Asher, he never seemed to take the safest route.

"Will you wait while I change? I just need to get out of these barn clothes."

With a reluctant sigh, she nodded. "I'll call the monitoring company and let them know you're coming with me."

He winked at her before departing for the bedroom. Lani's insides turned to mush as her gaze locked on his tight rear end. A sigh whispered out of her before she realized what she was doing. *Stop!* Sure, the man had a body to die for and a knack for getting beneath her skin with his cocky smiles and heated glances, but she shouldn't indulge in his candy-coated yumminess during the day. She was a professional with a job to do. She needed to stay focused on that.

Before she'd finished her phone call, Asher had reappeared in clean denim and a light gray button-down shirt with the collar open to reveal the strong column of his throat. Her gaze locked on his tan skin as she remembered nibbling her way along it the night before and the heady sounds of his groans. She'd been so entranced by the sounds he'd made that she'd continued exploring him with her lips, teeth and tongue far into the night. A familiar flutter of excitement awakened deep in her belly as she picked up her laptop case.

"Let's get going," she said tersely, hating the husky note in her voice and the heavy pulse of longing that made her want to tear off his shirt and taste him once more.

"After you," he murmured, a wry smile softening his hard masculine features into irresistible boyish charm.

Did he know what she was thinking? She was known for her poker face, but he had a knack for reading her emotions. As they walked down the stairs toward the barn, she surreptitiously touched the back of her hand against her cheek. Was she warmer than normal? Did a hot pink flush betray the heat rising in her? How could she remain professional when her body betrayed her at every turn?

"Do you want me to drive?" he asked as their feet crunched along the gravel path, leading from the back of the barn to a series of turnout paddocks. Asher gestured to their cars, sitting side-by-side.

"No, I will."

"Okay." He sounded disappointed.

Lani shot him an impatient glance. "What?"

"I thought maybe after last night…" The previous evening they'd discussed her need to be in charge all the time.

"When it comes to my case, what I say goes."

"Yes, boss." He coupled his snarky comeback with a long-suffering sigh.

"I'm not your boss."

His raised eyebrows said she was sure acting like one.

"You like being in control. It seems like having a minion would suit you." He shot her a wicked grin before heading toward the passenger side of her SUV.

He was right. She wanted staff. More investigators meant she could take on more clients, but she needed more cases to be able to afford to hire anyone. When she'd started her investigative business, she hadn't taken into consideration how important contacts would be. Which was why solving this case for Kingston Blue was so critical. Finding the missing festival funds and bringing the embezzler to justice would boost her reputation.

Which was why it made no sense that with so much riding on this case, she was sleeping with the one man who everyone thought was guilty.

"If driving is that important to you," she snapped, deflecting her self-reproach onto him, "then be my guest."

"Thanks."

This single word, spoken with gratitude and delight, further inflamed her heated emotions. All he was trying to do was be helpful. He wanted to participate in clearing his name and she continued to behave like a prickly pear cactus. It wasn't his fault that she'd made the mistake of crossing the professional line. She could've been stronger. Punishing him for her transgression wasn't fair.

Stewing, Lani slid into the passenger seat of his luxury sedan and tried not to enjoy the way she sank into the butter-soft leather.

"So how come you're meeting with Zach?" Asher asked as they sped through the estate gates and turned onto the highway. "Do you think he could be guilty?"

"I'm talking to everyone involved with the festival. And no, I don't think he's guilty. For one thing, he has a lot of money already."

"Yes, but he makes that money as a social media influencer. Something he's put on hold since moving to Royal. Maybe it was embezzling funds from the festival that gave him the ability to leave his life as an influencer behind."

Lani wasn't sure if she was more surprised by the fact that Asher had obviously been doing some research of his own regarding the festival's participants or the theories he'd developed for why Zach might be a suspect. She'd never given him credit for being capable of such serious, deliberate thought. And that certainly wasn't fair. Yet had he ever indicated that his thoughts were full of anything other than where the next party or exhilarating adventure was?

She winced. How often had she noticed that there was more to Asher than met the eye and then dismissed it as ridiculous? Had it been fair to look no deeper than his gorgeous appearance and his party-boy antics and assume that was all he had to offer? Five years earlier he'd given her a taste of his luxury lifestyle and she'd assumed because he hadn't earned his money that she was better than him.

Is that why she'd determined from the start that it would be a summer fling and nothing more? Because she didn't believe he wasn't capable of or interested in being more than that? She'd avoided discussing serious matters with him. Was that to keep from dwelling on his shallowness or dodge getting too attached? When she'd confessed her love to him, what had she expected would happen between them? Despite toying with the idea of not going on to grad school, the thought of altering her meticulous plans for the future had unnerved her.

Or had she done him a disservice? He hadn't seemed to mind their casual interaction. Lani thought about those true crime books sitting on his shelf. Had getting to know her that summer sparked a passion for unsolved murders? He'd asked a lot of questions about her process and thrown himself into helping her find the missing money. Would he be as interested if he hadn't been charged with the crime?

How come you haven't taken on any associates?

Was that just idle curiosity or was there something more behind the question?

Lani glanced at his profile and wondered what it would be like to partner with someone. To have another person to talk to about cases. To brainstorm ideas. To interact with clients.

No. She'd be crazy to even consider letting Asher get anywhere near her business. She was doing just fine on her own. She'd be doing better after the successful conclusion of this case. After that, she'd go her way and Asher would go his. It was what had happened before. It would happen this time too.

Eight

A merry bell sounded as Asher pulled open Royal Diner's front door. Both a welcome and a warning, the tinkle seemed louder than usual because the classic diner-style restaurant was only half-full. Asher braced as his shocking appearance stirred the atmosphere. For the last week or so he'd actually forgotten about his increased notoriety around town. But now, as the whispers began, Asher ground his molars. He wasn't used to so much negativity directed his way.

Twenty feet of black-and-white-checkerboard tile separated them from the red vinyl booth where Zach Benning sat. A dozen pairs of unfriendly eyes watched his progress as Asher followed Lani past the counter service area. Curiosity and contempt battered him, but he acted oblivious to the commotion he was causing.

Asher focused his attention on the guy they'd come to meet. His gray designer T-shirt gave him an LA vibe. Coupled with his expensive haircut, Zach looked every inch a city boy.

"Hi, Zach, thanks for meeting me." Lani glanced Asher's way before amending, "Meeting with *us*."

"Sure." Zach's eyebrows sank below the rim of his sunglasses as Asher slid into the red vinyl booth beside Lani. "You're out?" This he directed at Asher.

"On bail." Lani spoke up before Asher could explain and her quick explanation left him feeling defensive.

Retreating into sardonic humor, he stuck out his leg and showed off the edge of the ankle monitor. "I'm on a short leash."

This seemed to mollify the other man because after scrutinizing the device, he gave a short, satisfied nod, dismissing Asher as a threat. After that, Zach focused his full attention on Lani and the volume rose on his charisma as he pointed a lopsided smile in her direction. Asher bristled as Lani relaxed beside him.

The two men were close in age and similar in nature, each preferring a freewheeling lifestyle of parties, women and luxury. But where Asher was cavalier about his image, Zach had cultivated his particular bad-boy style into a huge social media following that had made him a multimillionaire.

Familiar with Lani's weakness for pleasure-seeking reprobates, Asher slung an arm across the back of the booth behind her shoulders and twisted his upper body so he could easily watch the pair interact.

"As I mentioned on the phone, I'm looking into the money that's gone missing from the festival."

Zach's gaze flicked toward Asher and the corners of his lips flattened in derision. "Shouldn't you be asking this guy?" He kicked his thumb in Asher's direction.

"I didn't take the money," Asher growled, letting his annoyance get the better of him. "I'm trying to figure out who did."

"You're trying to figure out…?" Zach looked from

Asher to Lani. "I thought you were the one doing the in-vestigating."

Lani gave Asher's thigh a hard nudge with her knee in warning and leaned forward, resting her forearms on the table. "I'm exploring the possibility that someone set Asher up."

While it wasn't a resounding declaration of confidence in his innocence, the tight knot of irritation eased in his chest. Most days he vacillated between relief that she was finally looking into alternate theories of the theft and worry that, without any evidence pointing to another's guilt, her logical mind would return to the most obvious theory that he was responsible.

"Somebody?" Zach echoed. "Like who?"

"Various people." She paused. "I'm talking to anyone who had a connection to the festival—"

"Wait one second," Zach interrupted vehemently, lean-ing forward. "I had nothing to do with the actual opera-tions and—"

Lani threw up her hands in a pacifying gesture. "Not you, of course." She softened her expression, but didn't actually smile.

"If you're going after Lila, I've got nothing more to say."

"No. No. It's nothing like that," Lani assured him.

Lila Jones was a member of the festival's advisory board in addition to working for the Royal Chamber of Com-merce. A hardworking, serious-minded woman, rather for-gettable in Asher's book, she'd engaged Zach to promote the festival through social media. Apparently seeing po-tential where no one else had, Zach had sprinkled some sort of fairy godmother dust on her and turned Lila into an Instagram sensation. The pair had become romantically involved and Lila had been seen around town sporting an enormous diamond on her left hand.

Although normally Asher paid little attention to the love

lives of those around him, he was beginning to see a pattern of couples finding each other thanks to the ill-fated festival. He glanced Lani's way. Would that same magic work for them?

"But you were around many who were involved," Lani continued, "and I wanted to hear your impressions."

"I don't know how I can help you." Zach's tension eased marginally. "Early on I showed up, did a photo shoot—not anywhere near the actual site of the festival because of all the construction for the stages and restaurants. I didn't meet all that many people."

Lani offered an encouraging smile. "I'll bet you know more than you realize."

"It was all pretty chaotic. Really disorganized." Zach looked thoughtful. "Wait. Now that I think back, I did catch wind of how materials weren't showing up because bills weren't getting paid. Money problems were delaying everything." Once again Zach glanced toward the guy who everybody thought was the guilty party.

Asher's gut tightened. He could almost hear Lani's brain whirring as she processed what Zach had to say. Okay, so obviously something fishy had been going on with the money all along. And yeah, he should've paid more attention, but the day-to-day details of the project had really not been his cup of tea.

"Besides the funding, did anything else strike you as unusual or wrong?"

"Not really." But Zach grew thoughtful. "Well, maybe this one thing. I kept seeing a guy that I thought I knew from back in LA."

Beside him, Lani stiffened, but her voice sounded nonchalant, almost blasé as she asked, "What guy?"

"Your brother's friend," Zach directed this remark to Asher. "I can't remember the name he introduced himself as, but I remember running into him several times in LA. The names didn't match. But I *swear* it was the same guy."

Ross's friend? Asher thought back to everyone who'd been to the island. When they were pitching it to various vendors and people they knew, they'd brought hordes of people to check out the site and hear the pitch. That had been the fun part... Entertaining the investors, painting a picture of the exclusive event, the delicious food, fantastic wine, the famous headliners like Kingston Blue set to perform, with all the proceeds going to charity.

Turns out he'd done too good a sell. In fact he'd oversold the festival. *Literally.*

The festival had suffered from neglect on the part of the principal players. Ross had been focused on his reunion with Charlotte and getting to know his two-year-old son, Ben. His attention was further disrupted by the major blowup this had caused with Rusty. Being disinherited can sure distract a guy. Sort of like being falsely accused of embezzlement.

Gina had been preoccupied with her mother's return to Royal after a nineteen-year absence and the family drama that had ensued.

That left Asher. His talents involved persuading people to trust him and painting their investors a picture of how awesome the festival was going to be. Initially he'd brought in a lot of the funds that had then gone missing.

"Which friend is that?" Lani asked, returning Asher's attention to the conversation. "Can you describe him?"

"Tall guy. Dark hair. Blue eyes. He seemed as if he knew the family really well. And he spent a lot of time sucking up to your dad."

It sounded like Billy Holmes. Ross's friend from college. He'd been a major player in the festival organization and always seemed to be around.

"You said you couldn't remember his name," Lani began,

but before she could go much further into the questioning, Zach snapped his fingers and cut her off.

"Howard Bond," he declared. "No wait, not Howard Bond…"

While Zach scrunched up his face and racked his memory, Asher struggled to keep from shouting at the guy to get on with it. What the hell was going on? Who was Howard Bond? And what did any of this have to do with the embezzled money?

"Bond Howard," Zach announced, looking pleased. "That's it. I remember meeting the guy at a pool party thrown by an executive producer at Universal. I usually meet a lot of people at these events, but he stuck out in my mind as being a first-class dick."

"Why was that?" Lani asked, her flat tone hinting at only casual interest while Asher's heart thumped like a pile driver at the unexpected direction this interview was going.

"The party was loud and I didn't catch his name at first so he repeated it. He's all like, *it's Bond, as in James Bond.*" Zach intoned this like an exaggerated imitation of Sean Connery. "I thought to myself, that's crazy because who names their kid Bond? More likely he was called Howard and his last name is Bond so because it was LA, and everybody changes their name, he switched it to Bond Howard, which is much cooler."

While Zach was telling this tale, Asher noticed that Lani's body had begun to hum with excitement. She was like a bloodhound on a scent and it totally turned him on.

"So, when I met him on the island, and he was introduced as something else, it struck me as odd. Especially when he insisted we'd never met."

Lani narrowed her eyes. "Did you doubt it was the same person?"

"No, I was pretty sure it was the same guy. He has a

fairly distinctive look. Do you know what I mean? Not like you'd mistake him for a bunch of other people."

Was this a legit lead? Asher glanced at Lani, but her expression remained inscrutable. He wanted to end this meeting with Zach and get her alone so he could figure out what was going on in that big beautiful brain of hers. Hope was tapping on the edge of his consciousness, wanting in. For the first time since his whole world came crashing down around him, Asher realized the level of fear he been suppressing. His hands began to shake as the truth of his reality struck him. In the back of his mind, he'd been grappling with going to jail for a crime he hadn't committed. Only now, as it was looking like someone else might be a suspect, did traction set in.

"Well that sounds promising," Asher said, keeping a lid on his excitement as they stood up and headed toward the exit of the Royal Diner.

Before they reached the exit, the chime above the door rang, warning him someone was coming in. Both he and Lani slowed to let the new arrival enter. Deputy Vesta entered, tipping his hat to Lani as she headed out past him. Asher started to follow, but found the deputy in his way. Before he could step aside, Vesta had bumped his broad shoulder hard into Asher's chest as he went by. Although the blow didn't throw him off balance, the hit jolted his ego, reminding him that in the eyes of the town, he was a thief who'd stolen from people who couldn't afford the losses.

In a much more subdued frame of mind, Asher lengthened his stride to catch up with Lani. "Why do you think Billy would've introduced himself as Bond Howard?" he asked, picking up their earlier conversational thread.

"First of all, we're not really sure if this Bond Howard and Billy Holmes are the same person."

Asher appreciated Lani's caution about as much as a

pie in the face. He wanted her to leap all over this lead and chase it down to prove she believed in his innocence and would go to any lengths to exonerate him. Instead, she showed every sign of proceeding with her plodding, methodical investigation.

"How do we go about figuring out if they are?" Asher asked, letting just a bit of his impatience show.

He unlocked his car and swung the passenger door open for Lani. She shot him the oddest look before sliding into the car.

"What?" he prodded.

"I can open my own doors."

"Stop being so damned independent," he growled, wishing she understood how much he enjoyed taking care of her. "Let me help once in a while."

Asher wasn't just talking about the car door. He wanted to impress upon her that he was someone she could rely on. She might be too proud to accept financial help from him, but he could be there for her in other ways. As a sounding board to bounce ideas off of. As muscle in case she got into another tight situation like the one with Mika Sorenson's husband.

"Whatever."

She pulled the door shut, leaving him standing on the sidewalk, staring at her through the side window. How could this woman be so sensual and yielding in bed and stubborn and prickly out of it? Naked in his arms, she gave every part of herself to the moment and to him. But heaven forbid he fixed her favorite cocktail or made her dinner or—*gasp*—opened her car door, because then she became surly and churlish.

By the time he circled the car and slipped behind the wheel, she had her laptop out and was madly clicking away on the keys. From her extreme focus he might as well not have been in the car at all.

"Where to?" he asked, starting the engine. If it had been up to him, he would've driven straight to Billy Holmes's house and demanded answers.

"Just a second."

Asher was growing accustomed to Lani's ability to block out all distractions when she was investigating and didn't take offense when she put him off.

Still, he decided to do some musing out loud. "Why do you suppose Billy was using a different name in LA?"

"We don't know that it was Billy."

"But Zach seemed pretty sure," Asher argued. "And he was right about Billy's look being distinctive."

Lani made some noncommittal noises and continued to work away at her laptop. With a weary sigh, he put the car in gear, signaled and pulled out of the parking spot. One way to find out about Billy was to ask the guy himself. A tempting move, but he suspected he would do himself no favors if he started confronting people and accusing them of the theft. However he could go ask the suspect's good friend, Asher's brother, Ross.

They were halfway to The Edmond Organization when Lani looked up from her laptop and realized they weren't on their way back to the estate. "Where are we going?"

"To talk to Ross. He's known Billy since college and they've kept in touch all these years. Surely he knows what his good friend has been up before he moved to Royal two years ago."

"Are you out of your mind?" She rolled her eyes. "We can't barge into Ross's office and start asking a bunch of invasive questions about his friend."

"Why not?"

When she didn't immediately answer, Asher glanced her way. Her pained expression was like a knife in his chest.

"Why the hell not, Lani?" he demanded, a sick feeling swirling through him.

"A few months back your brother was struggling financially."

"You don't seriously think that Ross was involved in this embezzlement, do you?"

He couldn't believe what he was hearing. Ross wouldn't do something like that to him. Yet even as he rejected Lani's inference, her logic began eroding his trust. Whom was he supposed to put his faith in? The man he'd called brother since he was a teenager? Or the woman he'd spent a fun-filled summer frolicking with? The same one who was currently investigating him for embezzlement?

"Let's put it this way, I suspect everyone." Her answer was a sharp kick that connected with his head and set his temples to throbbing.

"Including me," he stated flatly, gripping the steering wheel until his knuckles turned white.

"Yes."

Presuming he'd made inroads with her had been too optimistic. Just because they were sleeping together, didn't mean her opinion of him had improved. No. Just as it had been between them five years ago, he was little more than a walk on the wild side for her. She'd been clear from the start that she couldn't take him seriously. He wasn't relationship material.

While he'd been ruminating, she'd gone back to typing. If they weren't heading to the Edmond headquarters, he needed some destination. "So, where are we going?"

If Lani heard the tension in his voice, she made no sign. "I think the best thing is to head back to Elegance Ranch. I have some research to do on this Bond Howard character. We need to figure out if he and Billy are the same guy."

"And how do we do that?"

"Well, we can start with his social media."

"Billy's?" Asher had no idea how that was supposed to help.

Lani shook her head. "Bond Howard's."

Asher gave her space to work as he drove back to the estate. The moments of freedom he'd known while driving during his all-too-brief trip to the Royal Diner left him hyperaware of how little he'd appreciated his freedom until now.

As the estate gates loomed, he had a fleeting but overwhelming urge to turn the car around and head straight for the airport. He knew he wouldn't get anywhere with the electronic-monitoring device strapped to his ankle, but a jittery restlessness had taken hold of him. In the past he had exorcized his demons by indulging in some sort of risky action. That door was shut and barred to him for now. He would just have to face his reality and learn to make the best of it.

The thought actually made him grin. Was this what personal growth was all about? It figured it would take something as drastic as looming imprisonment to wake him up.

"Any luck finding Bond Howard's social media presence?" he asked as the car raced past the main house and made for the stable.

"Hmm."

It really was time for a change, he mused. As much as he enjoyed living close to his horses, he really should put the entire string up for sale and move away from Elegance Ranch.

"There's quite a bit actually," Lani said, clicking away on her laptop. "Turns out he has several online personas."

Asher mulled that bit of news as he parked beside her SUV. Her preoccupation with whatever data she was finding gave him enough time to shut off the car, exit and have her door open before she closed the lid. He smirked at her scowl and went the extra mile by offering his hand to help her out of the low-slung sedan.

The tingle in his fingers shot straight to his groin. He

pushed all thoughts of sex from his brain and asked, "How did you find the additional social media profiles so quickly?"

"I have software that allows me to find similar images on the internet. Already the search has yielded profiles for Bobby Hammond and Brad Howell, in addition to Bond Howard."

"That looks pretty suspicious," Asher said, hoping she agreed.

"Maybe." She started for the stairs to the apartment. "We'll need to do some more digging before that becomes clear."

"We'll," he echoed, grinning. "I like the sound of that."

Nine

For days after their meeting with Zach, Lani kicked herself for letting Asher think he was participating in the investigation. It was hers to handle. She shouldn't have involved him at all. And the excuse that she enjoyed his company was too lame for her to acknowledge even though it was absolutely the case. So much for her lone-wolf policy. Maybe she'd been too quick to downplay her need for associates. His determined approach to the task was altering her attitude. Sure, his style was different from hers. But that didn't mean his results weren't sound. Could she let go of her need to control the entire process? *Should* she?

Still, day after day they'd set up their laptops at his breakfast bar. Side by side, typing away in companionable silence. She'd done a deep dive into Bond Howard while Asher researched Bobby Hammond and Brad Howell. Sure enough, Billy Holmes had been living in various parts of the country under different names. They'd contacted anyone who had tagged him in their photos and a picture was beginning to form. The women were quick-est to respond. Asher and Lani discovered Billy had left a trail of jilted lovers and unsatisfied investors in his wake. Everyone was angry.

And now he was comfortably ensconced in the Edmond estate, living rent-free in one of the guesthouses and show-ing no sign of moving on. Lani gazed in the direction of the main house, wondering how a college friendship had translated into the relationship Billy now enjoyed with the entire Edmond family. From what she could tell, he was practically a member of the family. Did Ross know about Billy's multiple identities? She hadn't seen the two men in-teracting. Was it possible that they'd been working together to bring the festival down?

If so…why?

It was well-known that once Ross's former lover—and their child that she'd never told him about—had returned to town, his relationship with his father had completely fallen apart to the point where Rusty had disinherited his biologi-cal son. Would Ross's financial troubles have made him an unwitting pawn in Billy's schemes? Or had Ross gotten in over his head and chosen to frame his own brother for the crime to avoid taking the fall?

Either way they couldn't tip off either man until she gathered more information.

"It's not looking too good for our boy, is it?" Asher's delight broke through Lani's introspection. His lopsided smile had appeared. For the first time since she'd visited him in jail, he looked genuinely relieved.

Although she wanted to reassure him, her instincts warned her to be cautious. "Not at all."

Asher's good mood dimmed. "You don't sound all that sure."

"It looks bad," Lani agreed. "But nothing we've turned up is proof that Billy is connected to anything illegal with the Soiree on the Bay festival. Adopting multiple aliases and convincing wealthy women to invest in his business ideas might be sketchy, but not every venture is successful. Maybe the guy is better at ideas than execution."

"So I'm still the bad guy."

He'd raked his fingers through his hair frequently over the course of the last two hours and several unruly spikes poked up in various directions. She liked his disheveled look. It reminded her of all those mornings when she'd awoken in his bed and watched him sleep. She'd known such joy in those unguarded moments. Anything had seemed possible. Like she could have it all... The satisfying career she craved. A happy life with the man who showed her how to let go and have fun. Lani pushed away the fantasy. These dreams of the perfect future were a distraction she couldn't afford.

"Look, don't give up hope." She set her hand on his shoulder and squeezed. "We'll find something."

Asher took both her hands in his and faced her. His somber expression made her stomach drop. She traced his features with her gaze, absorbing the sensual curve of his lips, the strong bones of his face, the hint of stubble that blurred the sharp jut of his jaw. Naked emotion flickered in his dark brown eyes. Relief. Gratitude. And something... *more*. Her breath caught at the vulnerability she glimpsed in that unguarded moment. She set her palm on his chest. In the stillness that followed, her heart found a new rhythm and beat in sync with his.

A second later he lowered his thick lashes and the link between them snapped. The recoil stung. Neither one of them was brave enough to acknowledge the connection between them for long. Yet each day it grew stronger. The ache more acute when they were apart. And unlike when they'd been together that summer, she was losing the will to resist her longing to be with him. In the sensible moments when her emotions weren't in control, she wondered what would happen when this case ended.

"I hope you realize how much I appreciate that you believe in me," Asher said, covering her hand on his chest and giving a light squeeze. "I don't know how I would've gotten through this without you."

Lani's throat tightened, making speech impossible. This would be the perfect moment to tell him that she still had doubts about his innocence. Her last report to Kingston Blue had been objective and scrupulously professional. Afraid that she was letting her personal feelings interfere with her judgment, she hadn't voiced her suspicions that Asher might have been set up. Once again she had prioritized her career over her personal life and doubted Asher would understand.

Instead of facing her mistakes, she apologized to him in a way that they could both appreciate.

"Hey," she murmured, sliding her fingers through his hair and offering him her best come-hither smile. "I could use a snack."

Asher's sleepy gaze stroked her features. "I'm feeling a little hungry myself."

"You know I'm not talking about food, right?"

His wicked grin said it all. "What did you have in mind?"

She slid off the stool and snagged his waistband, drawing him toward the living room. "It's about time we christen this chair, don't you think?"

"Oh, yes. I'd been thinking that exact thing just an hour ago."

"And you didn't bring it up?" she teased, unfastening his belt, the button on his jeans and the zipper below. With her breath escaping her lungs on a languid sigh, she burrowed under all the fabric and dropped to her knees before him, taking his clothes with her. At her urging, he stepped out of each pant leg, letting her undress him. His fingers brushed a stray lock off her cheek. She knew he would tangle his hands in her hair later, riding the movement of her head as she brought him pleasure with her mouth.

Lani placed her hands on his thighs, palms skimming his hair-roughened skin, past his jutting erection and over the smooth, chiseled plains of his abdomen. There, she gave a gentle shove and he sat down in the armchair with a quiet grunt of surprise. Then she was parting his knees and sliding between them. Her fingers began working the buttons of his shirt. When she had them undone, she spread the fabric wide and leaned forward to press a kiss to his throat. His Adam's apple worked as he swallowed hard and she smiled as she nipped and nuzzled her way to his ear, across his jaw and finally to the corner of his mouth. He turned and slanted his head so their lips met. Their open-mouth kiss was a slow, sultry tease of breath and flicking tongue. Lani's hands tracked down his chest and stomach, savoring the splendid muscle beneath all his silken skin. The man was perfection in so many ways.

With her hot gaze on his arousal, she set to peeling off her own clothes. Stripped down to her underwear, she fondled her breasts through her lace bra before bracing her hands on the chair's arms and bending forward.

"Care to do the honors?"

"My pleasure."

He reached behind her and popped the bra clasp. The fabric fell into his grasp and she bestowed a saucy wink.

"Thank you."

As the ache between her thighs intensified, Lani skimmed her palm down her belly and beneath the edge of her panties. Because he loved to watch her like this, she threw her head back, rolled her hips from side to side and pressed her fingertips against her clit. Wetness soaked her panties. When he made a strangled sound, she opened her eyes and focused on his face.

A moment later she dropped to her knees once more and let her hair down, knowing he adored the seductive slide of the strands against his skin. With a brazen smile, she moved between his thighs and wrapped her fingers around his erection without warning or preliminaries. A breath ejected from his lungs, a startled curse that made her smile.

Lani eased her hold on his shaft. "Too much?"

"No." The single syllable wheezed out of him as her thumb circled the head of his shaft, sliding over the bead of moisture she found there before gliding her fingers to the base. "It's perfect."

Asher clenched his fingers over the chair's arms and settled deeper into the seat, offering his body for her to play with. She repeated the stroking motion, watching the way his head dropped back and his lips parted. He watched her from beneath heavy lidded eyes, tiny flecks of copper blazing in their depths. While his posture looked relaxed, his expression remained tight with anticipation. She understood. She couldn't wait to get her mouth on him. And why bother holding back when that's what he wanted too?

She licked her lips and lowered them over his blunt head, purring in delight at the salty taste of the velvety flesh. A growl tore from Asher's throat as she flicked her tongue over him, tormenting him the way he had done to her the night before.

"God, Lani."

Her name on his lips was heaven. She decided to reward him. Shutting her eyes to block out all distraction, she hummed and took him in, the vibration making him jerk in reaction. He was clutching the arms of the chair now, bracing to endure the wicked pleasure she was giving him.

Making her lips into a tight circle, she took as much as him into her mouth as she could handle. It was a lot, but she'd learned how to relax and open for him. When the head of his erection hit the back of her throat, his fingers slipped into her hair. He played with the strands, applying no pressure as she withdrew, circled him with her tongue and bobbed backed down again.

His appreciative murmur, punctuated with the occasional hiss of acute pleasure were the only sounds that came from him. He'd let her know when he was close. Communicate if he wanted her to finish him in this way or climb aboard. In the meantime she would make this a night to remember. By alternating between teasing and deep dives, she held him on the brink longer than she expected.

But his willpower was only so resilient and she'd mastered the art of pleasuring him this way. When he cupped her face in his hands and angled her head away from his erection, her body awakened with delight. He covered her swollen lips in a tender kiss that tangled their tongues and said without words how deeply he appreciated her.

"Come here."

He pulled her up off the floor and drew her onto the chair. There was just enough room for her knees on either side of his hips. His long fingers bracketed her hips, moving her into position. His thick shaft bobbed against her thigh, seeking the connection they both hungered for.

Lani gasped as he speared into her dripping heat. Utterly turned on, the full length of him filling her was nearly enough to trigger her orgasm. She was close...so close. Swollen with longing and impatient with need, when his mouth closed over the tip of one breast and sucked hard, she knew there would be no more holding back. Her hips bucked enthusiastically against him, grinding her clit against his pelvic bone, and a heartbeat later, her climax ripped through her.

She clutched his head against her breast, riding him hard, launched even higher at the scrape of his teeth against her nipple. The bliss seemed to go on and on, aided by the length of him driving into her over and over. Lani gasped and cried out, ridiculous incoherent chanting as her pleasure soared higher, so much higher. She could scarcely breathe. Surely she should have plateaued by now. But his persistent thrusts, so smooth and with perfect rhythm, made her muscles tense and coil as she ascended toward the peak of yet another orgasm. He'd done this for her before. Made her come and come and come again.

It's what made her crazy for him. His body, his soul, the heart he tried to protect. He was the one she'd dreamed about before they'd ever met and long after they'd parted. Fate had brought them back together. Now it was up to them to figure out how to make it work. Because this time she didn't want to say goodbye.

Had it only been three weeks since he'd been arrested for embezzling the festival funds? It felt like the threat of imprisonment had been hanging over him for far longer. How ironic that the worst thing that had ever happened to him resulted in something as wonderful as bringing Lani Li back into his life.

The last week together had been nothing short of magic. They'd returned to the playful camaraderie and sizzling passion of five years earlier. There were moments when he was convinced everything would turn out okay, but then he'd bump the electronic monitor on his ankle and the whole miserable mess returned to his awareness in a hurry.

Asher shook hands with the horse trainer who'd arrived to pick up Royal Flush. As they loaded her into the trailer for the journey to California, he walked away with a tight throat and a heart ready for fresh opportunities,

The money he'd gotten for Royal Flush would clear the debt between him and Lani. Sacrificing his favorite mount demonstrated his willingness to grow. As much as he'd loved them, the horses tied him to his old life. They had been his comfort when his relationship with Rusty floundered and offered direction when it came to his life's purpose.

Lani had been right to call him out all those years ago. He *had* been a directionless frat boy. But that had changed once he'd met her. And now that she was back in his life, he intended to evolve even more. New challenges awaited him and Lani was the key to what he wanted to do next.

Smiling, Asher attacked the stairs to his apartment, taking the steps two at a time. He was eager to share his new vision with Lani and see her reaction. She agreed with his assessment that The Edmond Organization wasn't the place for him. Tonight he was taking her to dinner, a celebration of the positive changes he was making in his life since she'd come back into it.

He'd chosen Sheen, not only because the restaurant was known for its exceptional cuisine, but also for being run and staffed by all women of various ethnicities. Ross's fiancée, Charlotte Jarrett, had returned to Royal to oversee the kitchen and had quickly made the restaurant a Royal favorite.

Lani had headed back to Dallas that morning to meet with a potential client and planned to return by six o'clock. That left Asher an hour to shower and get ready for their date. The word sent an electric zap through him. With his nerve endings buzzing pleasantly, he headed into the bathroom and the large mirror over the double vanity reflected back his goofy grin. He rubbed his palm over his stubbled cheeks, noted the sparkle in his eyes and remarked at the transformation joy had wrought. Damn, he was *happy*. Even to the point where he could appreciate the pain-in-the-ass electronic monitor clamped to his ankle, being charged with embezzlement and wire fraud had brought Lani back into his life.

Half an hour later Asher emerged from his closet dressed for dinner and realized he was no longer alone in the apartment. A cell phone was ringing in the living room. Eager to show Lani how much he'd missed her, he was halfway across the bedroom when he heard her answer the call.

"Hello, Kingston."

Asher slowed his pace as the name registered. Kingston, as in Kingston Blue? An image of the famous singer popped into Asher's mind. Above-average height with an imposing frame and a handsome face framed by long dreadlocks, his open and friendly manner combined with a wide white smile had disarmed and enchanted everyone. But it was his keen brown eyes that had told the real story as his gaze had scrutinized the construction happening at the festival site on Appaloosa Island, assessing the pros and cons before agreeing to headline Soiree on the Bay.

What was he doing calling Lani?

"What's up?" While she came across as calm and professional, Asher detected a wary note.

Moving carefully, he took several steps toward the door leading into the living room, the better to hear the conversation, aware that by eavesdropping he was questioning if he could trust Lani. In a flash he realized he was once again prioritizing his needs first and in doing so causing damage to their fledgling relationship. How could he hope to form a solid connection with her when the first time his faith was tested, he chose to doubt.

"…progress report," came the deep rich masculine voice. Lani must have had him on speaker.

Progress report? What progress report? Asher recalled how she'd avoided answering every time he asked her who hired her to look into the missing money. Was Kingston Blue that client? The man hadn't made all his money with his music. He was a savvy businessman, as well. And obviously one determined to locate what had been stolen from him.

"As I mentioned before," Lani said, "this case is a lot

more complicated than it seemed. The money vanished from the bank accounts right after the funds were transferred. The feds think the money was moved offshore, but there's no trace of those accounts on Asher's work or personal computers, his phone or in his house. If he was funneling the money away from the festival accounts, then he was very careful about it."

"If?" Concern deepened Kingston Blue's voice. "You disagree with the feds about Asher Edmond's guilt?"

"I know the evidence points to him. His name is on the house in the Maldives," she said, "and his online signature triggered the wire transfers. But he could've been set up."

A pregnant silence followed her words. Asher's heart hammered. While it sounded like she was defending him, this conversation drove home the fact that she'd ultimately come to Royal to find the missing festival funds. Something he'd conveniently put to the back of his mind.

"I hired you because of your previous relationship with Asher," Kingston Blue said. "I assumed you would use that connection to get information out of him about where the money ended up."

Kingston's words scored a direct hit. Asher set his hand on the wall as his thoughts reeled. All this time she'd been playing him for a fool. While he shouldn't be surprised, that didn't make the emotional blow less devastating. She made it very clear five years ago that her career came first and he was just a reckless playboy without a future. Well, one thing was true, obviously she'd gotten a lot better at acting.

"That's not how I work," Lani said stiffly. "I've been looking into various people involved in the festival and Asher isn't the only one with access to those funds. His brother Ross—"

Kingston Blue interrupted her. "It seems to me you're just offering me excuses why you think your ex-boyfriend is innocent. I'm not paying you to exonerate him."

"Asher was never my boyfriend." Her voice was stark and fervent on that point. "I'm not emotionally involved with him now if that's what you're thinking. You hired me to find the money and if you can be patient with me a little longer, that's what I intend to do."

"By chasing random leads."

"By doing a *thorough* investigation," Lani insisted. "As soon as investigators found the house in the Maldives, they stopped looking at anyone else."

"There's overwhelming evidence that Asher's the one who transferred the funds out of the festival account. Where they went is what I want to know."

"So do I," she said. "But I need to figure out who actually stole the money."

"Asher Edmond."

"Maybe." Lani sounded less than thrilled to be arguing with her client. "But I'm also looking into someone else. Billy Holmes."

"Who is that?"

"Friend of the family. He lives at the Edmonds' estate. I've discovered he has a suspicious background and I'd like to pursue the lead."

Kingston Blue paused before answering as if weighing his options. "You have three days. After that you're off the case."

Asher took several seconds to compose himself before emerging from the bedroom. Lani was standing by the large window that overlooked the extensive manicured grounds between the barn and the main house.

"You're back early," he remarked, crossing the room to pull her back against his body and place a kiss on her cheek. "How'd the meeting with the new client go?"

She stiffened momentarily before relaxing into his embrace. "Good. She hired me."

"Then we should celebrate." Asher headed into his

kitchen to pull a bottle of champagne from the wine cooler, and set two glasses on the breakfast bar. "You have a new client. I sold Royal Flush."

"You want to celebrate that?" Lani asked, drawing near. "That's been a big part of your life. I thought you'd be sad that she was gone."

Asher focused on pulling the cork from the bottle rather than look at her. He was still processing the call he'd overheard.

"It was hard to part with her, but she's too well trained to waste away here." Asher pictured the chestnut tearing across the polo field and smiled. "And since her new owner paid me a hundred thousand dollars for her, I can pay you back the money you put up for my bail and compensate you for the time you spent on my case."

This last part he'd added to test her reaction.

"I already have a client." She looked uncomfortable. "You know that."

"Is there some reason you can't have two?"

"I'm not sure that your goals aren't in conflict."

"It seems as if everyone wants to find the money. Including me." He extended a glass filled with bright sparkling liquid toward her. "I'd also like to find out who stole it. I don't see how we could possibly be in conflict."

"I just don't think it's a good idea."

Dismayed by the fact that she continued to let him think that Rusty had hired her, Asher chose not to push any further. No doubt she had her reasons for keeping him in the dark. The fact that they were at odds as long as this case remained open was not the problem. He was more concerned what would happen once everything had been wrapped up.

He lightly clicked his crystal flute against hers before taking a sip. He watched her surreptitiously while appearing to savor the champagne. She looked more miserable than he'd ever seen her. Obviously guilt wasn't a comfortable weight on her shoulders.

"Now that I've officially closed the door on any chance of a comeback as a professional polo player—"

"Was that a possibility?" she interrupted, arching one dark eyebrow.

"Hush. I've been thinking what I want to do next."

Retreating into his frat-boy act was familiar and would serve him better than venting his frustration over the investigation's slow progress.

"Next?" She looked resigned as she asked, "What about your position at The Edmond Organization?"

"I promised Rusty that I'd stick with it for two years. My time is up and after spending these weeks with you, I realize I rather enjoyed investigative work and I think I have a knack for it."

She gave an odd snort and then began to cough vigorously as if the champagne had gone up her nose rather than down her throat. "I'm sorry?" she wheezed. "Didn't you go to work for the family business after Rusty threatened to cut you off? How are you going to support yourself?"

"By partnering with you."

"Partnering…?"

"You're not the only one who can dig up information on people. I checked you out and it turns out your business is in a bit of a slump. It could use someone like me to bring in more high-profile clients."

Lani was staring at him as if had sprouted a set of horns. "Let me get this straight, you want to go into business with me?"

"Why so surprised?" He ignored the negative sweep of her head. "We work well together."

"I think you like dabbling in my investigation because it's a distraction. But once this case is over and if you're exonerated—"

"If?" Her meaning went through him like a hot blade. Without her on his side, eager to prove his innocence, he could still go to jail. Even if the money was recovered.

She continued speaking as if he hadn't interrupted her. "I'm convinced you'll lose interest in the kind of work I do."

Asher needed no further proof of Lani's low expectations about him and the hit blew a big hole in what he thought was developing between them. This constant feeling of not being good enough because he'd made mistakes in the past was getting old. No wonder he'd preferred traveling around the world playing professional polo to sticking around and seeing nothing but disappointment and disapproval in his father's eyes.

"Are you really worried that it's the investigative work I'm going to lose interest in?" he countered, frustration making him strike out at the one person he wanted to make happy.

She shifted her weight backward, a slow recoil from his insinuation. "What else?"

"Or is this about us?"

Ten

Us?

Lani stiffened at the question and leveled her gaze at him. The answer was too fraught with uncertainty to answer. Was Asher romancing her for the sole purpose of using her to change careers? She'd been worried that he wanted her on his side to clear him of the embezzlement charges, but now it seemed he wanted to move in on her business, as well.

"Is there an *us*?" she asked, unsure where to draw the line between reality and fantasy.

"You tell me. Are we going to keep seeing each other once the case is over?"

She could barely acknowledge to herself how much she wanted their sexual connection to develop into deep romantic love much less share that with Asher. Long ago she'd confessed her feelings and he'd rejected them. She couldn't face that same crushing disappointment again.

Lani bit her lower lip and grappled with how to answer

him. "I don't know." She wanted to, but once the prescribed proximity of the investigation ended, would Asher even be interested in a personal relationship anymore? His interest in her business seemed to confuse the situation. "You live here in Royal and I'm in Dallas..." It was an obvious dodge given how they'd broken up last time.

"Once you were open to a long-distance relationship," he reminded her.

"And you made it very clear that it wasn't your thing."

"What if I moved to Dallas?"

Hope barreled through her, but she shut it down. Was this about their relationship or a business partnership? Had she let herself be played?

"Are you serious about quitting The Edmond Organization?"

"It's not for me," he told her.

"What about your horse training?"

"I'm already in the process of selling the string." His gaze increased in intensity as he spoke. "I'd like to help you with your business, but it's more important that you want to take a chance on me."

"I tried that once." She could barely get the words out past the lump in her throat. "It didn't work out so well for me."

"So you're saying you can't trust me."

"I don't honestly know. All this is coming at me so suddenly and there's a lot of upheaval in your life right now. Who knows how you'll feel once the case is closed and things settle down." As much as she wanted to trust him with her heart, she'd been devastated last time.

"Don't make this about how I feel," he said, wariness entering his expression. "I want to know how you feel. What are we doing? Is it just casual sex or are we going to turn it into something real?"

"Something *real*?" She tried the phrase on for size, but couldn't find comfort in the fit. "I don't know."

Even though they'd reconnected physically, her resistance to baring her heart put a wall between them. A wall she was loathe to tear down. Sex was one thing—they had explosive chemistry and it was easy to lose herself in the magic of his touch. However, as long as the embezzlement charge hung over his head, he needed her help with the investigation. Once it was over, she would reconsider taking the risk of getting emotionally entangled with him. But for now she couldn't in good conscience commit to that.

"Because you're using me to close your case and make your client happy?"

"I'm *not* using you." That was true even if it had been her plan at the start. Once her old feelings had surfaced, she'd lost the battle with how much she wanted him. "But I really don't know if we can make it work."

"Sounds like you've made up your mind." He stared at her for a long time while a muscle jumped in his jaw. "So, I guess that means you're putting me in your rearview mirror once more."

"*I'm* the one putting *you* in the rearview mirror?" Was she hearing him right? "I recall that I wanted to try the long-distance thing and you thought that was too much of a commitment."

Asher's gaze intensified. "And so you called us done and walked away."

"You didn't give me a whole lot of choice. Basically, it was either give up on grad school and run off with you to Argentina or we were over." Her blood raged white-hot as unresolved resentment flared. A second later fear and panic kicked in. She was on the verge of losing him all over again. "You didn't want to do the long-distance thing."

"Okay, so maybe that was a mistake."

Maybe?

"Or maybe neither one of us was ready for a committed relationship" she said. "And so we did the best thing we could do for ourselves and broke up."

"It wasn't that cut and dry for me."

What did that mean? Lani sucked in a deep breath in an effort to calm her wildly fluctuating emotions. She hadn't expected the fledgling intimacy between her and Asher to be tested so soon.

"What do you want me to say?" *That you were my first love and I never got over you?*

"I want you to be honest with me about how you feel."

"Honest." Her chest heaved as she gulped in a big breath. "Okay, if you want the truth, the reason I don't think it's a good idea for us to become business partners or any other kind of partner is that I'm not sure I can count on you."

From the first she'd recognized that they approached situations completely differently. Where her personality was a bullet shot from a gun, a swift straight line from problem to solution, Asher was like air. A gentle breeze coming at her from one direction. Then moments later a gust of wind that smacked into her blind side, knocking her off her feet.

"You still see me as that irresponsible frat boy." Asher scowled. "That's not who I am and hasn't been for a long time."

Yet he couldn't stick with anything. Not polo. Not the job with The Edmond Organization. Not her.

"Really?" she challenged. "Look at the mess you're in because you didn't take your responsibilities with the festival seriously."

"You have no idea what I take seriously. Yes, I had access to the accounts…"

"And someone—probably Billy Holmes—was able to take advantage of that."

"But it could've been any of us. Gina. Ross. Even Rusty

given how close the two of them are. He chose me for some reason I don't get."

Lani heard Asher's sweeping frustration, but couldn't summon the courage to comfort him. "Hopefully I can figure that out. I'm heading to Las Vegas to meet with his mother tomorrow."

But Asher wasn't going to be thrown off topic. "What would it take for me to prove you can count on me?"

She dug her fingertips into the back of her shoulder where stress was pinching the nerves and gave her whirling brain a moment to process everything that was coming at her.

"I really don't know."

"Well, at least be straight with me on one thing. Do you think I stole the money from the festival?"

"No." At least she could give him a clear, decisive answer on that score.

He gave her a tight smile. "Well, I guess that's something. And the money for my bail. Do I return the hundred thousand dollars to you?"

Lani went cold. The intensity of the question put a hard lump in the pit of her stomach. Was he shooting in the dark or had he overheard her conversation with Kingston? She'd been careless when she didn't realize he was in the apartment.

When she didn't answer right away, he continued, "Or should I wire it directly back to Kingston Blue?"

Damn. Now he knew she'd been deceiving him from the start. "You can give it to me. I'll get it back to him."

His eyes narrowed. "Can I trust you?"

Although she knew it was a big show to get under her skin, Lani stiffened. "Of course."

"I'm not so sure. Knowing how complicated our relationship is, you let me believe my father hired you. How could you let me think he was finally on my side?"

Lani dropped her eyes to the floor. "I shouldn't have done that."

"No," he agreed. "You think you understand how messed up things are between us, but it's worse than you know. It was a big deal for me to believe that he wanted to help me out."

"Why such a big deal now when he's supported you since the day he married your mother?"

A sardonic smile ghosted across his lips. "He supported me. But there were conditions tied to it. Conditions I had no idea about until three years ago." Asher's grim expression made Lani's heart sink.

It was becoming clear that she'd made a huge error in judgment. "What sort of conditions?"

"He and my mother had a little side agreement regarding her alimony. She agreed that since I turned eighteen, any money he gave me came out of the payments he owed her. And as part of the deal, she wasn't allowed to tell me anything about what was going on."

Lani gasped. "Why would he do that?"

"Because he's a miserable excuse for a human being. I don't know if he regretted formally adopting me or if he just wanted to mess with her. A couple years ago, I found out she was nearly bankrupt and I couldn't understand why. She finally broke down and confessed what had been going on. I confronted Rusty and he offered me a bargain. He would pay my mother everything he'd withheld if I agreed to sign a five-year contract with The Edmond Organization."

"Did you?"

Asher kept his gaze fixed on the windows that faced the main house. "As much as I wanted to help my mother, I knew I wouldn't survive five years working for Rusty. Instead, I got him to agree to let me work for him for two and a half years in exchange for fifty-percent of the money he'd spent on me. That, and what I had in investments was enough to get her out of trouble."

"Why didn't you tell me this before?" Lani asked, her heart aching for all he'd been through.

"Why should I?" He shook his head. "When you already had more than enough reasons not to trust me."

He was right. She'd failed to believe him at every turn. And each time she'd been wrong.

"So now you know. I didn't quit polo because I was afraid to be cut off. I didn't join The Edmond Organization because I was trying to win Rusty's approval, and I'm not leaving because I can't stick with anything. I haven't sold off my horses because I'm tired of training. And I don't want to become your business partner as some sort of lark."

Lani had no words that could undo the damage she'd caused by not believing in him. "I'm sorry." It became immediately obvious this was the wrong thing to say.

"Don't be. It's my problem, not yours." With his lips flattened into a thin line, he raked his fingers through his hair. "Look, I don't feel much like celebrating tonight and it sounds like you've got a trip to get ready for. If it's okay with you, I think we should skip dinner and call it a night."

"Okay. I understand…"

And while she stood with her heart a lead stone in her chest, Asher headed into the master bedroom and closed the door behind him.

The morning after his fight with Lani, Asher woke with a headache and a really bad idea.

It was time for a party.

Not that he had anything to celebrate or was in the mood to be social. Lani had let him believe that she was on his side and that he had a reason to dream of a better future with her a big part of it. Nothing he'd done in the last three weeks had convinced her to give him a chance. She still perceived him as someone frivolous and shallow, unable to consider anyone's welfare but his own. Had he really thought by letting her in on his bargain with Rusty that her outlook toward him would suddenly be transformed? He was so tired of fighting everyone's bad opinion of him, of having to prove himself to people he loved.

The realization hit him like a piano falling from a very tall crane.

Damn.

He loved her. He loved Lani Li.

She was the one he let get away. Now he knew she was also the woman he couldn't live without. The one person he longed to spend the rest of his life laughing and fighting and making love with. The certainty had been building for days. It had taken a huge relationship-ending blowout for the fog to clear from his brain.

Was it any wonder he wanted to act out, to wallow in self-sabotage, letting everyone believe he was the same directionless jerk he'd always been?

He thought back to five years ago when he and Lani had first met. What if he'd been more serious back then instead of letting frivolous pursuits distract him? He could've saved his mother financial headaches and achieved a high level of success in his field. Instead he'd fallen short of expectations and reinforced Rusty's disapproval.

At the time he hadn't realized how he'd given his power away. Not until Lani had come along and opened his eyes to hard work and focused goal setting had he been filled by an optimistic sense of his own worth. How different things might've been if he'd had someone in his corner sooner.

Someone who could've channeled his ability to charm people into positive avenues. Much of what had appealed to him with the Soiree on the Bay festival was the chance to benefit others. How ironic that instead of helping people out, the whole situation had destroyed numerous lives.

Being the guy that everyone hated had been a wake-up call. Using his money and position to benefit others would be so much better than selfishly squandering everything he'd gained. When his accounts were unfrozen, he intended to make changes in his life. He would invest in other people's dreams, focusing his resources, time and energy on helping people.

But that was his future. In the now, the one woman he needed to believe in him couldn't. The agony lancing through his heart pushed him toward self-destructive behaviors. The old Asher would lose himself in fun. And nothing said fun like a lively party with a large group of friends. Since he wasn't allowed to go anywhere without Lani, he would just have to bring the party here.

Since he doubted very many people would show up for his benefit, Asher reached out to Gina for help.

"Call everyone you know. We're throwing a party at Elegance Ranch."

"Are you sure this is a good time?" she countered.

"It's the perfect time. Rusty's out of town and I'm stuck on house arrest."

"It's going to end up being a pretty small affair." She sounded as low as Asher felt.

They hadn't spoken much since he'd been released from jail, but he'd texted her often to check in. Despite still smarting over the way she'd turned her back on him, they were family and he loved her.

"Even if there's only twenty or thirty people, it will be a party." Easing up on the forced optimism, he added, "And I really need this."

"I'll see what I can do."

She grudgingly offered suggestions for a fun-filled, family-friendly barbecue with a guest list including their usual complement of friends from the Texas Cattleman's Club— or at least the ones who were still talking to them—but also those in Royal who'd suffered because of what happened with the festival. Fearing that no one would show up if they thought he was involved, he suggested that she leave his name off the invitation.

Fifteen minutes after he'd hung up with Gina, Ross's number lit up Asher's phone.

"A *party*?" Ross demanded. "Are you out of your mind? This is no time to celebrate anything."

It wasn't a celebration, but a distraction. A way to keep from brooding over the implosion of his relationship with Lani and the bleak future that lay ahead of him.

"I'm stuck here alone with nothing to do," Asher complained.

"You're on house arrest," Ross snapped. "I don't think throwing parties is going to enhance your reputation."

"I'm not throwing a party. You and Gina are."

Asher hadn't really expected his brother to understand. Practical Ross had never related to the restlessness that drove Asher. His identity had always been cemented in being the heir to one of the wealthiest men in the country. That Ross suffered the same neglect as Asher didn't negate the blood bond.

"This isn't a good idea."

"No, it's a *great* idea." And one that Asher hoped would prove to Lani that he would make an excellent partner for her. "Oh, and make sure you invite Billy. It wouldn't be a party without him."

Eleven

Still reeling from the fight with Asher the day before, Lani buckled herself into her seat for the three-hour flight from Dallas to Las Vegas. Her stomach flipped as her phone rang. Hoping it was Asher, she glanced down at the screen but the caller was Kingston Blue.

"Hey," she began as the plane filled up around her. "I'm on my way to Vegas,"

She'd snagged a window seat and watched the grounds crew load luggage under the plane. Since she only needed a few necessities for her quick trip, her own bag sat in the compartment above her head.

"What's in Las Vegas?" Kingston Blue asked, his voice hard and suspicious.

Apparently her people skills were in the toilet. Not only had she damaged her relationship with Asher, but her credibility with her client was dangling by a thread.

"A woman by the name of Antoinette Holmes," Lani explained. "She's Billy Holmes's mother."

A charged silence radiated from the phone. She gnawed on her lip, imagining the grim tension in Kingston's face. As much as she didn't want to argue with the musician, she believed in her investigative skills *and* in Asher's innocence.

"Look, I know you don't agree with the direction I'm taking the investigation, but you hired me to find the money and I really don't think Asher's your guy." Her voice heated as her confidence flared. "If you want me off the case, I understand, but I'm still going to investigate Billy Holmes."

"How much of this has to do with your personal relationship with Asher Edmond?" While the edge had come off Kingston's tone, he sounded no less dubious. "You were in love with him once. Can you assure me that's not interfering with your judgment now?"

Lani breathed a sigh of relief that her client was willing to hear her out. This she could handle. After all, for the last five years she'd been telling herself that falling for Asher had been a huge mistake and one thing she never did was screw up twice.

"When you first approached me with the job, I wanted him to be guilty. Things didn't end well between us and I thought maybe he was finally going to have to take responsibility for a mistake he'd made."

Initially, she'd intended to demonstrate to her treacherous heart that Asher was a lying, manipulative, selfish jerk who'd toyed with her for fun and thus banish him from her daydreams forever.

"So what changed?" Kingston asked.

"I'm a professional. I approached this case by looking at the facts." Never mind that one glimpse of Asher looking exhausted and defeated in that jail cell had started to change the polarity of her emotions. "Which resulted in me interviewing several people and finding out that Billy Holmes had a sketchy past and an odd fixation on Rusty Edmond."

"But what does any of that mean?"

"I don't know, but I'm hoping to find some answers by talking to his mother."

"Fine. Keep me updated."

Lani ended the call, relieved that the musician appeared appeased for the moment. As the announcement came to stow all electronic devices, her mind went back to the last conversation she'd had with Asher. She recognized that letting him think his father had hired her had been a mistake. When she landed in Las Vegas, she would let him know that she'd spoken with Kingston and relayed her opinion about Asher no longer being her prime suspect.

Not that she believed this would be enough for him to forgive her. She hadn't understood about the strained relationship between Rusty and his adopted son or the pain Asher had felt at being either ignored or criticized by the only father figure he'd ever had.

As the plane taxied toward the runway, she closed her eyes and mentally reviewed what she'd dug up on Billy Holmes.

He'd grown up in Las Vegas, raised by a single mom.

Without any luggage to pick up at baggage claim, Lani secured a rental car and was on her way to meet Billy's mom. Antoinette Holmes was a cocktail waitress at a downtown casino and lived just east of the city center in a second-floor apartment in an older complex.

Lani was careful not to trip on the chipped concrete as she strode past a pool in desperate need of refurbishing. Feeling the heat radiating off the sun-bleached door of apartment number twelve, Lani used the corner of her phone, instead of her knuckles, to rap.

The face of the woman who answered the door looked much older than fifty-nine beneath her heavy makeup. Years of harsh desert sunshine and hard living had taken its toll on Antoinette's skin. Yet Lani could tell Billy's mother had once been a beauty.

"Antoinette Holmes?" Lani spoke the woman's name like a question although she already knew the answer.

"Yes?" The woman rested her left hand on her hip. Her slender fingers were tipped with long bright blue nails adorned with rhinestones. They matched her blue workout pants and matching sports bra. Antoinette's face might've showed her age, but her trim body did not.

"My name is Lani Li. I'm a private investigator from Dallas, Texas, and I was wondering if I could speak to you for a few minutes."

When she had indicated she was from Texas, Antoinette's eyebrows had risen. Now, however, as she raked her gaze over Lani's jeans, pale blue T-shirt and boots, the older woman's expression shifted from surprise to caution.

"What about?"

Not wanting to fidget and give Antoinette any sense that this inquiry was anything other than routine, Lani resisted the urge to wipe at the sweat trickling down her temple. Dallas had been in the upper eighties when she'd left. Las Vegas was already well into triple-digit temperatures and the heat index continued to climb as the sun crept toward its zenith in a cloudless sky of vivid blue.

"I'm doing some background work on your son, Billy," Lani declared blandly. "And I have a few questions only you can answer."

"What sort of questions?" The waitress looked poised to slam the door in Lani's face if she didn't like the answer.

Lani suspected she'd get nowhere if she told the truth. "Did you know your son has been living in Royal, Texas, for the past two years? He's staying in a guesthouse at Elegance Ranch, a property owned by Russell Edmond."

The thing about wearing long false eyelashes was that they called attention to a woman's eyes and what Lani glimpsed in Antoinette's wide green gaze was longing, anger and a trace of fear.

"I haven't seen or heard from that boy in years so I don't know what I can tell you." The older woman studied Lani for a few seconds longer while curiosity and reluctance battled on her face. In the end Antoinette backed into the house with a curt gesture that invited without being welcoming. "You might as well come in. I don't need to be air-conditioning the neighborhood."

"Thanks."

Crossing into the dim interior of the woman's apartment was like stepping back in time. And not in a good way. Years of cigarette smoke clung to the '70s wallpaper and burgundy carpet beneath her feet. As Lani made her way across the grungy patchwork of spills and threadbare spots, she couldn't help but contrast the shabby one-bedroom apartment to the elegant guesthouse on Elegance Ranch where Billy lived.

"Can I get you something to drink?" Antoinette asked, leaving Lani to wonder if she was being hospitable or if a lifetime of waitressing made the offer a habit. "I've got diet soda or water, or I could make some coffee."

"I'll take a soda," she said with a polite smile after glancing at the dishes piled in the sink. Hopefully the drink would come in a can because she couldn't imagine there was a single clean glass in the place.

After Lani perched on the gold velvet couch her hostess had indicated, Antoinette headed into the kitchen to fetch the offered drink. This gave Lani a chance to glance around. Billy's mom said she hadn't heard from him in years. Obviously she hadn't benefited from any of the money he'd swindled as Bond Howard, Bobby Hammond or Brad Howell.

Spying a cluster of pictures on a side table, Lani leaned

over to peer at them. What she saw caused her to pull out her phone and snap several images.

These were obviously a collection of Antoinette's most cherished photos. They told her story, starting with a grainy shot of a somber-faced man and his beaming bride on their wedding day. Her parents, based on the fashion and quality of the photo.

Next in order was a shot of a fresh-faced teenage Antoinette, posing in a cheer uniform with two other girls similarly dressed. The trio triumphantly held a trophy in their grasp, indicating Antoinette had known better times.

Lani's favorite of the bunch was a charming image of the woman snuggling a boy of about four or five. From his mother's joyful smile, Billy hadn't lacked affection growing up. But the photo that stopped Lani's breath was the one in a fancy gold frame. It featured a beaming Antoinette and a much-younger Rusty Edmond.

"That's my boy," Antoinette said, handing Lani an off-brand diet soda before indicating a wall of photos from Billy's school years. "The last picture I took of him was the day he went off to college." She gave a bitter laugh that turned into a classic smoker's cough. "First one in my family to go."

"You must be very proud of him..." Lani trailed off, hoping Billy's mom would fill in the details without the need for direct questions.

"It gave him airs." Antoinette stared at the pictures on the side table. "What sort of background check are you doing on my boy?"

Lani resisted the urge to clear her throat. "The man who hired me is very particular about the people he does business with." It wasn't a lie. Kingston Blue had certainly had her checked out before hiring her.

"I haven't seen Billy in five years or so. He never came back much after he graduated college. Just walked away, as all men do…as his father did." Antoinette darted a glance at the man framed in gold. "I should've known better."

"Does Billy have much to do with his dad?"

Speculation gleamed in Antoinette's narrowed eyes. "Why do you need to know something like that?"

"It fills out the picture…"

The older woman assessed Lani's appearance once more. "I've said all I'm going to for free."

She blinked. "I'm sorry?"

"If you're a private detective, you've probably got an expense account." The waitress licked her lips and smiled. "If you want to know anything more, it's gonna cost you."

With Asher's freedom on the line, Lani had a lot riding on this interview, and a photo of Rusty Edmond with Billy's mother demonstrated there was a story here. To persuade the authorities to look at Billy, she needed something that piqued their interest.

Moving with deliberate intent, Lani opened her purse and added up everything she had. Would nine crisp one-hundred-dollar bills be enough to get all the information she needed? Lani pulled out one bill and set it on the coffee table in between them.

"Does Billy see his dad?"

Antoinette's hand shot out and drew the hundred toward her. The bill disappeared into her ample cleavage.

"No."

Trying not to let her impatience get the better of her, Lani plucked out another bill and set it on the table. She made sure to avoid glancing at the cluster of pictures as she asked, "Does his father know about Billy?"

"He knew I was pregnant, but he didn't believe Billy was his."

So the answer to that was no. The photo of his mother with Russell Edmond was the only one of Antoinette with a man. Billy obviously knew or suspected that Rusty was his father. What was Billy up to? Why hadn't he told Rusty that they were father and son?

"Why not?"

Antoinette crossed her arms over her chest and scowled. Another bill appeared in Lani's hand. She set it on the table.

"Tell me about Billy's father." She gestured at the picture in the gold frame. "Is this him?"

"A real charmer with a sexy drawl. He was from Texas like you. An oilman with deep pockets. Good tipper." The waitress purred, "He made me feel like the most beautiful woman on the planet."

While the woman relived what was obviously a high point in her life, Lani couldn't help but notice the similarity to how she'd met Asher. Antoinette waxed nostalgic about Rusty's hypnotic gray eyes and how his deep laugh had given her chills. Meanwhile Lani pictured how Asher had hungrily watched her through half-closed lids and wore down her resistance with his lingering, sensual smiles. "He liked to come to the casino where I worked and throw money around. He treated me good."

"That's great," she murmured, growing uncomfortable at their parallel experiences.

Yet was it a surprise that when a wealthy man wanted a woman, he used whatever means at his disposal to have her?

"Until I got pregnant," Antoinette said. "Then it was over."

Abruptly Lani felt sorry for the woman. If she and Asher hadn't been careful, that might've been her, pregnant and scared with an uncertain future looming before her. Given his restless nature and frat-boy attitude, would Asher have reacted any better to an unplanned pregnancy than his father had?

At least she knew things would be different today. If she got pregnant, she had no doubt that Asher would not only want to be an involved father, he'd probably insist on taking care of her, as well.

The thought warmed her. Even though she let him believe her opinion of him hadn't changed, the concern he'd shown for those harmed by the troubles surrounding the festival demonstrated that he could care about someone besides himself. And really, if she took a good honest look at everything that had transpired between them that summer on Appaloosa Island, she knew she never would've fallen for him if he hadn't treated her so well. In fact, once she stopped getting in her own way, she'd discovered that Asher made her feel secure.

Lani plucked the rest of her cash out of her wallet and placed it on the table. "This is everything I have. Just answer these last few questions." And then without waiting for Antoinette to agree, she launched into the rest of her inquiry. "Did you ask him for child support?"

"Never thought of it."

That was so obviously a lie, but Lani resisted the urge to challenge Antoinette.

"But you said he was wealthy. I would think you could've proved Billy was his son and benefited financially. How come you didn't run a paternity test?"

Suddenly Antoinette didn't look so eager to keep going. "You ask a lot of questions."

"I paid you a lot of money for answers," Lani countered in aggrieved tones as frustration got the better of her. Asher was counting on her to save him and everything hinged on what she found out. "Why no paternity test?" she repeated, slapping her hand over the pile of cash as the waitress leaned forward to snatch it up.

Antoinette kept her gaze riveted on the money as she mumbled, "There were other men around the same time."

Yet a paternity test would've provided definitive proof of whether or not Rusty was Billy's dad. Unless…

"How much did he pay you to leave him alone and forget about the paternity test?"

"You think you're so smart, don't you?" Antoinette snarled. She glanced at the money again and heaved a sigh. "Fine. He paid me ten grand to drop it and never contact him again. And Russell wasn't the sort of man you crossed."

"So, you don't actually know who Billy's father is," Lani mused.

But Antoinette obviously hoped it was Russell Edmond. The ornate gold frame around the oil magnate's image highlighted how much he'd meant to her. Billy had grown up seeing that face every day. It made perfect sense that he'd believe this man was his father.

Had resentment festered with each passing year? Growing up poor, had Billy become obsessed about his wealthy father living in Texas? Had he planned how he was going to make friends with his half brother and eventually worm his way into the family?

"Does Billy begrudge his father for not acknowledging him?"

"No. Why would he?" But something about Antoinette's answer didn't ring true for Lani.

With one last glance at the photo of Rusty and Antoinette, Lani lifted her hand off the cash and got to her feet. After a quick goodbye and no backward glance, Lani escaped the suffocating apartment with her thoughts whirling from all she'd learned. Finally Billy's motive was clear. Not only had he taken revenge on his father's family, but he'd also pulled off the biggest score of his life.

No doubt he wouldn't be sticking around for much longer. In fact Lani was surprised he'd stayed in town this long. With that thought came a rush of panic. She needed to get back to Royal as soon as possible and convince the authorities to take what she'd discovered and go after Billy. But first she needed to reach out to the one person who would benefit the most from what she'd learned.

This might be enough to save Asher and she couldn't wait to tell him.

But two hours and three phone calls later, Asher hadn't picked up once.

As her plane for Dallas began boarding, Lani ended the last call without leaving a third message. She was determined not to jump to the wrong conclusions as to why he wasn't answering her calls. But even so, anxiety sank its talons into her psyche, making her wince. There were a lot of possibilities for why he wasn't picking up beyond the one currently stuck in the forefront of her mind—that she'd hurt him badly. Badly enough that he wanted nothing more to do with her? Lani desperately hoped not.

Asher couldn't take his gaze off Ross, Charlotte and Ben. He'd never envied his brother as much as he did at this moment. That could've been him with Lani and possibly their own child if he hadn't been so afraid of the changes required to move forward with their relationship. Without offering her any sort of vision of an alternative, better future with him, he'd selfishly asked her to change her plans for grad school and follow him to Argentina and beyond. Was it any wonder that she'd balked? He'd known how driven she was.

If he'd put some thought into a plan, he might have found a better way to convince her than, *I have plenty of money. You'll never need to work a day in your life.*

He'd known immediately that was the wrong tact to take with her. But it wasn't like he could set his heart at her feet, tell her he'd fallen hard and couldn't bear to live without her. What if it didn't last? What if she woke up and realized he wasn't good enough for her? He'd dreaded the possibility that the love shining in her eyes would dim as disappointment set in.

She'd stopped criticizing his lifestyle once they'd started dating, but her desire to help people and her passion for justice was all he needed to recognize that she didn't approve of his lack of direction any more than Rusty did. And at the end of summer, when she left Appaloosa Island to live her mission-driven life, he'd been left wondering why he always seemed to be craving the love and approval of people who could never accept him for who he was.

Lately he'd been wondering a great deal about what might've happened back then if he had changed. Grown up. Become the man Lani needed. Would she have started to take him seriously? Would they have gotten married? Had a child? He'd sure wanted to be with her. To demonstrate what life with him could be like, he'd taken her on a magical journey through the extravagances his lifestyle afforded him. The big boat, fine dining and luxurious suites at the best hotels, a private plane to anywhere they wanted to go... But he'd mistaken her delight in the finer things he offered with a shift in her nature. She might've been able to appreciate the amenities he had access to, but that didn't mean those things would become more important to her than her schooling and the career in law enforcement she'd hoped to pursue.

"It's good to see Ross this happy, isn't it?"

While he's been observing the happy family, Gina had walked up beside him. Despite her upbeat statement, she looked as gloomy as Asher felt. He threw his arm around her in comfort. Over the course of Lani's investigation into the missing festival money, Asher and his sister had made a semblance of peace.

"Obviously fatherhood and being in love suit him." Asher noted a roughness to his voice. He swallowed a hard knot in his throat before musing, "Do you suppose either one of us has that to look forward to?"

"I don't know about you," Gina murmured, "but I'm pretty sure I don't."

"Why is that?" Asher turned his full attention on his sister and seeing her misery, took her hand in his. Squeezing gently in reassurance, he said, "You never know. Mr. Right could be waiting for you to notice him."

She responded with a bitter laugh. "With our family's reputation sullied by the festival scandal, who could possibly want me now?"

"Any man with half a brain would realize what a catch you are," Asher said, surprised by his sister's inability to see her worth. "There's more to you than being an Edmond. You know that, right?"

Not only was Gina beautiful and smart, she was kind and giving, as well. That she failed to recognize all she had to offer wasn't a surprise. None of the three siblings had been showered with the sort of approval and love that would've given them the confidence to take on the world. Rusty never acted as if he gave a damn about any of them. Was it any wonder the three of them struggled to find love and develop successful relationships?

"I really don't," Gina said. "I guess I never realized how much I benefited from being an Edmond until our name got dragged through the mud."

"I'm sorry this happened."

His sister looked stricken. "I know you. Stealing isn't your style. I feel bad that I ever believed you were guilty."

"Don't worry about it," Asher assured her with a warm smile. "The evidence was so damning that there were times I actually thought I had stolen the funds."

"Oh, Asher." She laughed at his joke as he'd hoped she would and his spirits remained high even as she sobered once more. "But what are we going to do about proving your innocence?"

"Lani and I have some ideas on that. In fact, we have a suspect."

Gina looked startled. "Who?"

He'd promised Lani not to tell Ross what they learned about Billy, but he could share the information with Gina without violating their agreement.

"We've been looking into Billy."

"Billy Holmes?" Her voice was louder and sharper than Asher would've liked and he immediately shushed her. "Why him?"

"We found out he's been operating under false names all over the country and getting women to invest in schemes before backing out and taking their money with him."

"Seriously?" she gasped, confusion blanketing her expression. "That makes no sense! He's been Ross's friend since college. I can't imagine him doing something like that or being that type of person without Ross realizing it."

Asher pondered how Rusty had embraced Billy when the cranky billionaire rarely approved of anyone, including his own children. "Well, he's obviously pretty good at charming people to get what he wants. I mean, he *is* currently living in the guesthouse on our estate."

"What does Ross have to say about this?"

"I haven't spoken to him about it and I need for you to promise me that you won't say anything either. I can't risk him tipping off Billy. He's already left a trail of missing funds across the country. Nothing on the scale of what was stolen from Soiree on the Bay, but it has all led up to this moment. And with me in jail, he gets away with it."

Gina's brown eyes grew wider as he spoke and Asher realized his voice had grown louder as he vented his frustration.

"You need to go to the authorities with this," his sister said, her eyes darting toward Ross and his family.

"With what?" Asher growled. "It's nothing but speculation at this point. I have no proof." Then he remembered that Lani had called him before the party started. Still smarting from their last conversation, he'd never picked up her calls or listened to her messages. He pulled out his phone and unlocked the screen. "Or maybe we do. Lani called me from Vegas."

"What was she doing there?"

"That's where Billy's mom lives. She went to see what she could find out. I haven't listened to her message."

"You've been with her a lot. I heard she moved in for a while," Gina remarked, her voice carefully neutral. "Is it all business? I mean, when you two dated before, it was pretty clear she meant a lot to you."

"It's not business on my part," he retorted, his clipped tone exposing his raw emotions. "She just doesn't see a future for us."

"Because...? I mean you were once in love, right?"

"Yes. And my feelings haven't changed on that front." Even though he was confessing to the wrong woman, it felt good to admit how he felt about Lani. "I just don't think I'm the man she wants."

"So become that man." Gina's advice was simple and hard-hitting. "That girl looked at you with heart emoji in her eyes. I'm sure if you put in the effort, she'd come around."

With his lungs constricting in reaction to his sister's words, Asher drew Gina into a hug and then hit the Play button on his phone.

Lani's voice came over the speaker, sounding excited and somewhat annoyed. "Will you please stop avoiding my calls? I know you're not unavailable so I guess I'm just gonna have to leave another message. I talked to Billy's mom and it turns out she had an affair with Rusty. He gave her ten thousand and told her to never contact him again. The thing is, she has no proof that Billy is Rusty's son. She never had a chance to do a paternity test and apparently there were several men she was seeing around the same time. I guess that explains Billy why was so unhappy when Ross and Rusty looked like they were getting along and why he set you up. He thinks he's Rusty son and resents the fact that he didn't have all the things growing up that you all did... Well, the plane's getting ready to take off so they're making me shut off my phone. I'll arrive in Dallas in three hours. I'll call you when I land and we can talk more then."

The whole time Lani had been speaking, he'd been staring at the screen. Now he looked up at his sister and saw his shock mirrored on her face.

"Wow," Gina said in awe.

"Wow is right."

"Now we have to talk to Ross. And tell the authorities."

"Absolutely." But his attention was on the dark-haired man making for the exit in a hurry. "Except I think we might be out of time." He indicated Billy's rapid departure.

Gina's eyes rounded. "Do you think he heard us?"

"Maybe." To Asher's relief, Billy's progress was halted by a trio of women. "Can you keep him busy for me? I need fifteen minutes."

"Where are you going?"

Asher thought about his apartment over the barn and the unlocked front door giving access to anyone on the property. "I'm going to search the guesthouse."

Twelve

The distance between the main house and the guesthouse where Billy currently resided was a three-minute jog along a tree-lined winding drive. Asher accomplished it in half the time. Heart pounding, his breath coming hard from the sprint, he trotted up the steps to the front door, keyed in the code to unlock the door and entered.

The house's cool stillness embraced him. Asher knew the housekeeper wasn't home. Anytime there was a party at the main house, she joined the staff, keeping the food and drinks flowing smoothly from the kitchen to the guests.

Still, running into someone was the least of his problems. He had no clear idea where to begin a search and a limited amount of time to execute it. What did he hope to find? A laptop with incriminating information would be great but he'd settle for a file marked *stolen festival funds*.

When they'd landed on Billy as a prime suspect, he'd proposed to Lani that they infiltrate the guesthouse while Billy was away, but she'd shut him down. Her methodical approach didn't involve breaking and entering. But it wasn't really breaking in when he had the code to the front door, right?

Asher made his way into the study off the foyer. He couldn't believe his luck. A laptop sat on the large wood desk and he made his way over to it. Even as he lifted the top and peered at the screen, he had to wonder if this was just a decoy. Surely Billy was too clever to leave a bunch of damning evidence lying around for someone to scoop up and run out the door with.

Seconds rushed by as Asher pulled up the browser history and quickly scanned through it. Asher couldn't see where Billy had used this computer to access any banks. Still, his search had been cursory at best and with time running out he looked around for a place to stash the laptop. If Billy intended to pack up and get out of town, Asher wanted to make sure he wouldn't be able to take this device with him. The quickest, most obvious spot was underneath the couch cushions. He was counting on the man assuming someone had walked off with the computer and that he wouldn't search the room.

The bedrooms were on a level above and Asher headed up the stairs, taking them two at a time. He found an identical laptop to the one downstairs, sandwiched between the box spring and mattress. With excitement pumping adrenaline through his bloodstream, he slid the computer into a laptop case that he found in the closet. With the thrill of the hunt surging, he riffled through the nightstand and dresser before getting even more creative with the search. From their careful concealment beneath shirts and socks, taped to the back of the drawer and even affixed behind the painting over the bed, he unearthed several passports— one with Billy's face but Asher's name that he dropped into his pocket—along with a wad of cash, two burner phones and a handgun.

This was *not* how an innocent man behaved.

Asher glanced at the closet, wondering how many goodies he could turn up there, but heard the front door open. With only one set of stairs leading up to the second floor, he was trapped. Fortunately he'd left everything except for the laptop where he'd found it. Asher eased out of the master suite and crossed the landing to one of the two guest bedrooms just as he heard Billy start to climb upstairs. With his blood thundering in his ears, he slipped behind the door out of sight and wondered if he dared try to slip down the stairs while Billy was packing.

Instead Asher glanced at the window. Maybe he could try to jump and hope he landed without hurting himself. Moving cautiously, he went to the window and opened it. He hadn't done more than drop the laptop into the bushes below before Billy started cursing. Asher barely had time to press himself against the wall when the other man raced past again.

Deciding this was his best chance to make his escape, and with his ears tuned for the slightest noise, Asher waited until he heard the front door open and close once more. Then he quickly, but quietly, descended to the first floor. After a quick detour to the study to collect the laptop, he headed for the kitchen and the door that led to the side yard. He needed to retrieve the other laptop, but when he opened the door, standing before him was Billy Holmes with a handgun leveled at his chest.

"You."

Asher was not at all flattered at the surprise on Billy's face. "Me."

Billy's gaze went to the laptop Asher held. "Give that to me."

"Or what? You'll shoot me?" He was rethinking his words as the other man smirked. "Fire that gun and everyone at the house will hear. Gina knows what you did.

She's probably already warned Ross. They'll lock the gates and you'll never get out."

"I guess I need a little insurance then, don't I?" Billy backed up and gestured with the gun toward the car parked in the driveway.

Unsure what the traitor had in mind, Asher decided to let the scene play out until he saw an opening to act. A suitcase stood beside the car. Keeping a close eye on Asher, Billy popped open the trunk.

"Give me the laptop and get in."

"The trunk?"

Asher took a tighter grip on the laptop, prepared to swing it at Billy's head, but the other man shook his head.

"Don't be stupid. If you make me shoot you, I might not get away, but you'll definitely be dead."

All too aware that would be true, Asher made a huge show of reluctance before handing over what he hoped was Billy's decoy computer.

"Get in," Billy repeated.

"Why? You have everything you need to get away clean."

"Except for a head start. So, to throw everyone into a state of confusion, you and I are going for a little drive."

And before Asher could summon another protest, Billy's hand holding the gun shot out and everything went black.

No three-hour plane ride had ever felt as long as this one.

How could she have told Asher he wasn't the right man for her? *Of course* he was. She loved him just the way he was. She didn't want to change him. Why would she? He was thrilling and adventurous and made her get out of her head and listen to her heart. Loving him was a wonderful chaotic ride and she was ready to spend the rest of her life on it.

The first thing she would do when she saw him again

was tell him that she loved him. No matter if he was angry with her or indifferent. She wouldn't hesitate, wouldn't play it safe. If he believed that the only reason she'd been waiting to speak up was to determine if he was innocent, she'd convince him that her change of heart had come the day they'd visited the festival site on Appaloosa Island. She'd just been too afraid to trust her emotions.

As soon as the plane landed, Lani turned her phone back on and watched the screen light up with notifications. She scanned for a message from Asher, but the only names that appeared were Ross, Gina and the Maverick County Sheriff's Department.

Cursing the love of her life for being impossibly stubborn, Lani dialed his number again and groaned in frustration when it rolled straight into voice mail. With Asher out of reach, she turned her attention to the rest of her messages, starting with Gina.

We think Billy overheard your voice mail. Ross and Asher are going to talk to him.

"Damn it!"

Lani's seatmate shot her a dark look and she offered the woman a tight smile and a mumbled apology as she checked the time stamp and saw that it had come in an hour earlier.

And as if that wasn't bad enough, she had three messages from Ross, each one worse than the last.

Billy knows we're onto him and he's running.

Asher went to the guesthouse to stop him.

I'm not sure what's going on, but Sheriff Battle just called to say that Asher is on the run.

What the hell was going on? Lani dialed Ross's number, but after several rings it rolled to voice mail the way Asher's had. She scrolled through her contacts and located the one for the Maverick County Sheriff's Department. Tapping her fingers against the armrest, she waited for someone to pick up.

"I'm looking for Sheriff Battle," Lani said when the receptionist answered. "My name is Lani Li and it's about Asher Edmond."

"One moment."

With hold music playing in her ear, Lani stared out the window as the plane taxied toward the busy Dallas/Fort Worth terminal, stopping repeatedly to let other planes pass. Her heart thudded hard against her ribs as her agitation grew by the second.

What had Asher been thinking to go after Billy? Didn't he know he was already in enough trouble? He and Ross should've called the sheriff and let the cops sort everything out. But sitting idly by when there was something adventurous to do wasn't Asher's style.

"Sheriff Battle." The man's calm, booming voice did little to soothe Lani's wildly fluctuating emotions.

"Sheriff, this is Lani Li. I've just landed in Dallas and I think I know who embezzled the money from the Soiree on the Bay festival and set up Asher Edmond to take the fall."

"I don't think you've heard, Ms. Li, but Asher Edmond is running."

"He's not running because he's not guilty." Lani couldn't imagine what had possessed Asher to take this sort of risk. What was he doing? This might ruin everything. "I think what he may be doing is trying to stop Billy Holmes from leaving town and disappearing."

"What does Mr. Holmes have to do with any of this?"

"I went to Las Vegas to visit Billy's mother. I found a connection there to Rusty Edmond."

A moment of silence followed her words, and then Sheriff Battle said, "Maybe you'd better fill me in…"

By the time she finished explaining everything, the plane had reached the terminal and the woman in the seat next to her was openly goggling. Lani ignored the eavesdropper and willed the passengers to disembark at a faster pace.

"So, you can see why Billy Holmes has to be stopped and questioned," she added, completely out of breath. "It's why Asher is chasing after him."

"If that's true, then they're both heading to the airport," the sheriff said.

"Billy can't get away." If that happened, the money would be gone forever and Asher's name might never be cleared.

"I'll get ahold of the special agents in charge of the case and my deputy that's following Asher and fill them in."

Lani hung up the call and got to her feet. As she joined the line of disembarking passengers, she chided herself for not calling the investigators before boarding the plane in Las Vegas. Yet how was she supposed to know that Asher would do something as reckless as go after Billy on his own? She ground her teeth as the people in front of her slowly shuffled off the plane. When she got ahold of Asher, she was going to kill him. Or kiss him senseless.

Once she reached the terminal, Lani looped her bag over her shoulder and began to jog toward the security gate that led to the arrivals area. She had no luggage, and no reason to follow the crowd to baggage claim. Besides, if Billy and Asher were on their way to the airport, the most likely spot to find them would be at the ticketing level. Only as she passed the doors leading to the shuttle that circled the five different terminals did the magnitude of the search area sap her hope. How could she hope to find Billy amongst the dozens of airlines and thousands of people checking in?

She was racing toward the arrivals area, scanning the faces around her, when she spied a familiar figure exiting TSA. Although he was wearing sunglasses and a baseball cap, she recognized Billy Holmes.

She angled in his direction, moving fast to intercept him. It wasn't until she stepped into his path that Lani realized she hadn't considered how to stop him.

"Billy Holmes."

To Lani's relief, he stopped.

His icy blue gaze darted in all directions before coming to rest on her. "Do I know you?"

"I'm Lani Li. I've been hired by Kingston Blue to look into the missing funds from the Soiree on the Bay festival."

His upper lip lifted in a snarl. "Good for you."

"I'd like to talk to you about your connection with the Edmond family."

"I'm sorry, but I have a plane to catch and don't have time to—"

Billy side stepped as if to go around her, but Lani was prepared for his evasion and kept herself in his path.

"I visited your mother today," she told him, hoping if she delayed Billy long enough, the police might catch up to him. "I know her connection to Rusty Edmond."

Billy shrugged. "They had an affair. So what?"

"So, you think he's your father. You think he abandoned you and your mother and you wanted payback. That's why you stole the money from the festival and blamed Asher."

"That's ridiculous. Asher stole that money. Everyone knows that." He gave her a cocky smile, but tension rode every line of his body.

"I also know about Bond Howard, Bobby Hammond and Brad Howell."

"Who?" Billy continued to regard her as if she were out of her mind, but Lani saw she had his complete attention.

Her cell phone began to ring. Hoping it was Asher, she

glanced down at the screen, but realized it was Ross Edmond. She answered the call, but by the time she glanced back up at Billy, he was gone.

"Damn it!" she growled.

"Lani? Is that you?" Ross sounded upset and confused.

"Yes. Where's Asher?" she demanded, searching all around her for Billy. She couldn't spot his tall figure anywhere. It was as if the man had vanished.

"He's being arrested."

Anxiety banished all thought of Billy Holmes from her mind. She had to get to Asher. "Where are you?"

"Outside Terminal A."

As luck would have it, Lani's plane from Las Vegas had landed at the same terminal.

She ran outside and gaped at the mob scene. Four police cars surrounded a sedan parked by the curb with its trunk open. They had one man down on the ground as another argued and waved his arm toward the terminal. It took her a second to realize that Ross Edmond was the one gesticulating wildly and Asher was face down on the pavement, his hands cuffed behind his back.

She ran over and added her voice to the cacophony. "Billy Holmes is in the terminal. I just saw him. He's getting away."

Ross turned to her with a relieved expression. "That's what I'm trying to tell them," he said, "but they're not listening to me."

Two cops lifted Asher to his feet. One wore the insignia of the Maverick County Sheriff's Department, the other was a state trooper.

"I was kidnapped," Asher protested, eyes widening as he spotted her. "Hey, Lani."

As she rushed toward him, the state trooper stepped in her way and stood with his feet planted shoulder-width apart, hands on his gun belt. "And you are?"

"Lani Li. I called and spoke with Sheriff Battle when I landed." She glanced at the deputy's name tag. "Deputy Vesta, didn't the sheriff get ahold of you? You have the wrong man."

"I don't think so," the deputy said, jerking his thumb at Asher. "He's trying to get away." His vehement glare suggested that there was something personal in his dislike of Asher.

"Look, I wasn't trying to escape." He tipped his head to one side, showing a bloody gash on his temple. "The bastard bashed me on the head and dumped me in the trunk."

"You weren't in the trunk when we pulled up." The state trooper pointed out.

"Because the car had finally stopped and I figured it was safe for me to get out."

"The man you're looking for is Billy Holmes," Lani put in, tearing her gaze from Asher's wound. She hoped it wasn't as serious as it looked.

"Don't know anything about that," the trooper said. "We received a BOLO from Maverick County that this guy was skipping town."

Lani glanced at the car the police cruisers had surrounded. Its open trunk seemed to substantiate Asher's claim.

"He wasn't skipping town because he's innocent," Lani fumed. "You need to go after Billy Holmes. I ran into him in there. He's getting away."

The trooper glanced toward the door leading into the terminal. "Who's this Billy Holmes character?"

The deputy started dragging his prisoner toward the police car. "Let's go."

"Can't you wait just a second," Asher protested, resisting. "I have something to tell Lani."

Heartsick, she moved to go after them, but the trooper

caught her arm, keeping her in place. She glanced around the police officer, trying to keep Asher in sight.

"Let me go with him."

Was that her voice sounding so desperate and anxious? Suddenly it had become crucial that Asher hear that she loved him.

"They're taking him back to Royal. You can see him at the sheriff's station."

"Please," she pleaded with the cop. "There's something he needs to know."

"Fine. Make it quick."

The Maverick County deputy was already urging Asher into the back of his patrol car when Lani drew near. The deputy had his hand on the door and was about to slam it shut when she spoke up.

"Wait." Irrational panic had seized her and wouldn't let go. "Just give me a second with him."

To her dismay he just smirked at her and started to close the door. A fraction of a second remained for her to confess the three words that had been hiding in her heart. Terrified, where she'd been bold moments earlier, Lani locked eyes with Asher and sucked in a breath for courage. But as she began to speak, Asher clearly had something on his mind as well and there wasn't time for both.

As the car door swung on its hinges, an instant before glass and metal blocked their words, their overlapping messages reached their targets.

"I love you."

"I got Billy's laptop."

Thirteen

Asher lay on his back staring at the damn jail ceiling once again. His head was throbbing beneath the hastily applied bandage on his temple. He'd stopped pacing an hour ago and resigned himself to spending the night. At least this time he wasn't worried about being stuck here indefinitely. He'd been told that they'd found Billy's laptop where he'd hidden it and the forensics team was combing the hard drive in search of the accounts where the funds had been sent. Thanks to Lani, a clear picture had formed of Billy's notorious past, stemming from his mother's affair with Rusty that suggested a reason for him to destroy the Edmond family's reputations and set up Asher to take the fall for the missing festival funds.

Unfortunately, in the midst of the wild and completely out-of-control scene at the airport, Billy had escaped into the crowds and it appeared as if he'd vanished into thin air. No doubt he had several different identifications to go with his aliases and with the festival funds squirreled away, he had the means to go just about anywhere.

But none of that mattered anymore. What preoccupied Asher was that he was stuck in here while Lani was out there doing who knew what. He was on pins and needles waiting to be released. And after he was set free, then what? He and Lani hadn't sorted out their problems. Before leaving for Las Vegas, she'd made it clear that she still didn't trust him.

As the hours passed without any word from her, he grew almost frantic with worry. Over and over his mind replayed those moments before Deputy Vesta had shut him into the back of the patrol car. Once again Asher had screwed up. While Lani was confessing her love, he'd been bragging about securing Billy's laptop. She was sure to think that he was only worried about saving his own ass, not that he'd done it for her so that she could find the missing money and solve the case.

And now she was avoiding him, no doubt guessing that he didn't love her in return. Would she ever give him the chance to explain? Or was it already too late? Maybe she wasn't busy with the authorities. Maybe she'd already gone back to Dallas, putting him in her rearview mirror once again.

Nor could he blame her for leaving him to rot. Hell, if he'd confessed his love to her only to discover she was solely focused on saving her firm, he'd be pretty messed up too. Hopefully she would give him another chance. He would shower her with I love you's from now until eternity if she would just show up.

The door leading to the rest of the police station opened and Asher's heart gave a painful wrench. He was on his feet and across the small cell before realizing his visitor wasn't Lani, but the stocky deputy who despised him.

"Hello, Deputy Vesta," he said in his most droll tone. "I thought you'd forgotten all about me."

Vesta shot him a disgusted look. "Someone's here to see you."

Asher grabbed the bars and held on as relief washed over him. His head spun as Lani slowly advanced into the room. Strands of dark hair framed her exhausted features and her shoulders slumped as if burdened by an enormous weight. She looked as if the news she'd come to share was so bad she couldn't bear to speak it.

"What is it?" he demanded. His stomach knotted. "What's happening?"

"You look like hell," she said, stopping halfway toward him.

Her unwillingness to meet his gaze coupled with her delay in coming to see him made his heart plummet. Either she'd been unable to convince the authorities that Billy was the true thief or her part of the case was concluded and this was goodbye.

"Well I've been locked up in jail for…" without his watch or a clock to gauge the time, he'd lost track of how long he'd been in this cell "…a while now," he concluded wearily, wondering how he could possibly convince her they had a future if he remained locked up. "You, on the other hand, look glorious."

Her lips flattened into an unhappy line. "I'm tired and in desperate need of a shower so…"

More than anything he needed to touch her, to crush her in his arms and deliver his heart into her keeping. But this time he knew he needed more than his easy charm. She needed—deserved—the honest message of his heart.

"About what happened at the airport," he began.

"Billy got away." She shook her head. "We're not sure if he's actually Rusty's son, but it's clear that he believes that's the case and that he wanted Rusty—your whole family, really—to pay for abandoning him and his mother."

Asher could care less about Billy Holmes or the damned case. All he knew was that his future happiness was slipping through his fingers. He needed to be clearer, to make her understand how mad he was at himself for screwing up again. Hopefully it wasn't too late to make her understand that he regretted not speaking from his heart. It was what *she'd* done in that tense, chaotic moment. Would she believe him now?

"I don't care about that right now," he insisted, wishing she'd stop staring at his chest and see his earnest expression. He blustered on, "I want to explain about what happened when you said I love you and I told you I got Billy's laptop. What I was really trying to say was that I love you too."

After flicking her gaze to his face, she took a single step closer. Her bowed head and tightly clenched hands gave her a look of uncharacteristic uncertainty and Asher took that as his chance to spill all of it.

"I've loved you since the first time you called me frat boy," he rushed on, baring all his fear and regret, his joy and hope. He needed his sincerity to reach her, to encourage her to give him—*them*—a chance.

He stretched out his arms as another slow, shuffling step brought her almost within reach. She continued to remain silent, but her willingness to hear him out gave him hope.

"From here on out, I'm at your command," he declared, the words tumbling out of him. She'd given him this chance and he would not fail. "Whatever you need. Whoever you need me to be. I'm that guy. I swear you will never be disappointed in me ever again."

She'd moved near enough that he could wrap his fingers around her jacket lapels and pull her forward.

"I love you," he murmured, putting his whole heart into the phrase.

Lani caught his wrists as he tugged her toward him, but to keep her balance rather than to resist him. Still, it was pretty obvious that more kept them apart than the steel metal grid between them.

"I love you just the way you are," she whispered, lifting her gaze to his at last.

The amount of anguish in her mink-brown eyes made Asher catch his breath. Throat tight, he cupped her cheek and cursed the mess he'd made of things. If only he'd been able to find the courage years ago to give her his heart.

"But I'm already different because of you," he said. "Being with you that summer five years ago changed me. Oh, I resisted. I was still an arrogant ass, asking you to give up on your dream when I wasn't ready to grow up and take responsibilities for the decisions I'd made." He shook his head in disgust. "Looking back, I was so stupid to persist in trying to win Rusty's approval, too caught up in my resentment when I couldn't."

"We both had a lot of growing up to do." Her smile was both sad and filled with regret. "With grad school ahead of me, I wasn't ready to be in a serious relationship. I didn't think I could have it all. A successful career *and* you."

Optimistic that she hadn't barred her heart to him, the knot in his chest eased slightly. "Maybe I'm reading this wrong," he teased, "but I'm not sensing you thought being with me was gonna be a picnic."

"Oh, it would've been a picnic, all right," she muttered with a quiet snort. "Including fire ants and an unexpected thunderstorm."

"You're not wrong." He accepted the accuracy of her claim with a wry smirk. "Being with me won't be without its surprises."

When it came to consistency and predictability, he would not be her ideal choice. They approached things in completely opposite ways. She was methodical. He was spontaneous. Yet they both loved a challenge and never let fear stop them from engaging in thrilling adventures.

"At least it will never be dull." She thrust her knuckles

into his stomach. The jab didn't hurt, but her message was clear. *Don't make me regret this.*

"I swear I won't," he murmured, pressing his face into the gap between the bars, but finding her lips remained out of reach. "I don't suppose there's any way you could get me out of here so we could seal our new partnership with a kiss."

"Oh," she said with a playful lilt in her voice. "Did I forget to mention that you're free to go?"

The news shot through him like a lightning bolt. "This is the second-best news I've had all day."

Her left eyebrow lifted. "And the best news?"

"Deputy Vesta promised me meat loaf for dinner."

As her eyes blazed, Asher was really glad to have the protection of the cell bars between them. A second later, however, before she could voice the murder flashing in her eyes, the aforementioned deputy reentered the room and unlocked the cell door.

"See if you can stay out of trouble this time," Vesta grumbled, looking as if he'd tasted something really bad.

With a cheeky smile for the deputy, Asher grabbed Lani's hand and pulled her toward freedom. This time, his incarceration had only been a few hours, but while waiting for Lani to come visit him, it had felt like an eternity.

He intended on making a beeline for the front door, but Lani resisted. When he looked back at her, she shook her head.

"We need to get that off first," she said, indicating the monitoring device on his ankle. "You are officially no longer a suspect in the theft of the festival funds."

Asher wrapped his arms around Lani and swept her off her feet. As he whirled her in a tight circle, she wrapped her arms around his neck and laughed merrily in his ear. Nothing had ever felt as good as her body pressed up against his, her breath warm on his neck, her joy filling him with giddy delight.

When he set Lani back on her feet and dipped his head to hers, she rose up on tiptoe to meet him half way. Her lips parted on a groan and he sent his tongue dancing forward to meet hers. They clung together, the fierce, thrilling kiss making his head swim. His throat tightened on a rush of joy. This woman in his arms was all the contentment that had been missing from his life.

"I take back what I said earlier," he declared, breaking off the kiss. "*This* is the second-best news I've heard all day."

As he spoke, he towed her toward the room where the electronic device had been attached a month earlier. Half an hour later he emerged into the humid evening and sucked in a breath of fresh air.

"We have to celebrate my freedom," he said. "Where should we go? New York? Buenos Aires? Tahiti?"

"How about we go back to Elegance Ranch and start figuring out how this new partnership of ours is going to work."

"When you say partnership…" He held his breath, wondering what she had in mind. Did she mean a business partnership? Or a personal one?

"I've been thinking about hiring an associate and I could use someone like you with the sort of connections that could bring in a better paying clientele." Her fingers tightened on his as she added, "It doesn't pay well, but if you work really hard, we might be able to grow the business."

"I appreciate your willingness to mentor me," he teased, drawing her toward the parking lot, eager to get her alone and show her without words just how much he adored her. "And I am grateful for your faith in me, but…"

"But?" she prompted, doubt creeping into her tone.

"But…" They reached her SUV and she reached into

her pocket for the keys. "I have a little different take on our partnership," Drawing her into his arms, he lowered his forehead to hers. "One that involves rings and vows and kids. To summarize, it's us living happily-ever-after."

Lani chewed on her lower lip for several suspenseful seconds before her lashes lifted and she met his gaze. "Are you sure you're ready to take on that sort of partnership?"

"I've been thinking about it a lot. Someone needs to keep me in line. And I think you'll agree that no one is better at it than you." He grew serious as he stared into her eyes, willing her to see the fervent truth of his love. "And then there's the part where I adore you and can't bear to live without you. I want us to have kids and be a happy family."

The words came faster and faster as her muscles tensed. She seemed reluctant to take him seriously and his breath grew ragged as a tight band around his chest kept his lungs from fully expanding.

"I know this may seem like it's coming too soon. What can I say to convince you I can't live without you?" A lightbulb went off in his head and he dropped to one knee before her. Taking her hand in his, he offered her solemn sincerity. "Lani Li, I offer you my heart. Will you accept?"

To his dismay, she began to laugh.

"What's so funny? I'm trying to be all romantic."

"This is you being romantic?" She twisted her features into a skeptical expression, but a slight twitch at the corner of her mouth hinted at a smile.

"Give me a chance," he rasped. "Marry me."

For several heartbeats the only sound between them was the harsh, irregular pattern of their breathing. As he waited out the silence, Asher knew this wasn't the moment that would make or break them. He wasn't going to give up if she said no. She was too important to him to so readily accept defeat. He would fight for her. Fight for the amazing future they would have. But when her words came, it became clear that any battle she intended to wage would be at his side.

"Yes. I'll marry you."

Relief slammed into him. Leaping to his feet, he banded one arm around her waist and startled her with a quick spin and a dip. "At last you'll be mine."

"I've always been yours," she gasped. "Now, can I please get up?"

He set her back on her feet, but kept her in his arms. Setting aside all levity, he cupped the side of her face. "I'm done with running away because I'm too scared to face rejection. I intend to stay put and put in the effort."

"I love you, Asher Davidson Edmond." She framed his face with her palms and set fire to his blood with her earnest gaze. "I'm sorry I didn't give us a chance five years ago. I was afraid to choose you over my career because I didn't trust what we had could be enough. I never even considered fighting to have both. I know now that my life isn't fulfilling without you in it. Let's make a life together. With kids and a successful business." A brilliant smile bloomed. "We can have it all."

"We absolutely can." He brought his lips to hers. "And we will."

* * * * *

SECRETS OF A
ONE NIGHT STAND

NAIMA SIMONE

To Gary. 143.

One

Achilles Farrell had been called many things in his thirty years.

Dumb fuck.

Ex-con.

Bastard.

That last one behind his back since most people were leery of insulting a six-foot-four-inch-tall, 214-pound man to his face.

But never had he been called an heir.

Brother.

And in the space of one afternoon, he'd become both.

After a shock like that, he needed alcohol. Lots of alcohol.

Achilles stared at the neon red signs advertising the various beers on tap as well as framed posters declaring this pub the best *and* worst Beacon Hill, Massachusetts, had to offer. Hopefully, that ambiguity didn't translate to its liquor quality.

It'd been a couple of hours, but he could still feel the

judgmental gazes of "polite" Boston society on his skin like a thousand ants. The sensation deepened his thirst for the coffee-and-caramel flavor of a perfectly drawn Guinness, sharpened his anticipation for the burn of whiskey down his throat. Had him damn near demanding the bartender bring him another round when he hadn't even requested his first drink yet.

"What can I get you?" The bartender leaned on the scarred bar top. Despite the colorful tattoos running the length of both arms, the young woman barely looked old enough to drink the alcohol she was serving.

"A shot of Jameson and a Guinness."

She nodded. "Coming up."

Only when she turned around to start building his drink did he exhale, some of the tension in his shoulders leaking out of him like a slowly released valve. Maybe once that Irish whiskey hit the back of his throat, the cold in his bones from that mockery of a funeral would finally dissipate.

To think, just three days ago, he'd been in his small cabin, alone except for his computers, just the way he liked it. That's when he'd received a certified letter about the death of a man his mother had always refused to talk about although she'd given Achilles his last name. Achilles hadn't given a damn then, just like he didn't now, about a will or an inheritance. But morbid curiosity about the man who'd impregnated his mother had compelled him to accept the paid-for plane ticket and travel thousands of miles across the country.

As soon as he'd stepped off the plane and met the glacial expression of the chauffeur, Achilles had regretted his rash decision. He'd thought landing in prison had cured him of his hot, impulsive behavior. Apparently not. And now he was paying for his spur-of-the-moment decision to attend the funeral and the reading of the will for his so-called father.

A year.

He had to give up an entire year of his life, remain in Boston, with half brothers he didn't know, and run a company he had no clue how to operate. A company he wanted no part of.

That was the price his father demanded Achilles remit.

Even from the grave, Barron Farrell was a selfish, narcissistic asshole.

When he was growing up, Achilles had begged his mother to tell him who his father was, to introduce Achilles to him. She'd always refused both requests. He'd resented her then. If she were alive, he'd thank her.

He propped his elbows on the bar top and ground his thumb and forefinger into his eyes. What he wouldn't give to be back in Tacoma, Washington, in his cabin less than a mile from the Cascade Range. So far away from affluent Beacon Hill, Massachusetts. And not just in location

Yeah, Tacoma had its wealthy, but as the son of a waitress, he didn't have any use for them. In his experience, the rich either fucked you or fucked you over.

But as he'd stood in that mansion's ridiculously huge library with its hardwood floor, leather furniture, fireplaces large enough for even him to stand in, spiral staircase and floor-to-ceiling bookshelves, it hadn't been just his black thermal shirt, faded jeans and battered brown boots that had differentiated him from the other men in the room.

Cain Farrell—his older brother, the heir, the son Barron Farrell had kept and acknowledged. Kenan Rhodes—the youngest son, biracial and the other bastard besides Achilles. But both men hailed from the same world. Boston's elite. It was in the razor-sharp yet elegant cut of their suits. The cultured speech. The arrogant demeanor.

Achilles had encountered people like them. And had ended up despising every one of them.

Now he had to call them brother.

Life should really offer him a cigarette when it decided to fuck him.

Again.

"You starting a tab or paying for these now?" The bartender set a mug filled with dark, cold brew topped with a creamy head that spilled a little over the rim. Next to it sat a short, smooth glass of amber whiskey.

Perfect.

"A tab." Because yeah, he was just getting started. The whole purpose of this trip entailed not thinking. And several rounds should accomplish his mission.

"I'll be back, then."

She cocked her head, running a dark blue gaze down his frame. He'd hit six foot his sophomore year of high school and had kept growing. He'd become used to that glint in a woman's eyes. And he didn't shy from it. The only thing better than losing himself in alcohol was hot, dirty, nameless sex.

His height, his build and his eyes—those were the only things his worthless sperm donor had passed down to him, and women seemed to eat that shit up. He picked up the shot of Jameson and knocked it back, never breaking visual contact with the pretty brunette. The corner of her lips lifted, desire flickering in her gaze as it dipped to his mouth.

"Let me know if you need to order food. Y'know, to balance all that alcohol. Can't have you too wasted just in case you have later...plans." She smirked before sauntering off to the other end of the bar.

"Hmm. That was subtle."

Achilles stiffened.

That voice.

Like a fire beating back the coldest winter winds.

Like fingernails on a chalkboard.

As silken and sexy as skin sliding over bare, heated skin.

As jarring as crashing cymbals directly in the ear.

He longed to curl up against it, roll around in it.

He wanted to snarl at it, hurl himself away from it.

His heart smashed against his rib cage like a caged beast. His pulse, in sharp contrast, a sonorous warning at the base of his throat. Something primitive inside him warned that he should go find that bartender with the invitation in her eyes, pay for his drinks and get the hell out.

But the impulsive, destructive streak that had brought him to Massachusetts must have still been alive and kicking because he didn't heed that warning. Instead, he slowly turned around on his barstool.

Jesus Christ.

That sense of self-preservation had been right.

This woman was everything he usually avoided.

Gorgeous. Pampered. Rich. He didn't need to see the price tag on the purple pantsuit that conformed to her abundant, wicked curves to know it cost more than everything he'd packed in his suitcase back at the hotel. Including the luggage.

A Trojan horse.

That's what she was.

Designed to appear like one thing—something innocuous—while inside was a virus waiting to strike, to infect…to destroy.

He dealt with those deadly viral strands during his job as a software developer. He'd suffered the poison of one after tangling with a woman like her.

Her dark gaze slid over him, and—in spite of knowing

who she was, what she was—his breath snagged on the ragged resentment in his chest. Blood heated in his veins… pounded in his lengthening dick.

Apparently, his cock could give two damns what tax bracket she fell in.

She lifted a slim hand, hailing the bartender over to her. And in the magical way her kind had, the bartender abandoned the person she was talking to and headed their way.

Flicking a glance over Achilles, the brunette hiked her chin at the woman next to him. "What can I get you?"

"I'll have…" She narrowed her eyes, tapping a pale pink–painted finger against her tad-too-full bottom lip. "I'll have the bacon cheeseburger with a side of onion rings. Make that an extra-large order. And a Budweiser."

Well…damn.

As if she'd heard the astonished words in his head, she arched a dark eyebrow.

"They have wonderful hamburgers here and the best onion rings in Boston." She dipped her head in the direction of the bartender, who disappeared through a swinging door on the other side of the bar. "She was right, you know. You might want some food. I recommend one of the burgers or the fish 'n' chips. Make sure you're sober enough for—" the barest hint of a smirk whispered over a corner of her mouth "—later."

Was she flirting? If so, teasing him about fueling up to fuck another woman had to be one of the weirdest come-ons…or the hottest. Possibly both.

His dick twitched as she flicked a tight, honey-brown curl away from her cheek.

Definitely both.

Disgust for himself trickled through him, and he picked up his Guinness, gulping the sweet and bitter ale until nearly half of it disappeared before he settled the glass mug back on the bar top. But the cold alcohol did nothing to douse the flickers of lust in his gut. Not when wisps of her scent—an earthy musk carrying hints of lavender, cedar and something more elusive—drifted to him, taunting him. Not when a glance down ensnared him in the dichotomy of a lush thigh and a delicate ankle. One invited his hungry teeth and the other his gentle fingers.

He had no business being tempted by either.

Women like her... They only wanted one thing from men like him. And while he didn't mind a night of hot, no-strings sex, it was being looked at like trash afterward that didn't work for him. Being someone's dirty secret tainted the soul, and that kind of stain was hell washing out.

She sighed, and out of the corner of his eye, he caught her folding a napkin until it formed a tiny square.

"I'm sorry. I didn't mean to be so flippant or rude." She broke off as the bartender reappeared and set her beer in front of her, removing the cap.

The woman smiled at her in thanks, and Achilles glanced away as another bolt of lust speared him in the chest. And lower. A dimple. Of fucking course. Because cheekbones as sharp as broken glass, eyes the color of melted dark chocolate, a mouth a shade too wide and a sinner's prayer past too full weren't enough. Because tight, springy curls the shade of sun-warmed honey wasn't overkill. She needed dimples.

"I'm usually not so forward. I'm blaming it on jet lag." She shook her head, picking up her beer and raising it to her lips.

And by all that was holy, he should've looked away. Shouldn't have stared so openly, so...so eagerly at how that beautiful mouth pursed around the opening. Or how her delicate throat worked as she swallowed. His fingers tightened around the handle of his mug. Either that or do something that would get him booted out of the bar and possibly arrested. Like lean forward and wrap his hand around that elegant throat so he could feel every swallow against his palm. Feel the vibration of that husky contralto when she spoke.

He fixed his gaze on the rest of the ale in his glass. "Jet-lagged from where?"

He didn't glimpse her surprise, but it crackled over him just the same. As did her soft delight when she said, "London. I was there on business, and you'd think after being away from home for a week the first thing I'd want to see is my own bed, but I can't go—" She broke off, and Achilles glanced at her. But she didn't continue the sentence, instead taking another sip, then setting the bottle on the bar, studying the dark brown glass with a small frown. But her expression cleared as she looked at him. "Anyway, I found myself craving a greasy burger and a beer from my favorite bar."

As someone who'd learned early in life that detecting a lie could save him from being backhanded by whomever his mom happened to be dating, he could sense an untruth when he heard it.

"You sat down by me," he said.

She nodded. "I did."

"You started talking to me."

The corner of her mouth twitched because the "uninvited" went unspoken but might as well as have been shouted to the ceiling. "True."

"And you're never going to see me again after tonight."

"Also true."

"So you don't have to bother with bullshit. Either you tell me the truth or tell me you don't want to get into it. But don't lie."

She stared at him, pretty lips parted. She wasn't the only

one surprised. He lived and worked alone for a reason: he didn't really care for people. Liked talking to them even less. Developing computer software encompassed designing algorithms, producing code, testing applications and troubleshooting existing systems. Challenging, but it came down to numbers, to science.

Not emotions. Not baggage. Not history. Not on which side of the tracks a person resided.

People were messy as fuck and he wanted no part of them.

Which didn't explain why he'd decided to engage Ms. Beacon Hill in conversation.

That dimple flashed again as her lips slowly curved into a smile that had his chest seizing and his dick hardening.

"You're right. There's something to be said for the gift of having only the 'right now,' isn't there? It's temporary, which somehow makes it more special, exciting." She extended her hand toward him. "Mycah."

After a brief hesitation, Achilles accepted that slim, smaller hand in his own. And exhaled a low, long breath when his completely encompassed hers. "Achilles."

"Achilles," she repeated, and he clenched his jaw when she emitted a little hum afterward, as if savoring his name on her tongue and finding it satisfying. "I like that name. Well, Achilles." She picked up her beer bottle once more and tipped it toward him in a toast. "Here's to strangers meeting for a night."

He lifted his mug, tapping it to her beer. And he couldn't prevent his rebellious gaze from traveling down the graceful column of her neck, past her slim shoulders to a pair of beautiful breasts that might not fill his hands but would damn sure make their presence known. Her open suit jacket offered him an unhindered view of high-waisted pants and a slightly rounded belly that he found sexy as hell. A woman who ordered the kind of meal she had, who didn't starve herself...

He shifted his scrutiny to her face of contrasting angles and curves and narrowed his eyes, studying her anew. Her clothes, those shoes with their red bottoms that even a fashion idiot like him recognized, her flawless makeup and smooth, pampered, almond-brown skin—all of that shouted wealth.

But the decadence of her food order, the roundness of her stomach, the gorgeous lushness of curves that society dictated she diet away, even her laid-back choice in beer and bar... Those all pointed to a woman who indulged herself. A woman who knew restraint but also understood that abandon wasn't always the opposite of losing control.

What would it be like to have this woman lose control all over him?

"To strangers and one night."

As they sipped their respective drinks, and the Guinness flowed over his tongue and down his throat, he couldn't shake the sense that his words had never been more prophetic.

Good thing he didn't believe in that shit.

Two

"Team Dean or Team Sam?"

Achilles lifted his mug of Guinness to his mouth, and for some odd reason Mycah Hill found herself studying the length and width of his fingers. Before she'd entered her favorite Beacon Hill bar tonight, she'd always considered herself a shoulders-and-arms woman. God knew, Achilles had that covered, as well. Massive. That black thermal cotton showed off the wide, tight, big perfection of both.

But his *fingers*.

She'd never been so fascinated by the proportion, length and…elegance of a man's fingers. Until tonight.

"Dean." His answer snatched her from her inspection of his blunt-tipped fingernails. "Natural-born leader and selfless. Let me guess." He arched a dark, thick eyebrow. "Sam."

She scoffed. "That wasn't the least bit condescending."

He stared at her.

"Oh, so what?" she snapped. "Sam was resilient, and he had a lot of obstacles to overcome. Being half demon. Losing his soul. And through it all he learned discipline, had to work through guilt and remorse and learn to forgive himself. Plus, he was self-sacrificing."

"You loved his abs."

"They were straight out of the God's Handiwork Supermart, aisle eight."

Oh, wow. The corner of that deliciously carnal mouth twitched. All night, images of his face wreathed in a full-out smile had fluttered through her head. And all night, she'd hungered to see one. That desire hadn't been fulfilled. Yet each quirk of his lips like the one she'd just been given lit her up. Ridiculous, considering they'd just met, and she didn't know him and wouldn't see him again after they both left this bar, but still…

A gift.

It'd taken greasy bar food, a couple of rounds of drinks and several rounds of "Who's better?" to break the sheet of ice between them, but she was enjoying herself. And even the buzz of her cell phone in her pants pocket for the sixth time—yes, she'd kept count—couldn't ruin it.

Surrender to the demands of her parents to arrive at their home and perform like a perfect show pony? Or sit here and indulge in this brooding, bearded, sexy enigma with long, dark hair and piercing bright eyes?

Her Harvard education wasn't needed to make this decision.

And in a year where she'd been questioning so many of her choices—her career trajectory, her relationships, hell, the flavor of jelly on her English muffin—tossing out her usual reserve to talk up this fiercely beautiful stranger had been her best decision yet.

Even if initially everything from the stiff set of his

massive shoulders to the cold of his stark facial features to the grim line of his carnal mouth had initially told her to fuck off. Although, someone should really inform him that lips that full, that sensual could never truly flatten…

"You're staring."

Mycah hesitated, beer-bottle-number-three a couple of inches away from her mouth. The blush tried to crawl up her throat to her face as she lifted her gaze from his lips to his narrowed blue-gray eyes. And if it hadn't been beer-bottle-number-three, maybe that rush of heat would've met its destination, but a little liquid courage and a lot of I-don't-give-a-damn went a long way toward eroding modesty.

Besides, Achilles hadn't said those two words as other men would've—flirtatiously, with an invitation for her to tell him more about how hot she found him.

No, his words had been a statement of fact, as no-non-sense as his black Henley and scuffed boots. Almost a challenge…an accusation. Why did that have arousal eddying low in her belly?

"I am." Challenge accepted. She sipped from her beer. "Why does that bother you? Because it does. Bother you, that is."

His eyes narrowed even farther. "Because I'm not an animal in a zoo."

She rocked back on the stool, only her fingers clutching the edge of the bar preventing her from losing her balance. Blinking, she gaped at him. Shocked. Stung. Angry.

Slowly twisting around, she signaled for the bartender. When the woman who'd been eye-banging Achilles all night approached, Mycah swirled a finger around his empty shot glass and nearly empty beer mug. "Another round for him, please. On me." His eyebrows jacked down low over his bright gaze, but Mycah shot up a hand, forestalling any argument. "Oh, no, this is about me, not you." Glancing at the woman behind the bar, Mycah flashed her a tight smile. "Please bring those drinks."

"What the hell is that supposed to mean?" Achilles demanded on a low rumble that rippled over her skin, vibrated in her taut nipples and echoed lower, much lower.

That voice of thunder had been wreaking havoc on her all night, and though he'd pissed her off with that unfair comment about treating him like an animal, her body apparently didn't give a damn.

"Hold on." She drank from her beer, waiting until his shot of Jameson and Guinness had been replenished. Only then did she lean forward and meet his gaze, unflinching and all business. "Was she Black?" When he stared back at her, confusion flickering in his eyes, she explained, "The woman I'm the substitute for and getting thrown attitude at on her behalf. Was she Black?"

His scowl could've peeled the paint off the Longfellow Bridge. "What the fuck? Are you actually calling me racist?"

She crossed her legs, cocking her head to the side. "If the bigotry fits..."

"Woman, I know the lighting in this place is for shit, but this skin is brown. My mother was Hawaiian."

Of course, she'd suspected Hawaiian or maybe another Polynesian culture. It was in his high forehead, bold cheekbones, beautiful wide mouth, his thick, dark hair, in his skin kissed by the sun and wind.

And yet, right now, she focused on none of that.

Was.

That *was* shimmered with grief even as *mother* and *Hawaiian* rang with pride. Hurt for him echoed in her chest. For his loss. His pain.

"And your father?"

A shutter fell over his face, and that, too, echoed inside her.

"My father was an asshole."

She nodded. God, did she get that. But that particular trait transcended race, religion, creed and culture.

"You're not a misogynist. Or rather, you don't resent all women. Because when I arrived, you and the bartender—" she dipped her head in the direction of the tattooed brunette on the other end of the bar "—were basically eye-banging each other—in a respectful way. So there's something about me that's had your back up from the moment I sat down and opened my mouth."

He didn't say anything, but he did knock back the shot of Jameson.

"The tattoos?" Mycah tapped her fingernails on the bar top, swinging from side to side on the stool, scrutinizing that impassive face. "But for all you know, I could have ink underneath this pantsuit…" The truth slammed into her, and she straightened. "That's it, isn't it? The pantsuit. You think I'm slumming it."

He still didn't say anything. Didn't confirm her guess.

But he damn sure didn't deny it, either.

And it hurt. More than it should considering he was a stranger, and she didn't even know his last name.

"You don't know me," she whispered.

"Then tell me why you're here." He propped an arm on the bar and leaned forward until she could detect the ring of lighter blue around his dark irises. Until she could inhale his woodsy pine-and-fresh-rain scent underneath the beer. "And don't lie this time," he ordered in a soft tone that a less discerning person would've called kindness. And that person would be an idiot.

She was tempted to tell him to go fuck himself. That

she didn't owe him answers, and he didn't deserve any part of her.

But there was a part of her that wanted—no, *needed*—to prove him wrong. Needed to share something with this man, whom she wouldn't see again, that she couldn't with anyone else. Maybe *because* she wouldn't see him again. He couldn't use the information against her. Couldn't throw it back in her face. Couldn't call her ungrateful or disloyal.

She needed to be…honest. For once in her life, she needed to be honest with someone and with herself.

"Family." The confession slid out of her before she could corral it. "I'm hiding from family."

She could tell him so much more. Like how as soon as her plane had landed at Logan International Airport, her parents had been blowing up her phone, leaving increasingly…vociferous voice mails insisting she join them at their home for their latest dinner party. Or how it didn't matter that she'd just arrived home after an eight-hour flight and a weeklong business trip. There wouldn't be welcoming messages of "welcome home" for her. No "We missed you." Just "Get here because we have an odd number of guests and Janet Holloway is bringing her son who's in wealth management. Be presentable, and for the love of God, don't embarrass us with talk of your boring job."

She could share how since she didn't put it past either one of her parents to send their butler—yes, in this day and age they still had a *butler*—to Mycah's house to hunt her down, she'd escaped to the bar.

But Mycah didn't tell him any of that. She just left it at hiding. Because that alone was incredibly…sad.

And the second after she uttered the word, she fought the pointless urge to snatch the truth back from between them.

Achilles's expression didn't alter; it remained as still,

as stony, as it had when he'd basically dared her to prove him wrong. Yet his eyes… His eyes no longer resembled shards of ice. They were heated. And fierce with an emotion that surpassed sympathy.

"Me, too."

She stared at him. Shocked. Two simple words. But like a decoder ring from a cereal box, the words unlocked the meaning of his gaze.

Connection.

Affliction.

Gratification.

"Who would've thought we would find ourselves here?" She surrendered to the desire that had been pulsing within her since spotting him the moment she'd entered the bar. Reaching out, she captured a dense lock of his long hair, rubbed the silken strands between her thumb and forefinger. Her palm itched to scrape over that thick beard. Achilles's sharply indrawn breath echoed between them, but he didn't pull away. Instead, he watched her, those lupine eyes steady and unblinking on her face. On a trembling inhale, she released his hair and leaned back, reaching for her beer and moistening her parched throat. "On common ground," she added, her voice uneven as she attempted a note of levity.

Mimicking her, Achilles lifted his own ale and drank from it. The taut moment vibrated with tension, but then he arched an eyebrow and said, "Yeah, amazing, considering you believe Daniel Craig is a better James Bond than Sean Connery."

She snorted. "I said what I said."

Achilles shook his head. "Blasphemy," he muttered.

Mycah laughed, and when his beautiful mouth quirked again, she mentally chalked in a point for her. She was a

businesswoman, and even if her parents refused to acknowledge it, a damn successful one.

Yet... In this moment, all her accomplishments seemed
to fade in comparison with one faint, reluctant smile.

Oh, she was in deep.

And she wanted more of him.

The thought jolted through her before she could cage
it. There was no getting rid of it. Not when the idea had
already sown deep and even now its roots were spreading,
reaching, growing...

Her heart thudded against her rib cage, a heavy bass
that reverberated in her sex. In the space of one breath to
the next, the arousal that had been frolicking in her veins
all evening had flashed into a serious, I'm-not-fucking-
around fire.

For the first time in her twenty-nine years, she wanted
to jump into the flames and burn.

"You're staring again."

"I am." She switched her legs, recrossing them. And
damn his too-observant gaze; he didn't miss the gesture.
Probably knew why she did it, too. Not that the action alleviated the sweet pain pulsing inside her. "Does it still
bother you?"

"Depends."

"On?"

"Why you're staring."

She slicked the tip of her tongue over her lips, an unfamiliar case of nerves making themselves known. Again,
his eyes caught the tell, dropping to her mouth, resting
there, and the blast of heat that exploded inside her damn
near fused her to the barstool. What he did with one look...
Jesus, it wasn't fair.

"Because you're so stareable. Don't do that," she insisted, no, *implored* when he stiffened, his eyes going gla-

cial. Frustration stormed inside her, releasing in a sharp clap of laughter. "This is ridiculous. The ability to communicate is literally in my job description but I seem to fuck it up with you." She huffed out a breath, shaking her head. "You should grant me leeway because you don't know me, and I don't know you. And you—all of you—" she waved her hand up and down "—are a lot."

"A lot of what?" His body didn't loosen; his face remained shuttered. But that voice...

She shivered. Her breath caught. Her breasts swelled. Her thighs squeezed. Was it possible to orgasm from a voice alone? She might be the test case.

"A lot of—" she spread out her arms the length of his shoulders "—mass. A lot of attitude." She exhaled, her hands dropping to her thighs. "A lot of beauty," she murmured with a tremble she hated but couldn't erase. "A lot of pride. A lot of..." Fire. Darkness. Danger. Shelter. Passion. So much passion. And sex. A promise of hot, burn-her-alive-and-leave-nothing-but-ashes sex.

Her fingers curled into her palm.

"A lot of intensity," she finished.

Achilles stared at her. And she fought not to fidget under his hooded gaze. Struggled to remain still as he leaned forward. That tantalizing, woodsy scent beckoned her closer.

"Mycah, come here."

She should be rebelling; she should be stiffening in offense at that rumbled order. Should be. But no. Instead, a weight she hadn't consciously been aware of tumbled off her shoulders. Allowing her to breathe deeper...freer. Because as Achilles gripped the lapel of her jacket and drew her closer, wrinkling the silk, he also slowly peeled away Mycah Hill, the business executive who carried the responsibilities of several departments... Mycah Hill, the eldest daughter of Laurence and Cherise Hill, who bore the burden of their financial irresponsibility and unrealistic expectations.

In their place stood Mycah, the vulnerable woman who wanted to let go. Who *could* let go. Just this once.

So as he reeled her in, she went willingly, until their faces hovered barely an inch apart. Until their breaths mingled. Until the fire from his bright gaze heated her skin.

This close, she glimpsed the faint smattering of freckles across the tops of his lean cheeks and the high bridge of his nose. The light cinnamon spots should've detracted from the sensual brutality of his features. But they didn't. In an odd way, they enhanced it.

Had her wanting to dot each one with the tip of her tongue.

"What?" she whispered.

"Say it again." He released her jacket and trailed surprisingly gentle fingers up her throat. "I want to find out for myself what the lie tastes like on your mouth."

Lust flashed inside her, hot, searing. Consuming.

God, she liked it.

If she wasn't careful, she could easily come to crave it.

"Do you still think I'm slumming it?" she murmured.

Achilles stared at her. "I don't care."

She blinked, not certain how she felt about that answer. "Why?"

"Because." He didn't remove his gaze from hers as he lifted a hand to her lips, stroked a thumb across the bottom one. "I want be buried inside here." He pressed against her. Hard. "I want to get lost in there." His eyes flicked down to her thighs. Between them. "I want that more than I dislike your...suit."

No man had ever talked to her like that. And his words hurled kindling on the inferno already burning inside her.

She wasn't a stranger to men. Even enjoyed them. But never had she felt so desired. No, that didn't describe this. Never had she felt so *vital*. As if she were as necessary to him as food, as water…as oxygen.

She knew what she looked like. Knew what she brought to the table. Also knew her connections, her name, her pedigree were as much an enticement as her face or her body. Sometimes even more so.

Yet this man wanted her in spite of those trappings. Those…albatrosses.

That deepened her hunger for him.

She didn't analyze it. Just accepted it.

More than that. She ached for it.

"So… Am I closing out tabs here or what?"

Mycah jerked straight, her head snapping to the side to meet the narrowed gaze of the bartender. Out of her peripheral vision, she caught Achilles slowly leaning back. Behaving much less "caught in the act." Which was ridiculous on Mycah's part since it hadn't been her who'd been making visual promises to get naked with the bartender.

"Yes," he said to the other woman without the least bit of guilt or regret coating his voice. "You can close out both of them." He reached into his back pocket.

"That's not necessary—"

He shot her a hooded glance. "Oh, it is." Returning his attention to the bartender, he removed several bills that appeared more than enough to cover the tabs and laid them on the bar top. "Close out both and keep the change."

Rising from the stool, he held out his hand toward Mycah, palm up. For a long moment, she stared at that big hand with its long fingers and clean nails. Not only was she about to place her hand in his, but so much more. Her body. Her pleasure. Her safety.

All of that with a man whom she'd known for less than three hours.

It was crazy. Nonsensical. So not her...

She slid her palm over his. Tangled her fingers with his.

And when he tugged her to her feet, she went, her chest brushing his, her thighs nudging his. The heavy weight of his cock branding her belly.

She closed her eyes, lust spiraling through her in a heated glide that incinerated breath and any lingering doubt.

"Let me hear you say it." His other hand gripped her waist, squeezed it. She locked her jaw to contain the whimper that climbed her throat. With a will she hadn't known she possessed, she forced the needy sound back down. "Use that pretty mouth and tell me this is what you want."

"If you expect me to cry foul tomorrow, I won't. No regrets, Achilles." She inhaled a deep breath and tilted her head, studying him. "Now, if you'll let me go, we can get out of here. I can grab a room at whatever hotel you're staying at for whenever we're...finished for the night."

"Finished for the night," he enunciated, a note of incredulity imbedded in his voice. But in the next instant it was replaced by a darker, hungrier tone that vibrated through her, thrumming in her breasts, low in her belly, high in her sex. "What dickless wonders had you in their bed and were satisfied with being *finished for the night*?" He snarled those words with such a healthy dose of scorn that even if she'd suddenly lost her hearing she wouldn't have missed it.

Maybe she should've been embarrassed at his astonishment. But the fact that he seemed insulted on her behalf and angry at the men who'd shortchanged her alleviated some of the sting.

"I think..." She cleared her throat, but the lust thickening her voice didn't evaporate. To hell with it. "I think you should stop talking so we can get out of here and go catch a cab."

He made a sound low in his throat that could've been a laugh or a grunt.

Both had warmth spilling inside her.

Both had her chest squeezing tight.

Both had danger alarms blinking like warning signs on an unlit road.

And allowing him to guide her from the bar, she didn't heed them.

Three

For the first time since arriving at the luxurious five-star
hotel with its over-the-top decor, Achilles was thankful
for the arrangements his father's estate had made. While
he still cringed at the floor-to-ceiling windows that had
him itching to yank the drapes closed against the Boston
skyline and terrible feeling of exposure, Mycah no doubt
appreciated the panoramic view.

What would she think of his cabin? Or the mountains
that surrounded it? Would she appreciate the beauty there?
Or would the silence, the solitude, the lack of amenities
bore her inside a couple of days?

He mentally shook his head. Why was he even entertaining those questions? They were pointless because
this—Mycah in his hotel room, the sex that would happen—
wouldn't go past tonight.

But they did have tonight.

And from the moment she'd stood up from that stool,
confirming every fantasy about her body, he'd been ex-

ceedingly grateful to deities both Christian and pagan for
tonight.

As she glided across the sunken living area into the
dining room, the lights from the crystal chandelier hitting her tight, raw-honey curls, his hungry gaze dropped
to the sensual sway of her round hips. To the tight perfection of her full ass. The thickness of her thighs. And when
she peeled off her suit jacket, laying it over the back of a
dining room chair, his fascinated stare rose to the pull of
material across her breasts. His fingers curled, straightened. He didn't even have to close his eyes to imagine the
feel of her undoubtedly firm yet tender flesh.

Unbidden, like an animal scenting its mate—there he
went again with the fanciful shit—he followed her. But
not to touch her, even though the need to do so rode him
hard. Like a child with sticky fingers and his face pressed
against a candy store window, he enjoyed looking at her.
Because no matter how much he wished it didn't, her
beauty captivated him. Dark brown, heavily lashed eyes
that seemed full of secrets yet brimming with a vulnerable
truth. Arrogant cheekbones, a patrician nose, stubborn but
delicate jaw and chin, and a carnal mouth that he couldn't
stop staring at. Couldn't stop picturing working him over
until he trembled and begged…

"Do you want me to get rid of my clothes so they don't
remind you of who I am? Would that make this easier for
you?" she asked, turning away from the wall of glass, her
fingers fiddling with the top button of her nearly sheer
shirt.

A teasing note infiltrated her voice, but he caught the
hint of stiffness beneath. The…insecurity. And he'd put
it there with his words, his personal hang-ups. It was his
responsibility to erase that doubt. It didn't belong between
them. Not here. Not tonight.

"Is that what you think?" He edged closer, cocked his head. Pinching a curl, he tugged it and watched as heat flared bright in those chocolate eyes and her carnal lips parted on a soft gasp. "That you can just strip off that suit, slip out of those shoes and I won't be reminded of, what? How soft and delicate this skin is?" He rubbed the back of his finger down the satin of her cheek. "Of how cultured and sexy this voice is?"

He lowered his hand to her throat, necklacing the slim column. If she'd stiffened or shoved at him—protested the hold in any way—he would've released her. But she didn't. No, Mycah's lashes fluttered, and she slightly leaned into his palm, as if relishing the show of dominance. His cock jerked behind his zipper, blood roaring south to fill his flesh in a flood that left him almost light-headed. He ground his teeth against the lust that scalded him.

Inhaling, he dipped his head, dragged his nose up the tendon that ran along the side of her neck. "What? You think taking off your clothes will somehow erase this scent that's grace, woman…sex?" He shook his head, brushing his lips over the line of her jaw and nearly growling at the skin-to-skin contact. "No, Mycah. Stripping can't make me forget who you are. And it for damn sure wouldn't make things easier for me. Just. Fucking. Harder."

"Achilles."

"Yeah?" He grazed another caress over her jaw, her chin, unable to help himself. Not sure he wanted to.

"Kiss me. Please."

So demanding.

So polite.

And both had him crushing his mouth to hers in a greedy onslaught.

That first taste. It crashed into him like a meteor set on a collision course with Earth. Hot. Cataclysmic. Fatalistic.

She opened for him without hesitation, and he dived deep, taking immediate advantage. The kiss was...carnage. It left him wrecked, wide open and damn near shaking. He sent mental orders to his hands to be gentle on her hair, to not fist the strands so tight, to not pull so hard. But they didn't listen. They didn't loosen. Thank God Mycah didn't seem to mind. No, the opposite. From the hot, tiny whimpers that he swallowed directly from her greedy tongue, she appeared to want it...crave more of it.

So he gave it to her.

He tugged on those rough silk curls, hauling her head back, angling it and diving deeper. Consuming more. Leaving nothing untouched, undiscovered. Every lick, every suck, every lap stoked a need that crackled and raged. But he wasn't satisfied with burning in those flames. He wanted to be devoured by them.

Untangling one hand from her hair, he lowered it to her throat again, feeling the mad thrum of her pulse under his palm. Reveling in the rush of it. Because it was for him. He sent blood pumping through her, excitement and lust rushing through her. *Him.*

The knowledge lit up his veins, and he snatched his mouth from hers, ignoring her small cry of disappointment to latch on to that thin patch of skin. He tongued it, tasting the richness of her scent, grunting at the bite of her nails in his shoulders. His hips punched forward at that hint of pain, mating with the pleasure twisting and bucking inside him. He ground his cock against the soft swell of her belly, growling like an animal. His gut clenched, lust a vise clamping tighter. And tighter.

"Fuck," he muttered against her damp skin.

Lifting his head, he captured her mouth once more, unable not to. He *needed*... God, he hated saying that word even in his head. Hated that it was true. But he did. He

ached for her taste on his lips. Hurt for the cushion of her
flesh against his throbbing dick. Hungered for the almost
plaintive sounds that escaped her—that let him know he
wasn't in this struggle by himself.

Though it cost him, he levered back and away from
her. But just for a moment. Long enough to reach behind
him, grab a fistful of his shirt and pull it over his head.
Lips swollen and eyes hooded, Mycah watched him. And
as he dropped the bunched cotton to the floor, she lifted
her hands to the top of her own shirt, but he stopped her
with a hard shake of his head.

"Let me." With fingers that suddenly felt too big, too
clumsy, he plucked at the little pearl buttons, pushing them
through the corresponding holes.

His heart kicked against his rib cage in steel-toe boots
as he revealed smooth brown flesh encased in light purple
lace. All moisture fled his mouth, and he didn't stop until
he skated his palms over her shoulders, sliding her shirt
down her arms and to the floor.

"Fucking beautiful." The last word scratched against
his vocal cords as he traced a path along the pretty edge
where lace met skin.

Gooseflesh broke out where his fingertip tread, and he
jerked his gaze up to her face, amazement sparking inside
his chest. Yes, she'd allowed him to strip her of her shirt,
let him touch these gorgeous breasts, but still… Part of
him still couldn't believe it. Still wondered when she'd
change her mind.

"Whatever you do tonight," she said, grasping his
larger hand in her smaller, more delicate one and pressing it harder to her flesh, "don't treat me like I'll break. I
can take it, take you. Give me all of you, Achilles. Don't
hold back on me."

"You don't know what you're asking, Mycah, telling a man like me not to hold back."

As…ominous as that sounded, he'd gone into that bar to forget about his dead sperm donor, about brothers he hadn't known existed, about being forced into a world he wanted nothing to do with.

About being rejected, scorned by that world—again.

So yeah, he'd gone there seeking nothing more than to lose himself in oblivion—alcohol and sex. And that didn't lend itself toward control or setting limitations on himself. And once he got his mouth on that dusky valley between her breasts or that dip where her torso and thigh connected—or her dark, wet sex… Yeah, control would be a pipe dream.

Mycah shifted closer and lifted her arms, burrowing her hands into his hair, her nails scraping over his scalp.

"Do your worst."

He shuddered, at her words and at her touch. Pleasure streaked through him. Groaning, he gripped her hips and, hiking her in the air, nudged the chairs out of the way and set her on top of the dining room table. Her soft, startled gasp segued into a sharp cry as he bent over her and sucked a diamond-hard, lace-covered nipple between his lips.

His own low moan almost drowned her out, his mouth insistent, impatient. Ravenous. He pulled on the beaded tip, drawing on her. The pinpricks dancing across his scalp from her restless fingers only stirred him, encouraged him. With his free hand, he unsnapped the front clasp of her bra and quickly removed it, cursing as he cupped her flesh.

"Achilles," she whispered, twisting against him, thrusting her breasts into his mouth. "Please."

There was no way he could deny such a pretty plea. Switching to the other mound, he nuzzled the neglected nipple, then plied it with licks and sensual laps. By the time he finished, skimming his lips down her damp torso, her chest heaved, her stomach going concave under his tongue. But he didn't pause, couldn't. Not when passion and need swept him up in an undertow so fierce, he was powerless against it. Not when lust clawed and howled inside him like a voracious beast that demanded to be satisfied.

Not when he doubted he could ever be satisfied.

Even as the sacrilegious thought skipped through his head and his heart thudded in protest, he pressed a hand to her chest, gently urging her to lie back on the table. She watched him, a wary expression flashing across her face.

"Trust me?" Why he asked that, he didn't know. He didn't need her trust; that's not what tonight was about. But he didn't try to retract the question. Partly because, though it didn't make sense, he wanted it. He wanted her assent.

After a moment, she slowly dipped her head, sending relief coursing through him. "In this—" her gaze flicked down her bare torso to where his fingers lightly gripped the tab at her waist "—yes. I trust you."

It was enough.

In quick work, he freed her of the pants, taking her panties with them, pausing only to remove the heels from her slender feet. Placing fleeting kisses along her instep, he trailed a worshipful path back up her inner thighs. He closed his eyes, inhaling her earthy musk, savoring it. Craving it on his tongue.

"Achilles." Mycah cupped his head, her beautiful legs tightening around him. Preventing him from moving. "I haven't… I've never… I don't— Hell."

He stopped, settling into one of the dining room chairs as if having a woman spread out before him like a delicious buffet was a common occurrence. No, not a woman. Mycah. And there was nothing common about her. Trying not to stare at her trembling breasts with their beaded, dark nipples or the lush beauty of her thighs or the soaked, swollen folds of her sex was a struggle that defied human strength and veered into something out of mythological trials.

"You haven't what, Mycah? Had a man's mouth on you? Do you want me stop?" Jesus Christ, it might kill him—especially when he could *see* the evidence of how much she wanted him on her flesh—but he would. Cold anger pulsed inside him for the selfish pricks who hadn't given her this.

"No, of course I've…had a man's mouth on me. I can't believe I'm having this conversation with you while you're literally sitting between my legs," she muttered, pressing the heel of her palm over her eyes. She propped herself up on her elbows, curls wild around her face and shoulders, her face an adorable mixture of confusion and surprise.

"Do you want me to stop?" he asked again. Because to him—and his dick—that was the most important issue here.

"No," she whispered, her eyes glazing over.

"Then what have you never done, Mycah?"

"This." She waved a hand down her body, encompassing him. "On a table. With the lights so…bright," she finished, her voice containing a tinge of embarrassment. "Could we possibly go to the, I don't know, couch or bed, where I don't feel so…exposed? I mean, people eat on this table."

"No."

She stared at him. Blinked. "No?"

"No." He shifted to the edge of the chair, simultaneously gripping her hips and tugging her closer to the end of the table. "You told me not to treat you like you're fragile, like you'll break. Light won't break you. Pushing you out of a comfort zone won't break you." He pushed his face into the fragrant space where her torso and thigh met. Inhaled. Growled. "Like you said, people eat on this table. Well, so will I."

He dived into her.

Palming her thighs, he spread her wide and feasted on her. He dragged his tongue through her folds, losing himself in the sweet, spiced taste of her. Taking his time to lick and nibble. To explore and discover what made her legs tremble, that little bud of flesh flinch. What drew whimper after whimper. He became a connoisseur in everything Mycah.

Though his dick ached, he could stay here, his mouth buried against her, pleasuring her. An inane thought crept in his mind, there and gone before he could banish it: purpose. *I've found my purpose. Giving this woman ecstasy.*

"Achilles." Once more her fingers had found their way to his hair, tangling and pulling, holding him close. Her hips bucked, rocked, demanded. There existed no ambiguity about what she needed from him. "Please. I need…" A sound between a whimper and a cry escaped her but the abrupt flex of her ass telegraphed her request. "Please," she whispered.

Before, he'd thought her pleas pretty. This time, they shredded him. And that primal part of him that desired— hell, was *obligated*—to provide what she asked of him. Sucking the bundle of nerves that crested her sex, he thrust two fingers inside her. Deep. Hard.

She screamed.

She clamped down on him and, between his mouth and fingers, he gave her every measure of the orgasm, not stopping until she fell limp on the table. Her pants lanced the quiet of the room, and his harsh breaths underscored hers.

Fuck. Lust strung him tight, and if he didn't get inside her, he was going to snap.

He shot to his feet, the chair beneath him falling backward. With his body moving before his mind could fully deliver the order, he scooped Mycah up in his arms, cradling her. He calculated the distance to the bedroom, but his cock determined the couch was closer, and he headed there. Mycah didn't open her eyes as he gently deposited her on the sofa that was easily double the size of his at home. But he didn't remove his gaze from her while he quickly stripped his remaining clothes and boots, pausing only long enough to remove a condom from his wallet.

"Hey." He knelt beside the couch, cupping her face and tilting it, sweeping his thumb over her cheekbone. "Look at me."

Her lashes fluttered, then lifted. Satisfaction punched him in the chest when her pleasure-glazed brown eyes met his. Because he'd put that look there. The feeling was primitive. It was arrogant. But fuck if he didn't own it.

"You good? You still with me?"

She blinked, the haze clearing. Her gaze roamed over his face then lower, down his shoulders, chest and lower still, taking in his dick that stood at rock-hard attention. He didn't try to hide from her, fisting his erection, stroking it. Letting her see just what she did to him.

"Yes, I'm still with you." She reached for him, covering his hand with hers. Replacing his hands with hers.

A full-body shiver racked him as her delicate fingers wrapped around him, squeezed him. His head bowed, palms flattened on his thighs. And he watched her—watched her touch him. Undo him.

"Enough, baby," he ground out, gently sweeping aside her devastating fists. "I want to finish inside of you."

Picking up the protection, he ripped it open, swiftly sheathed himself and then climbed onto the couch. He crouched over her, one knee separating her thighs, the other planted on the floor. The head of his dick kissed the wet, tiny opening of her sex, and he shook from that barely there caress, yet he paused.

As much as it cost him, he gripped the arm of the couch and pressed his forehead to hers, carefully crushed his mouth to hers…and breathed Mycah in. As he parted his lips, slowly slid his tongue into her, he mimicked the action with his cock.

Thrust.

Penetrated.

Buried deep.

Heat. A liquid heat that scalded and had him drowning at the same time.

He clenched his jaw, his fingers curling around the couch's arm so tight they pulsed in protest. His muscles howled with the need to move, but the stranglehold she had on his dick… Too tight. Almost painfully tight. And too fucking perfect. He didn't want to break it.

Tearing his mouth from hers, he scattered hard kisses to the corners of her mouth, chin, cheekbones, temples, forehead.

"Talk to me, Mycah." He studied her, searching her face for any sign of discomfort. Her sex fluttered around his dick, as if acclimating to his width, his length. And he granted her that time. Still, before he did anything else, he wanted those words to move. "You okay? Tell me what you need from me."

Her tongue wet her full lips, and she met his gaze. "Don't hold back with me."

Groaning, he hooked a hand underneath her leg, and withdrawing until only the tip of him remained notched inside her, he thrust home. Their twin groans saturated the room, snapping his control. Her nails bit into his waist, and that added a flare of pain to the sensory overload that catapulted him into this erotic storm.

He didn't fight it. Didn't want to. No, he willingly became a part of it. He let go, sweeping Mycah up with him, riding her, fucking her with an abandon that should've alarmed him. And if he'd cared enough to slow down, to analyze why this woman affected him in a way no other did, he might've been scared. But he didn't slow. Didn't analyze. Didn't care.

Flipping them over together, he buried his hands in her curls, dragging her head down and fusing their mouths together as he slammed up inside her, urging her to take him even as he did the taking. And she obeyed that unspoken command. Her hips crashed into his over and over, she rose and lowered, doing a lewd dance that threatened to send them into the sweetest, dirtiest oblivion.

Mycah trembled, her sex quivering around him, and heeding that signal of a looming release, Achilles reached between them and circled that slick, swollen button between her feminine folds. Circled, rubbed. Pinched.

With a high, hoarse scream, she came.

And a couple of strokes later, he went with her.

Even as he hurled over that edge, he knew one truth...

Once wouldn't be enough.

Four

The elevator doors opened with a quiet hiss and Achilles stepped onto the executive floor of Farrell International. It'd been three months since he'd attended the reading of his *father's* will. He barely managed to suppress a shudder. God, even thinking that word still had a fist of disgust and anger lodged in the base of his throat. It'd been three months since he'd arrived in Boston to find out about Barron's death. Since he'd gained two half brothers. Since he'd become a billionaire who owned and ran one-third of an international conglomerate.

But in those ninety-and-some-change days, he'd yet to stop feeling like an impostor. Yet to stop feeling like the fifty-first part of a fifty-piece puzzle that the manufacturer mistakenly added to the box.

The Feral Farrell.

That's what they called him.

Not to Achilles's face. No, Boston's so-called polite

society and his older brother Cain's many business associates weren't brave enough to risk their reputation or bottom line to do something as stupid as blatantly insult a Farrell. Bastard or not.

More specifically, insult Cain, the rightful heir, the son Barron Farrell kept and acknowledged. They really couldn't care less about offending a man they didn't believe would be around a year from now.

They weren't wrong.

Sliding his hands into the front pockets of his suit pants, Achilles kept his gaze focused straight ahead, not glancing around and taking in the quiet but obvious wealth of the executive floor. It wasn't the first or the fifteenth time he'd been here. But the art on the walls that cost more than his entire cabin or the furniture that had most likely been handpicked by some interior designer who catered to celebrities and presidents alike unnerved him *every time* he stepped foot up here. Hell, even the smell would make a great candle labeled "Money to Burn."

Achilles silently growled, battling the urge to yank the tie from his hair, rip this restricting suit jacket from his shoulders and flip one of these desks like an enraged reality housewife. That would give these people a show. That's why they watched him like a hawk, after all. Waiting for him to lose his shit like an uncivilized sideshow act. Just so they could say, *I told you so. He's not like his brothers. Not like Cain, the heir. Or Kenan, the charmer. He's not one of us.*

Again... They wouldn't be wrong.

He wasn't Cain, who, unlike Achilles and Kenan, Barron Farrell had kept instead of abandoned, and trained from day one to run his international company. Achilles wasn't Kenan Rhodes, who, though he was another illegitimate son, had been adopted and raised by an influential and powerful Boston family.

No, Achilles was the ex-con, semireclusive bastard who preferred the company of code and computers to people.

There'd been only one time since he'd arrived in this city that he'd felt wanted…needed. As it often did, more than he cared to admit, his mind flickered with images of that sex-soaked night in a five-star hotel with a beautiful woman he was half-convinced he'd conjured up. Only the scratches he'd carried on his shoulders and on his waist and the chafing on his dick the next morning had proved to him that he hadn't. Those and the dreams that continued to haunt him like erotic wraiths all these months later.

How many times had he woken up, shaking with lust, back bowed, lips twisted in a snarl? How many times had he found himself searching the crowded streets for that familiar, stunning face? Or cocking his head, listening for a certain low, sultry voice?

One night. That had been the limit he'd set. And he didn't regret it. Because as his unconscious mind revealed, Mycah could've become an obsession with him. And he didn't need anything—not obligations, not promises, not brothers, not obsessions—holding him here when his year came due.

Nothing would hold him back. He would be free to return home, unfettered.

Fuck.

He deliberately inhaled a breath, quieted the riot of morose thoughts swirling in his head.

None of this mattered. None of it changed the fact that he'd promised to remain in Boston for a year to helm Farrell International with half brothers he hadn't known existed three months ago.

He'd made his billion-dollar bed and now he had to lie in it.

"Good morning, Mr. Farrell." Charlene Gregg, Cain's executive assistant, greeted him with a warm but professional smile as he approached her desk. "They're waiting for you in the conference room."

Achilles nodded and strode past her. Why Cain insisted on including him in these business meetings eluded him. Contract negotiations, board or acquisitions meetings... Having Kenan there since he was a marketing genius made sense. But Achilles? He couldn't give a damn about any of it. Just leave him to ride out the next nine months on the IT's eighth floor, where he'd carved out a place for himself, and he would be fine.

Clenching his jaw, he grasped the handle to the conference room door and pressed it down.

"...reputation precedes you— Here he is." Cain stood from one of the black leather corporate chairs that flanked the long wood table, Kenan rising, as well. "We were waiting on you to arrive before we started the interview, Achilles."

Achilles dipped his head in acknowledgment, quietly shutting the door behind him.

"Sorry. I had a call and was held up," he said.

Partly true. He'd been on the phone with one of the sales reps about possible new virus protection software, but it'd ended nearly a half hour earlier. It's what he'd started working on after the call that had consumed his attention and made him lose track of time. But he couldn't share that with Cain and Kenan. Not with anyone.

He moved toward the chair next to Kenan and avoided his younger brother's too-sharp gaze. God, for someone who constantly seemed to wear a smile the man was too fucking perceptive. It annoyed the hell out of him.

As if reading Achilles's mind, Kenan smiled wider, a gleam in his eyes. "No problem. We know how much you insist on attending these meetings, so we didn't want to go forward without you."

Thank God he'd been an only child for thirty years.

"Achilles, we were just starting," Cain said. The corner of his mouth twitched as if he were attempting to imprison a smile at Kenan's not-so-subtle smart-ass dig. Three months ago, Cain Farrell would've seared the paint off the walls with a scowl at Kenan's antics. But now, he fought back a grin. Funny what falling in love and getting engaged did to a man. Cain turned toward the woman rising from the seat across the table, sweeping an arm in her direction. "Let me introduce you to Mycah Hill. She's interviewing for the VP of operations position."

Mycah.

Shock, icy and rough, slammed into him. Every muscle in his body locked as he stared at the woman across from him. The woman who had let him lose himself in her body on several surfaces of a hotel room. The woman who, months later, refused to be evicted from his head.

Goddamn, she was…gorgeous.

As if Fate were having a slow day and decided to play a game of "Whom Can I Fuck with Now?" Mycah could've been plucked right from his memories and set down in this conference room. The same tight, honey-brown spirals that even now he could feel over his palm. The same beautiful face with its oval-shaped, dark brown eyes, sculpted cheekbones, lush, decadent mouth and delicate but stubborn chin. The same thick, curvaceous body that conveyed a sensual strength that had his chest squeezing and his dick hardening.

What the hell was she—what had Cain said her full name was? Mycah Hill?—doing here? No, wait. A job.

The position of vice president of operations. At the company Achilles owned a third of. His company. What were the odds she hadn't known?

Even if she hadn't been aware of his identity that night in the bar—and he believed she hadn't since the news about him and Kenan hadn't broken yet—she damn well did now. The media scrutiny on the sudden appearance of the two Farrell bastards had been hell since the funeral. And from the moment they met, Mycah had struck Achilles as a smart woman. And she wouldn't apply for a job without first thoroughly researching the company and its owners.

Yes, she would've walked into this building forewarned and armed with the information that she would be sitting across from the person she'd seen biblically naked.

That made one of them.

He narrowed his gaze on her, meeting those level espresso eyes. To her credit, she didn't avoid him. Admiration and anger tangled in his chest.

What was her plan now? Admit that she knew him? That she'd spent a night under him, over him, spread wide for him?

Or pretend that she'd never laid eyes on him before?

"Mycah, this is Achilles Farrell, our third brother, and Chief Digital Officer of our IT department," Cain continued with the introduction.

Mycah nodded, offering Achilles a polite smile. "It's a pleasure to meet you, Mr. Farrell."

So it was to be option B.

The well-mannered thing to do would've been to reply, but at the moment that was beyond him. He was too busy strong-arming the disappointment and anger barreling through him like a rampaging bull.

Which didn't make any sense.

This disappointment in her. This rage. He'd been more than aware whom he was taking to bed. Known that her pretty talk aside, that if he'd met her on the cobblestone streets of Beacon Hill in the light of day, she wouldn't have anything to do with his rough talk, rough hands and rougher demeanor. Her kind with their flawless pedigree, upper tax bracket, superior education and untouchable society.

Although, he'd proved just how…touchable she was, hadn't he? No matter how much she probably wanted to forget.

Too fucking bad.

Still, he dipped his head, rolling one of the executive chairs back and lowering into it. Kenan shot him an exasperated glance and Achilles returned it with an arched eyebrow.

"Since calling all of us Mr. Farrell could become a little confusing," Cain said, reclaiming his seat, as well, "why don't we go with Cain, Kenan and Achilles?"

Another smile from her, and Achilles curled his fingers into his thigh under the table, remembering how those lips had curled against his own. Had parted so easily and greedily under his own. *Shit.* He shifted his gaze from her to the wall of windows over her shoulder. This interview had to end before he did something monumentally stupid.

Like beg her to give him one more taste of that heady lavender-and-cedar scent…

"I can do that," she agreed.

"Great. Let's get started." Cain passed Achilles a folder, and with no choice he opened it, finding her résumé inside. "We've gone over your résumé, and I'm very familiar with your reputation, which is impeccable. Over at Ryland & Co., you were key in restructuring their policies and departments. Thanks to the programs and streamlined procedures you implemented, the company substantially created higher ROI as well as optimization of workflow. I have to admit, I spoke with certain management personnel over there, and they spoke highly of you and admitted that you helped attain growth and profit for the business. That's a glowing recommendation, but one I already knew. The question is—" Cain rested his forearms and clasped hands on the table "—why are you looking to leave Ryland to come here?"

Mycah didn't immediately answer, instead mimicking Cain's position and meeting his steady gaze, before making visual contact with each of them. Though his eye contact was shorter. Still, Achilles found himself leaning forward, impatient to hear her reply. This woman—professional, reserved, confident—he'd glimpsed that night in the dive bar. But damn if he wasn't reluctantly fascinated by this facet of her.

"Ryland is a good, stable company. I wouldn't have stayed with them for seven years, the last three in the position of VP of operations, if they weren't. But Farrell International isn't just good—it's the best. And here, *I* can be the best. I can start at vice president of operations, but that's just the beginning and not the end of where I can go. I've done all I can at Ryland, and one thing I can't abide is stagnancy. And—" she arched an eyebrow high, the corner of her mouth twitching "—there is the matter of the salary you're offering, which is almost double what I'm making now."

Kenan chuckled. "Honesty. I like it."

Cain cocked his head. "So you wouldn't be satisfied with the position of vice president of operations?"

Again, Mycah copied him. "Would you?" she retorted smoothly.

Cain slowly smiled. "No."

Ambitious. Probably ruthless. Achilles silently snorted. Why wasn't he surprised? Virtues both his half brothers would admire. Achilles had seen those same qualities in the inmates who'd come into the jail and desired to rule the pod, make life fucking miserable for the rest of them who just wanted to get through their sentence with their heads down and as little trouble as possible.

He didn't trust ambition. Didn't trust those who hungered for it and what it brought.

The rest of the interview progressed with no input from him and more questions from Cain and Kenan about her work experience, what she could bring to Farrell International, what she would implement, how she would handle certain business situations. Achilles sat back, wishing he could tune them out. Trying to ignore her presence.

But that was an impossibility.

Her voice vibrated inside him like a tuning fork. Her scent might as well have infiltrated the central air system because it seemed to circulate in the conference room, saturating the air. Why his brothers couldn't sense it confounded him.

He'd tried not looking at her, but... That hair. Those eyes. That mouth. Even her damn throat. There wasn't a damn part of her he could tear his gaze from. Wasn't a part of her he could stare at and not...remember. Not relive.

By the time Cain started to wrap up the interview, Achilles pretended not to notice Kenan's curious sidelong glances at his bouncing leg or the vise grip he had on the chair's arms.

The walls weren't closing in on him; he would've recognized the signs of a panic attack. After his release from jail, he'd suffered them often enough. Being locked in a six-by-eight-foot cell for hours on end could do that to a person. But this wasn't that.

No, what pressed in on him now was the weight of her indifference. What twisted his stomach and squeezed his rib cage was the loathing for himself because he fucking cared.

He needed out of here.

Shoving his chair back, he shot to his feet.

Cain frowned, concern darkening his blue-gray eyes. "Achilles, you—"

"I forgot about a phone call I'm expecting," he said by way of explanation for his erratic behavior. "It was nice meeting you, Ms. Hill."

He shoved the words out, and they emerged sounding scraped and rough. Nothing he could do about it. Just as he couldn't do anything about the bemused looks Cain and Kenan threw him. No doubt they were wondering if there was any truth to that Feral Farrell bullshit.

Especially Cain.

They were all in a better place than they had been when Kenan and Achilles first entered Cain's life, but Achilles didn't fool himself. A man as brilliant and as guarded as his older brother didn't allow wolves at his door without first having them at least collared. Cain would've had a background search done on Achilles. His brother had to know about his criminal background. About *why* he'd been locked up.

Unable to meet their gazes any longer—and definitely unable to look at the woman whose very presence drove him away—he strode out of the conference room.

No, that was a lie.

He fled.

Five

Mycah stared down at her new badge, her solemn image gazing back up at her. It belied the nerves buzzing inside her like a swarm of bees.

A day.

Only twenty-four hours after the interview with the three Farrell brothers, and Cain had called, offering her the position of VP of operations. Even though she clutched the badge that granted her access to the office building and executive floor, even though the company handbook and employee contract claimed space in her briefcase, part of her still couldn't believe she was now an employee of one of the most powerful, influential and wealthiest conglomerates in the world.

Her predominant emotion should have been joy or excitement.

Or definitely satisfaction.

A twenty-nine-year-old Black woman in a field dominated by older white men, and she was already making her mark? And this was just the beginning, as she'd told Cain Farrell. So yes, satisfaction should definitely be coursing through her.

But no. The main feeling that she had to lock her knees against, lest she crumble to the elevator floor in an undignified heap?

Relief.

Because as soon as she'd received that call, she could breathe again.

In the interview, Cain had asked about her reasons for wanting to work with Farrell International. She'd been truthful. But not fully.

After all, how could she explain to a prospective employer that she needed this job so that the huge stone wheel slowly grinding her rib cage to dust could finally, *finally* lift? And the name of that stone wheel?

Family.

Right. That wouldn't have gone over well. They would've all stared at her as if she'd suddenly sprouted six fire-breathing heads, then politely ushered her to the conference room door.

Well, maybe one of them wouldn't have. Maybe one of them would've understood.

She briefly closed her eyes, and an image of Achilles Farrell instantly appeared. Not that it required much to summon him to her mind. Physically, they might've indulged in a one-night stand, but mentally? Mentally, she'd conducted a three-month-long affair where he invaded her bed most nights, not leaving her dreams until he'd left her aching and wet—and empty. So damn empty.

Huffing out a breath, she shook her head, staring at the lit elevator button for the eighth floor. As it dimmed, the doors hissed open. Her heart thudded against her sternum, stomach twisting as she stepped out onto the deserted floor. She'd waited until after seven to access the building, checking with security downstairs to make sure the person she needed to see hadn't yet left for the day.

Preparing herself for coming face-to-face with Achilles for the interview had been difficult. And she'd still barely pulled it off. God, the power, the vitality the man emanated... It was a force that slipped under her dress to hum over her skin, skim over her nipples, dance over her belly, slip between her legs... She'd nearly rocked under it, betraying herself to Cain and Kenan Farrell.

Whether in jeans and boots or a perfectly tailored suit, Achilles was potent.

And when his lupine eyes had locked with hers?

She'd lost all thought. Well, not *all*.

Memories of how he'd laid her out on that dining room table to make a feast of her had bombarded her. Of how he'd carried her so tenderly to the couch before taking her so fiercely.

Of how he'd followed through on his promise of not being finished with her for the night.

She hadn't stumbled into her own hotel room until early the next morning, deliciously sore and tired.

And yet somehow, she'd met Achilles's gaze in that conference room and not revealed that she shook with those memories.

If her mother had been there, she would've beamed with pride over her daughter's ability to lie.

A dull pounding took up above her right eye, a sure sign of a pending migraine. The sooner she got this task over with, the better. She started her position at Farrell International in a week. This wasn't a conversation she could avoid.

The thick carpet silenced the footfalls of her heels as she approached the closed office door. The open blinds on the windows offered her an unfettered view of the long-haired, wolf-eyed giant frowning at the bank of computers on his desk. She stuttered to a halt, her breath catching in her throat. He was so, so... So damn *too*.

Too gorgeous.

Too virile.

Too sexy.

Too wild.

He was the eye of the hurricane, a false calm. One shift, one step either way, and he would devastate you with all that he was.

And God. She closed her eyes, pinched the bridge of her nose. She needed to lay off the late-night Netflix binges.

She lifted her lashes and a bright gaze immediately ensnared hers.

Lowering her arm, she deliberately exhaled.

Hell.

Fixing a smile to her face that felt brittle and fake, she forced her feet forward and opened the closed office door. He rose from his chair, as if the good manners of standing for a woman were reflexive rather than voluntary. The scowl creasing his forehead remained.

"Achilles." Wonder whispered through her that her voice didn't tremble. Because, damn, that glare could burn hydrogen off the sun.

"Kenan told me you were hired. Congratulations." The flat tone carried no sarcasm, no venom, no...nothing. And that bothered her. More than she wanted to admit.

"Thank you." She hesitated, studied him. "You didn't...?"

"Have anything to do with the decision?" he finished her question, then shook his head. "No. I told them whatever they decided was fine with me."

Once more, relief rushed through her, and she glanced

away from him. The last of her uncertainty that she hadn't earned this job on her own merit faded away.

"Is that why you're here?" He circled the desk and leaned back against it, crossing his arms over his wide shoulders. She pretended not to notice how the sleeves of his plain white dress shirt strained against his powerful arms. Pretended not to notice the corresponding pull low in her belly. "To make sure I didn't influence the outcome?" He cocked his head. "Or to make sure I did?"

Hurt, dagger sharp and bright, pierced her chest, and she blinked against it. "Is that what you really think? That I wanted you to use our past…association to give me this job?"

"Why are you here?"

Another flash of pain. But this time, she buried it beneath a sheet of ice. She'd learned the coping mechanism early; with parents like hers, she'd acquired defensive skills that would impress a five-star general. If she survived Laurence and Cherise Hill, she damn well could endure this conversation with Achilles Farrell.

"To clear the air. If we're going to be working together—if I'm going to be a vice president for your company—we need to be on the same page. Especially about where we stand as far as being employer and employee."

"Make it plain, Mycah. You're not going to be fucking the boss, and you don't want anyone to know that you have in the past. Is that what you're saying?"

How was it possible to go up in flames that were equal parts embarrassment and lust? It seemed like he twisted everything she said to him. But God, just hearing him growl the word *fuck* and recalling his saying it to her at another time under very different circumstances…

She shook her head. "Look, Achilles, can we start over? It seems like I keep offending you—"

"Why did you pretend not to know me yesterday?" He pushed off the desk, straightening, but he didn't come near her.

Shame flickered through her, and she forced herself to meet his gaze. She'd like to say that she was an honest person, and at her core, she believed she was. God, she had to cling to that belief. But in her family, lies had their many uses. For her parents, lies were tools, a stock in trade. For Mycah and her sister, they were a necessity for survival.

And that's what yesterday had been.

Survival.

"I'm sorry that I misled your brothers—"

"You lied."

"I lied," she murmured. Exhaling a soft breath, she spread her hands out, palms up. "And I'm sorry for the position it put you in. I really am, Achilles." She shifted closer to him, but the ice in his eyes warned her not to come nearer. A shiver worked its way through her. With effort, she forced her hands to her sides instead of rubbing them up and down her arms to ward off the chill. "I'm not asking you to understand or accept my reason, but I'm a woman in a male-dominated business. Even with all my education, the successes that I can recite alphabetically and chronologically, if anyone discovered that I'd had sex with an employer or supervisor, none of what I accomplished would matter. I would be seen only as the woman who made it to the top on her back."

Achilles didn't reply, but he jerked his chin at her, and she took that as the universal man sign to continue. Sighing, she ran a hand through her curls.

"I don't know if your brothers would've fallen into that misogynistic category, but I also know I couldn't chance it."

Because she needed this job.

Not just because she desired to bust through a glass ceiling.

Not just because of the prestige of being an officer with a company that consistently appeared on the Fortune 100.

No, she desperately needed this job because of family. Specifically, her parents.

While the Hill name might belong to old wealth and an older lineage, thanks to Laurence and Cherise's overindulgent lifestyle, the quarterly business profits of their family company couldn't support them. And so, her parents had come to depend on Mycah's employment—or rather her salary—even as they derided her for that dependence. They considered her job common; it shamed them. Yet they expected her to foot the bill when their allowance ran out. What was an overdue mortgage or car payment or the household staff's salaries going unpaid when the living room had to be redesigned with what was au courant? Why should they concern themselves with inconsequential bills when they had her to cover them?

If it were just them, she might say to hell with it. But it wasn't just them. There was Angelique. Her brilliant fifteen-year-old sister had started high school this year. And not just any high school. A prestigious private academy whose academics rivaled Harvard—and so did the price tag. But she deserved every advantage. And for Angel, Mycah would willingly pay...

Even if it meant continuing to foot the tab for their parents, too.

The throb above Mycah's right eye intensified, and she caged the impulse to rub it. At one time, she'd willingly stripped naked in front of Achilles, had been as vulnerable as a woman could be with a man. But that was then, not now. She couldn't afford to be weak, exposed. This man, so unlike the one who'd taken her mouth even as he'd tenderly and passionately taken her body, offered her no quarter with his merciless stare. He sought a flaw to exploit.

"Was lying the only length you were willing to go to?" He moved forward, closing the distance between them.

He stopped just short of looming over her, but still near enough that his pine-and-fresh-rain scent wrapped around her, invading her nostrils. Since not breathing wasn't an option, she had no choice but to inhale him, dragging him into her lungs. She remembered how his sex-dampened skin tasted on her tongue.

Damn.

Shaking her head to rid her mind of those thoughts, she murmured, "What are you talking about?"

"You're too intelligent not to have researched the company. You had to know there'd at least be a chance I would attend the interview. Ambushed, Mycah. That's what I felt. But was that your plan? What would've happened if you hadn't been offered the job? Would blackmail have been the next step?"

Outrage scorched a path from her stomach up to her throat, temporarily incinerating her ability to speak. Hurt fueled the flames. She didn't deserve that—she *didn't*. And damn if she'd take it.

"You're correct," she said quietly, straightening her shoulders. "I did research Farrell International. But I didn't need to do any regarding you and Kenan Rhodes. I was well aware of who you both were since the media has covered you ad nauseam over the last three months."

The anger continued to simmer inside her, and maybe it fed a vein of recklessness as she shifted forward, eliminating even more space between them. Something flickered in his eyes, but he hid it behind a hooded expression before she had a chance to decipher it.

"I've apologized for not being truthful in the interview, and I'll do it again if you need me to. I'm sorry. But I won't apologize for some imaginary extortion plot that I had no intention of carrying out. I don't know whether to be offended or flattered that you've given me credit for something so ingenious. Criminal and devious, but ingenious, just the same." She tapped her bottom lip, narrowing her eyes. "Oh, wait. Offended." Then, she leaned into his space, cocking her head, and refusing to allow the anger or the pain to reverberate in her voice. "Why do I have the feeling that I'm once again being punished for the actions of another woman?"

His nostrils flared, and this time she had no trouble cracking the mystery in his gaze. Because it mirrored the same emotions zigzagging through her. For a second, she almost regretted her question. Almost lifted her hand to cup his lean cheek, tell him she didn't mean to pry, to forget she asked.

Almost.

But if he could lob bombs, then so could she. And she would be lying *again* if she claimed not to want the answer.

Not that she expected him to give it to her.

Besides, if he offered her an explanation, she might be expected to tender one in return. And damn if she was going there.

"You came looking for me for a reason, Mycah. I'm beginning to suspect everything you do has an agenda. So get on with it, because I have work to get back to. What do you want?" he rumbled, taking a step away from her.

She detested that one step felt like a rejection.

A slap.

"I didn't want...this," she said, waving a hand back and forth between them. Suddenly she was tired. And sad. So inexplicably sad.

"I could've saved you a trip." He turned away, striding back behind the desk. For a moment, he studied the monitors in front of him, a frown creasing his brow. As if she'd been forgotten, dismissed. But he glanced up at her, his blue-gray gaze pinning her to the spot. "When I didn't say anything at your interview, that was me agreeing to never bring up our past—how did you put it?—*association* again. Believe it or not, I understand your reasons for not being honest. I get it. I also get that you want to make sure what happened between us in the past stays there. No slap and tickle with the boss. Got it. My mother was a waitress who worked twelve-hour shifts on her feet in a diner delivering food to truckers who thought her ass was on the menu along with the steak and eggs. And then, as if dodging handsy customers wasn't enough, she had to deal with bosses who believed she was fair game because she was a single mother who desperately needed that job. So no, you won't be getting that shit from me." He arched his eyebrow. "So if that's it?"

Only a fool would think he was inviting more conversation. And while a number of things could be attributed to her—liar, masochist, walking ATM—fool wasn't among them.

Nodding, she pivoted on her heel and exited the office. What else could she say? He'd nailed why she'd approached him—to establish a working boundary for them.

And yet...

Yet she left feeling as if gauntlets had been cast down and swords drawn.

Why did she sense this would be war?

Six

"How's the second semester shaping up, Angel?" Mycah asked her sister, leaning back in her chair as Beth, one of her parents' staff, ladled lobster bisque into her bowl. Mycah murmured her thanks at the young blonde. Picking up her spoon, she nodded, smiling at her little sister. "Last time we talked you were telling me how much you were enjoying your computer science class. Is that still going well?"

Angelique quickly patted her mouth with her cloth napkin, beaming at Mycah. "I am *loving* it! Ms. Ferrara is amazing and I'm learning so much from her." Angelique leaned forward, dark brown locs almost skimming the lobster bisque as she gushed over her favorite teacher. "And guess what?" she nearly squealed. Not allowing Mycah time to speculate, she charged ahead. "We're developing our own computer games! How cool is that, right? Ms. Ferrara said colleges and future employers will look at our portfolio of games as evidence of our design ability, so high school is the perfect time to begin building it. We're going to download the Unity engine—"

"Angelique, please," Cherise Hill interrupted, a slight snap in her voice even though she didn't raise it. A lady never, *ever* raised her voice. That was a sign of poor manners and upbringing. As was vulgar language, laughing too loudly and showing up to an event uninvited. "Eat your dinner before it gets cold. Now, Mycah," she said, an ingratiating warmth infiltrating her words as abruptly as a light switch being flipped, "this is the first time you've had dinner with us since you started working at Farrell International. Our feelings have been a little hurt that you haven't been by to tell us about your new job."

Irritation crept through Mycah, and she tightened her grip on her spoon. She saw the embarrassment and pain that flashed across her sister's face before she bent her head, her locs swinging forward. Mycah shot her mother a glare, a hot rebuke burning the tip of her tongue, but at the last instant, she extinguished it. Not only would Cherise deny how dismissive and hurtful she'd been to her youngest daughter, but bringing attention to her bad behavior would only mean negative consequences for Angelique. Consequences Mycah was very familiar with—arctic silent treatments, ostracism or cutting criticisms.

No, if she could help her sister avoid that, at least for tonight, then she would.

Her heart ached with a yearning to reach across the table and pull Angelique into her arms. She crossed her ankles to keep herself seated.

"Well, starting with a new company, becoming acclimated to the culture there and learning my responsibilities, has been a little time-consuming. But in my defense, you haven't shown an interest in my job in the past. I didn't think you would be interested now."

Yes, it was a dig. One she should've been above. But she wasn't.

"That was before you started working for Cain Farrell," her father said from the head of the table.

Laurence believed in coating shit in sugar and talking out both sides of his mouth with other people, but not with his daughters. With business associates or guests at the endless parties he and Cherise attended, those dark brown eyes would glimmer with humor. But with his daughters, that gaze sliced with the precision of a surgeon's scalpel, exposing insecurities, faults and failures.

In spite of her employment helping to maintain their lifestyle, apparently, her job only *now* had any worth because of Cain. Because the Farrells were Boston royalty. If the Hills were considered earls or viscounts, then the Farrells were powerful dukes. And Mycah had suddenly become her parents' "in" to that rarefied circle.

Unease swirled in her belly like sour alcohol. She set her spoon down beside her bowl.

"Have you met Cain Farrell yet?" her father demanded.

"Of course," she said, keeping her tone level. Revealing her disquiet to her parents would be like throwing bloody chum into shark-infested waters. "I interviewed with him."

"And?" Cherise raised a perfectly arched brow.

Mycah blinked at her mother. "And I got the position of vice president of operations."

"Being deliberately obtuse doesn't become you, Mycah," her mother said, ice dripping from each syllable. "I have one daughter who is wasting the money we're paying for that exclusive school by focusing on computer games. And when our other daughter—the one who is pushing thirty and is still unmarried and doesn't even have any prospects—finds herself in front of a single, handsome billionaire, all she cares about is a *job* instead of a potential husband."

"Do you understand the influence, the power, the business a match between you and Cain Farrell could bring to Hill-Harper Inc.?" her father asked.

Hill-Harper, a holding company that had been founded by Mycah's maternal great-grandfather, enjoyed a respectable, conservative reputation here in Boston and nationwide. But for someone who only visited the office two or three days a week and was more or less a figurehead, Laurence always sought more. More wealth, more connections, more renown. And he viewed his daughters as tools to achieve his goals. "For a woman who claims critical thinking as one of her best skills, you fail to see the big picture here. The most advantageous picture. Fine, get your foot into the door with this *job*. But that isn't the endgame. Cain Farrell is."

Jesus Christ. Briefly closing her eyes, Mycah leaned back in her chair. Silently counted to ten. Fifteen. Stopped at twenty. Ticking off numbers wasn't going to calm her when dealing with her parents.

Mycah inhaled a breath, held it, then slowly exhaled. "One. I went to Farrell International to interview for a very important position that would benefit my career, not to scope out a husband. Two. Even if I weren't a professional, it would've been pretty difficult to flirt, hit on or climb over the conference room table and sexually harass Cain Farrell as his two half brothers were also in attendance. And three—and perhaps most important—Cain Farrell is engaged to Devon Cole. And has been for months. Which you both very well know."

Cain's sudden fairy-tale-esque engagement to the little-known Devon Cole had taken Boston society by storm. Some people had doubted the relationship, giving it mere weeks before Cain broke it off with the pretty but unassuming woman who worked at a local community center. But three months later, they seemed as in love as ever. Even more so.

Making her parents' assertion that Mycah romantically pursue Cain even more ridiculous.

"That little nobody?" Her mother waved a hand, laughing, the tinkling sound all the more cruel because of its beauty. "Please. He can do better. All he needs are options."

"So you've met the famed Farrell bastards?" her father asked, a smile curling his mouth. A gleam entered his dark eyes, lines fanning out from the corners, and he barely noticed as Beth cleared his bowl. "What was your impression?"

The Farrell bastards.

God, she hated that stupid, disrespectful name. With a passion.

How high society had taken such glee in salivating over news of Barron Farrell's illegitimate sons. Achilles, a giant of a man with his long hair and tawny skin. Kenan, biracial, tall, with smooth brown skin, a close-cropped beard and a lean but powerful build. They both shared the same distinctive blue-gray eyes of all the Farrell men, though, including their brother, Cain.

"They were fine," she said flatly, trying to dissuade him from the topic.

"Frankly, I'm surprised he let them sit in," Laurence continued, not discouraged by her tone at all. He chuckled, and it held an ugly undertone familiar to Mycah. "I know Barron's will stipulated Cain had to keep those two on at Farrell International for a year, but to include them in business decisions? I can almost see Kenan Rhodes since his family actually runs a company, even though it's nowhere near the level of Farrell. But that other one?" He shook his head, his grin widening.

"The Feral Farrell?" Cherise chimed in. "All that long hair and that hideous beard? And have you seen how big and...coarse he is? I don't care if Cain stuffs him in a suit—he's not fooling anyone. He looks like a thug."

"Did that one speak in the meeting?" Laurence snickered, leaning back as Beth set down his plate filled with filet mignon, sautéed asparagus and risotto. "Or did he just grunt?"

Her mother's laughter joined Laurence's, and it pounded against Mycah like pebbles striking her skin. Anger brewed inside her chest, a raging storm gathering wind and speed. And underneath...currents of shame coiled. These were her parents. She wasn't responsible for their actions, for their snobbery. But that didn't stop her from feeling tainted.

Sullied.

You don't know him.

She wanted to hurl those words at them. To make them understand and see the intelligent man who could be tender yet defensive, sensitive yet guarded. She'd glimpsed those pieces of him even as he actively shut her out. And just from the shreds of information he let slip about his past—only to be surrounded by people like her parents—she didn't blame him for those rock-solid walls topped by barbed wire.

Hell, she had her own barriers designed to prevent others from getting too close. Because people, starting with her own parents, had taught her that when they did, it was with an agenda.

Yes, she had trust issues.

Scanning her parents' smirking faces, she didn't have to wonder why.

Shaking her head, she pushed back her chair and rose from the table. "If you'll excuse me," she said, setting her napkin next to her forgotten bisque.

"Where do you think you're going?" Laurence frowned. "Dinner isn't over. And we're not finished talking to you about this new job."

"I'm afraid I am through, though." Mycah injected regret into her voice that was pure bullshit, but the alternative—revealing to her parents that their jabs at Achilles sickened her—wasn't an option. "I just remembered I have an early meeting to prepare for. I'll make sure to come by next week for dinner. I'll call you later."

Before they could object, she strode from the room, ignoring her father's strident calling of her name. Neither of them would pursue her. Not only would they refuse to grant their staff anything to gossip about, but etiquette would keep them in their seats. And nothing—not even a fleeing daughter—trumped etiquette.

Sometimes Mycah detested their devotion to manners.

Then sometimes she was grateful for it.

Like now.

Within moments, she accepted her coat from their butler and stepped into the frigid January night. She paused on the top step of the Back Bay mansion and breathed deep.

How sad was it that she didn't inhale the scent of crisp air as she walked away?

No.

All she tasted was freedom.

Seven

Achilles plowed his fist into the punching bag, sending it spinning away and swinging back. He struck it once more, the power singing up his arm and into his shoulder. He welcomed the vibration that carried a subtle, sweet burn. He sought it, chased it as he pummeled the bag again and again until his arms trembled with fatigue and sweat dripped off his face and bare chest.

The gym in Farrell International had quickly become Achilles's favorite area of the building, next to his office. In both places, he lost himself either in code or in the numbing exhaustion of exercise. He could lock himself away… lock everyone else out. Even Cain and Kenan.

Guilt flickered in his chest, and he smothered the urge to rub at the spot, as if he could erase it like a smudge of dirt. If only it were that simple.

He scowled, stalking over to the weight bench where he'd left his towel and bottle of water. Snatching both up, he wiped off the perspiration and downed almost half the water. At seven o'clock at night, he had the place all to himself. After a long day at work, most of the employees champed at the bit to leave. Not him. He delayed going back to that luxurious penthouse that had come with the appointment of co-CEO. Luxurious and cold. Three months he'd lived there, and he still felt like a squatter. To be fair, though, he had no desire to be there.

The cavernous apartment with its floor-to-ceiling walls, fireplaces huge enough for a man his size to stand in, a kitchen that would make Emeril Lagasse weep in envy, a library that his mother would've wrestled Belle to get...

It didn't make sense that he could live in a place so huge and still battle claustrophobia.

Nine more months.

That had become his mantra.

Nine more months, and his promise to Cain would be fulfilled. And then he could return to his cabin. His life. His peace.

Twenty minutes later, showered and dressed in battered but comfortable jeans and a long-sleeved T-shirt, he moved behind his desk, his mind already focused on work. Not for Farrell, though. No doubt it violated about ten company rules, but he used his after-work hours when all the rest of the staff had gone home to return to his pet project—the one he'd been laboring on for over a year now.

A high-fantasy, open-world, action-adventure video game geared toward at-risk youth. With world building that was a cross between the inner city and Middle Earth, he aimed to challenge players, teach them teamwork, decision-making, discipline, problem-solving, to think outside the box.

Six months of that year had been working with a psychologist on Achilles's mission and figuring out what elements he needed to include in the game to reach the kind of youth he'd once been. The youth he'd met and lived with for two years while locked up. This game wasn't just a possible moneymaker for him; it was his passion. He didn't want to hear why it wasn't marketable. Or that while his ideals were laudable, they weren't realistic. That's why he hadn't told anyone about it.

He might now be a millionaire, living in a penthouse at the top of a high-rise, but that didn't expunge lessons learned from bullies' fists or slaps from his mother's boyfriends: No one cares how smart you are. Keep it to yourself.

Achilles sank into his chair, reaching for his mouse to bring up his programs on the three monitors on his desk. His fingers flew across the keyboard, and within minutes he became engrossed in the script.

"Hey, Achilles." A fist rapped the top of his desk, reluctantly dragging him out of the world of code. "I'm not above doing something completely immature to get your attention. We both know this."

Sighing, Achilles leaned back in his chair and met an identical blue-gray gaze. Kenan smiled at him, dropping into the visitor's chair, his long legs sprawling out in front of him. Unlike Achilles, his half brother still wore a dark blue, beautifully tailored business suit that appeared as fresh as if he'd just donned it minutes ago instead of hours.

"What're you doing here?" Achilles asked.

Kenan heaved a theatrical, loud sigh. "Aging well before my time worrying about you. I'm too young and pretty for these lines of concern to be etched in my forehead." He circled a finger over the nonexistent wrinkles. "So I'm asking you the same question. What are you doing here so late?"

Achilles snorted. Both at the dramatics and the deflection. Kenan might be better at hiding his ambition and hunger behind his charm and magnetic smile, but the other man didn't fool Achilles. Demons pursued his younger half brother, too. Achilles just didn't know Kenan well enough to identify them by name.

"Working." He jerked his chin up at Kenan. "Your turn."

"I'm wrapping up a couple of things." Kenan cocked his head and studied Achilles through shrewd eyes that belied his smirk. "But unlike you, Jan, I don't make a habit of burning the midnight oil. What gives?"

"Jan?" Yeah, he was stalling, but still... What the hell?

"Y'know, Jan. Middle child. *Brady Bunch.* 'Marcia, Marcia, Marcia!'" he chanted in an impressive falsetto. "You exhibit classic middle-child syndrome." He returned to his normal voice with a wide grin. Holding up a hand, he ticked off each point with a finger. "Unsocial behavior. I mean, instead of choosing an office on the executive floor with Cain and me, you purposefully chose to be down here in the basement in a closet."

"It's not the basement," Achilles muttered.

Ignoring him, Kenan continued, "Trust issues. In spite of Cain trying to include you in Farrell business and showing you he's trying to make an effort to build a relationship with us, you're as cold as a hundred years of winter." When Achilles arched an eyebrow at his *Narnia* reference, Kenan scowled. "What? I read. And third, and the one that will possibly get me thrown out of here on my really great ass, but I'm going to say it anyway..."

Kenan leaned forward, planting his elbows on his thighs, his gaze losing all hint of humor and trapping Achilles behind his desk. In this moment, Achilles sympathized with a butterfly mounted on a corkboard.

"You don't want to get too close to Cain and me. Hell, you probably have your plane ticket already bought for the one-year anniversary of the reading of the will when you can return to Washington. But whether you admit it to yourself or not, you want us as brothers. You're just afraid we won't want you back. Which is bullshit. Because we're not Barron. Or…" Kenan's mouth hardened, locking away whatever else he would've said, but the flint in his eyes remained. "Like I said, we're not Barron."

Achilles stared at him, stunned. And if he could move, then maybe he would've kicked Kenan out of his office as he'd predicted.

His brother's words echoed through him, pounding inside his head like hammers. He longed to lash out at Kenan, order him to mind his own business. To stay out of his. That DNA didn't give him the right to go digging around in his psyche or play armchair psychologist. Or better yet, to tell Kenan he didn't know what the fuck he was talking about. Not about the office. Not about trusting him or Cain. And damn sure not about wanting their love or brotherhood.

Achilles was doing them a favor by staying. Wasn't that enough? What more did Kenan want from him? It was all he had to give. All he was willing to give.

All he could afford to give, goddammit.

His breath roared in his head. It lifted and dropped in his chest.

Slowly, he straightened fingers that he hadn't even realized had curled into tight fists. And second by second, he deliberately relaxed his body. Only then did he dare to meet Kenan's steady gaze. He expected challenge or even smug satisfaction to be in that Farrell blue-gray gaze. Instead, a disarming and disquieting compassion greeted him.

Part of him would've preferred the smug satisfaction.

"I think somewhere in California, Dr. Phil is sighing in relief that his job is safe."

The corner of Kenan's mouth quirked, and he shrugged a shoulder. "He better keep an eye on that wife of his, though.

Robin's hot." Standing, he stretched. "I'm about to head out. What about you? Are you going to be here much longer?"

Saying yes would only invite more unwanted analysis so he shook his head. "No, I'm going to shut it down in a few minutes."

"In that case, join me for dinner."

Well, shit. He'd walked right into that one.

As if reading his mind, Kenan grinned. "You would be doing me a favor. My parents called and nagged me about not coming home in forever. With you there, they wouldn't dare air dirty laundry in front of a guest. It simply isn't done." Something flashed in his eyes, there and gone before Achilles could decipher it, but the grin remained. "Say you'll be my beard."

"As tempting as that sounds—" A buzz echoed in the room, and Achilles glanced down, noting the flashing red light on the company IT help line. Looked like someone else was working late, too.

Kenan snorted. "Huh. Saved by the bell. Literally. If only I had that excuse." He gave Achilles a mock salute. "Talk to you later, Jan."

Kenan strode out of the office with a chuckle. Glaring after him, Achilles picked up the phone and jabbed the blinking button.

"IT."

"Oh, thank goodness. I hoped someone was still there."

Oh. *Fuck.*

He closed his eyes, pinching the bridge of his nose. God hated him. Had to. Otherwise, why would *that* voice stroke his ear?

"Hello?" Mycah asked. "Are you still there?"

Lowering his arm, Achilles gripped the receiver tighter. "Yes, Mycah. I'm still here."

Her soft gasp echoed across their connection. "Achilles?"

"It's me," he said, impatience sliding into his voice. "What do you need?"

He didn't miss her brief hesitation, and he fully expected her next words to be "never mind." But this was Mycah.

"My computer just made this weird buzzing noise, then the screen did this even weirder staticky thing. I rebooted it, and now I can't find the most recent copy of the document I was working on. And I'm trying not to panic."

Trying and failing, because he clearly caught the thread of it in her voice.

"I'll be right up."

"Wait."

He paused, listening to her agitated breath over the line. "What?"

"You can't..." She emitted a sound that landed somewhere between a cough and a groan. "...you can't just tell me how to fix it over the phone?"

"No, I can't." He barely managed to swallow his snort. "What's the matter, Mycah? You have a problem being in the same space with me?"

"Of course not," she snapped. This time he didn't bother containing the snort. "Fine. See you when you get here."

The line went dead, and for a moment, he continued to hold the receiver to his ear. A grim smile curved his mouth.

He must be a glutton for punishment.

Because he could most definitely accomplish the task remotely, and with any other employee, he would've fixed her problem that way. But at the thought of seeing her, slivers of excitement stirred to life in his chest for the first time in two weeks.

Definitely a glutton.

Achilles ground his teeth together as he tried to focus on the computer monitor in front of him. And not on the woman behind him. Which was damn difficult to do when her lavender-and-cedar scent taunted him with what he'd once tasted but could never allow himself to have again.

Next time, he didn't care if he had to text her a Power-Point. He wasn't coming up here to this office.

"What're you doing again?" she asked, leaning over her his shoulder.

Not breathing wasn't an option. Dammit. "Locating your autorecovery folder to see if your documents are in there." His fingers flew across her keyboard. It sounded simple, but there were multiple steps required. He worked in silence, and in minutes found the folder. "What are the names of the files?"

Mycah pressed closer, her lush hip brushing his arm. He locked down a growl and forced himself not to flinch from the glancing touch that had lust blazing a path straight to his cock.

Employee. She was his employee now.

Off-limits.

Besides, she'd made it perfectly clear that their night together had been an aberration. For him, it had been, too. Because he'd been looking for a one-night stand and instead it'd ended up being the most intimate, emotional connection he'd had with someone in a very long time. And if that wasn't sad as fuck, then he didn't know what beat it.

Sadder still because he couldn't wrangle control over this need for her, even knowing she was a liar.

And not because she preferred to keep their relationship professional.

He hadn't misled her when he'd said he understood her reasons. He also hadn't meant to reveal all that he had about his mother, yet it didn't change the fact that he did get it.

No, she was a liar about the *why*.

And the *why* was always the most important.

"Damn, you are good," she breathed. "Those right there." She tapped the monitor. "'Release Policies and Procedures.' 'Operations Agenda Quarter One. Grisham Inc.'" She exhaled and it ended on a short burst of laughter. "Thank you, Achilles. I was a nervous wreck thinking I would have to re-create all of those files."

"You're welcome." He quickly pulled up the documents, then opened and saved them. "You should be fine now."

Shoving back her chair, he rose, but a small, delicate hand on his forearm might as well as have been a steel manacle, it stopped him that effectively. He stared down at that slim, long-fingered hand with its neatly polished nails. Branded. The heat, the intensity—it dug past flesh and seemed to scar. He fully expected to see the imprint of her palm on his skin when she removed her hand.

Yet he didn't move.

Because masochist that he was, he enjoyed the pain of the burn.

"Achilles," she murmured, hesitated. Then, as if remembering she still touched him, glanced down and lowered her arm. Didn't matter. The phantom imprint remained behind. "I was just about to, uh—" she stepped back, rubbed her arms up and down "—order food. Would you like to have dinner?"

He stared at her. Noted that she wouldn't look at him.

"Doesn't dinner cross the professional line you've drawn?"

That brought her head up, those gorgeous curls falling away from her face. And when her espresso eyes narrowed on him, something like satisfaction flared bright inside his gut.

He recognized it.

Had experienced it often when he'd grown big enough to fight back. And win.

The light of battle.

"Not when we're just two colleagues sharing a meal," she said evenly, though her gaze clearly ordered him to fuck off.

Did it make him perverse to be delighted by that visual middle finger?

Maybe.

But it was probably the lesser of two evils.

The second evil being his hard dick kicking against his zipper.

"One, we can never be 'just two colleagues.' Not as long as I'm me. People won't allow that." He planted one hand on her desk, fingers splayed wide, and gripped the back of her office chair with the other. Leaning forward, he said, voice low, "And two, you're a much better actress than I gave you credit for if you can sit across from me, talk about office gossip over chicken Parmesan and pretend you don't know how it is to have me swallow your moan as I push inside your body." He slowly shook his head. "Sorry. I'm not that good an actor."

Her eyes dilated, the pupils nearly engulfing the irises. "So you don't need friends?" she asked.

"Not you."

She barely flinched at the blunt answer, but he caught it. And part of him—the part that hadn't been cauterized in that jail and by the equally harsh life lessons that followed—almost reached for her. Almost cupped her jaw and thumbed the patrician slope of her cheekbone.

Almost apologized, even knowing she, an illustrious Hill, didn't consider him worthy enough of the word *friend*.

"Do you need anyone?" Mycah murmured.

The *no* hovered on his tongue, abrupt and definite in his head. But he couldn't utter it. Because as loud as the *no* roared in his mind, a small voice whispered underneath that it was a lie.

"Achilles—"

"Oh, honey, I'm so glad I found you," a feminine voice purred.

Surprise rippled through Achilles, and he stiffened, shifting away from Mycah and glancing toward the office door.

Mycah's mother.

He didn't need an introduction for her identity to be confirmed. Even if he hadn't done a deep dive on Mycah after the interview, it would've required only one glance at the older woman to determine their relationship. Though instead of her daughter's riotous curls, she wore her dark brown hair ruthlessly straight, they shared the same oval-shaped, chocolate eyes, elegant facial features and wide, generous mouth. The same smooth, brown skin. There were subtle differences, too.

A calculating hardness in her mother's eyes that Mycah hadn't yet adopted.

Faint lines fanned out from the older woman's mouth, as if she spent an inordinate amount of time with it pursed in disapproval. Which was a shame.

One day, would Mycah wear the same lines? Carry identical shrewdness in her gaze?

He glanced at her, and a weight settled on his chest. So heavy he fought the urge to rub it away.

"Mom." Mycah briefly met his gaze, and he caught a flash of emotion that on anyone else he would've labeled concern. But that couldn't be right. Why the hell would she be worried about him? "What are you doing here? At my job?" she asked, an edge in her tone.

Her mother laughed, a delighted, charming sound that grated across his nerves.

"To see my daughter, of course. Is that any way to greet your mother? Your friend will think we're heathens." She strode farther into the office, her arms outstretched.

If Achilles hadn't been studying Mycah so closely, he might not have noticed her hesitation, but he did observe the pause before she crossed the room and briefly embraced her mother, air-kissing both cheeks, then stepping back.

"That's much better," her mother admonished, brushing at the shoulder of Mycah's pale green shirt. "Getting you to return a phone call is a minor miracle, so you left me no other choice but to come hunt you down." Then, as if remembering Achilles's presence, she switched her attention to him with a warm smile. "I'm sorry for just barging in and interrupting. I'm Cherise Hill, Mycah's mother. And you are?"

"Achilles Farrell."

Recognition glinted in her dark eyes, and unease crept down his spine. Instinct warned that his identity hadn't come as a surprise to her.

"It's a pleasure to finally meet you, Mr. Farrell. You and your family have caused quite a stir these past few months." She approached him, her arm extended.

His chest tightened, everything in him repelling at the idea of grasping that hand, but despite the rumors circulating about his nature, he did have manners.

Enveloping her hand in his, he lightly squeezed it, then released her. "It's nice to meet you, Mrs. Hill."

"Hmm."

She studied him, and manners or not, he returned the favor. He knew her type, had come in contact with it even before arriving in Boston. If she expected him to cower and fidget underneath that analyzing, patronizing inspection, well, life was full of disappointments. The days when he bent for any man or woman were long gone.

"Mom, I'm sorry you had to come all the way downtown. But what is it that you needed?" Mycah pressed, drawing Cherise Hill's focus away from him and back to her.

Why did he get the sense that she had that maneuver down to a fine art?

"Well, like I said, if you'd have returned my or your father's calls, you would've known that we are planning a dinner party for a week from tonight."

"A party," Mycah repeated, tone flat. She crossed her arms, and Achilles frowned at the gesture that didn't strike him as annoyed but rather reeked of self-protection.

"Yes, honey, a party." Flint slid into Cherise's voice. "And consider this your official invite. And you, too, Mr. Farrell." She whipped around, aiming another of those hostess smiles his way, the warmth of it belied by the hint of frost in her gaze. "We would absolutely love if you joined us."

"Mom—"

"Thank you. I accept."

The words leaped out of him before he could cage them or consider the ramifications. But he didn't rescind them. Even when he noted the flicker of satisfaction in Cherise's eyes.

Even when he caught the glint of disquiet in Mycah's.

A glutton.

He was most definitely a glutton for punishment.

Eight

Pride goeth before a fall.

Jesus, how many times had Achilles heard that from his grandmother while growing up? And she'd immediately followed it up with "Don't be like your mother."

Achilles snorted. God knows Natia Lee had enough pride to have a few proverbs written about her. And he'd adored that about her.

Sighing, he nodded a thanks to the driver, who'd opened the back door of the sleek black Lincoln town car. Another amenity Cain had insisted Achilles accept. This one he didn't mind having so much as the others. The drivers in Boston were another level of crazy. And he didn't relish taking his life in his hands by getting behind the wheel among them.

"Thanks, Dave. If I don't call by ten, assume they have me trapped in the Sunken Place and send in reinforcements."

Dave snorted, closing the door behind him. "Will do.

In the meantime, try not to scowl too much and remember bathrooms are for pissing, not the carpets."

Achilles snapped his fingers before smacking his forehead. "Damn. Thanks for the reminder. I almost forgot that."

They looked at each other and snickered. After bonding over Seahawks and Patriots football, classic rap music and old mafia movies, the older man had become a friend in the last three months. Dave gave him a small salute, then returned to the car, leaving Achilles to stare up at the imposing Back Bay mansion. Unlike the other brownstones on the street, the Hills' home was composed of a white, marble-like material that stood out like Cinderella among the other belles at the ball. Large, intricate bay windows adorned three stories and even he, who knew nothing about architecture, could tell a fine and skilled hand had paid loving attention to the detail on the building's facade.

He approached the iron gate that separated the sidewalk from the property, and a black-suited staff member stood there. To let the guests in and bar the undesirables from entering, Achilles mused. And as he neared the man, he still didn't know which one the Hills considered him.

Minutes later, when he handed another young man his long wool coat, resignation filled him. His pride had dug this hole, and now he had to stand knee-deep in it. Three hours. He could get through three hours of small talk, drinks, dinner and mind-numbing boredom—

"Achilles."

He turned at the sound of his name and froze.

The air in his lungs stuttered, stalled. Hell, the air in the ornate lobby came to a halt, as if stunned into utter stillness.

Mycah.

He should probably turn away, stop staring. Stop devouring the elegant column of her neck and the bared length of her delicate shoulders revealed by the upsweep of her curls in a crown on top of her head.

Stop worshipping the beautiful mounds of her breasts that he could map blindfolded with his hands and lips. A black corset-style top lifted them, cinching in a waist that was already small and drawing attention to the feminine flare of hips that had his fingers flexing to grab, dig into...mark. The formfitting skirt molded to her gorgeous curves, thick thighs and strong calves. Impossibly high stilettos completed the stunning visage of a confident, sexy woman who could willingly and joyfully bring a man—or woman—to their knees.

Lust burned through him. He pulsed with it. And if chatter and laughter didn't echo down the corridor, he would have wrenched that tight skirt over her gorgeous hips, pressed her against the dark paneled wall and released it into her.

Goddamn, he hurt.

"Achilles." She neared him, the heels of those shoes clattering on the marble floor. "Thanks for coming. Are you...okay?"

Okay? No. Unless *okay* had suddenly become synonymous with *hard as fuck*. "Yes, I'm fine." Because he wasn't able to help himself, he flicked another glance over her, devouring her in one quick look that he hoped she didn't catch. "You look beautiful."

Her fingers fluttered across her bare neck, and he couldn't help remembering when his hand had been the only necklace she'd needed. Shit. He really needed to get himself under control.

"Thank you," she murmured. "You do, too."

He arched an eyebrow. "Beautiful?"

She met his gaze even though a tinge of red painted her cheekbones. "Yes."

They stared at one another, the air between them charged, vibrating with tension, riddled with unspoken words.

Never one who gave a damn about his appearance, for once, he'd listened to Kenan's browbeating and worn the slim-fitting black three-piece suit and ice-blue shirt and tie. He'd bound his hair back in a bun and, though he'd refused to cut his beard, he had allowed Kenan's barber to trim it. Spying the glow of appreciation and—a fist clenched in his gut—desire in Mycah's gaze, he was glad he'd put forth the effort.

"This must be our guest of honor."

The intrusion of the deep, cultured baritone dropped between them like the blast of an arctic wind after a balmy summer. Dragging his attention from Mycah, Achilles met the piercing hazel stare of a distinguished, tall, older Black man. Again, no introduction was necessary, although it would undoubtedly be forthcoming. Laurence Hill, president of Hill-Harper Inc. Mycah's father.

And just like his wife, he sent a frisson of disquiet skipping down Achilles's spine. Something in the eyes. In the too-wide smile. In the too-welcoming tone.

Lies.

He glanced at Mycah, saw her shuttered gaze. This family was built on lies.

"Laurence Hill." Mycah's father extended his hand toward Achilles. "Welcome to our home. We're delighted you could attend our little party."

"Achilles Farrell. Thank you for inviting me," he said, accepting the hand, and as he'd done with Laurence's wife, he shook and released it as quickly as possible.

"Of course, of course. When my daughter told us she

landed a job at Farrell International, we couldn't have been prouder. It's a company with a long history based on tradition and family. And family is everything, isn't it?" Laurence said.

The words were innocuous enough, but the voracious gleam in his gaze...

So this was what Achilles had to expect tonight. God, the rich. Rage and bile churned in his gut. But damn if he would reveal how this asshole angered him. That's what the man wanted. A reaction. Strip away the money, the lineage, the connections and nothing separated people like him from criminals in jail.

If they got a rise out of you—if they pinpointed your weakness—then they had you.

Well, fuck them back in County then. And fuck Laurence Hill now.

"Yes, family is important," he said, conjuring up an image of his mother and his grandmother to keep his voice even.

Without his conscious permission, another picture wavered in his mind. Of Kenan and him standing in the library of that Beacon Hill monstrosity Cain called a home, supporting their older brother as he purged an old wound about their abusive bastard of a father.

Family *was* everything.

"There you are, darling." Cherise Hill sailed up to their trio, beautiful in a gold cocktail dress. She threaded her arm through her husband's and smiled at Achilles. "Mr. Farrell, it's wonderful to see you again. Do you mind if we call you Achilles? After all, there are so many of you Farrells now. It could get confusing." She chuckled.

God, these people.

"Achilles is fine."

"Mom, Dad, if you don't mind, I'm going to give Achilles a tour of the house and introduce him to the other guests." Mycah mimicked her mother's hold and weaved her arm through Achilles's. "Excuse us."

Not waiting for their reply, she led him past her parents and down the corridor. They passed a curving staircase, a wide fireplace with a sitting area and several doorways that opened to luxuriously appointed, empty rooms. Tension emanated from her, and just as they paused in front of the entrance to a room filled with milling, formally dressed guests, she turned to him, tilting her head back and pinning him with a dark, unfathomable stare.

"Why are you here?" she asked, tone low, almost vehement. "Why would you come here tonight?"

He didn't pretend to misunderstand her questions.

"Because she didn't want me to."

Mycah blinked. Exhaled a breath that ended on a short, humorless chuckle.

"It amazes me how certain people continue to underestimate you," she said to herself, shaking her head. Then, pasting a replica of her mother's hostess smile on her mouth, she waved a hand toward the room. "Ready?"

No. Not in the least.

"Lead the way."

Stepping into what Mycah had called a great room, he couldn't rid himself of the sense of being on display. He'd once accused Mycah of staring at him like he was an animal in a zoo. He'd been wrong. As he circled this room with Mycah guiding him from person to person, group to group, he sympathized with those caged beasts. Felt the weight of curious, assessing eyes. Heard the murmurs and whispers. The three months in society with his brothers had taught him how to hold his own with polite small talk, but that didn't make it any less suffocating.

And Mycah had remained by his side through it all.

That had surprised him. He'd expected her to make a few introductions then leave him to mingle as she knew far more people in attendance than he did. But she didn't. She'd stayed glued to his side, refusing to abandon him.

The last person who'd done that had been his mother, when he'd been in jail.

He jerked his thoughts from going down that road.

He might be thankful to Mycah in this moment, but she had nothing in common with his mother. Nothing in common with him. They were from two different worlds. Wanted different things. All he had to do was look around this house to see what was important to her, to her family.

All of which he wanted nothing to do with.

"Does that happen often?" Mycah asked, passing him the whiskey he'd requested from the bartender.

"What?" He accepted the drink, sipping the amber alcohol and welcoming the burn it left in his throat and stomach.

"That." She dipped her head toward the small group of men they'd just left. "When you meet people, they use the opportunity to engineer a meeting with Cain or extract information about him."

He considered her over the rim of the tumbler, taking another sip. "Often enough." All the time.

"It pissed me off. As if your whole identity is comprised of being Cain Farrell's brother." Her full, sensual mouth thinned. "As if you're not a brilliant software developer and designer in your own right who was courted by one of the most popular and successful computer systems design companies directly out of college. You've won numerous industry awards and cash prizes that total more than five million dollars. Hell, you were a millionaire before you even arrived in Boston. But they don't bother to learn that about you. All they care about is your last name and

who your brother and father are," she fumed, fingers fisting her wineglass.

Achilles stared at her, shock ricocheting through him.
"You've done your research."

She glanced away from him, shrugging a slim shoulder. "My sister, Angelique, is a computer science whiz.
When she discovered I worked with you, she might've
raved about you. Fair warning. My parents didn't allow
her to attend this party, but I can't promise she might not
crash it anyway just to meet you. I'm not saying she's a
stalker, just very enthusia—"

"Mycah." He pinched her chin between his thumb and
finger, turning her head back to him. Her lips parted, trembled, and heat flashed in her dark eyes. "Thank you."

"For what?"

"For wanting to defend me." The corner of his mouth
quirked. "With information received from your stalker
little sister."

Mycah laughed, and he chuckled with her.

"Achilles, Mycah. Dinner is ready to be served." Cherise appeared next to them, her gaze zeroing in on his hand
still gripping her daughter's face. He slowly released
Mycah, turning to meet her mother's narrowed eyes. "As
our special guest, we've reserved a place of honor at our
table for you."

Achilles didn't trust that smile or the cold gleam in her
eyes. And forty-five minutes later, he knew he'd been right
to trust his instincts.

The "place of honor" was a seat at the far end of the
table stuck between the gallery owner with several failing shows on his left and the aging society maven on his
right... Or the maven would've been on his right if Mycah
hadn't insisted on switching with her much to the barely
contained fury of her parents. Achilles hadn't been privy

to the brief but furiously hushed conversation, but from the glares they'd shot his way, Laurence and Cherise had placed the blame of their daughter's etiquette rebellion squarely on his shoulders.

"So, Achilles, tell us," Cherise said, her voice clear and loud in the sudden silence of the dining room. Over twenty-five pairs of eyes focused on him, and though frigid skeletal fingers crept over his skin, he calmly met her gaze. "How are you enjoying Boston? It must be so different from… Seattle, is it? That is where you're from, right?"

Achilles set his spoon down next to the chocolate cherry mousse that had been set in front of him moments earlier and centered his attention on Cherise. Because only a fool didn't direct all his focus on a snake when he came face-to-face with one.

"I was born and raised in Seattle, yes, but I've lived in Tacoma for the past few years. As far as Boston, it's a beautiful city. Same as Seattle. They have their similarities. Some differences, too."

"Similarities?" Laurence chuckled, surveying his guests as if polling them. "How so?"

"Both cities have a lot to offer as far as culture, arts and business. Their histories are different but proud and they're rich in ethnically diverse neighborhoods. Classism exists, but for the most part, at least from my experience, the people are the heart of each city."

Only a lone uncomfortable cough from somewhere to Achilles's left broke the thick silence. Even from the length of the long dining table, he caught the tightening of Laurence's mouth and the flash of anger in his hazel eyes. But then he laughed again, leaning back in his chair.

Beside Achilles, Mycah stiffened, the cadence of her breath shifting. Almost as if she were warning him. But he didn't need her to caution him.

Italian suit or orange jumpsuit. Glenlivet or Wild Irish Rose. Socioeconomic differences didn't matter. Predators were predators. He'd been educated long ago on how to handle them.

And he'd graduated with honors.

"Still, this must be all so new to you. This world. *Our* world." Laurence waved a hand, gesturing toward the crystal chandeliers suspended above the table, his bejeweled guests. "Correct me if I'm wrong, but wasn't your mother a...waitress?"

Rage poured through him. When Laurence had said "waitress," the connotation had been synonymous with *prostitute*. The bastard had said it that way on purpose, seeking a reaction from Achilles. No doubt attempting to get the Feral Farrell to make an appearance for his guests. And from the low murmuring around the table—not to mention the smug smile Laurence didn't even try to hide—they were eating it up.

"Dad, this isn't—"

Achilles closed his hand over Mycah's.

"Yes, my mother was a waitress," Achilles said, none of the fury that roared inside him evident in his tone. "Just as your great-grandmother was a domestic. And your grandmother—" he glanced at Cherise "—was a server in a speakeasy." He ignored the gasps that echoed in the room and deliberately picked up his spoon and slid a serving of mousse into his mouth. He paused and savored it as if the dessert was the most delicious thing he'd ever eaten, but in reality, it tasted like a mouthful of ashes. "They were admirable professions that all three of us should be proud of because of the women who worked hard to provide for their families and made sure they didn't go without."

"Damn," Mycah whispered next to him.

Yeah, Achilles silently snorted. Damn. Computers were

his life, and there wasn't anything he couldn't do with them—or find on them.

"There's a big difference between your waitress mother and our ancestors, isn't there?" Cherise sniped, anger threading through her voice. "What happened with Barron Farrell? She must've thought she hit the jackpot when she met him. And yet she ended up stuck in some truck stop. Abandoned."

"Mother," Mycah snapped from beside him. "What the hell?"

Cherise gasped. "Mycah, excuse me?"

"No, I won't. Achilles is a guest in our home."

A sneer curled her mother's mouth, curdling her beauty into something spoiled, ugly. "Oh, please—"

"My mother was a single parent who worked her fingers to the bone to provide for her son. Because she loved me. She died still working and doing what I'd witnessed her do all my life—sacrifice so I could go further, do more, be better. She was the best person I've ever known. Did she believe she'd hit the jackpot with Barron? I don't know, since she never told me who he was and to my knowledge never received a check from him. Would she have liked to live like this?" He mimicked Laurence's earlier gesture and waved a hand toward the lavish room.

Meeting Cherise's and then Laurence's gazes, he compared them to parasites. Insects feeding on the labor, the sweat, the dignity of those they considered beneath them. Getting bloated until there was nothing left, and then preening as if they hadn't left destruction and carcasses in their wake.

"Possibly. Probably," Achilles continued. "But there's another difference between you and my mother. She didn't understand generational wealth or privilege. She didn't comprehend reaping the benefits of someone else's hard work simply because of the coincidence of birth and DNA. She believed in the efforts of her own hands and the satisfaction that comes from a hard day's work. So yes, maybe she might have enjoyed your beautiful home and your seven-course dinner—because she always loved great food—but I don't know if she would've stayed long in your world. She wouldn't have been content with being kept."

A silence so deafening rang in the room, it assaulted his ears. No one moved. Not even the servers, who stood behind the guests, their carafes of coffee frozen aloft in their hands. The stone of the mountains around his home possessed softer facades than Laurence's and Cherise's faces. That same flint hardened their eyes and Achilles didn't flinch from it. No, they'd sought to humiliate him, to tear down his mother in front of their guests. Undoubtedly, he'd made enemies of the Hills tonight, but he couldn't find a single fuck to give.

"We're ready for coffee, please." Cherise nodded to her staff, dismissing Achilles.

Or pretending to. The angry, stiff set of her shoulders contradicted her attempt to resume normal dinner conversation.

Everything in him demanded that he abandon this house and this farce of a party. He wasn't wanted, had never been anything but the planned entertainment, like a tragic circus clown. But pride kept his ass in the chair. Damn if they would run him from the table. He would stuff down the rest of this tasteless mousse and pretend just like them. Pretend that he belonged. Pretend that his skin didn't itch with the need to tear this suit off like the costume it was.

Pretend that all eyes weren't on him, watching, waiting… judging.

"Achilles." Mycah laid a hand on his thigh under the

table, and the muscle bunched so tight, it ached. "I'm sorry."

She was part of this world. Belonged here. And yet, dark heat radiated from under her palm. He hated his body in this moment. Detested that it responded even when his heart, his head wanted nothing to do with this place—with her.

"Let it go," he ordered, shifting away, dislodging her touch.

He didn't need her apology. Or her pity.

After another excruciating twenty minutes, he finally stood from the dinner table and escaped into the drawing room with everyone else. But he didn't stay. He'd done his penance for the evening.

Past caring what the Hills or other members of Boston society thought about him, he slipped into his coat in the foyer, not bothering to wish his hosts good-night. They could forgive him or not. Most likely not.

Again. Didn't give a damn.

And as he strode out into the January night, preferring to wait out on the curb in the frigid winter cold for Dave rather than spend another second inside that mausoleum of a house, he swore that would be the last time.

The last time he returned to this house.

And the last time he gave a damn.

Nine

Anger was a wonderful motivator. Shame a close second.

Enough of a motivator to walk out on the rest of her parents' dinner party, bear the brunt of their outrage, brave the freezing January night and the judgy eyes of this security guard.

Wasn't the security for multimillion-dollar buildings supposed to be of the see-nothing, hear-nothing variety? After hesitating too long, he picked up the phone and punched in numbers on the keypad.

"I'm sorry to disturb you so late at night, Mr. Farrell, but this is John Ward at the security desk. There is a young lady here asking to see you. A Mycah Hill." He paused, suspiciously eyeing Mycah as he nodded, listening to whatever Achilles said on the other end. "Right. I'll send her up, then. Thank you, sir." The guard hung up. "If you'll just enter your information here and sign in."

Mr. Ward slid a black registration book toward her and

flipped it open to a clean sheet, setting a pen on top. Moments later, she followed him to a bank of elevators. He slid in a key card to a private car off to the side and a pair of doors opened. Stepping forward, he pressed a button, and shifted aside, motioning for her to go inside.

"This will take you to the penthouse. Good night, Ms. Hill."

With that, the doors closed, and she rode thirty-two floors. In seconds, the doors opened once more, and she came face-to-face with Achilles.

It'd been less than an hour, but it might as well have been days. The impact of him slammed into her like a cudgel to the chest. He'd removed his suit jacket and tie, but the ice-blue shirt remained, and the black vest hung open over his massive chest, and the slim-fitting pants clung to his hips and powerful thighs. The hem broke over his bare feet.

God.

Why did the sight of his bare feet reverberate through her like two cymbals crashing together? Maybe because it reminded her of the man and the intensity, the raw strength barely leashed beneath the civility of the suit?

Maybe. Did it matter when her nipples tightened under the cups of her corset top and her sex swelled and dampened beneath her skirt? When her belly tightened, as if in hunger, but not for the dinner her parents had served nearly an hour earlier. Only the man in front of her could sate her.

She inhaled, swerving her gaze away from him, over his shoulder. To the relative safety of the apartment behind him. It served to distract her, because *good Lord*. She was used to wealth, but this… Just the glimpse of the expanse of glass, marble and stone had her softly gasping in amazement.

Achilles shifted to the side, silently inviting her in. He didn't speak, just slid his hands into the pockets of his suit pants and trailed her as she wandered into the penthouse, gaping—yes, gaping—at the home that made her parents' home look like a hovel. Okay, maybe not a hovel. But definitely a single-family home.

Three glass walls invited the dark sky and Boston skyline into the apartment, granting the illusion of living among the clouds. Floating, freestanding structures separated rooms into different living areas—couches, a white piano, fireplaces, a chrome dining table, random sitting areas with low-slung furniture designating the purpose of the rooms. A steel and veined marble state-of-the-art kitchen encompassed the back end of the penthouse, while a suspended, curving, glass-encased staircase led to the second level.

She jerked her awed glance from her surroundings to Achilles. His mouth twisted into a caricature of a smile.

"Go ahead and say it. I'm a hypocrite."

She blinked. "What?"

"Lecturing your parents on excess and benefiting from the work of someone else and living here." He wore that same dark smile. "I believe that makes me the definition of a fraud."

"Since a fraud or a hypocrite would be the last persons to admit they were as much, I doubt it." She tilted her head. "Let me guess. Cain?"

His eyes narrowed on her, and she chuckled, shaking her head.

"It's not difficult to guess. Kenan is from Boston. You relocated to Boston and wouldn't have had a place to stay. And unknown half brother or not, Cain wouldn't have had you living in a place he wouldn't live in himself. And this place—" she pivoted in a small circle, again taking in the glass palace in the sky "—has Cain Farrell written all over it."

"And what has me written all over it?"

She knew a challenge when she heard it. Knew when she was being set up for failure, too.

"Keep some of the glass and the sky. More walls. Less steel and chrome and all the amenities. I don't think you mind the fireplaces, but not gas. I think…" She paused, cleared her throat and considered the wisdom of her next words, but what the hell? "I think you're like how you described your mother tonight. You like to see the product of your own hands. So you would want to chop your own wood for your fireplace. Which means trees, nature and not a glass castle on the thirty-second floor. How am I doing?"

He didn't answer, just stared at her with that bright gaze that both unnerved her and set her ablaze.

"Why are you here?" he rasped.

"To make sure you're okay."

Once more he studied her with that unblinking, measured scrutiny. Then, after a moment, he gave his head a hard, abrupt shake and stalked toward the living room. "Do you want a drink?"

"Since I skipped after-dinner drinks, definitely."

He glanced at her over his shoulder, eyebrow arched. "I'm sure that went over well."

She flashed him a dry smile. "Swimmingly. If you can call dire warnings of ruining my family's reputation by running after you like a common trollop—who even says *trollop* anymore, I ask you?—'well.' If so, then yes, it went over very well."

"That's…dramatic." He reached the built-in bar and removed a Sam Adams for himself from the fully stocked mini-refrigerator. "What can I get you?"

"I'll have what you're having."

He didn't comment on her choice, just twisted off the cap of his beer, handed it to her and retrieved another for himself. Only after she lifted the bottle to her lips for a sip and downed the ale, did he ask, "Why are you really here, Mycah?"

Slowly, she lowered the beer, met his piercing gaze.

To apologize for my parents' behavior.

To look you in the eye and see for myself that you don't despise me.

All true. All answers she could give him, and he would most likely accept them. All she had to do was say them. Just say them, dammit...

"Because I didn't feel safe in that house."

Oh, God. Why had she said that?

Lightning flashed in his eyes, and she wanted to hide from it.

She wanted to hurl herself at it. Be struck by it.

"And you feel safe here? With me?" he asked, a low rumble in his voice.

"Yes."

As inane as it was, as tumultuous as their past and our rent...relationship might be, she did. She harbored zero doubts that he'd ever intentionally hurt her, exploit her. If she'd come seeking shelter, he'd not only give it, he'd use his own body to provide it. That was his nature.

No.

It's who he was.

After witnessing the pettiness, the cruelty her parents were capable of tonight, she needed that haven. She craved that security. She'd come here on the pretense of making sure Achilles was okay, but really, she was the one who desperately wanted to be assured.

Did that make her a user? Did that make her selfish?

"Stop, and no."

She blinked, snatching herself from the downward spiral of her thoughts. "I'm sorry?"

"Wherever you were going right now in your head. You had a deer-in-headlights look in your eyes."

"I'm selfish. A user," she whispered.

"You're going to have to explain that one." He cupped her elbow and led her to one of the sitting areas, guiding her to a black armchair. "Sit. Because you look like you're about to fall over."

"I convinced myself I was coming here for you. When it was about me, *for me*, all along. Selfish," she repeated, tilting her head back to meet his gaze. "I came here to use you."

She expected his disgust at her admission. At the very least annoyance. Not that flicker of...*oh, God*, desire.

"Use me in what way, Mycah?" Another man might have hunkered down next to the chair, minimizing his size so she didn't feel towered over or intimidated. Not Achilles.

And she didn't feel intimidated or overpowered.

No. She felt covered. Protected.

And so aroused she could barely breathe without taking in his scent—pine, fresh rain and sex.

"Mycah."

"I want... I would..." She couldn't say it. Couldn't push it out.

In her family, asking for what you needed—other than the latest season's fashion line or the newest car—was akin to exposing your neck to an apex predator. It was revealing a weakness. When he'd been a stranger, someone she hadn't expected to see after a night together, it'd been easier. But he wasn't a stranger anymore.

If he'd ever really been.

And as much as she'd run to him tonight...as much as she trusted him not to intentionally hurt her... What this man could inadvertently do to her heart would make a natural disaster look like an April shower.

"We'll table it for now." He sank into the chair across from her, his sprawled long legs bracketing hers.

He didn't speak as he tipped the bottle to his mouth and drank. And she did the same, watching him, mesmerized by the oddly sensual sight of his ale-dampened lips and the dance of his Adam's apple as he swallowed. Maybe it was the alcohol she'd barely sipped, but she longed for nothing more than to lean forward and slowly close her teeth around that strong throat and flick her tongue over his skin. Taste the earthy, salty flavor of it.

User, a small, smug voice rustled in her head. The apple didn't fall far from the tree.

"I'm sorry, Achilles," she whispered, tracing a fingertip through the condensation dotting the bottle. "You didn't deserve that kind of treatment tonight. I know you didn't want my apology earlier, but I need to offer you one. Or try to."

"Look at me."

She lifted her head, meeting his gaze, a flicker of annoyance at her immediate obedience to his order mingling with a flash of lust.

"I didn't want to hear it earlier because it wasn't yours to give. The same now." He leaned forward, setting his beer on the floor before propping his forearms on his thighs. Pinning his bright eyes on her, he said, "And yes, I was mad as fuck and trying to hide it with everything in me so I didn't end up giving your parents and everyone else at that table the satisfaction of proving I was who they believed. The beast. The thug. The Feral Farrell."

"You know about that?"

He snorted. "I'm not deaf or blind, Mycah."

"No, I know that." She waved her hand, frustrated. "I guess I hoped you hadn't…"

"My mother always told me, it's not what they call you,

but what you answer to. Your parents or any of the people here in Boston don't define me." He paused, studied her, and she fought not to recoil from that incisive stare. Fought not to hide lest it perceive too much. Slice too deep. "So why are you allowing them to dictate who you are?"

"I'm not…" Damn him. She closed her eyes. Hiding. And not caring if he knew it. No, screw that. She reopened them, glared at him. "I told you before that you don't know me. So stop presuming that you do."

"Then tell me."

If he'd scoffed at her, she might've left. Might've ordered him to fuck off as she stalked out of there in righteous indignation. But his quiet offer full of curiosity, of genuine interest, deflated her anger.

Soothed her hurt.

"In the interview, Cain asked me why I wanted to work for Farrell. The answers I gave—promotion, opportunity, experience—all were true. But he asked the wrong question. It should've been why I *needed* to work there. Because I do. I *need* this job." She huffed out a laugh, holding the cold bottle between both of her palms and rubbing it back and forth, back and forth. "That party my parents threw tonight? Do you know who paid for it? Me. Or I will at the end of the month. Because the monthly allowance that they receive from Hill-Harper will be gone, spent on clothes, jewelry, lunches, spa appointments, gifts for their friends. And it will be up to me to cover the mortgage, household bills, staff salaries and any other outstanding debts they owe. See, my parents deride my career, but they depend on it."

"You're enabling them, and they're taking advantage because they know you'll pay their way." He growled, anger radiating off him. "That isn't love. That isn't sacrifice."

She shook her head. "It's family," she insisted. "If your mother—"

He slashed a hand through the air, cutting off her argument. "My mother would never have asked that of me. Which is why I would gladly have given her the world if she'd lived. And you know what she would've done, Mycah?" He leaned forward, his blue-gray eyes burning into hers. "Told me no. She would've fought me on it until I wore her down. C'mere." He crooked two fingers, beckoning her closer, and she slid forward on the chair cushion. "You don't even believe the bullshit you're telling me," he said, his voice impossibly gentle, brutally blunt.

Tears sprang to her eyes, stinging them.

But then, the truth tended to do that.

Sting.

"What is it, baby?" he whispered. "You're safe. Tell me."

The truth grappled with self-preservation in her throat for approximately five seconds before it burst from her.

"Three and a half more years. That's all I have left. Three and a half more years before my sister graduates from high school and goes to college. Then I'm free. I'm paying for her tuition, and I can't abandon her. She's brilliant, Achilles, and deserves the best education possible. I won't take that away from her, and I can't lose her. She's the only real relationship I have. I don't put it past my parents to prohibit me from seeing her if I stop paying their bills. But in three and a half years, she'll be through with high school and she'll be eighteen, an adult. And I'll have what I've dreamed about for years."

"What have you dreamed of, Mycah?" he pressed when she hesitated.

She threaded her fingers through her curls—or attempted to. Remembering too late the strands were secured in an updo, she clenched her hands tight before dropping them to her thighs.

"Mycah."

"Freedom." As the word echoed in the room, she winced, emitting a hushed, embarrassed chuckle. Turning, she set her neglected beer bottle on the side table. Anything to avoid looking at him. "Freedom," she repeated less vehemently, with a much heavier dose of self-deprecation. "You must think I'm dramatic."

"You think I don't understand the need for freedom?"

She jerked her head back to him, shock ricocheting through her.

He slowly nodded. "You know the terms of Barron's will. By now, everyone does. For most people, it would seem like a dream come true. Co-run a multibillion-dollar company. Instant billionaire. But I never asked for it. Never wanted any of it. And I'm counting down the months, the days until I'm out of here. Out of Boston. Until I'm free from it all."

He surged from the chair and strode to the window, yanking the tie from his hair on the way. Burrowing both hands through the thick strands, he fisted them, yanking so hard, she winced in sympathy. He splayed his fingers wide on the sheet of glass. As if attempting to reach through it to the sky beyond.

"Do you know the reason I hate the name *Feral Farrell* so much?" he rasped. "Because a part of me fears that there's some truth in it. Sometimes I feel like I'm going crazy within the confines of this…world. After—" he broke off, his hand balling into a fist against the window, his head bowing between his shoulders "—I left Seattle, I deliberately chose a specific way of life for myself. A quieter life, a simpler one. This one… It's too loud. Too harsh. Too mean. I know Cain and Kenan think I'm

NAIMA SIMONE   105

pulling away from them, that I'm distancing myself from them, but I can't let myself become too attached because I can't stay here. They were both born here. This is home for them. I don't belong here."

She rose and went to him, unable to remain in her chair any longer. Without questioning the wisdom of what she was doing, she crossed the room and didn't stop until she stood behind him. So close, her forehead pressed into the indentation of his spine. So close, the toes of her stilettos nudged the bare heels of his feet. So close, her hands slipped under the edge of his vest and cupped his slim waist.

Achilles's body went rigid, but he didn't move away from her. Taking that as a positive sign, she closed her eyes, breathed him in. Dragged that decadent scent of the outdoors into her lungs and held on to it like a drug. Then as she exhaled, she already craved the next hit.

"You asked me how I wanted to use you," she murmured, her words puffs that fluttered against his vest. "I came here because I needed you to hold me. To touch me. To shield me from the world just for a little while before I have to go back out and face it again." She slid her hands over his stomach, up the ridged ladder of his abs until her palms covered his pounding heart. Turning her head, she pressed her cheek to his back. "I think we can give each other that. I don't see anything wrong with both of us using each other."

For the longest moments, he didn't stir. The *thump*, *thump* against her hand the only movement. But in a sudden explosion of action, he wrenched out of her embrace, turned and damn near leaped on her.

Excitement and lust combusted within her, and she met him in a clash of lips, tongue and teeth, his beard abrading her chin and mouth in a sensual caress. God, it'd been so long. So damn long since she'd been touched. No, that was wrong. Not just simply touched. So long since she'd been touched by *him*. By *Achilles*.

The whimper that escaped her throat should've embarrassed her, but she was beyond that. Tunneling her fingers through his thick, cool strands, she fisted them, dragging his head down so she could feast on the mouth that had been taunting her for weeks. Impatient and so damn hungry, she licked him, demanding he give just as much—no, more—in return.

His big hands gripped her head, angling this way. Then that way. Then this way again. As if he couldn't get enough. As if he'd never be satisfied. Join the club. He could suck at her tongue, nip at her lips, lick the roof of her mouth, and she would still yank on his hair, claw at his scalp, silently beg for everything.

This wasn't a kiss.

It was war.

And goddammit, yes, she wanted to be a casualty.

"This dress. It's been fucking killing me all night. How do I get you out of it?" he muttered against her mouth, his hands roaming her breasts, belly, hips.

Chest rising and falling on labored breaths, she turned, giving him her back. "Hooks at the back. Zipper at the hip." She glanced over her shoulder at him. "Hurry."

The next few moments were an exercise in patience as he worked his way through the delicate hooks of the corset-style top, but the brushes of his fingertips over her spine and the caresses of his coarse curses in her ears only heightened the rush of burning arousal in her veins. By the time the top loosened around her breasts and the skirt dipped around her waist, she trembled with lust, and gooseflesh pebbled her skin. And when he lowered the dress, the black material pooling around her shoes, leaving her clad only in a silk thong and thigh-highs, she sank her teeth into her bottom lip to imprison the sob of need that clambered at the back of her throat.

"Turn around." He paused. "Please."

That *please* in his gruff voice, with a note of the same need that burrowed through her, nearly sent her to her knees. Before she could do as he asked, though, he grasped her elbow.

"Wait."

He knelt in front of her, and the air evaporated from her lungs. Her body and mind were of one accord as they both recalled the last time his face and that beautiful beard of his had been between her legs. But this time Achilles's attention wasn't focused on her sex but on her feet. Carefully, he removed her stilettos and swept the dress to the side. He sat back on his heels, staring up at her. Her body had never been the "perfect" size four, much to her mother's dismay. Even so, over the years, Mycah had come to not just accept but to love her body, regardless of others' opinions.

And as Achilles's gaze caressed her thighs, which had never been slim, her hips, which had always been rounded, her belly that had never been completely flat and her breasts, which had always been fuller than an A cup, she felt desired. Worshipped.

Perfect.

"You're beautiful."

Truth ran through his voice, in every syllable. And no matter what might pass between them elsewhere, here, in this, she believed him.

"You're overdressed." She hiked her chin toward him, arching an eyebrow at his shirt, vest and pants.

His hands went to his vest, and he shrugged free of it. When his fingers gripped the top button of his shirt, she sank to her knees. Lust pumped through her, hot and heady, as she brushed his hands aside and took over the task. With every slice of inked brown skin revealed, her arousal ratcheted higher. She squeezed her legs against the sweet pain in her sex, knowing her flimsy lacy thong hid none of the evidence of the desire dampening her upper thighs. And as she pushed his shirt from his shoulders, Achilles confirmed as much when he dipped a hand between her legs, stroking a fingertip across the skin just below her folds and lifted glistening fingers to his mouth.

Deliberately, he slid them between his parted lips, licking them clean. His dense, black lashes fluttered close, and he moaned, the sound ravenous. She whimpered, an aching tug pulling hard in response.

"Touch me," she pleaded, past pride. "Touch me, please."

His arm snaked up, hand cupping the back of her neck and hauling her forward. Their bare chests collided, his mouth covering hers. She tasted herself on him, and the faint musk enflamed her. She opened wider for his possession. He cupped her behind with both hands, squeezing, and she arched into his hold, loving how he told her without words how much he enjoyed her body. Adored her body.

Tearing her mouth from his, she trailed her lips over his jaw, down his strong throat. She paid special detail to the swirls, geometric patterns, lettering and biomechanical art covering his shoulder, arm and chest. He was beautiful, and she closed her eyes against the sting of tears. Silly. God, she was being silly.

"Mycah?"

He cradled her face. Or tried to. She dodged those big palms, ducking her head and flicking her tongue over his flat, brown nipple. His groan rumbled under her mouth, and she raked her teeth over the nub, then sucked it, drawing hard.

"Damn, baby." He carefully removed the band and pins from her hair, then drove his hands through the curls, tangling his fingers in them, tugging, sending darts of pain scattering across her scalp. "Again. Do it again."

She complied. Gladly. Placing her palms against his wide shoulders, she lightly shoved. One of his muscular arms wrapped around her, and he fell back to the carpeted floor. She took swift advantage, crawling on top of his giant frame, straddling his abdomen and moaning deep as those ridges pressed against her wet, swollen folds. Another moan rolled out of her, and she couldn't have stopped herself from grinding against him if inhaling her next breath depended on it.

Why did she need to breathe when pleasure so intense was turning her into living ecstasy?

"No?" Achilles growled, circling her neck, applying just enough pressure to have a dark, erotic wave swirl through her lower belly and pool between her legs.

"Yes," she damn near whined, leaning into his hold. Another buck of her hips, another, and another, and she shuddered, so close to coming just from grinding over him and that illicit grip on her throat.

How was that possible?

Because it was Achilles.

"I don't want to want you." He accompanied the admission with a sweeping caress of her nipple.

Electricity sizzled in her veins, the sparks echoing in her head, but she still clearly heard him. And underneath the pleasure, hurt vibrated within her. She lifted her hand, preparing to shove him away from her breast, but when he pinched the tip, tweaked it, her hand fell away. She surrendered to the pleasure even as she couldn't escape his words.

"You're everything I told myself I shouldn't have. Everything that's destructive to me. And yet—" he cupped her, levered up and sucked her into his mouth, his tongue licking and circling her flesh before crushing a kiss to her lips "—you've become my fantasy."

"And you hate us both for it," she whispered against his lips.

He stared at her, his wolf eyes so bright, so intense it almost hurt.

"Yes. Almost."

A pain carved into her, sharpened by the tender care he gave her. She wanted to hate him back, to strike out at him for making her care. This was sex. Ill-advised sex, at that. Nothing more. But her pounding heart whispered *liar*.

Good thing her heart held no power over her head, just as only her body could rule her for tonight.

Breaking the kiss, she slid down his body, scattering kisses down his torso, her fingers grasping the tab of his pants, undoing them, then tugging down his zipper. Scooting farther down, she settled in the vee of his thighs and fisted his cock. His guttural growl broke on the air, and satisfaction flooded her. He might hate desiring her, but his dick didn't. This part of him—she freed him from the confines of his black boxers—loved her.

She didn't waste time teasing him. Not when his dense, earthy musk teased her, and her mouth watered for the taste of him. Arrowing his length downward, she swallowed him. Another of his harsh moans rippled through the room and two large hands cradled her head, oddly gentle, and a contradiction to the barely leashed control of his straining body.

Closing her eyes, she lost herself in him. The feel of him sliding over her tongue. The threat of him nudging the back of her throat. The power of him pulsing in her hand. The taste of him she coaxed on each glide back up the length of his cock.

In this moment, as he bunched her curls in his hands, lifting them away from her face so he could glimpse every hard suckle, she was…powerful. He was hers.

And she was his.

In this moment.

"Enough." His gravel-roughened order came seconds before he grabbed her by the shoulders and hoisted her up and off his body. But only long enough to shuck his pants, remove a condom from the wallet and sheathe himself. Then he reached for her, pulling her back on top of him. Grasping one of her hips with one hand, he squeezed his cock with the other, holding himself at her entrance. "Take me, Mycah."

It could've been a demand. It could've been a plea.

She gave in to both.

Slowly, she sank down over him.

Her breath snagged in her throat at the impossibly tight fit, and she paused, shaking. Yes, she'd done this with him before. But this position made him seem bigger, thicker. Her fingernails dug into the dense muscles of his chest, and she shook with the increasing pressure as she pushed down, taking more.

The stretch. The burn.

And underneath? The pleasure.

Pleasure, simply because it was Achilles inside her, filling her, branding her flesh, marking her.

"Shh. Easy, baby. Take what you need." He cupped her breasts, whisking his thumbs over the beaded nipples, his long hair tangled around his head. His hooded gaze seemed to miss nothing—not her struggle, not even her pleasure. His face hardened into a mask of such fierce lust, it stole what little air she had left in her lungs. "You're so fucking tight. So wet. Months I've been dreaming about this, and nothing came close to how perfect you are."

Months? So she hadn't been alone in not forgetting that night?

A silent cry echoed in her head, and she sank lower. Oh, God. She had to move. Had to…do *something*. Using his chest as leverage, she rose off him until just the tip of him kissed her folds, then she took him back inside, the wide, thick length of him claiming her just as she claimed him.

Twin ragged groans penetrated the room, and with his hands still caressing her breasts, she rode him. Cautiously, at first, but gradually, with more abandon until he filled all of her and her behind slapped his thighs. It was so damn *good*.

Achilles replaced his hands with his mouth, drawing on her, sucking on her, torturing her as his big hands encouraged her to fuck him…to break him.

He tunneled a hand into her hair, pulled her head down as he reached between them and circled a blunt fingertip over the nub of flesh at the top of her sex.

"Let me feel you come all over me, baby."

This was all demand. And she obeyed. He gave that engorged, pulsing flesh two more hard, relentless circles and she exploded, came apart for him. For herself.

And as he followed close behind her, his giant body surging and pitching beneath her, she clung to him, wringing out every last bit of the orgasm snapping through her like the hottest of lightning bolts.

Just like this release, she would claim all of tonight for herself because tomorrow she had to start the process of letting go all over again.

"Will you tell me about her?"

Beneath her, Achilles's body jerked, then stilled, as if he hadn't meant to betray his reaction to her question but hadn't quite managed to hide it. His heart beat solidly, but at an elevated rate under her ear.

They continued to lie in his bed, the sheets twisted around their bodies from their last bout of sex. At some point during the night, he'd carried her from the living room up the stairs to the bedroom, and she'd discovered once more that slow, tender sex with Achilles was just as hot and mind-blowing as when it was fast and intense. But now, as the sweat dried on their skin and her thoughts had started whirling again, she couldn't stop them.

And couldn't keep them from tumbling out of her mouth.

Mycah didn't repeat the request or say anything else to expound on the *her*. She didn't need to; they both knew to whom she referred.

He remained silent so long, she assumed he decided not to answer her. Disappointment flashed inside her chest, but not surprise. Sex didn't mean he would suddenly confide in her. Especially about someone who'd obviously had such an impact on his—

"What do you want to know?" The words erupted from him as if he'd propelled them out. Get them out or never say them at all.

She blinked, part of her unsure she'd actually heard him, but she quickly recovered, not willing to squander this opportunity.

"Are you still in love with her?" *Oh, for God's sake.*

She mentally cringed. That's what she led with? Dammit, she sounded…needy.

"No." Gently grasping her shoulders, he lifted her. Sitting up, he slid across the mattress until his back hit the headboard. His hair tumbled about his face and shoulders, that piercing gaze narrowing on her. "Why would you ask me that?"

She shrugged. How could she answer that, when she didn't know herself? "When someone remains so angry with another person it's usually because they still have strong feelings for them."

"I'm not angry with her." His dark brows slashed down in a frown. "She taught me a valuable lesson I'll never forget, but I'd have to care about her to be angry. And I don't give a damn either way."

"What was the lesson?" Mycah whispered, certain she already knew.

He watched her for several long, quiet moments, then said, voice flat but soft, "Most rich women will toy with someone out of their tax bracket, but when it comes down to it, they're not settling for the dirty little secret."

Each word landed like a solid punch, and through sheer will she didn't flinch from the blows. Did he believe she saw him as a dirty secret? Second class? Out of her league? She scrolled through their interactions, beginning at the bar and ending with the evening at her parents' house. Here, in the living room with his confession about hating himself for wanting her.

Yes, he did believe that.

Pain and anger sizzled inside her, but as quickly as it flared, she extinguished it. This wasn't about her. And as much as she longed to defend herself, she couldn't make it about her.

"Will you tell me what happened?" she asked.

He cocked his head, surprise flickering in his eyes. "Why is it important to you?"

"Because I want to know who I'm being punished for. And why." And maybe, just maybe, though he claimed he wasn't angry, speaking about it could lance this obvious wound.

Again, he didn't immediately reply, but after a long

pause, he finally nodded. Turning his head, he shifted his gaze from her to the glass wall that, during the day, would provide a phenomenal view of Boston Harbor.

"I met her not long after my mom died," he began. "My mom and I were living in Tacoma by then, and it'd been just us. You might not have noticed, but I don't play well with others—" a slight quirk of his lips, there and gone in an instant "—so I didn't have anyone among my coworkers that I'd call friends, just acquaintances. So with Mom gone, I was alone, and when this beautiful, sophisticated, cultured woman approached me at one of my company's investors' parties, I fell. And I fell hard."

Okay, maybe she didn't want to hear this story. Jealousy sparked and writhed inside her, and though she reminded herself she'd literally asked for this, she couldn't snuff it out. Couldn't abolish the thought of this *beautiful, sophisticated, cultured woman* with this virile, gorgeous man.

"She claimed to love me, said she was interested in my career, concerned about my well-being. Even encouraged me to see a grief counselor about my mother. But the moment the counselor cautioned me about jumping into a relationship so soon after Mom's death, she found a way to shut that down. Told me the counselor was against us. And stupid-ass me believed her. Fuck." He loosed a harsh bark of laughter. "I was so goddamn dumb and needy."

"Stop it." For the first time since he started relaying his story, she spoke, scooting closer and grabbing his hand in both of hers. He turned from the window, dipping his head to stare down at their clasped hands. "The fact that you recognized you needed a counselor is brave. You actually going? Even braver. That she manipulated you into stopping, using your trust and love to further her own agenda, is her shame, not yours. So don't you dare take that on you."

He lifted his gaze to hers. He didn't nod, but he didn't refute her, either. Mycah took that as a win.

"We were together a year and a half, although that was a year too long. In that time, I never met her family, although she promised I would, I just needed to be patient. She did take me around her friends, though. Bought me new clothes, dressed me up, trotted me out to the clubs, bars, parties. Though she said she cared about my career, if my work interfered with her social events, she resented it. Even tried to sabotage it by calling my supervisor and insisting I be placed on less demanding projects, and expecting to be obeyed since she was an investor. See, she believed her money and pedigree would solve any problem or situation. Including me. Because I was her toy to play with, dress up, bend and, when the time came, to put on the shelf."

"Achilles." Part of her didn't want him to finish. But again, not about her. Not about the hole he ripped in her chest with each word. So she didn't say anything else. Just continued to hold his hand.

"I finally ended it, but not because I woke up or got fed up. Only because a coworker who knew we were dating took pity on me and emailed me the engagement announcement in the Tacoma society pages. Her engagement announcement to the heir of a financial empire." His mouth twisted into a sardonic caricature of a smile. "When I confronted her about it, she waved it off. As if her upcoming marriage meant nothing. Because to her, it didn't. She expected me to remain her fucking side piece. As I'd been all along, I just hadn't known it. And she actually appeared shocked when I told her hell no. Seems no one had told her that before."

He sighed, pinched the bridge of his nose, then tunneled his fingers through his hair, dragging the strands back from his face.

"I grew up in the roughest parts of Seattle, considered myself street-smart. I'd been through—" something hard... haunted flickered in his eyes "—some shit. But the first time a beautiful woman other than my mother showed me compassion, attention, I lost myself. I became someone I didn't recognize. And I've never forgiven myself for it. I don't know if I can. Because if I do, I'll forget and I'll do it again. I can never go back to that place. Ever."

The vow came out impassioned, almost furious. But that fury was reserved for himself, the man who'd fallen for a woman who had betrayed him.

Mycah understood that kind of betrayal. The path of it might be different, but that pain? Oh, she was very familiar.

And it could break a person's spirit. Their belief and trust in other people. In themselves.

"What was her name?" she asked.

He studied her for a moment, head cocked to the side. "Yvette. Why?"

"They say if you give the devil a name and say it aloud, he—or she—no longer has power over you."

He snorted softly. "That's what they say, huh?" He shook his head, a faint smile lifting the corner of his mouth before disappearing. "Yvette." He said her name again, lower this time, and if she hadn't been so tuned in to him, she might not have caught it. He hiked his chin at her. "What's the name of your devil, Mycah?"

A spark of panic flared in her chest. Oh, God, where did she start? Easy. She didn't. Because she was afraid if she did, she wouldn't be able to stop.

"I don't have any."

"Liar," he murmured, calling her out.

His arm shot out, curling around her waist, hauling her across his thighs. He arranged her so she straddled him, and she moaned, her sex notching against his rapidly hard-ening cock. But before she had time to roll her hips and get ready for round—what, three or four?—he cradled her face between his hands and tipped her head down so she had no choice but to meet his unwavering scrutiny.

"You, Mycah Hill," he said, sweeping his thumb over her cheekbone, "are a liar. But that's okay. We've had enough revelations for one day. But when you're ready, I'll be here. And you're going to tell me. Because we both know you have demons. You let me know when you want to name them."

Then he took her mouth.

And took her under.

And she let him.

Ten

"I swear, one day you're going to have to explain to me why you prefer this office in the basement when there's a perfectly good one with fucking windows on the executive floor."

Achilles sighed as Cain strode into the office, scowling as he surveyed the workspace as if it were the first time he'd seen it. Which it wasn't. His older brother just never let pass an opportunity to bitch about the size and location. For some reason, it really irked Cain that Achilles preferred to be down in the IT department instead of on the thirty-second floor with Cain and Kenan.

When he asked, Achilles gave him his rote answer of feeling more comfortable with the people who "spoke his language." And it wasn't a complete lie. But neither was it the truth.

He couldn't tell Cain, or Kenan for that matter, that even something as inconsequential as taking an office next to them and appearing as a unified Farrell front constituted bonds he wasn't comfortable forming. Not when he had no intention of strengthening or tightening those bonds.

Not when he planned on returning to Washington in a matter of months.

Doing so would just make it that much harder to cut ties when the time came. And if losing his mother and Yvette's betrayal had educated him in anything, it was that love hurt.

Whether due to abandonment, lies, fists, betrayal... death.

Love always ended in pain.

No attachments. No love. No hurt.

So no, he'd keep his office here on the eighth floor and his brothers at a careful distance. It would be better for them in the long run. And definitely better for him.

"As I've repeatedly told you and Kenan, it's not the basement," he said, shifting his attention from Cain, who had dropped into the visitor's chair, and back to his monitor.

"Did I hear my name being taken in vain?" His younger brother appeared in the doorway, carefree grin in place. "Or were you saying it in total adoration? I get that a lot."

Cain snorted. "This office is already cramped. We damn sure don't have enough room in here for us and your ego."

"I told you we should've had this meeting in the broom closet down the hall. It's more spacious." Kenan shrugged, claiming the other chair next to Cain.

"Are you two finished?" Achilles snapped. "If you feel so claustrophobic, there are perfectly good phones in your offices, and you could've used them to call me."

"What would've been the fun in that?" Kenan asked. "Besides, I love the smell of fresh asbestos in the morning."

Achilles growled, and Kenan laughed, holding up his hands, palms out.

"Fine, fine. I'm done. Cain, can we get on with this before he forgets that I'm his brother?"

As if he could. Achilles curled his fingers into his palm to prevent himself from rubbing at the pang in his chest Kenan's words generated.

"Here, Achilles." Cain leaned forward and slid a manila folder onto the desk. "I emailed you a copy of this, but here's a hard copy, too. Don't say it." He turned and jabbed a finger at Kenan, then pointed the same one at Achilles. "I know, I know. And so what? I still like to have things in my hands. Sue me."

And in the hands of others, too, but okay, he'd keep his mouth shut. That was an argument for another day.

"Anyway, we're looking at acquiring a software company out of San Francisco. Just from what we're seeing and hearing, they're really turning the software-as-a-service industry on its head with their backup technology. They're making on-premises backups obsolete with their third-party backup software app on the cloud There haven't been security issues and it cuts costs. I'm sure there are variables we haven't uncovered, and that's where you come in. And before we invest one hundred and fifty million dollars, we need to make sure it's sound. And that we're going to make a profit, of course. Can you look it over and give us your opinion on not just the software but the company?"

Achilles blinked. Cain had requested his presence in meetings, but he'd felt like a figurehead. He hadn't offered his opinions, and he hadn't been asked for them. Here, in the IT department, he was at least useful, able to answer calls, offer help and fix problems, even install software when needed because he wasn't afraid to get his hands dirty.

But this...

He glanced away from Cain for a moment, unable to maintain eye contact with the same penetrating gaze he met in the mirror every morning. His brother, who'd suffered through too much at the abusive hands of their father, saw too much. Cain, accepted heir of Farrell and renowned businessman, wouldn't lay the fate of millions of dollars in Achilles's hands if he didn't trust him. And Achilles feared Cain would glimpse how much this show of trust, of faith, meant to him.

Because it did.

There went those bonds. Tightening. And he fought them like a man drowning, even as an image of his passion project—his video game—popped in his mind. As did the inane urge to tell his brothers about it. The longing shoved at his rib cage, growing in pressure. He needed to share it with the two people who just might be those closest to him. Who might understand him if he just opened up and let them in...

Love always ended in pain.

No attachments. No love. No hurt.

The reminder whispered through his head, echoed in his heart. And it was sharp, leaving an ache behind.

"Yes, I'll do it." Achilles picked the folder up. "When do you need the info back?"

"Next Monday work?" Cain asked.

That gave him a week, which would be more than enough time. "That's fine."

"Good." Cain stood, sliding his hands into the front pockets of his gray tailored pants. "Also, just wanted to give you a heads-up. Devon's going to be calling you. She's starting a computer class at the community center since a new donor anonymously donated PCs."

Kenan coughed.

"Shut up, you," Cain snapped. "Anyway, I didn't want you to be ambushed." He paused. "But you should know, my fiancée has a soft heart. And even if you decide to tell her no, let her down gently or I'll steal those Dr. Who collectibles in your desk drawer that you think we don't know about and sell them online for a penny."

Achilles gaped at Cain, caught between shock and laughter.

"I think you broke him," Kenan whispered.

More of those bonds.

"Okay, got it," Achilles rasped.

Moments later, his brothers left, and Achilles still stared at the door. Finally, shaking his head, he got back to work. And if his chest felt a little lighter, well, he attributed it to the challenge of a new project, nothing else.

Hours later, a knock at his office door brought his head up, and another kind of warmth streamed through him. Molten. Greedy. Which made sense, since Mycah stood in his doorway. It'd been a couple of days since he'd seen her, sharpening the need inside him to a knife's edge.

He glanced at the clock at the bottom of his computer monitor. Several minutes after seven. That meant they were most likely the only ones left on his floor. He rose from his chair as she stepped inside, closing the door behind her.

It'd been almost two months since that night at her parents' disastrous dinner party—since they'd had sex on his living room floor. And on his couch. And in his bed.

Not that it'd been the last night they'd spent together. More had followed. Many more. But by tacit agreement, they'd kept it between them, a secret, not allowing what they did to each other after hours to cross the boundaries into the office. Since they rarely saw one another, no issues had arisen. Still, he was cognizant that he was an owner of the company…at least for the next several months. And because she'd made her worries about her professional reputation very clear, he ensured he didn't cause any tongues to wag by behavior on his part.

Still… He would be lying if he didn't admit that the secrecy irritated him like a pebble in an ill-fitting shoe. After Yvette, he'd vowed never to be someone's dirty little secret. Never to allow anyone to make him feel as if he were unworthy. And while he understood Mycah's very valid concerns for her career, he couldn't help the seeds of doubt that had never been fully uprooted; they'd been sown in hurt and betrayal. The similarities between then and now crept into his mind after the passion cooled and she curled next to him or left his apartment.

Coming to him in the cover of darkness.

Pretending they weren't lovers around others of influence.

Conscripting him to live a lie.

But then she'd touch him. And the need trumped what he'd ever experienced with any other woman, even Yvette. The loneliness that he'd convinced himself didn't bother him disappeared.

Maybe he was worrying over nothing, though. Unlike with Yvette, he recognized this…arrangement with Mycah couldn't go anywhere. It had an expiration date and a definite conclusion. For both of them.

"Hey," he said, rounding the desk. "What're you doing here? I thought we were meeting at the— What's wrong?"

He pulled up short, for the first time noticing the stark look in her eyes and the tension holding her body unnaturally rigid.

She parted her lips, and they moved but no sound emerged. Unease pulsed through him, and he stepped toward her, but she shook her head, holding up a hand, and he stopped. Though everything in him demanded he go to her, pull her to him, slay and then fix whatever it was that had darkened her gaze to nearly black.

"I'm pregnant."

Eleven

I'm pregnant.

Her announcement reverberated in the room like a shout. Except instead of gradually quieting, it seemed to gain volume, growing louder and louder until it assaulted her ears, boomed in her head. Of course, that was her imagination, but staring into Achilles's stern face, the honed slashes of his cheekbones and jaw jutting out in stark relief under his taut, golden-brown skin... Well, she could be forgiven for her dark flight of fancy.

Not that she could blame him.

She'd had two days to absorb the fact that she—a twenty-nine-year-old professional woman well versed in the mechanics of sex—had fucked up and ended up pregnant. Yes, *she*. Because ultimately this was *her* body, *her* responsibility. No one would love it, care for it, protect it like she could—was supposed to. No, it wasn't all on her, because hell, he'd been there. But she'd known she hadn't been on any other contraception; there hadn't been any need since she... She squeezed her eyes shut. Damn that heat of the moment and that one and only time that had seemed so harmless... Turned out, it hadn't been.

Fear slicked a path through the highway of her veins, leaving dangerous black ice behind. Oh, God, she was scared. So fucking scared. And alone. For two days, she'd called in sick, claiming a stomach flu when in truth, she'd lain curled up in bed, shell-shocked, grappling with her new reality. A new reality that had twisted and warped into this alternate universe with a plus sign on a stick.

Her job. Her lifestyle. Her family. Those had been her first thoughts, as selfish as they'd been. And she could admit that they had been selfish. She'd worked hard for years to get where she was now. This was just the beginning. There were so many more years of work to put in, and regardless of the foolish woman she'd been years earlier, she hadn't imagined a man and baby in her life now. Some women wanted all of that and managed it beautifully—she wasn't one of them. Besides, she enjoyed the freedom of being single, of not having to answer to anyone. Of doing something as simple as going out to dinner or to the store when she wanted—by herself. Or going on vacation. She'd heard enough from friends with kids to know she could kiss that carefree lifestyle goodbye.

And then her family. Jesus. A child out of wedlock. They'd disown her. Even discovering the identity of the father wouldn't appease them. Finding out Achilles was the father might be worse because he was the bastard, the thug, in their eyes. The nobody. Anger rushed through her. Not that they knew what they were talking about since they'd never even given him a chance.

As suddenly as the anger entered, the emotion evaporated like smoke, leaving her exhausted.

None of those reasons that had bombarded her mattered in the end, though.

Because as she'd stared at another dawn creeping over the horizon, chasing away the night, a certain bone-deep knowledge drove away her doubts.

She was keeping the baby.

Her baby.

Along with that knowledge had come a love so simple, yet so profound. And now, standing in front of Achilles, that love for something—someone, because it was already someone to her—the size of a bean had already consumed her whole.

"You're pregnant."

He stated it rather than asked, but she nodded anyway, instinctively crossing her arms low over her stomach where their child slept. Of course that perceptive but inscrutable gaze didn't miss the gesture, and his gaze dropped to her belly, remaining there for several long moments before returning to her face.

"What're your plans?" he asked, voice even, calm.

Too calm.

His guarded expression, careful tone... They revealed nothing of his thoughts, and she couldn't gauge him. It was the Achilles from the bar, and her heart thudded against her sternum. *What do you want?* her mind railed. *Tell me if you want this baby.*

But she didn't loose those words. Didn't go to him, pound her fists against that brick wall of a chest and act a fool. Maybe he had the right of it. Emotions didn't belong here between them. After all, hadn't messy *emotions* gotten her here in the first place?

If she'd spent only that one night with him like she'd promised herself instead of... *Say it,* her ruthless mind insisted. If she'd stuck to the one-night rule instead of giving in to how he made her feel, they wouldn't be in this situation. Not just the physical pleasure. As amazing as that was, the hedonism of stripping free of the "Hill" layers and just being Mycah, just being herself, had proved far more addictive. She hadn't been ready to give that up.

And now they both had to pay the cost. Or at least she did. And she would, willingly and gladly.

Notching her chin high, she straightened her shoulders and met that cold, lupine stare.

"I'm keeping it." Her arms tightened around her middle. "I'm keeping the baby."

Fire blazed in his gaze, melting the ice. "Good."

"Good?" she whispered, shock whipping through her. She hadn't been expecting that. Or the... Wait... "You're happy about this?"

For the first time since she'd dropped the bombshell, he betrayed a reaction. Well, no, that wasn't exactly true. There'd been that breath-stealing flicker of heat in his eyes. But he dragged a hand through his hair, dislodging the tie at the back of his head. He removed it, tossing the band on the desk behind him, and didn't immediately turn back around. Instead, he braced his hands on the desktop, his broad back straining against the material of his white shirt.

Finally, he pivoted, and the shadows in his eyes... Her chest seized, an invisible clamp reaching inside and squeezing her ribs so she could barely breathe.

"Happy. I think that's too easy." His fingers flexed next to his thighs before he seemed to catch the movement and deliberately stilled it. "You know who my father is—a man who impregnated my mother, then abandoned her. Threw her away like she—like we—were trash. But the men who followed? Barron was the kindest."

That clamp around her sternum clinched tighter and tighter. And she ground her teeth together to imprison the whimper that clawed at the back of her throat. She didn't think Achilles would appreciate the sympathy it conveyed. He'd probably mistake it for pity when it wasn't. There was absolutely nothing to pity about this man.

"I didn't have a good male role model. Most of the boys I knew growing up didn't, either. I had my mother and grandmother, but they couldn't teach me about fatherhood. What I learned about manhood, I got from the men my mom brought around. And they taught me what I didn't want to be, what not to do. How not to treat a woman and a child. But was it enough? I don't know." He shook his head, spread his hands wide, studying the big palms as if they contained the answers that hadn't been passed down to him growing up. After a moment, he lifted his head, looked at her. "So am I happy? Yes. Maybe. But more than that I'm terrified I'll fuck up."

"You've met my parents, right?" Mycah murmured. When Achilles blinked, then snorted, she softly laughed. "I've had two days to process this. And I'm scared, too. I grew up with two parents in a wealthy home, affluent neighborhood, great schools, with every privilege and opportunity afforded me. And yet, I'm what some might call emotionally stunted, care too much what others think, seek validation in my career and am terrified of my parents' rejection even knowing they are elitists, classists and just damn mean. So I have baggage, too, and yes, am equally terrified of fucking up. But maybe that's what will make us good parents. If we believed we were going to be perfect, we would be setting ourselves up for failure. If we go into this knowing we're going to make mistakes, that we're far from perfect, then we'll be vigilant, careful and, most of all, we'll be forgiving. Of ourselves and our child."

He exhaled a breath. Nodded. "Okay, that makes sense." He paused. Nodded again. "Thank you." Clearing his throat, he stretched an arm toward her, then dropped it.

Frowning, he asked, "Where do we go from here? Have you seen a doctor?"

"I set up an appointment for tomorrow morning. I—" She crossed her arms over her chest, rubbing her hands up and down as if she could warm herself. Impossible when the cold emanated from within. "I don't want to exclude you from the pregnancy, I promise you I don't. But you might not be able to go to my doctor appointment with me tomorrow."

His frown deepened, lightning flashing in his eyes. "Why?"

"Because I share the same ob-gyn as my mother, and while doctor-patient confidentiality is supposed to be sacred, I don't want to risk it. So I'm going to confirm the pregnancy tomorrow. I'll find another doctor's office so we can both attend the appointments."

Slowly, his expression cleared, but shadows remained in his gaze. Still, he nodded. "Fine."

"Also," she continued, blowing out a puff of air. "If you don't mind, I want to keep the pregnancy a secret for now. At least for the first trimester. You might not understand—"

He leaned back against his desk, curling his fingers around the edge. "Then make me."

Thrusting her hands through her curls, she paced away several steps, gathering her chaotic thoughts. How to make him see without once again making this about her? But in a way, it *was* about her. Because as Barron had shown with his mother, at any point, Achilles could walk away, and she would be left alone, her life irrevocably changed.

She drew to a halt several feet in front of him.

"Call me superstitious but the first trimester is the most fragile time of a pregnancy, where miscarriages can occur. And I'd rather wait until we're free of it and in the second trimester before telling anyone. Second, I just started this job at Farrell. I need to figure out how to tell your brothers that not only am I pregnant but by their brother, co-CEO of the company—a man I pretended not to know during my job interview. And then deal with how that will appear to the employees and the business community as a whole, and how it will affect my reputation. Third, I have to decide how I'm going to tell my parents. And prepare myself for that fallout. So yes, I'm asking you for time."

He silently studied her, and finally he pushed himself off the desk and strode the short steps toward her, eliminating the small space separating them. His chest brushed against hers, his thighs grazing hers. Despite the situation, his scent, the firm pressure of his big body touching hers, lit her up.

"It really sucks that you got knocked up by the Feral Farrell, doesn't it?" he asked softly. Almost gently. Which made the question even more blasphemous.

"Don't you say that," she said, her voice vehement, furious. "Don't you ever fucking say that again."

He arched a dark brow, his bright gaze impenetrable once more. "Don't worry. I won't say a word. Now, is that it? Any more conditions?"

She shook her head. "Achilles—"

"Good. Call me after the appointment and let me know what the doctor said."

He turned away from her and stalked across the office, returning to his desk. Dismissing her. The punch of pain to her chest shouldn't have surprised her; she wasn't a stranger to it. Yet it still drove the air from her lungs.

But damn if she'd let him know it.

She'd promised herself long ago that she'd never allow herself to become emotionally entangled again. To never give anyone else the opportunity to reject her. She'd failed herself on both accounts.

She wouldn't do it again.

Not when she now had too much to lose.

Twelve

I'm on my way over. I need to talk to you. It's important.

Mycah stared at the text and debated pretending that she didn't see it. No, that wouldn't work. Her mother would see that she'd read it.

She glanced down at her long-sleeved white shirt, black lounge pants and bare feet. If she shoved on sneakers quickly, threw on a coat and grabbed her car keys, she might be able to make it out of the house before her mother made it over here.

The doorbell rang, dispelling that hope.

Shit.

Mycah clapped a hand to her forehead.

Why? Why had she bought a condo in the same neighborhood as her parents' home? She should've taken that cute apartment in Charlestown like she'd wanted. Right. Because of Angelique. When she was her sister's age, she'd wished for a place to escape to when her parents had become too overbearing. Mycah had wanted to give that haven to her sister. Too bad Laurence and Cherise knew the location, as well.

Sighing, Mycah headed across her hardwood floor toward the front door, the exhaustion that had sent her home from work early suddenly feeling heavier.

Her first doctor's appointment had been earlier in the week, and it seemed like as soon as she'd officially confirmed the pregnancy, all the symptoms she'd ever heard and read about—morning sickness, fatigue, breast and abdomen soreness—had visited upon her like plagues. Achilles had been supportive: asking questions about the appointment, inquiring about her health, even picking up her neonatal vitamins after work when she'd been too tired to do anything but go home.

But one thing he hadn't done—*they* hadn't done—was resume their former relationship. If their secret, no-strings, sexual arrangement could be called that. Whatever it'd been, it was over. He hadn't tried to touch her, hadn't asked to spend the night, hadn't asked her to come over to the penthouse.

She should be grateful.

Because any kind of attachment other than co-parenting wouldn't be wise.

And they hadn't even had a chance to discuss the mechanics of that yet. How he planned to co-parent from across the country. Literally.

Until I'm free from it all.

His words continued to haunt her, even months later.

He was leaving. She couldn't forget that.

Couldn't forget the reality of it. What it meant not just for her, but for their baby.

Before... Before a plus sign turned up on a stick, flipping her world on its head, she'd been in danger of forgetting that the "just sex" relationship she and Achilles had didn't have a fairy-tale ending. Even then, the odds had been stacked so high against them that she would've needed an Atlas-sized ladder to see over them.

Achilles's resenting anything or anyone having to do with the wealthy world she came from. Their employer/employee relationship. The potential damage to her professional reputation if their intimate relationship ever got out.

Still… She'd forgotten the main issue that trumped everything else.

There'd been no "them."

Because Achilles had never intended on staying in Boston. His home was back in Washington, where he belonged.

And if she were honest with herself, could she give up her career, give up this part of herself for him? She'd been ready to do that for a man before. To place his happiness, his career, above her own. She'd loved him so much that she'd willingly turned a blind eye to his character, even when he'd shown her who he was. And when he'd stolen her proposal for a new diversity, equity and inclusion program, submitted it as his own and ended up receiving a promotion for it? She'd been devastated, damn near destroyed by the betrayal.

That heartbreak had taught her that men, parents, colleagues could disappoint and even crush her. But only she could control if she allowed it. Only she could control herself.

They couldn't hurt her if she didn't permit them access to the core of her. At some point in her life, she'd let each of them have that access, and they'd betrayed her. Almost destroyed her. Used her.

Never again.

Achilles hadn't committed any of those sins yet.

Yet.

But he more than any of those in her past had the power to wreak the worst damage—a damage she might not be able to recover from.

So yes, she was grateful they hadn't resumed that part of their relationship.

It was for the best.

No physical entanglements meant she didn't open herself to messy emotional ones. If she didn't protect herself, no one else would. God knows, history had proved that one out.

And if she didn't protect herself, then how could she be there for her baby?

The doorbell rang again, more insistent this time.

No more putting off this visit. Hell, the sooner she got it done, the quicker it would be over with and she could return to bed.

She paused to glance through the peephole—this was Back Bay but still not immune to crime and she was no fool—then unlocked the door and opened it to her mother.

"Mom."

"Hello, honey." Cherise swept inside, her light floral scent swamping Mycah as she brushed kisses over both her cheeks. "I'm glad you were home. You claim to be so busy lately. Too busy for your parents."

Guilt Trip 501. Graduate level.

"Your text said you needed to see me about something important." Mycah shut the door and moved toward the living room. Her mother frowned in disapproval as Mycah sank to the couch cushions, but God, she was *tired*. And call it sixth sense, but something told her she needed to sit down for the bullshit that was headed her way.

"It is important, honey." Lowering to the armchair across from the couch, Cherise perched on the edge, perfect and immaculate in an elegant, dark green pantsuit even at six o'clock in the evening. "Margaret Dansing mentioned she saw you and Cain Farrell downtown having lunch last week."

Mycah arched a brow, irritation sparking inside her. "The eagle-eyed Mrs. Dansing would be correct. It was a business lunch. That's the important issue?"

"No, I just thought it was interesting. She commented on what a striking couple you made. I have to admit, I agreed." Cherise toyed with an earring, but Mycah wasn't fooled by the casual gesture or tone.

"Mother, please tell me you shut that gossip down. For the millionth time, Cain is just my employer. If Margaret Dansing had stuck around a little bit longer, she would've seen a couple more people from my department join us. And for the millionth and one time, Cain has a fiancée. One he looks even more striking with."

Her mother waved a hand. "Engagements end all the time. All I'm saying is you need to keep your options open."

"Mother," Mycah ground out between gritted teeth. "What was so important?"

Cherise sighed. "Fine. Mycah, your father and I are worried about you."

Out of respect, Mycah managed not to roll her eyes. Barely. This "we're worried about you" speech came about once a quarter. It was a little early, but not unexpected.

"I'm fine, Mom. Now, if that's all—"

"Mycah, first this insistence of working at all these jobs—"

"Two, Mom. I've worked at two. One for seven years."

"It would be one thing if you at least worked for Hill-Harper."

Mycah snorted at that. No way in hell. And be under not just her father's thumb but at the mercy of a board of people who remembered her when she was in Pull-Ups? Zero chance of respect.

"Then you bring home that...that man to dinner," her mother sneered.

"If memory serves me correctly, and it does, you invited him to dinner, and you did it to be spiteful. Just to humiliate him for the entertainment of your guests." Fury rose inside Mycah as she uncurled her legs from under her, leaning forward and pinning her mother with a glare. "You and Dad are just angry because he turned the tables and threw your snobbery back in your faces and embarrassed you in front of your guests."

"As if he could." Her mother sniffed, picking nonexistent lint off her pants. "He just exhibited his poor breeding and manners."

"I'm sure that's what he said about you two."

"Mycah Hill," Cherise snapped. "Don't you dare talk to me like that. I'm your mother and you'll show me respect."

"Believe me, Mom, I am." She blew out a breath and shook her head. "You and Dad disappointed me that night. Why do you think I haven't been back since then?"

"Well, the feeling is entirely mutual," her mother said, voice as cold as the winter wind. "Taking his side over your family. Chasing after him. You barely know that thug and we're your family."

"You don't know him, either, and don't call him another name in my house or in front of me."

Her mother's chin snapped back a little at Mycah's equally cool tone, then her eyes narrowed, mouth thinning.

"Well, is that how it is?" She tilted her head to the side, studying Mycah. "Are you involved with this...man? Is that why you've appointed yourself his zealous defender?"

"No, we aren't involved." *Anymore. But he's the father of your grandchild.* God, how she longed to say it. But by sheer will she bit back the words. "But he doesn't deserve your antipathy. You've made him a target because of who his mother is and where he's from and what he wasn't born with. When, if circumstances were different, given the color of your skin and the country you live in, you stripped away your money and fancy address, some of the people you call friends would talk to you in the same way."

Face tight, Cherise rose from the chair, anger vibrating off her stiff form.

"Your father and I have only wanted what's best for you. We've tried to guide you in the right direction, yet you've rebelled, slapped our hands, scorned our efforts at every turn. Have you ever looked down from your high horse to wonder how that made us feel? You're ungrateful. Excuse us for loving you."

With the regality of a queen, she swept from the room and out of the apartment, the door closing softly behind her. Because even in her anger, her mother would never slam a door.

Mycah stared at the empty living room entrance, numb.

You're ungrateful. Excuse us for loving you.

You're ungrateful. Excuse us for loving you.

The accusations played over and over in her head like a scratch-free, newly minted record. And each time they rebounded off the walls of her mind, the ice in her body spread a little further, capturing another part of her in the emotional frostbite.

Good. Because she didn't want to feel.

"Mycah?" A hand cupped her cheek, and she jerked from it, the warmth of that palm almost too much for the cold. She needed the cold. "Mycah?" Another hand cradled the other side of her face, forcing her to focus, to look at the person who refused to leave her in the comforting cold. "Baby, look at me. What's wrong?"

With no choice, she looked. Focused. And met an all-too-familiar sight. Achilles's frown. "Achilles?" she murmured. "What are you doing here?"

"I knocked but you didn't answer. And the door was unlocked." Reproach colored his tone but, again, she was too numb to take offense. His thumbs caressed her cheekbones. "I called your name, but you didn't answer. What's wrong? You seem...off."

Nothing.

It sat on her tongue, because God. She was so damn tired of explaining. Of saying the wrong things that set people off and hurt them. "Nothing" seemed the safest, but when she parted her lips...

"She called me ungrateful. And maybe I am. I've said that about myself often enough. I'm selfish, too. Look at what I've done with you. Used you for your body, even though you did some using, too. But we both got orgasms out of it, so I think the exchange rate was pretty fair there. But ungrateful with them? How? Tell me how. By trying to be the perfect daughter even when I wanted to run away to a circus. A literal fucking circus. I was ten, on a class trip, and I snuck behind the tent and was five minutes from sneaking into a clown's trunk. Only fear of being the circus's tigers' next meal made me go back and find my class."

Achilles choked. "Mycah—"

She gripped his thick wrists, clinging to them as if his solid body were the only thing anchoring her to the earth. "No, I'm serious. By getting straight As and graduating top of my class and going to the best college? Supporting them for years with the job they scorned? I'm not worthy because I don't have a billionaire husband and head several charity committees and host social events of the year? My ring finger, vagina and womb are more important than my brain. Yet, without me, they would be out on the street.

But *I'm ungrateful*. They destroy me with their criticism. Their dismissal of my successes. Their derision of my perceived lack of femininity. Meanwhile, sometimes, I think I'm strangling from the responsibility of carrying this family and their expectations. And yet I do it. You asked me why I do it. Do you remember that?"

"Yes, baby, I remember," he whispered.

"Because I want their love. I want them to accept me for who I am, to love me for me. But that means sacrificing my own dreams, my own desires, and conforming to theirs. Just like they're already starting to do with Angelique. She said to excuse her for loving me. I can't." Mycah tightened her grip on him, tugging, closing her eyes. "I can't excuse her. Because their love comes at too high a price. My identity. My peace. My...soul."

When the last word left her, she wilted, as if the outpouring sapped the last of her strength. Achilles caught her, hauling her against his chest. He rose, holding her in his arms as if she weighed nothing, and took her place on the couch. And when the numbness cracked down the middle, and the hurt, anger and sorrow gushed in, drowning her, she didn't fight it.

She sobbed her disappointment, her outrage, her pain, her fear. How long she curled on his lap, pressed against his chest, she didn't know. But by the time she glanced up, the sky outside the bay windows had deepened from purple to black, casting dark shadows across Achilles's face.

A chasm of emptiness yawned wide in her chest, but unlike the numbing from earlier, this was...cleansing. Sighing, she shifted, wincing at the weariness that weighed down her limbs. She should get up, move, say something. At least apologize to Achilles for losing her shit, then crying all over him.

Before she had a chance to decide which one to do first,

he stood, still holding her in his arms. She gasped, wrapping her arms around his neck, and even that effort was almost beyond her at the moment.

"Bedroom?" he asked.

"Down the hall. Last room on the right."

He didn't speak again, just followed her instructions. In moments, he entered her room. Not bothering to turn on the lights, he set her on the bed and left, making his way to the en suite bathroom.

The light flicked on, and seconds later, the sound of running water reached her. Surprise whispered through her, but she didn't have time to dwell on it because he returned, gently grasping her waist and bringing her back to her feet. With a quick efficiency that didn't contain sensuality but only tenderness, he removed her clothes and once more lifted her against his chest.

No words were spoken as he settled her in the warm bath, removed the tie from his own hair, gathered her curls on top of her head and bathed her. In other circumstances, she would've objected. She'd always been the caretaker, the provider, the one in control. But now, as Achilles smoothed the bath cloth over her shoulders, arms and breasts, she handed that control over to him. Let him care for her. Wash her. Pick her up out of the tub and pat her dry.

When he carried her back to her bedroom, slipped her between the sheets and climbed in behind her, she didn't protest. No, she welcomed his hard, protective body curled around her. This wasn't about sex. It wasn't about expectation.

And as she drifted to sleep, for the first time in longer than she could remember, peace filled her.

Thirteen

Achilles raised his arms above his head, stretching them toward the beautiful, vaulted ceiling of Mycah's living room. Groaning at the burn in his muscles, he lowered his arms, exhaling and surveying the room he'd temporarily commandeered as his workspace.

As soon as Mycah had fallen into a deep sleep, he'd slid out of bed, retrieved his laptop bag from his car and set up just down the hall so if she needed him, he could hear her. After that meltdown, no way in hell he was leaving her alone tonight. She shouldn't be alone. He had the feeling she was alone too often.

And yeah, he definitely caught the pot-calling-the-kettle-black hypocrisy of that.

Leaning back against the couch cushion, he took in the surprisingly warm, cozy apartment. If a person could call huge bay windows with ornate designs, a massive fireplace that nearly spanned one wall, beautiful hardwood walls, floor-to-ceiling fully packed bookshelves and gorgeous molding something as simple as an apartment. Still, he liked it much better than the penthouse where he stayed. Here, trees filled her view, and in her spacious bedroom with its exposed brick walls, he'd snagged a glimpse of a garden outside her window. Even her kitchen looked like an actual kitchen—homey, lived in, with a table, chairs, wood cabinets, windows—instead of something out of a futuristic sci-fi movie.

Mycah had even decorated it with furniture meant for comfort instead of appearance. The overstuffed couches and chairs, earth tones and jeweled pillows, throw rugs, standing lamps, Afrocentric art—they all invited a person to sit down, curl their feet underneath themselves, talk, stay. A far cry from her parents' house that screamed "this is staged so you know how affluent, powerful and important we are."

The apartment wasn't the only surprising aspect he'd learned about Mycah.

Jesus.

Her pain.

So much of it, she'd cracked under the weight.

He propped his elbows on his thighs, digging his thumbs into his eyes, rubbing them. How could her parents not look at her and be proud of the woman she was? Not appreciate all that she sacrificed for them? Despite how they chose to show it, he didn't doubt that Laurence and Cherise loved Mycah. But that love came with conditions. And those conditions were asphyxiating the relationship with their daughter as surely as weeds choking the life from flowers straining to reach the sun.

A muted sound came from the direction of Mycah's bedroom, and he tilted his head toward it, frowning, listening. Several seconds passed, and just as his muscles loosened and he returned to his laptop to resume working, the sound reached him again. He recognized it.

Surging from the couch, he strode down the corridor, entered Mycah's bedroom and headed for the bathroom. He spotted her, hunched over the toilet and clinging to it as she vomited into the porcelain bowl.

Kneeling next to her, he murmured her name, rubbing soothing circles on her back, feeling…helpless. Not an easy thing for a man to admit. As soon as she'd told him about the pregnancy, he'd read everything he could about it—especially that first trimester. So he knew morning sickness—a misnomer if he ever heard one—was normal for most women, but he hated to see her suffer like this and not be able to do anything to help her. He'd witnessed his fair share of people puking. Some of the men his mother had dated. In high school. In jail. College. But this was different. With them, he hadn't wished he could trade places, take their misery on for himself.

Standing, he moved across the large bathroom, grabbed a bath cloth from the linen closet and wet it under the faucet. He folded it a couple of times and returned to her, settling it on the back of her neck as his mother had done for him when he'd been sick.

"You don't have to—" Another bout of retching cut her off, her back bowing under the force of it. She moaned as the last of it passed, a tremor shaking her.

"Yes, I do." He shifted behind her, curving his body around hers, lending her his strength, even though, realistically, it was an impossibility. Still, she could lean on him. Know he was there for her. He kissed the top of her curls. "I'm not leaving, baby, so don't ask."

Another groan. "I don't want you to see me like this."

He scoffed. "I've seen those birthing videos. In seven

months, I'm going to see you looking a hell of a lot worse. This is nothing."

She reached behind her and weakly slapped him. "That's a really messed-up thing to say. And don't re-mind— Oh, God."

For the next ten minutes they remained in the bathroom, and when they finally emerged, with her tired and clothed in fresh pajamas, Achilles led her to the living room and tucked her in on the couch. He rummaged in her kitchen, and soon returned to her with a steaming cup of pepper-mint tea and a slice of toast.

"It's not much," he said, sitting both the cup and the small plate on the table in front of her. "But it'll settle your stomach. And from what I've read, both are good to help ease the morning sickness."

"Thank you," she murmured, reaching for the tea and sipping from the cup. "That doesn't surprise me."

"What?" He lowered to the couch next to her, shifting his laptop, bag and manuals over to give her room.

"That you've been reading up on it. Watching videos." She studied him over the rim of the cup. "I don't think I've met anyone with a hungrier brain than yours."

"That sounds...disturbing."

The corner of her mouth quirked in a sardonic half smile. "It's a compliment. You're voracious for informa-tion. It's what makes you so brilliant. And so intimidat-ing, too. People look at the hair, the ink, the size—" she waved a hand up and down in front of him "—and un-derestimate you. For instance, my parents' party. I didn't even know that about my ancestors. Not that I'm ashamed of it. I think it's cool as hell. Still, I didn't know. But you did. Like I said. Information. And you wielded it like a double-edged sword."

"Unexpected?" He heard the edge in his voice, wished

he could dull it. But years of being on the "You're smart for being poor/brown/an ex-con" end of the stick was hard to shake.

"For them maybe," she admitted softly. "But not for me."

Silence thrummed in the room, and they stared at each other, a tension thick with words unspoken, desire a living, breathing entity right there with them.

"Eat," he finally said, nodding toward the plate and the untouched toast. "You need to coat your stomach."

"More things you read?" she teased, that faint smile touching her sensual mouth. But she did pick up the bread and nibble on it. "What are you working on so late?" she asked, dipping her head toward his laptop. "Is there a project from the office that you had to bring home?"

Achilles shifted his attention to his computer. He stood on a precipice, one of trust. No one knew about the video game. Not even Cain and Kenan. He glanced at Mycah, who slowly frowned the longer he remained quiet. His heart thudded, echoing in his head until all he heard was its bass rhythm. His tongue thickened, nerves twisting in his gut like a nest of snakes.

This was important because *she* was important. As much as he wanted to deny it, Mycah had crawled beneath his skin, into his bones, into his soul. She wielded the power to hurt him like no other, not even his brothers. And exposing this vulnerable part of himself to her—this project that encapsulated his passion, his hopes, his dreams—meant taking a leap of faith in her.

In the faith that she wouldn't reject the truth of him.

He touched the mouse, bringing the screen to life, and with a few more taps, opened the file with the video game art. For several moments, he studied the digital image of a ravaged land, a castle in the distance, a forest with malevolent blinking red eyes glaring from its depths, and in the foreground, a lone Black teenager, his locs falling around his face, in a white T-shirt and light blue jeans and a long, gleaming sword in hand. Inhaling a deep breath, he turned the laptop toward her. She scanned the monitor, then shifted wide eyes back to him.

"What is this?" she breathed.

"Mine." And again, hearing the defensiveness in his tone, he tried again. "A video game I've been working on for the past year. It's a high-fantasy, open-world, action-adventure video game."

She huffed out a soft laugh, returning her gaze to the laptop. "I have no idea what that means. Except for high fantasy. But the rest of that? I'm lost."

"Open world is where players can explore the game and choose for themselves how to approach the world and its particular challenges. Action-adventure games combine the best elements of both kinds of games. Just-adventure games have situation problems for players to resolve but little to no action. And action games center on real-time interactions between players that test their reflexes. Action-adventure games combine both—problem-solving and testing the reflexes."

"Angelique would be crushing so hard on you right now." Mycah flashed him a smile. "I really need to introduce you to her."

A banner of warmth unfurled inside him, even though a voice cautioned him that it was probably a throwaway comment on her part. To introduce him to her sister meant telling her parents about the baby and his being the father.

And she's too ashamed of you to do that.

Right. She needed time to prepare herself and them. Months.

The reminder doused that flare of warmth.

"Why this world?" she asked, her finger circling over the screen. "Why did you choose this particular setting?"

He hesitated, but said, "I'm not sure what you know about my past…"

"Only what the media has reported."

"I grew up in a rough neighborhood of Seattle called White Center. Back then crime, gangs and drugs had a grip on the area. Mom worked most nights, and by the time I was eleven, my grandmother had died, and I stayed in our apartment by myself. It wasn't anything to hear drug deals, fighting or gunfire in the alley behind our building. I was so immune to it, I'd just turn up the TV to drown it out. There wasn't any calling the cops."

The memories worked themselves back in, vines sprouting from seeds he'd thought long dormant. The fear of being home alone, wishing his mother was with him. Missing his grandmother.

"Still, with all that around me, my mother made sure I never got caught up in drugs or gangs. Even though she came in dragging, dog-tired and bleary-eyed at five o'clock in the morning after a night shift, she got me up, made my lunch, walked me to the bus stop, met me there after school, helped me with my homework, fixed dinner and then went to work. When she noticed I had an aptitude for computers, she took on more shifts and found a way to enroll me in college-level computer courses because I wasn't being challenged enough in high school. She always made a way. I graduated high school in the top ten percent of my class because of her. I was accepted to college because of her… And then I failed her by going to jail."

He remained silent, watching the shock wash over Mycah's face. Waited for the disgust or at least the unease as she realized she was in a room—that she'd gotten pregnant by—the thug her parents, the media called him.

But the disgust never came.

Compassion did.

And he had to battle past his first instinctive defense—slam up his guard. Reject what he perceived as pity.

Then she touched him. Covered his clenched hand with her smaller, more delicate one, and his walls cracked and tumbled down.

"Tell me," she said, her thumb brushing over his knuckles.

And he did. The story he'd never shared with anyone pouring out of him as she held his hand, his gaze and his heart.

"My mom... Like, I said, she gave me everything, all of her. So I never begrudged her the little bit of life she grabbed for herself, even if the men she chose were...lacking. It's like she had a radar for unemployed, drunk users. Most of them were jerks but harmless, but the last one..."

A fine tension invaded his body as he traveled back to that night ten years ago in their White Center apartment. His mother and her boyfriend arriving home after a night out at the local bar. Both had been drinking. Arguing. Getting louder and louder.

"Achilles, look at me." A hand cupped his cheek and he opened his eyes. He hadn't realized he'd closed them. "Keep those beautiful eyes on me. Go ahead. Finish it."

He nodded, squeezed her hand and drew it down to his thigh.

"One night, Mom came home from a date with her new boyfriend. Matt." His mouth twisted around the name, a thin layer of grime covering his tongue. "They'd been dating for two weeks and he was different from the others. There was nothing harmless about him. He had an edge to him. Mean. Hard..." Achilles shook his head. "They were a little drunk and were arguing. I was in my room and tried to ignore it. She wouldn't have appreciated me interfering, anyway. But then I heard her cry out in pain. I bolted out of my bedroom into the living room and he had her on the floor, hitting her. I… I snapped. I punched him. And I kept punching him. I found out later that the neighbors overheard and called the cops. Next thing I know, I was in cuffs and hauled off to jail."

He slid his hand out from under hers. He spread both of his hands out and stared at his fingers as if he could still see the bruised and swollen knuckles stained with Matt's blood. Could still feel the pain from beating a man unconscious.

It didn't take much to conjure the horror that had filled him at his actions.

"I ended up serving two years for the assault. Only my mother's testimony, my clean record and Matt's not-so-clean record kept me from more time. But while I was in, I saw men—boys, really—just like me who'd made mistakes. One bad decision that had led them there. Whether it was made in the heat of the moment or done years ago and set them on a path of more poor decisions. Yes, some of them belonged right where they were, there's no denying that. But others? Others didn't have the ability to see anything different. And when I was locked up in that cell, I started dreaming about this game. And the idea stayed with me after I graduated college after I was released from jail, and years later after I started working with the software design company. What story could I tell? But more importantly, for youth like me, like the men I was locked up with, like the girls I went to school with who were told they were worth no more than their bodies and smile… What could I get them to see?"

He grabbed his laptop, clicked a few keys and pulled up more game art. This one depicted the same teen stepping through a portal. One side was the world from the previous art and on the other side was a present-day urban inner city. A kid from one world stepping into an unknown one.

"You asked why the high-fantasy setting?" Achilles asked Mycah. "Think about every movie or book you've seen or read from that genre, set in that world. When you meet the characters, they don't know their purpose yet. The most important thing for all of us is finding our identity, our reason for being. Because when we do, we begin to understand why we're here. We begin to have hope."

He shook his head. "I'm not saying this game will give kids those answers, but I am saying research has proven that video games stimulate the brain. Can actually change it in some regions. So instead of giving them a game that aggrandizes what they see every day—crime, violence, debasement of their community and people—what about a game that will awaken their brains to more? Create a different mindset and passion for something that elevates them above the reality they already know? Spark a vision in them where they see themselves as heroes, warriors, kings, queens, where they make connections and fight as a team for a common goal instead of against one another? I want to create a game where they can escape the horrors of their current environment long enough to glimpse something different, something greater. To connect with it. To see they have potential and purpose."

As the last word echoed between them, he braced himself against the regret that tried to creep in. From the vulnerability of exposing that part of himself.

"I'm so damn awed by you," Mycah rasped. She sucked in an audible breath and leaned back, pressing the heels of her palms to her eyes. "Give me a minute. It's the freaking pregnancy hormones."

Huffing out a short laugh, Achilles cuffed her wrists and

gently drew her arms down. She kept her eyes squeezed closed, but after a moment she opened them, and her dark gaze glistened.

"I'm serious." She rose on her knees, tunneled her fingers through his hair, fisting the strands and tipping her head forward until it pressed to his. "What was your mother's name?"

"Natia Lee."

"Natia Lee," she breathed. "Without even meeting her, I know she was very proud of the boy she raised. And I'm certain she would've been extremely proud of the man you've become."

He blinked, staring at her, struck silent.

"You're beautiful," she continued. "Your soul is so beautiful, and screw anyone who can't see it. Who refuses to see it."

"Mycah." He clasped her hips. To push her away, draw her closer, he didn't know.

"No." Her grip on him tightened. "I'm not finished. You're brilliant. You're scary brilliant. And I hope our baby has your brain." She brushed a kiss over his forehead. "Is the game finished yet? Have you shown it to anyone yet? Have you told your brothers about it?"

"It's almost done, and no." He shook his head, leaning back, releasing her. "Cain is a thorough man, so I can't imagine him not knowing about my past, but I haven't told either him or Kenan about the game—or me being in jail."

"Achilles." She sighed. "They would be your biggest supporters. If you would just let them. And I agree with you. Cain probably knows about your imprisonment. Which means he doesn't care and has accepted you anyway. Let them in."

Fear etched a jagged path through him. In spite of his resolve to keep them at arm's length, the two men had become important to him. He couldn't bear their rejection. But what if… What if they… Hope glinted underneath the doubt, the dread like a bright penny hidden in freshly turned dirt.

"It's a lucky person who you let in," she said, and he narrowed his gaze on her. At the note of—well, on another person, he would've called it wistfulness. "They must pass tests that make the ones in your video games look like child's play."

He cupped the back of her neck, drew her forward until their lips brushed. Until their breath mated. "Do you want in, Mycah?"

Uncertainty shifted in those mocha eyes, and her lips parted, moved, but no sound emerged. An ache, swift and sharp, sliced his chest but he smiled against her mouth.

"Better question, baby," he said, arranging her so she straddled him. "Do you want me inside you?"

A beat of hesitation, but she nodded, and he raised the short hem of her nightgown, balling it in one fist, revealing her pretty flesh to his greedy gaze. He lowered his hand between her spread thighs, spearing her folds with his fingers. In seconds, her wet heat bathed him, and they both groaned. She rode his hand, clutching his shoulders, her nails digging into his skin.

"Take me out," he ordered. "Take what you want."

She didn't hesitate this time. Quickly, she complied, and in seconds, she'd freed his cock and notched him at her entrance. Their gazes met, a silent question in her eyes, and he was sure the same occupied his. This was the first time they would have sex since she'd told him about the pregnancy. The damage, so to speak, had been done. They could go bare, and fuck, all he craved in this moment was to have her tight, hot sex squeeze him with nothing separating them.

But it had to be her decision, too.

She nodded. Again.

And it was all he needed.

With a groan that emanated from his gut—hell, his soul—he thrust high and deep inside her. And entered heaven.

And God help him, he never wanted to leave.

Fourteen

"So if you want to look through the presentation I emailed you later for more detail, you can. But to sum up—" Achilles set his tablet on the coffee table and propped his elbows on his thighs as he leaned forward and addressed Cain and Kenan "—Jacobi is a solid investment. It permits the client to manage backup and recovery through a single service. They have a full support team, and it removes the resource drain from the client as well as any significant time for training, leaving the client companies open to focus their attention on other matters."

"I'm just skimming through the presentation now—" Cain swiped over the screen of his own tablet, frown creasing his brow "—and I'll pass it on to Marketing and Legal, but I agree with you. And I trust your opinion. Kenan?"

"I looked it over before the meeting." His younger brother poured more coffee into his cup from the carafe in the center of the table. "Given you're the expert on this and not me, you still broke it down to make sense. The money saved in time alone would make the return on investment worth it. I'm going with your recommendation."

"That's settled, then." Cain set the tablet down on the table and picked up his own coffee. "Thanks, Achilles, I appreciate it."

"You're welcome. It wasn't a problem."

Shock suffused him. Shock and a warmth that originated from a place he couldn't quickly identify. Probably because he'd never experienced it.

Acceptance.

Trust.

These two men—who shared his DNA but were as different from him as cotton from silk—unconditionally trusted his opinion. Accepted *him*.

"One last thing, Achilles," Cain said, hesitating a beat. "Since you did the research and understand it and the company better than me or Kenan, would you feel comfortable presenting it at the next acquisitions meeting?" Before Achilles could answer, Cain set down his cup and held up a hand, palm out. "Don't feel pressured, but I believe you would be the best man for it."

"I'll do it."

Cain blinked and Kenan stared at him, both looking as surprised as Achilles felt. Yeah, he hadn't expected to say that, either. But it was…right.

So was this leap of faith.

They would be your biggest supporters. If you would just let them... Let them in.

"Well, okay, then—" Cain smiled.

"If you two don't have anything scheduled and can give me a few minutes, I'd like to show you something."

Kenan shrugged a shoulder. "I'm free."

Cain studied him a long moment with that incisive stare. "Even if I did, I'd cancel it."

Another burst of that damn warmth. Throat tight, Achilles nodded and surged from the couch, grabbing his laptop bag. "Can I use your desk?"

Forty-five minutes later, he had his computer set up on Cain's desk, his program pulled up, and he'd explained everything about the video game—the setting, the target audience, the potential marketing...and the origination of the idea.

As he revealed his stint in prison neither Cain nor Kenan interrupted him, just let him relay his story until he completely finished.

And neither Cain nor Kenan looked shocked.

"You knew," Achilles flatly stated, not angry, not glad. Not... Hell, he didn't know how he felt.

"Of course I did," Cain said from his perch on the edge of the desk, arms crossed over his chest, no trace of remorse in his voice. "I had both of you investigated by the company's private investigator the moment after the will was read."

"And my father had you two investigated to rub in my face the kind of men I'd abandoned Rhodes Realty to align myself with." Kenan smiled, but the amusement didn't reach his eyes. "You two are real reprobates, by the way." His lips twisted. "I fit right in."

"I'm a reformed reprobate," Cain drawled. "Love has changed me."

Achilles shrugged. "Three hots and a cot changed me."

"Great." Kenan scoffed. "What kind of brothers are you, leaving me out here being a degenerate on my own?" He shook his head, but the mock disgust melted away, and his scrutiny turned speculative. "So is the supposed 'jail secret' why you've kept your distance from us?"

Dammit. Leave it to Kenan to get to the awkward heart of the matter. Pinching the bridge of his nose, Achilles rose from Cain's chair and strode to the floor-to-ceiling window of the CEO office. His brother's office. Where he fit. Where he was born to rule. How did Achilles explain that to a man who knew from the cradle that he would be king?

He didn't know, but he had to try. Because the time for secrets, for remaining silent and shutting his brothers out, had passed.

Turning around, he met their identical gazes.

"When I received that letter telling me about Barron's death, I honestly don't know why I used that ticket. I hadn't thought of my so-called father in years. I didn't care about him—"

"Stop lying to yourself," Kenan interrupted softly. "You came to that will reading for the same reason I did. Because your whole life you felt something was missing. And you were hopeful that maybe, just maybe, you might find it."

Achilles parted his lips to object, to claim that his mother and grandmother had always been enough. But the denial wouldn't emerge. Because seeds of truth lay in that statement. Curiosity and, yes, hope had propelled him to get on that plane and come to Boston.

"Okay, I'll give you that. And I'll even give you that I found the something that had been missing my whole life. Brothers. But you're right. I have tried to keep my distance, tried not to become attached to either of you because after this year is up, I'm leaving Boston. I..." Even as he surveyed the luxury of the office, the paintings, furnishings, obvious signs of wealth and power, a small voice whispered—was it still true? With the baby, he hadn't allowed himself to think that far in advance. "I don't belong here. Not in Boston. Not in Farrell International. You two were born into this world. You know how to maneuver in it. You know its language, its rules. I don't. I love computers, codes, software, design. It's where I'm happiest, not negotiating contracts, closing deals, attending parties or learning how not to offend some person with how I talk or just being...me. This isn't my world."

"That's bullshit," Cain snarled, shoving off his desk and stalking over to Achilles. "The man who endured the childhood he did... The man who survived fucking jail and then forged a successful career for himself... The man who created that brilliant video game so youth like he once was can see themselves as courageous and heroic. That man will not run from some assholes who have nothing better to do than sit around, pick out napkins for their next dinner party and gossip about people who are too busy changing the goddamn world."

Cain got in Achilles's face, his frown fierce, fire burning in his gaze. "I know what it is to turn everyone away. To be alone and convince yourself that's what you want. That you're better off that way. I won't let you do it. Not while I'm here. I'll fight for you. Me. Kenan. Devon. You have family now. And we'll fight for you. You're not going anywhere. Not if I have to keep flying all the way across the country to that forest and camp outside that damn cabin until you give in and come home. Because *this is* your home now. Go visit the mountains to get away for a few days or weeks, but you come back. You're always going to come back to us. Goddammit."

Achilles stood there, rigid with tension, staring at Cain, who glared back at him. Both of their hands curled into fists at their sides, and out of his peripheral vision, he caught Kenan standing a couple of feet away, glancing back and forth. Probably waiting to see whom he would need to tackle first.

Inhaling a deep breath through his nose, Achilles nodded. "Okay."

Cain blinked. "Okay?"

"Wait, okay?" Kenan parroted.

"Yeah." Achilles exhaled and a weight lifted from his chest. A weight so heavy, he shouldn't have been able to breathe all of these years. "I'll stay."

A smile slowly spread across Cain's face. "Yeah. Okay."

"Well, just out of curiosity, what was it that convinced you?" Kenan propped his fists on his hips. "The 'we'll fight for you' or the 'goddammit'? Both were equally compelling."

"Never miss a good chance to shut up," Cain growled at Kenan before turning back to Achilles. "One more thing. Your video game. I don't know what your plans are for it as far as distribution, but I'd like to sit down and talk to you about it. Because I want Farrell to do it. And not just yours. But more like it. Matter of fact, I want you to do the research on either acquiring or founding a company specifically to design games with the mission and vision you described to us. And I want you to run it."

Achilles turned to look at his laptop, at the art, the game he'd been working on for a year but that had been in his head for nearly ten. And now he could be part of bringing to life more like them and putting them in the hands of millions of kids?

"Yes," he rasped. "I accept."

Cain clapped him on the shoulder, then pulled him into a tight hug. "Welcome home," he murmured into his ear.

"Does this mean you're finally going to leave the basement and take an office on this floor?" Kenan asked.

Achilles snorted. Then laughed. And it felt damn good.

"Come on, show me more of this game. And what timeline are we looking at as far as getting it into beta testing. Can I be one of the betas?" Cain rubbed his hands together.

A chime echoed in the room, followed by a loud vibration. Frowning, Kenan removed his phone from his pants pocket. "Sorry, I need to check that. It's my notifications set to alert me if our name is mentioned in any..." He swept his thumb across the screen and tapped it a couple of times. His frown deepened as he scanned it, then his nostrils flared wide, his head jerking up. Eyes wide, he gaped at Cain. "Oh, shit, Cain."

"What?" Cain barked. "Kenan, what?"

"The society columns, gossip blogs, *Boston Noise* and the *Brahmin Post* are all publishing a story that Cain and Devon ended their engagement because he cheated on her and she found out."

"What the hell?" he demanded, his face darkening.

"That's not all," Kenan murmured. "They're all reporting Devon discovered you got another woman pregnant. Mycah Hill."

"Are you kidding me?" Cain thundered, stalking across the floor and tearing the phone out of Kenan's hand. "Where in the hell would they get this shit from?"

Shock spread through Achilles like frost on a windshield, dread curdling in his gut. Dread and suspicion. He didn't know how they could've found out about the pregnancy, but he had an idea where the story could've originated.

Achilles had promised Mycah he wouldn't tell Cain and Kenan about the baby, but with Cain facing the potential damage to his relationship with Devon and his reputation, he didn't have a choice.

"Cain, Kenan." He waited until he had his brothers' attention on him. "I have something to tell you."

Fifteen

Achilles stared at the penthouse elevator doors, waiting for them to open. The security guard had called minutes ago, informing him that Mycah had arrived asking to be let upstairs. He'd been expecting her since the story about her and Cain's supposed "love child" had leaked three hours earlier.

His brothers had taken the news about Mycah actually being pregnant and Achilles being the father better than he'd expected. And they'd even been happy for him. Hugged him. But they were still confused how Cain's name had ended up involved in the story instead of his. That part—his suspicions—he hadn't revealed and couldn't without talking to Mycah first. But he had promised to try to clear up the mess. And that meant convincing Mycah that they could no longer maintain this secret about the baby. Not if it meant that others would be hurt by it.

You'll find out if she's ashamed of you.

He briefly closed his eyes as the ding announcing the arrival of the elevator rang in the apartment.

He'd finally know if he'd been only a dirty secret for the woman he'd fallen in love with after all.

If he'd repeated a history he'd promised himself never to revisit.

If he'd given a woman his heart again only to be told it wasn't enough. That *he* wasn't enough.

Yes, he would have his answer.

The doors slid open, and Mycah rushed out of the elevator, and though he braced himself for what the next few minutes would bring between them, he soaked her in. The sensual explosion of curls that graced her shoulders and framed her beautiful face. The long, cream wool coat that opened over a dark purple sheath dress. The color reminded him of the one she'd worn the night they first met. And he tried not to let that strike him as an omen. Because he couldn't determine if it would be good or bad.

"Achilles." Breathless, her lovely mouth twisted down at the corners, her espresso eyes dark with worry, she crossed the floor to him. She slid her hands over his waist, clutching his hips and tipping her head back to gaze into his face. "I'm so sorry. God, I'm so sorry."

"What are you apologizing for?"

She frowned. At the question or his even tone, he couldn't tell, but her grip tightened on him. "Don't pretend we both don't know who's behind that story being leaked to the media," she said, voice grim. "Who else could it be but my parents? I don't know how they found out about the pregnancy, but it's them. Since I started at Farrell, they've been on me to cozy up to Cain. Maybe this is their twisted way of doing it, of forcing us together."

"If that's true, then you shouldn't be apologizing for them. These are their actions, and they need to own them.

Not you." When would she get tired of doing it? Anger sparked inside him, but he tamped it down. That wasn't his battle to fight; he'd gladly wage it for her if he could, but he couldn't. "But their actions have put us in a difficult position. And now we have choices to make."

She stepped back, her arms dropping down by her sides, and he almost reached for her, demanding she put her hands back on him. Let him absorb her warmth. Let him touch her when he dropped this bomb on her. Because physical connection seemed to be all they had—at least for her.

"What do you mean?" Her gaze searched his face. "What else happened?"

"I was with Cain and Kenan when the story broke. I had to tell them about us and the pregnancy."

She exhaled, the gust of breath long and soft. Crossing an arm protectively over her stomach and palming her forehead with the other hand, she paced away from him, crossing the living room to the window. He followed at a slower gait, allowing her space and time.

"Okay," she said after a couple of minutes. "I pretty much expected it had to happen. Especially since Cain and Devon are directly affected by all of this. I'm just so sorry they were dragged into this mess."

"Mess?"

She pivoted, frustration suffusing her expression and voice. Waving a hand, she shook her head. "You know what I mean."

"Yes, I do. And you're right—this is a mess of our making. Because we've failed to be honest. With our families. Our coworkers. Each other. Ourselves."

"What are you saying, Achilles?" she whispered, the barest hint of panic in her tone. A flash in her eyes.

"I'm saying we can only build a future on truth. No

more hiding, no more secrets. Because they have a way of crumbling and leaving people broken."

"Time." She splayed her fingers wide over her belly, and this time there was no mistaking the alarm in her voice. It darkened her eyes to near black. "You promised me time to reveal this how I needed to..."

"That was before a hatchet job about my brother fathering my child hit the fan," he growled, anger surging inside him, hot and possessive. The thought that people believed his baby belonged to Cain. That his brother had touched Mycah, put his mouth on her, seen what she looked like lost in pleasure... Dammit. He scrubbed a hand down his face, his beard abrading his palm. "Mycah, you can't hide your pregnancy any longer. It's impossible. And we have to address the misconception of Cain being the father. For him and Devon as well as for the reputation of the company."

"I know, I've thought about this," she said in a rush, the words piling up on each other. "I'll make a statement confirming the pregnancy and debunk the lie that Cain is the father."

"And when they ask who the father of the baby is? Because they will ask, Mycah." His body stilled, everything in him waiting for her answer.

"I'll tell them that information is between me and the father and we wish our privacy to be respected."

Pain, anger, sorrow, regret—they crowded into his chest, squatters claiming room and shoving against his rib cage for more space. They filled him, the pressure so great, he breathed the emotions, tasted them, became them.

"You do know not giving them a definitive answer will only flame the fire, not put it out, right?" he asked, surprised at how calm he sounded when a storm raged inside.

She shook her head, curls grazing her shoulders. "Not if we handle it correctly—"

"Are you that ashamed to admit that I'm the father of your baby?"

Her chin jerked back as if his accusation had delivered a verbal blow. Shock widened her eyes, parted her lips, and she blinked at him as if slow to comprehend his question.

"Achilles," she finally whispered, lifting an arm toward him and shifting forward. "That's not true. I could never—"

"Be embarrassed by me?" He arched an eyebrow, the corner of his mouth quirking. "Try again, Mycah. You forget, I've done this before. I'm familiar with the script. Intimately."

"I'm not her," she said, her fingers curling into her palm. "I'm *not* her."

"I know that. I've known that for a while. Doesn't mean history isn't repeating itself."

Accept me. Accept us.

"You're not being fair," she accused, and he hardened his heart at the desperation there. "The reasons I explained to you still stand. They're still valid. Even more so now that this story leaked the way it did. Which, I suspect, was part of my parents' reason for doing it. I'm unsure about my position with Farrell. Can Cain afford to keep me on with rumors of his supposed mistress working for him? And what about my professional reputation? Now more than ever I need to control the narrative and not allow them to steal that from me. To destroy years of hard work, to ruin how my coworkers and peers look at me. And while I haven't slept with Cain, if it comes out that I did sleep with the other CEO of the company, it would undo everything. I don't get a second chance at this. All I'm asking for is time, Achilles. You can't just flip the script because it's convenient."

"Convenient?" He stepped closer to her, then stopped.

Getting nearer to her so he could inhale her scent, touch her—that was a mistake. Then…fuck it. He eliminated the distance between them, not stopping until his chest pressed to hers, his thighs bracketed hers. She tipped her head back, meeting his gaze. He ached to brush his fingertips over her elegant brows, those sharp cheekbones, that trembling, sensual mouth. But even he had his limits. "You're not the only one out on that limb, Mycah. I'm right there beside you. Fuck, I want to be there with you. Just like you told me to do with my brothers—let them in. Now I'm asking you. Let me in. *Let me, baby.* This—" he gave in, stroked a hand down her hair "—there's nothing convenient about this."

"Isn't it?" she asked softly, her eyes dark with shadows, heavy with sorrow. "And what happens when you decide that I'm not enough anymore? That I've disappointed you? What then? What will I have left? My baby and my career. You're leaving Boston, or have you forgotten that, too? I'll co-parent long-distance, and my career, it's the only thing I have complete control over. I sacrificed it before, for a man. And I nearly lost everything I worked so hard for. Nearly lost all trust in myself and who I was in the process. I'm not willing to do that again."

Achilles dropped his arm. Took a step back. Damn near stumbled as pain and grief punched a hole in his chest, his heart. For him, for her.

For whom they could've been.

"You have so little faith in me—in yourself."

A sense of futility swamped him, and instinctively he battled it, almost reaching for her, needing to hold her, make her see that if she'd just fight for him…

Love him.

He briefly closed his eyes and pressed his fist to his chest, rubbing the ache there. Her gaze dropped to the movement, and he stopped, walking past her to take her former place at the window, blindly staring out at the view that so many people would—and did—pay millions for.

And him? He'd give it all away to wake every day to her.

"It amazes me that you don't see in yourself what I do. What everyone else does. You've been at Farrell for a matter of weeks, and already you have the respect of those who work under you and who are over you. I'm not minimizing your concerns, but I am saying that you're not taking into account how fiercely people will go to bat for you because of their respect for your work ethic, your record and your character. And you as a person. You don't just change procedures and cultures in a company, Mycah, you change people. You changed me."

He turned, faced her. As the glutton for punishment he'd called himself before, he needed to look into her eyes for this.

"I arrived in Boston alone, closed off, mistrustful, bitter, angry and looking for the exit back to Washington. I'm still not what anyone would call a people person, but I have family now—brothers. And not just in name only. Brothers who I trust, who trust me, who I want to become closer to. Not only do they accept me but they want to support me. Like my game. Cain wants to fund it, distribute it."

"God, Achilles, that's wonderful," she breathed, delight for him briefly dispelling the shadows in her eyes. "I'm so happy for you."

"You gave that to me. Because you encouraged me to trust him and Kenan. I'm letting go of the past, of the hurts, the anger. And today, I told Cain I would stay in Boston." As shock flashed across her face and her fingers fluttered to the base of her throat, a faint smile curved his mouth. But without humor. "I might have said I would today, but truthfully? I'd made the decision when you told me you were pregnant. I couldn't be a part-time father. And by then, the thought of leaving had me sick inside. Because it meant leaving you. It meant leaving the woman I was falling in love with."

"Achilles," she whispered.

He shook his head, cutting her off. "This isn't for you, baby," he said. "It's for me. I love you. And yes, maybe I'm not being fair to lay this on you, either. But I'm not asking you to do anything with it since at this point, you don't believe you can—or you don't want to. I settled for a half relationship in secrecy once. I won't do it again. I want more. I want it all. Because I'm willing to offer you everything I have and am in return—a husband, a friend, a protector, a lover, a father to our baby. I deserve more than scraps of you."

He glanced away from her, from the stricken expression that damn near brought him to his knees.

"Achilles, you don't understand. Just give me—" She stretched a hand toward him, but when he stared at it, she slowly lowered her arm.

This was a matter of survival. And if she put that hand on him, he might not have the strength to do them both the favor of ending this before they hurt each other beyond repair. They still had to be parents to their baby.

"And then what, Mycah? Another month? Another excuse? I can't." He slid his hands into the pockets of his pants. "Please let me know when your next doctor's appointment is. We'll probably have to be more careful given the publicity with the story, but I won't be shut out. I still need to be part of the pregnancy."

She wound her arms around her torso, and after a moment, nodded. And after another longer moment, she turned and walked across the apartment, stepped into the elevator and left him.

How long he stood there, staring out the window, he didn't know. But when he did stir, the pain, the sorrow crushing his sternum, hadn't eased. Only this time, he didn't have to face it alone.

Removing his cell phone from his pocket, he dialed his brothers.

Sixteen

Mycah glanced up from blindly studying her computer screen when she heard the knock on her open office door. She forced a strained smile, waving Kenan Rhodes inside, although her stomach tightened, and it had nothing to do with morning sickness.

He returned the smile, closing the door behind him.

Her belly pitched harder.

If they were going to fire her, they would send the charmer to do it. Sugar with medicine and all that.

She should be worried about losing her job, but as she met his blue-gray gaze, all she could think about was another man with those eyes. A man she hadn't seen in two eternally long days and nights. A man she couldn't evict from her thoughts. A man who'd entered her life, ravaged it like a midnight storm and left her irrevocably altered.

He'd claimed she'd changed him.

No, Achilles had it wrong. He was the perfect storm. And her?

Apparently, a storm chaser.

But that was over. And she stood alone. Again. Shivering in the cold. By choice? Maybe. Yes. God, but it didn't feel like it. She'd just been trying to protect herself, protect her career. Was that so selfish?

Protect yourself?

Or hide behind your career?

She silently cursed at that annoying voice that wouldn't shut up—that had refused to shut up—these past two days.

"I just wanted to stop by and see how you're doing." Kenan dipped his head toward the visitor's chair in front of her desk, silently requesting permission to sit. She nodded, and he sank into it. "You did a great job at the press conference."

She grimaced at the mention of the short press conference the PR department arranged that morning to address the article. It'd been held in the lobby of the building. Mycah had made a short statement and had refused any questions.

"Thank you. It's a sad day when a businesswoman has to make a public statement about the status of her womb." She released a sound somewhere between disgust and relief. "I'm just glad it's over. At least that part of it. How are Cain and Devon doing?"

Kenan rolled his eyes, a smirk tugging the corner of his mouth. "Disgustingly okay with going around exhibiting extra displays of public affection to dismiss rumors of his defection." He sobered, the smile fading from his lips. "They'll be fine. Neither one of them are strangers to public scrutiny. How are you doing? In the spirit of full disclosure, Cain and I spent the evening with Achilles a couple of nights ago."

A deep, bright ache bloomed in her chest, and she shifted her gaze from his, unable to look into those eyes any longer.

"How is he?" she rasped.

"Not good," he said bluntly. She whipped her head back toward him. "But he'll be okay."

"I suppose you and Cain resent me. I can't say that I blame you."

"For what? Giving Achilles a reason to stay here in Boston?" Kenan arched an eyebrow. "Cain might think he did that with his caveman 'You stay here' speech, but I know it was you. You and the baby. His love for you. You brought my brother to life. I could never resent you for that."

"I broke his heart," she whispered.

"Yes, you did."

"C'mon, Kenan." She leaned forward, her fingers curling into her palm. Her chest rose and fell on her elevated breaths. What game was he playing? Part of her wanted, *needed*, him to lash out at her. Punishment? "He had to tell you my reasons for not wanting to reveal he's the father of our baby just yet. Or why *he believes* I don't want to tell anyone."

"I understand what he believes. I also understand your reasons." Kenan reclined in the chair, elbows propped on the arms, fingers steepled under his chin. "Mycah, do you watch football?"

She frowned, confused at the sudden switch in subject. "I live in Boston. Will saying no get me fired?"

"Possibly. Probably. So just plead the fifth. Anyway, nearly seventy percent of the NFL players are Black. But fewer than ten percent of the coaches are Black. And if one of those coaches are fired? It's almost impossible for them to acquire another coaching position in the league or even college. While if a white coach is let go, he might have two or three more jobs with different teams, just in the league alone."

He lowered his arms, his gaze bright, intense. For the

first time since meeting the youngest Farrell brother, she glimpsed another side of him.

"The society we exist in isn't set up for minorities to win. And when we do make our own opportunities and lose them for some reason? Fail? That same system isn't set up for our recovery. It's different for the white male— and to an extent, the white woman—because they can fail, can come back for a second and third chance, and go even higher, achieve even more. But not us. We won't be the first rehired, and chances are slimmer that we'll achieve that pinnacle again within the same company. Is it any wonder we're in a constant dogfight where we battle like hell not to give in, never to fail because we know the odds of recovering aren't there? That if we're going to make it, we're going to have to do it outside a rigged system? So yes, Mycah, I get it." He nodded. "I get why you guard your career so fiercely. You're a Black woman who has a lot to lose." He paused, cocked his head, studied her for a long moment. "And if that's all there was to it, I would leave it alone. Because as a Black man in the same society, I'm the last person to stand in your way."

The relief from being *understood* chilled at his cryptic words. "What're you talking about, if that's all there was to it?"

His expression softened. "I meant it when I said we're from the same world, Mycah. Our families are…very similar." An emotion too quick to decipher flashed in his eyes. "Another thing Achilles can't really understand but I do. The responsibility toward them. And I may be a complete hypocrite right now, but you can't live your life for them. For an approval that is based on conditions. Because there will always be more conditions. Unachievable stipulations. Impossible goals. And you'll lose yourself trying to obtain them. And one day you'll wake up and realize that while they've been living their lives, yours has passed you by with nothing to show for it. Nothing but the reflection of someone else's dreams for you instead of your own."

"Yes," she said, fear, sadness and pain clogging her throat. Pressing against her chest. She briefly closed her eyes. "Yes."

That's all she could say and yet, it captured everything. Just as Kenan had.

Achilles believed she was ashamed of him. That she didn't want to tell her parents about the pregnancy because of that shame, and nothing could be further from the truth. She couldn't be more proud to have him as the father of her baby. There was no other man she wanted but him. The embarrassment belonged to her. Because as soon as she shared the news with her parents, they would use it…twist it. She harbored no doubts about that, about who they were. So she'd longed to keep this special news—their baby—between them for just a little while longer before she had no choice. Keep it pure and just theirs.

But her parents had managed to ruin it anyway.

No. The truth opened up inside her like a lamp clicking on, chasing away the darkness. No, she couldn't place all of this on them.

Because in the end, these were her choices, and the time had come to accept the truth and own those choices.

Yes, she'd worked all these years to establish a career she could be proud of, to provide for her family. But she also used both as a way to protect her heart from further hurt, to shield herself from rejection and the pain of being deemed unworthy, never good enough. While her parents had never said the words, while her employers had never written them on a review, the implications had always been that she'd had to work twice as hard, be twice as good…

And she'd done everything to achieve a goal that would always be this dangling, golden carrot.

But Achilles… She huffed out a chuckle that ended on a soft sob.

Achilles had never asked her to be anyone but herself. He'd never asked her to decrease herself so he could be increased. He had loved her for herself—flaws and all. He'd worshipped those flaws, loved her *because* of them, not in spite of them. But she'd allowed her fears to prevent her from claiming him for herself even though she so desperately longed to.

Because she loved him.

God, she loved him.

And she was living in fear of rejection, of disapproval. Of loss.

No matter the consequences of living in the light and out loud, she'd willingly face them. If that meant whisper campaigns from business colleagues, a hit to her reputation, ostracism from her family—so be it.

She was going to claim the life she wanted and finally, finally live it. And if he'd have her, she was going to claim the love of her life.

"So are we going to do this?" Kenan asked.

She startled, almost forgetting he still sat in the office with her. Glancing at him, she smiled.

"Oh, we are so doing this."

"Good." He clapped his hands together, rubbing them, a grin of what could be called only glee spreading across his handsome face. "Did I ever tell you how I single-handedly saved Cain and Devon's relationship? True story."

Seventeen

For what could possibly be the last time, Mycah climbed the front steps to her parents' home. Enough anger flowed through her that the thought of never entering the house again was okay with her. But underneath, the love for them that she could never eradicate made her hope it wouldn't be the final time she entered the place where she'd grown up. The last time she was with her parents.

But that would be their decision.

She used her key and let herself in, then removed it, setting it on the mantel. Odd not to have the key she'd had since she was twelve on her ring, but it was only the first of many changes in her life. Heading toward the rear of the house, she inhaled a deep breath to calm the nerves that fluttered against the walls of her stomach like a flock of migrating birds.

I can do this. I am *doing this.*

Because it needed to be done.

There was no going back.

She paused in the entryway to the small family room. As she'd expected, only her parents occupied the room; her father sat on the couch reading one of the murder mysteries he loved, while her mother commandeered the antique writing desk. At three o'clock, Angelique wouldn't arrive from school for another hour or so, depending on if she had play practice. Good. Because this wasn't a conversation her sister needed to overhear.

"Mom, Dad." Mycah entered the room.

"Well, this is a surprise." Her father set aside his book, smiling.

"It certainly is." Cherise rose from her chair and crossed the room to pull her into a hug, air-kissing both her cheeks. "A good one, though."

"Is it really?" Mycah asked. "You two should've expected me sooner or later."

"I don't know what you mean, honey." Her mother waved a hand, retracing her steps to lower to the couch next to Laurence. "Why don't you sit down, and I can—"

"No, that won't be necessary. I'm not staying long, and this isn't a social call."

"Mycah, interrupting your mother is unnecessary," Laurence admonished. "We didn't raise you to be rude."

"I hate to disappoint you, but I'm afraid that might become the norm, so you might need to become used to it." She cocked her head, coolly eyeing them. "Which one of you did it? Which one of you went to the media and told them I was pregnant?"

They didn't even have the grace to appear remorseful. Not even a little bit. If anything, annoyance crept across her mother's face. Annoyance that Mycah bothered her with this?

Jesus.

As if she didn't have the right to be angry.

"Is that what all this is about?" Cherise flicked a hand. "Neither one of us went to the media. I did happen to mention to Margaret Dansing that you were expecting while we were lunching. I'm not responsible for what she did with the information."

"Margaret Dansing. The same Margaret who told you about seeing me with Cain. The same Margaret whose daughter is a columnist with the *Brahmin Post*." Mycah seethed. Paused. And reminded herself this was her mother. She couldn't disrespect her even though, God knows, the woman couldn't give a damn about the word *respect* when it came to Mycah. "How did you find out?"

"Dr. Luther's office. The nurse there congratulated me on becoming a grandmother. Do you know the embarrassment you caused me when I had to pretend to know what she was talking about?" Cherise frowned. "Really, Mycah, I should've been the first person you told."

"Because of what you did with the information when you did find out?" she snapped. "How could you, Mom? Did you even care about the damage you did? To me? To Cain and Devon? To Achilles? Did you even care that it wasn't Cain's baby? Or that people only believe it was. That's all that mattered to you."

"I didn't say who fathered it," she said calmly. "I let Margaret draw her own conclusions. And since she'd just seen you dining with Cain..." She shrugged a shoulder. "But yes, anyone else is better than people believing *that man* fathered *our* grandchild," she bit out. "What were you thinking, Mycah?"

"I wasn't thinking about you."

"That much is obvious," Laurence said, shaking his head. "What's done is done. And you still get to keep your little job because Cain couldn't very well fire the mother of his child and look good in the public eye. It all works out in the end and it's for the best, if you ask me."

"It's for the best?" She stared at them. Gaped. Good God. She loosed a disbelieving laugh. She'd been protecting them all this time when they were ready to sacrifice her—her happiness, her well-being, her future—for themselves. "The best for who? You? You're connected to the Farrells, but through the *right* Farrell. And I still work and support you with my 'little job.' Well, I hate to break it to you, but that ends here."

"What are you talking about now, Mycah?" Cherise asked, leaning forward and picking up a magazine off the table in front of her. "You're being so dramatic about this, but like I told you before, you'll see we've only ever wanted the best for you. Eventually, you'll understand that."

"Oh, I see more than you think now. My eyes are wide open." She reached into her purse and withdrew a check she'd written out beforehand and set it on the table. "That's a check that should be enough to cover your household bills for three months. I'd spend it wisely because after it's gone, it's the last money you'll receive from me. I'm through supporting you."

"What are you talking about, young lady?" Her father surged from the couch, his book tumbling unheeded to the floor.

"Just what I said. I'm done. I'll continue to pay Angel's tuition and any of her needs because she doesn't deserve to be penalized, but the tuition will be paid directly to the school. As for you two, I suggest you actually start going into the Hill-Harper office or downsize or actually learn to live off a budget. Because I'm done allowing you to use me. This relationship is toxic, and I can no longer afford it—emotionally or financially. So you're cut off."

She turned and headed for the entrance to the family

room, ignoring their indignant calling of her name. But at the last second, she pivoted, holding up her hand, palm out.

"One last thing. Achilles Farrell is going to be in my life. And not just as the father of my baby, but as my husband, if he'll have me. And if you can't accept that, then I'm sorry. I'm even sorrier that it's a decision you're making not to be in your grandchild's life. Because I won't have you disparaging my child's father. If you can't respect him, my choice of a husband and the father of my child, then you don't have to be a part of that family. It will sadden me, but again, that's your choice."

With that, she left and didn't look back.

She only looked forward.

Because only the future lay ahead.

Eighteen

"Is all this really necessary?"

Achilles scanned the huge office with the floor-to-ceiling windows, the sitting area with the dark brown couch, matching chairs, rug and coffee table. Black, glossy built-in cabinets surrounded a wide, flat-screen television on one wall, and a large, curving glass desk with a bank of computers that, admittedly, had him drooling, encompassed only half the space. There was plenty left for him to add whatever he wanted, because yes, this was *his* office.

On the executive floor.

He'd *finally* made the move.

But it wasn't the furniture, computers and amazing view that had him scowling at Kenan and Cain.

No, that honor belonged to the streamers, balloons, food and people crowded into the office.

"Yes, it's necessary. You're finally out of the basement and up here with your brothers. Now stop glaring at us.

This is a no-glare zone," Kenan commanded, passing him a cup of—something red.

"Not to mention, you hired two people to help you work on your game and finish it. Think about that. You officially have the first two employees for your new company. Even before you have a name for it," Cain said, sipping from his own cup.

"I have a name for it." Achilles scrubbed a hand over his hair, then slid it in his pants pocket. "Farrell Brothers Incorporated."

Cain and Kenan stared at him. Then slow, wide smiles lit both of their faces.

"I love it." Cain nodded.

"It's fucking perfect," Kenan agreed. "Now you really have to drink up, because we have to toast to Farrell Brothers Inc."

Achilles lifted the cup—still didn't know what he was drinking—to his mouth when movement from the doorway caught his eye. He glanced up...and froze.

Mycah.

It'd been four days since she'd left his apartment, and fuck, it might as well as have been four months. Four years.

Or four minutes.

He missed her.

Like an amputated limb, she was gone—he knew she was gone—but he felt her phantom presence in the living room where they'd made love, in the bedroom where he'd told her about his past, in the kitchen where he'd fed her.

Because they were on different floors at work, it'd been easy to avoid her, and he hadn't attended the press conference. Hadn't watched it, either. As it was, when she'd emailed him the date of the doctor's appointment three weeks from now, he would need every day of that time to prepare himself to see her.

He hadn't been ready for four days.

God, she was beautiful.

In another one of those pantsuits that were both professional and sexy as hell. What would she wear when she started showing? Excitement and greed spiked inside his chest, low in his gut, because dammit, he wanted to know. Wanted to be there with her in the mornings when she dressed, to caress and hold her belly, wait for their baby's movements under his palm.

But she didn't want that.

At least not with him.

He drew back, mentally and physically.

Glancing around, he noted the looks thrown her way and heard an undercurrent of whispers. His gut tightened, and he remembered her worry about the hit to her reputation. Anger ignited within him. Yes, she'd broken his heart, but damn if she deserved this.

"Mycah." He held up a hand, waved her inside. "Come on in. Grab a plate and something to drink."

Relief flashed across her face, and she briefly smiled, stepping into the office. He spied the two gift boxes, one medium-sized and the other smaller, she carried as she neared, and his gaze flickered from the packages to her.

"I'm sorry to just drop in without…"

"Mycah, you don't need to apologize," he murmured. "Everyone's welcome."

"Right." An emotion that could've been hurt flickered in her eyes, but before he could ascertain it, she handed him the larger gift box. "For your office, and a belated gift for your new company."

Setting his cup down behind him, he accepted the present. For several seconds, he just held it, staring down at the gaily wrapped package. Finally, he lifted the top and pushed aside the tissue paper, revealing a framed picture.

No, concept art.

From his video game.

Speechless, the bottom part of the box dropped from his hand, unnoticed.

It wasn't one of the images he'd shown her, but something completely original that she must've had commissioned.

She'd plucked the vision straight out of his head. His teenage hero, wearing a hoodie, jeans and sneakers and bearing a shield and sword, stood on an inner-city street, the landscape of old buildings, cracked streets and dim shadows surrounding him. And in the distance, a dark castle, thick forest and maze.

He wrenched his gaze from the framed art to the woman in front of him.

"I commissioned it after you showed me your video game. I thought it would make great cover art for the game. But you're under no obligation to use it. I just wanted you to know I'm one hundred percent invested in your dreams in you. And..." She sank her teeth into her bottom lip, and his fingers clenched around the frame, needing to thumb the sensual flesh free. "This is for you, too."

She handed him the second box.

"I'll hold that for you," Cain murmured, taking the art.

Reluctantly, he turned it over, his heart thudding in his chest as he accepted the smaller gift. He didn't hesitate this time to open the present. Lifting the top, he removed the tissue paper, and as he stared down at the tiny item nestled inside, shock and then joy exploded in his chest.

He picked up the yellow onesie and read the bright green stitching on it aloud. "My daddy makes heroes."

Around them, a couple of gasps and more murmurs filled the room before it fell into total silence. But he didn't care. All of his attention remained focused on her. The woman who had just announced in front of his brothers and an office full of employees that he was the father of their baby.

"I know I asked for time, but over the last few days I've realized that time can be our greatest gift…and our worst enemy. I don't want another day to go by with you believing that I'm ashamed to declare to whoever will listen that you're the man who will teach our child what it is to be strong, respected and good. You're the man who will raise our baby with me, guide him or her, show them what true character is, what kindness is. Show them what it is to be loved. Because you've shown their mother all of those things. And I'm sorry I ever let you doubt it. I've allowed fear to run my life for too long, and I want to step out on that limb with you. Please forgive me, Achilles."

"There's nothing to forgive." And there wasn't. Because he'd forgiven her as soon as she'd left the penthouse.

"Yes, there is. I hurt you. But, Achilles, if you offer me your heart again, I'll take care of it. These past few days—" she shook her head, spreading her hands wide, palms up "—they've been so empty because you haven't been in them. My job, my family—they're all important. But not more important than my love for you. The life I want to build with you and our baby. *Our* family. I love you. So much more than I thought it possible to love a person. I don't just want you in my life, I *need you*. And I would be proud to stand beside you, with you, and claim you as mine, to be claimed as yours. If you'll let me."

Before the last word finished, he swallowed it with his mouth, tasted it on his tongue. Once more, he crushed those curls in his fingers, having missed their rough silk texture almost as much as he missed the flavor of her, the perfect fit of her pressed against him.

"I never rescinded my heart, baby," he whispered against her lips. "It's always been yours."

She laughed, the sound a bit waterlogged, and he cherished it. Had never heard anything as special, as wonderful. Not even the spontaneous outbreak of applause around them. Or Kenan telling everyone to stop being creepy voyeurs.

Achilles leaned his head back, joining in the laughter, his chest light, heart free. For the first time in...years. His heart was free. Because it belonged to another.

It belonged to Mycah.

"Tell me again," she whispered, brushing her fingers through his beard, her eyes glistening.

He smiled, covering her belly and their child.

"I'm yours. And so is my heart."

* * * * *

COMING SOON!

We really hope you enjoyed reading this book.
If you're looking for more romance, be sure to
head to the shops when new books are
available on

Thursday 2nd September

To see which titles are coming soon, please visit

millsandboon.co.uk/nextmonth

MILLS & BOON

MILLS & BOON

THE HEART OF ROMANCE

A ROMANCE FOR EVERY READER

MODERN

Prepare to be swept off your feet by sophisticated, sexy and seductive heroes, in some of the world's most glamourous and romantic locations, where power and passion collide.

HISTORICAL

Escape with historical heroes from time gone by. Whether your passion is for wicked Regency Rakes, muscled Vikings or rugged Highlanders, awaken the romance of the past.

MEDICAL

Set your pulse racing with dedicated, delectable doctors in the high-pressure world of medicine, where emotions run high and passion, comfort and love are the best medicine.

True Love

Celebrate true love with tender stories of heartfelt romance, from the rush of falling in love to the joy a new baby can bring, and a focus on the emotional heart of a relationship.

Desire

Indulge in secrets and scandal, intense drama and plenty of sizzling hot action with powerful and passionate heroes who have it all: wealth, status, good looks…everything but the right woman.

HEROES

Experience all the excitement of a gripping thriller, with an intense romance at its heart. Resourceful, true-to-life women and strong, fearless men face danger and desire - a killer combination!

To see which titles are coming soon, please visit

millsandboon.co.uk/nextmonth